WAXED EXCEE

Joshua Humphreys was born in ...lbourne in 1985. He was miseducated at La Trobe University where he read Modern and Ancient History. He spent two years writing and performing in comedy plays and doing stand-up before deciding that he should be writing novels. So he has spent the last few years gallivanting around Europe, Southeast Asia and the US. In 2015 he published his first novel, *Waxed Exceeding Mighty*. For six weeks he smuggled copies of it into London bookstores and exhorted his social media followers to steal them. Thus was born #stealthisnovel. He is extremely fond of watermelon. The ferocity of his tap-dancing is unrivalled, except in China, where his style is derided as only semi-ferocious. In 2009 he traveled to East Africa, where he was one of the first white men to see an ostrich eat nails. His favourite films are Lethal Weapon 2 and Dragonheart. He is currently writing the screenplay for Armageddon 2—Liv Tyler's emotional journey in learning to forgive Ben Affleck for leaving Bruce Willis on that asteroid. In 2012 Humphreys went to the Holy Land where he, like fellow monarchs Edward VII and George V before him, had a Jerusalem cross tattooed on his forearm; he brags now about how good his hummus is. He was for a brief interlude in 2013 the royal wolfcatcher to His Highness The Duke of Bavaria and later that year went to Capri, where he assaulted a woman in the forehead with a crayfish. In 2014 he traveled through Central America—in Belize he was taught how to make rice wine from a donkey's unhappiness and in Guatemala learned that the wearing of weasel's testicles as a necklace is more of a superstition than a contraceptive. He may or may not work for MI6 and can run really, really fast. He is fluent in Armenian, Cherokee, and Gibberish, and can read Latin, though he does not know what any of the words mean. He is a qualified mahout. He is very happily banned from France. He has not ever lost at paper-scissors-rock. And despite his own frequent assertions he is neither Mel Gibson's son nor Hugh Jackman's nephew. He currently divides his year between London, Italy and Vietnam.

WAXED
EXCEEDING
MIGHTY

JOSHUA HUMPHREYS

Dear Ellie,

I wrote that book in Vietnam, right before I moved to my beloved England, and it provided me with fond memories. I hope it may create new ones for you, and inspire you to great things.

Yours,

ISBN: 978-1-505-44777-4

Cover artwork by Samuel Humphreys

joshuahumphreys.net

And the children of Israel were fruitful, and increased abundantly, and multiplied, and waxed exceeding mighty; and the land was filled with them.

THE FIRST BOOK OF ADAM ATHELSTAN, CALLED
DILUVIUM

CHAPTER 1

1

'Just have a look at her. I don't care where she's from, she's the best corruption lawyer in the country. And twenty-eight years old, Adam. Can you believe that? The money this girl saved me. So I thought, what would be the ultimate thank-you present for my rare Chinese flower? And who do I find's the only person in the country that grows them?'

'Who grows them.'

'What?'

'*Who* grows them.'

'You do.'

'Gabriel, that's a non-defining clause in a sentence with two nouns, isn't it? You should have said *who* grows them. Otherwise you're saying that there's only one country that grows them and I'm the only person in it! What a boring old something of a place that would be!'

Often was Adam's enthusiasm met with suspicion and bewilderment. 'You are a strange kid,' said Gabriel, staring. 'But the only person in the country with a Golden Dragon Daffodil.'

'It's really a beautiful flower,' said Lian, trying to alleviate with kindness the perceptions of brutality she assumed Adam was having of the man she was currently allowing to lavish her with what she thought were high-class things.

'You charge an arm and a bloody leg for it though, don't ya? I didn't know flowers could cost that much. But have a look at her. She's worth every dollar, mate. Isn't she beautiful?'

'Stop it,' said Lian, darting her head from his affectionate hand precisely as she did from impertinent wasps.

'Look at that complexion. Our girls just don't have it. There's not much that makes a man my age feel young again, Adam. But she does.'

In a gesture which belied the fortunes of men spent on keeping her hair at its very precise point between wavy and curly Lian scrunched up her nose and presented to Adam a great deal of her tongue.

'How do I make you feel?'

Lian half rolled her eyes. 'I told you already. There's only one way to really live the high life, Adam. When you're young. And the only way a girl our age can do it?' She leaned in to whisper. 'Sleep with a millionaire.'

A waiter brought out a tray of drinks.

'Two glasses of incrocio manzoni? There we are. And a lemon squash.'

Adam looked down into his glass. Already his drink resembled a floe that had ventured too far from the Arctic and was racing, its members rapidly and tragically diminishing, for the equator. Flecks of ice dissolved before his eyes. He gave an anxious groan and lifted a signalling finger. 'I *am* sorry...'

'Hm?' said the waiter, almost turned to walk away.

'I'm sorry. This ice. Do you have–. This is umm–.'

'You asked for extra ice?'

'I did, yes. But I thought you would have ice *cubes*, at the very least. These... You don't have spheres, do you?'

'Spheres?'

'Ice spheres rather than cubes. Spheres have the lowest surface area to volume ratio, you see. They melt a lot slower and so they give less dilution *and* the highest chill factor. Chips like these actually have the *highest* surface-area-to-volume ratio, higher even than tetrahedrons. It's just that my lemon squash will be half water in around three and a bit minutes. I don't expect you–. You don't have um–. No. Do you have cubes? Ice cubes?'

'I'll see if I can find bigger ice?'

'That would be wonderful, thank you. Yes, the bigger the ice cube the lower the surface-area-to-volume ratio.'

'So the slower the ice melts.'

'Exactly. … You're a scientist.'

And the waiter removed the offensive refrigerant.

Lian put an elbow on the terrace balustrade and rested her chin on her palm. Dark and blustery night had come in. Glimpses of an amber Flinders Street Station shone dimly through the flapping leaves of the diseased elms which obscured most of their view. Each window of the city's proud towers was one long amber wiggle in the black river below. Above the trees the logos of an airline owned by an Arab tribe, of two American banks and one Chinese, a German financial services company, a Swiss-Dutch-British provider of healthcare, burned. Uncountable antennae, grossly illuminated, stuck out of the skyline like acupuncturist needles. The one spire, dwarfed and unlit, was a shadow barely discernible from the darkness.

'I love this city at night,' said Lian, sighing. 'It's almost like the less you see of things the more beautiful they are.'

'Not you,' said Gabriel.

She ejected her tongue quite further than she had previously and looked vacantly down to the furthest view of the river. Gradually she came up against the current. She leaned out to look at the tops of the heads below. Then she pulled away from the balustrade as though it were burning hot. 'Should we look at a menu?'

'What?' said Gabriel.

'What?'

'What did you see?'

'Nothing. When?'

'Right before you pulled away from the balcony like it was on fire.'

'Did I?'

'It's not your husband is it?' He looked at Adam. 'That'd be bloody awkward. … It *is* your husband?' He gave a short high hoot and laughed: 'I hope he doesn't come up here.'

'You have a husband?' said Adam. He so loved learning of the contentment of his acquaintances.

'Yes, but shh,' she said as though she were letting him in on a little prank. 'Now what are we all going to order? Let's be ready for when the others get here.'

The waiter returned with Adam's lemon squash. He had

procured some cubes of very dubious capabilities. Adam resigned the temperature of his drink to their powers and picked up a menu. Lian looked briefly at hers then slowly turned her head to look inside.

They were sitting at Akkadia. From floor to ceiling and all the way around, inside and on the terrace, the walls were covered in metallic blue tiles, interlaced like bricks. A frieze of golden bas-relief aurochs, of lions and daisies and mushussu and painted-on Immortal Median archers paraded around the restaurant. The mouldings were painted as simple crennelations, like four stacked children's blocks. Statuettes of Ishtar and idols of Marduk sat stubbornly guarding the wine bar and the dessert case. Denying the barrenest location of its inspiration the restaurant was verged in every niche with trees of tamarisk, of juniper and terabinth, of quince and bashan oak, cedar and holy bramble.

Akkadia's menu consisted of recondite culinary verbs preceding very expensive Levantine petals and demanding nuts and sour fruits, all used to conceal the flavour and soften the gristle of several otherwise inedible animals such as are forlornly stomached by bedouins in times of famine.

And the place was packed. Only Gabriel's generous bribe had secured them a table for five on the terrace.

Her head moved mechanically down the menu until Lian turned again to look across Gabriel and into the restaurant.

'He's not coming up here, would you relax?' Gabriel put his arm on the back of Lian's chair and stroked her shoulder blade with his thumb. 'I am wondering where the other two are though. He's never late for dinner, not when it's on me. Speaking of on me...' Gabriel lowered his voice to a very audible mumble. 'I can't wait for later.'

'Gabriel?'

At the threshold, between young palm fronds, a very bejewelled and very surprised middle-aged woman pulled a lilac pashmina tight around her bare shoulders. Gabriel's arm jerked from Lian's chair as though it too were burning hot. Looking up at this serenely livid woman, his face squirmed and curdled before ossifying at a settlement of eyebrow and pucker that was his attempt to appear defiant. 'You told me you had a dinner tonight.'

'I do. Here.'

'You hate ethnic food.'

'Who's this?'

'This is Adam, a new business associate. He's in rare flowers. Adam this is Ariel.'

Adam turned and began to rise from his seat.

'Not him. The comfort woman.'

A man stepped out onto the balcony. 'The *maître d'* said they're out here on the b—. Lian? Gabriel?!'

'Uh-oh,' said Lian.

'You said you were bringing your new girlfriend,' said Gabriel.

'I was,' said Michael. 'This is her.'

'My wife?'

'You're married?' said Michael to Ariel.

'You're *still* married?' said Lian.

Almost at menu's end, Adam put his mouth to his straw and took a big sip of lemon squash.

'Flew her in with your last load of refrigerators did you, Gabriel?'

'Hey, that's my wife.'

'She keeps you grounded, Michael?' said Gabriel. 'Yesterday you said she gives you a sense of historical continuity.'

'She does.'

'With what, the Middle Ages?' said Lian.

'Hey! That's my wife,' said Gabriel.

'Did you know that it's actually the Middle *Age*,' said Adam, a feeble and unheeded voice. 'There was only one, you see. It's from the French, *moyen-age*. It's actually not a plural. Though most people do…'

'She's like a hundred, Michael. Aren't things…' Lian put her hands palms-up in the air and closed her fingers as she pulled them down. '…hanging?'

'What happened to us, honeybuns?' said Michael.

'You can't give me the life I want.'

'Now I know how you know how to say so many dirty things in Chinese,' said Ariel to Michael.

'He's a giant spindly nuff-nuff, Ariel. Look at him. What could you possibly be getting from him?'

She pulled out the chair beside Adam's. 'Gabriel, you fulfilled me sexually but while you were buying me *things* did you ever once ask how I felt?' And Michael took the seat opposite Lian. 'We were young together, Gabriel. Weren't those memories enough for you?'

Adam had long ago decided on the khouzi ala timman. From all he could gather it was grilled lamb with prunes and mint. Adam loved mint. But now he sensed that perhaps the encircling disputes allowed little place for him; he could see no reason why they would be done with anytime soon. He tried to catch Gabriel's eye, that he might thank his host before excusing himself. Gabriel was busy insulting Michael. He tried to get Lian's attention so that he might bid her a pleasant evening. She too was caught up in crueller matters. So Adam Athelstan rose slowly from the table and left Akkadia and walked home.

1:2

Edith Athelstan, Adam's delightful grandmother, was reading in her armchair under the ruby light of one of two heavy wooden floor lamps. She was very glad to see her only grandson and she closed her book and pulled the knitted blanket off her lap and got up to put the kettle on.

'How was dinner, dear?'

'Oh, I didn't get to have any.'

'What do you mean, dear? Why not?'

'Well I was there with the man who bought the narcissus zephosii, and with the girl he'd bought it for, and then *his* wife turned up with *her* husband.'

'Oh no, dear. Not again.'

'Yes. And arguing does seem to be the most common reaction in that situation, so I got up and left.'

'Oh, you poor dear. You must be starving. Do you want me to fix you something to eat?'

'No, I probably shouldn't. If I eat this late I'm liable to have dreams again.'

'All right, dear.'

'Goodnight.'

'Yes, goodnight.'

CHAPTER 2

1

Shaved, bathed and dressed, Adam walked out into the combined kitchen, dining and living room that had been so recently marketed to Edith as their 'primary living space'. He fiddled at his tie pin and chimed, 'Good morning.'

'Good morning, dear.' Edith lifted Adam's toast from the bacon fat and covered them each with an egg.

Adam took his usual place at their small darkly stained dining table and folded the *point de venise* table cloth under itself so that it would not tickle the tops of his legs. He inspected the giotto larkspurs he had yesterday evening arranged in the fruit bowl among the cherries, the blackberries, the pomegranates, the figs. He held a blue and violet petal between his thumb and fingers and stroked it once, slowly, and was delighted.

The kitchen, demarcated from the dining area by the cessation of tiles and the commencement of beige carpet, was obtrusive; only habit prevented Edith from hitting her head on a looming cupboard each time she turned from stovetop to cutlery drawer. She put Adam's breakfast in front of him and sat over an empty bowl.

'Ooh, this looks delicious, Grandma. Thank you.'

Edith topped off a tall glass, already a third filled with whisky, from the milk jug and said, 'Of course, dear.' She stirred it and licked the spoon clean. 'I gave you an extra egg and double your bacon. I thought you'd be hungry after last night.'

'Positively starving.'

Adam stirred an overflowing teaspoon of condensed milk through his iced coffee. Edith sliced fruit into her bowl.

'And how did you sleep then?'

'Oh, well enough.'

'You couldn't stop thinking about last night.'

'For a time.'

Edith drizzled honey over her fruit and added a great dollop of yoghurt. 'The wickedness of the world is not to be abhorred, dear, but overcome by good example.'

'And that horrific ice they had! But I suppose that's what people do get up to. Now what have you got on for today then?'

'We've got a luncheon at two for one of the pastoral candidates.'

'Lovely.'

'Asian fellow, I think.'

'Oh, very lovely.'

'Yes, it should be. I don't know how the congregation will like him though. A bit young, I think.'

'Is he?'

'Only a year out of the seminary.'

'Oh, *very* young.'

'Yes, but we'll see. Luncheon will be impeccable regardless. Mrs Gladstone's bringing her shepherd's pie.'

'Oooooh,' said Adam. Only once had he had the privilege of tasting this renowned pea-ridden marvel.

'And how about you?'

'Well, I've a man coming to look at a Gibraltar campion on Tuesday so I'll have to start getting that looking as ebullient as I can. The macrobotrys is starting to choke one of the top corners of the frame, I'll have to put that in its place. Let me think. There should be a few strawberries to come in. Oh, and today's the twenty-ninth. The oxypetalum opens in a month. I'll get started on that today too. And I expect that'll be my afternoon.'

'That sounds a lovely day, dear.'

Adam had cleared from his plate all evidence that it ever contained a breakfast. 'Grandma, that was delightful.'

'Of course dear. Sweets?'

'Ooh lovely.'

Edith went merrily to the freezer and scooped some chocolate ice-cream into a cone. Adam pulled gently at the bottom of his waistcoat as he went to the front of the apartment.

The dining area was the brief interlude to the living, which began at the black-fringed crimson shades of the two floor lamps at either wall. Their tiny bedrooms and bathrooms were at the rear of the apartment. The walls of their primary living space (adorned by three oil landscapes of glistening temperate rainforest half-cleared of trees by Edith's grandfather, and a sepia photograph of long-bearded men and petticoated women stamping a foot on a newly felled eucalypt) were low and almost the same colour as the carpet. Four unmovably heavy arm chairs of dark wood, their leather fraying at the arm and head rests, faced one another and had each a side table. Edith's was between a white *art nouveau* writing stand and the crystal cabinet that sheltered from torrential dust one shelf of crystal and three of books, the most cherished of which was the family Bible—commissioned, bound and inscribed for the dolorous rupture of emigration.

Adam pulled the plastic curtain chain and exposed, through the wall-to-wall and floor-to-ceiling window, the day. Edith handed him his sweets; he smiled and gave a lilting, 'Mm-mm,' and licked the thing.

The sunshine of late morning meant none of the harbour's beauty could hide. Illuminated in all its splendour, overexposed and nearing white rather than golden, the vista was dominated by the girders of an enormous football stadium whose most prominent feature was the adorning logo of an airline operated for the profit of a Sheikhdom. A low line of storage sheds, long devoid of any maritime function and now with an exhibitive one, was the horizon of this no-man's land. In its distance a dozen proud cranes stuck out like dropped titanic spears. Logos of national banks and foreign insurance companies high in the sunlight glowed. There occasionally appeared above the fence-line, rocking on the water, the satellite dishes, radio antennae and canopies of the unused boats of a hundred zealous businessmen.

The residential buildings with which Adam and Edith shared the harbour-front were outwardly of coloured glass, placed over the façades at the onset of construction and out of fashion before the interiors were complete. Most were somehow, vaguely, nautical-shaped—this like a sail, that like an exhaust funnel, Adam and Edith's as the stern and bow of an ocean liner. Ignored in presale by the local inhabitants they consisted almost entirely of apartments, penthouses and incense-stunk hovels kept for the preferred prostitutes, indentured strippers and deserted mistresses of a thousand Asian businessmen for whom the same confinements at home would mean poverty, ostracism, the self-immolation of family members. Their ground floors were all given over to restaurants. Edith kicked up a small fuss, her only in the whole ordeal, in order to obtain for the sake of her grandson the ground floor of their own unlovable tower.

It was sold to Edith at a slightly reduced price by the construction company awarded the Athelstan pre-federation townhouse by the state government. Ilminster, or, as it was affectionately called by the final three generations of Athelstans who lived there, Ilmey, was demolished in a day. Erected in the place of it and twenty others like it was an immense building of pejorative architectural merit, the one-hundred-and-thirty-first floor of which was visible on an exceptionally clear day from the window at which Adam now stood.

Having pushed the scoop with his tongue down into the cone, he put the last inch of ice cream-filled crunchiness into his mouth and wiped his hands on his mustard-yellow handkerchief.

He slid the built-in door across and descended to the patio. But for the wind it was silent. No water was heard lapping, no ship bells, no flapping sails, no creaking masts. Occasionally there came a profanity screeched by a bumpkin or the underwhelmed exclamations of a tourist. The patio, twice the width of their apartment and three times as long, was tiled with terracotta. In the corner closest to the sliding door four garden chairs and a table, all of white ornate cast-iron, rested beside a matching lady bench. The walls which gave them privacy from the boardwalk below were made of a tinted material heavier, sturdier and uglier than glass.

The patio's purpose, and the reason for Edith's ado about their having the ground floor, was Adam's glasshouse. Half the length of the patio and almost its width, it was his livelihood, his vocation, his sanctuary. Old, leaden glass which when broken shattered into very malevolent-looking pieces, through age tinged green at the corners, full of burps and bumps and inconstancies of thickness, creaked and yawned in its ageing frame of cast and wrought iron. At sunrise and at sunset a mist went up from the sprinklers and watered the plants for half an hour. Over its door hung a wooden board painted, when the last panes had been transferred from Ilmey, with an inscription from Ruskin in white paint and Adam's hand: *'Roses and lilies would grow for us side by side, leaf overlapping leaf, till the Earth was white and red with them, if we cared to have it so.'*

Inside there were indeed roses and lilies—wild and of the valley were Adam's favourites and the most numerous—and, as Adam told anybody who asked, one-hundred-and-thirty-seven species of flowering plant besides. About half were ornamental and for Adam's pleasure, about half extremely rare and wildly valuable. A bench divided the glasshouse into four long rows. From them and under them and over them and along them there burst forth leaves, blades, fronds, branches, vines, fruits, buds, stems, flowers, roots, in so many shades of green that Adam often found that among them he was exhilarated. Each morning he started at the right wall and walked its length, found a small spot of rot here, evidence of an aphid there, a slug trail, a trip, rust, early signs of mould, botrytis—walking the four aisles with meticulous exuberance and taking note of each plant to which he would have to attend before his day's work could be considered done. The scent was all day of flowers, of wet soil, of steaming wood, of warmth and humidity, of open stomata and various other floral goings on which only Adam knew about. He described it fondly and often as the smell of life old and new. When his inspection reached the end of the last aisle he came to his grandfather's gramophone and the one record he kept beside it – *Life Is A Bowl of Cherries* by Al Bowlly.

Adam lifted the plastic cover which kept it dry and flipped the record over and wound the thing. He lowered the needle onto the record's outer edge. As a violin wafted he changed his shoes for gumboots, tied his garden apron at his waist, and made his way to whichever of the day's tasks was the most urgent. Today it was the jade vine warping the glasshouse frame. He sang, high and softly, to himself and the flowers:

> *Love is the sweetest thing,*
> *What else on earth could ever bring,*
> *Such happiness to everything,*
> *As love's old story?*

At eleven he turned the crank to open the ventilation flaps. The panes at knee height lifted down along the length of the greenhouse, the topmost rows of pane hinged up from the ridge.

At one o'clock Edith brought him an immaculately iced lemon cordial. As he did every day he asked if she cared to join him. Today she said, 'Athelstans are not made for the tropics, dear,' and Adam sat in his rocking chair with his cordial and reflected on how happy he was.

In summer he was in full sun from midday until four, in winter from eleven until three. When all too soon the sun disappeared behind the jib-shaped tower he remarked to a candycane sorrel upon how quickly his days seemed to go and then headed back to the gramophone and returned the needle to his record. He sang joyously as he changed out of his workwear.

> *Love is the greatest thing,*
> *The oldest yet the latest thing,*
> *I only hope that fate may bring,*
> *Love's story to you.*

2:2

At Adam's back gate Noah Dulrich used his beanstalkish height to reach over and pull across its bolt. On hearing Adam's warbling he thought he might give him a little bit of a fright. He crouched beside the glasshouse door, where the foliage might hide him where transparent walls could not. Adam finished covering the gramophone and emerged humming. His best pair of secateurs needed an oiling. Noah sprung up and said with raised hands and very loudly, 'Bleh!' Adam jolted at the noise and his arms flew into the air. Were they not his very best pair of secateurs he might have let them go, saving Noah's looming hand from their still quite sharp thrust.

Noah yowled from pain and gawked at the drop of blood which appeared immediately in the centre of his palm.

'I've stabbed you in the hand,' said Adam.

'You've stabbed me in the hand!' said Noah. 'There's blood.' His face drained instantly of colour; his ill-shaped head became as an upturned white peanut m&m. He began to droop.

'Are you all right?'

'Blood,' he quavered.

'That's what happens when you scare people, isn't it? Oh it's only a drop. It is very nice to see you. What brings you over? Come to see the glasshouse I expect?'

'No, not to see the glasshouse.' Adam helped him stumble over

12

to the white chairs. 'Oh that's better.' He gripped his wrist and held it to his chest. Adam put his beloved secateurs on the garden table. 'Mummy's throwing me a party on the boat.'

'That sounds like fun for you.'

'And I couldn't make party without inviting you. I know you don't like them though.'

'No, your parties are always rather populated by your mother's friends.'

'Yes.' Noah turned to unpleasant reflection.

'So many… improper men, on one boat.'

'Yes I do sometimes think that Mummy throws me parties just so she can meet men. But she promised this time there wouldn't be too many of them. This one's strictly for me. I've decided what I'm going to do with my life.'

'Oh, wonderful. Congratulations. What have you decided on this time?'

'I'm going to be a novelist.'

Adam gave the light chuckle and attendant appreciative sigh that he typically reserved for when somebody made a very good pun.

'Why are you laughing?'

'Why am I laughing?'

'Yes.'

'Oh you're being serious. I am sorry.'

'Yes I'm being serious. … What?'

'No, nothing.'

'What?'

'Nothing.'

'*What?*'

'Well it's just… No, nothing. '

'What!?'

'You write a novel?'

'Why does everybody keep saying that? Yes me write a novel.'

Edith pulled across the heavy glass door and, bearing a plate abundant of cucumber sandwiches, said, 'Good evening, Noah.'

'Hi Mrs Athelstan. Are they–? Oh, Mrs Athelstan. My absolute favourite.' As soon as the plate touched the table Noah began popping the crustless fingers into his mouth as though he were trying to fill a canyon with marbles.

'I'll just get you your cordials.' She brought two glasses brimming with spheres of ice and a jug of her lemon cordial as near to frozen as possible.

'Noah's having a party on his boat, Grandma.'

'Ooh, that sounds nice. It is *very* chilly once that sun goes. I'll just get you boys some cardigans.'

'And what's your novel going to be about then?'

'About anything.'

'You've not decided what kind of novel?'

'No. But I am gonna be a novelist.'

Edith returned with cardigans. 'What's the occasion then, Noah?'

'You gonna come for a drink, Mrs Athelstan?'

'Oh, Noah,' she said, whacking him gently on the shoulder. 'No I will not be joining you thank you. Why the party?'

'I've decided what I'm going to do with my life.'

'Good boy. And what's that?'

'I'm going to be a novelist.'

'A novelist. Good for you, dear. More sandwiches? I've got plenty of cucumbers.'

'Ought we to get moving?' said Adam.

'We? Are you gonna come?'

'I think I might just join you, Noah, for a quick celebration. It's a big day for you, isn't it? And I'm in a *very* good mood. You should *see* the Vietnamese gardenias that are just coming in. The softest white you've ever seen. You'd think that heaven just fell on the earth.'

'We have to wait for Jacob though. He's coming after work.'

'That wicked boy's not coming here is he?' said Edith. 'Last time he was here he went on and on about liberty.'

'You know he doesn't mean it, Grandma.'

'Then he shouldn't say it if he doesn't mean it.' She took away the empty plate. 'Ooph, that ghastly boy.'

Adam asked what Noah had been up to since they last saw each other. Noah said, 'Nothing really.'

'Nothing?'

'Yeah, not really anything. No. Just... No, nothing.'

A very long silence set in. Were they anywhere near the natural world the rubbing together of some insect's wings or the contraction of some other's tymbals would have been heard, loud and demonstrative.

The patio was awash now with the cold blue of early evening shaded by concrete, made colder by an ardent breeze.

Noah stared in one direction and Adam in the other. After a few minutes they both changed their staring directions, catching one another's eyes as their heads turned. They stared for a while longer. Eventually Adam said, 'Jacob's working on a Saturday then?'

'Dinah's quit her job. So he's had to start working weekends.'

A fumbling hand began making a racket over the back gate. It was struggling to reach the bolt. 'Adam!' called the turbulent voice which probably belonged to it.

'Speak of the devil,' said Noah and he went and unbolted the gate. Jacob Barron stepped through it and clasped their thumbs together.

'Adam! What's crackin'?' His dark face, groomed each morning to keep his stubble at his ideal, off-putting length, resembled, with his nose like a water-slide, that of a cartoon wolf.

'I haven't seen you in *quite* a long time.'

'No you haven't.' There was often something condescending in what Adam was returned by Jacob's whiney voice.

'And you're working Saturdays I hear?'

Jacob cursed his wife and said, 'Wants to be a bloody hippie wedding planner. And apparently I have to do whatever makes her happy and she starts that full time on Monday. But until we actually get any money from it I have to work nights and weekends. But not tomorrow. Let's get pissed!'

'Do you know what Noah's party is for, Jacob?'

'It's for getting pissed.'

'Noah's going to write a novel.'

Jacob cackled. 'Oh you're serious? *You* write a novel? You're terrified of your own boat. You've been out of the country once, you visited an auntie who bathed you the whole time you stayed with her. Why don't you use some of mummy's money and go away for a while? Live a little, get in some trouble. Then write a novel.'

'I've lived,' said Noah, most indignant.

'Have you?' said Jacob with high-pitched condescension.

'And I was thinking I'd write a book about how you want your wife's sister.'

'That–. That's not t–.' Noah laughed and Adam smiled. 'All I'm saying is, is that you may need some stories of your own.'

'Well I think I figured out about the story. I read the blurbs of all the current bestsellers. You just have to make it about something that the government, the press and the people all believe in but which we don't have yet. Best-sellers are for progress. The plight of this minority, the injustices suffered by gays there, the horrors of smacking a child. Whatever's the hottest topic of the day, we have to bring it to light for the people and make them feel good about believing in the right thing and tell them that they absolutely *do* deserve to have whatever they want.'

'We?' said Adam.

'Novelists.'

'We,' said Jacob. 'That's not the purpose of literature, Noah. You need to give them entertainment. You have to excite the people. To get them to see that there's more to life than offices and insurance and elections. You need stowaways on boats and swimming in Italian fountains, affairs with foreign aristocats, bar fights in Tunisia with the Foreign Legion, Russian roulette and journeys up tropical rivers. Those are the people that write novels.'

'Who,' said Adam.

'Those people.'

Adam so rarely agreed with Jacob, on anything, that he could here only do so with the greatest reluctance. 'Jacob mmmay have a point.'

'Do you remember Kylie Perkins? Her dad was SAS jungle extraction. *She* had interesting stories. *She* could write a novel. Go out and collect stories like that, then you can write one. You know she's bald now?'

'Kylie's bald?'

'Leukaemia. I saw her at Marc's engagement party. She wears an old-fashioned hat all the time.'

'You know she was my ideal girl in high school?'

'And now she's mine,' said Jacob.

'What?'

'Always had a fantasy about a bald woman. Just rubbing the scalp with your –.' Jacob looked at Adam and cut himself off.

'Anyway, you know my ideal girl.'

'Leah.'

'No. Not Leah. Voluminous blonde curls, skinny but bosomy, chirpy.'

'That's Leah.'

'It is not Leah. She's –. Well maybe it is kind of Leah.'

'All my ideal girls will be flocking to me soon because I'm a novelist.'

Edith, whose hair was short and grey and permed, walked outside with an iceless glass and put it in front of Jacob.

'Hello, Mrs Athelstan.'

'Jacob.'

'Mrs Athelstan, you don't have any of those cucumber sandwiches lying around do you? I'm starving.'

'Oh, I'm just out of cucumbers. I'm sorry, Jacob.' Noah laughed and Adam smiled.

'You know what I was thinking on the way over here, Mrs Athelstan?'

'Oh please don't start carrying on. I thought you were going to burst a blood vessel the last time I saw you.'

'I was thinking that Australian civilisation is as great as all the great civilisations that have ever graced the earth.'

'I'll bet you were.'

'The Egyptians, the Romans, the Ottomans, and now us. Just think about it. Think about what we have in common with them and then about how much richer we are than they were and how much more egalitarian we are. And all the superstitions that they had that we don't have. And then I thought, we should think about what's holding us back from *surpassing* them? Don't you think? That's more important. What do you think?'

'*They* were all slave-owning societies,' said Adam.

'Were they?' Adam nodded. 'Slaves,' Jacob reflected, and became lost in his own reason.

A loud splash echoed from the harbour. It was quickly followed by the laudatory whooping of a small crowd.

'I think it's began,' said Noah.

'Begun,' said Adam.

Somebody yelled something insulting. Soon there came a few obscenities.

'Yep,' said Jacob.

'I'll leave the back door open for you, dear.'

Noah stood and took off his jumper and kissed Edith on the cheek. Jacob was offered a handshake. 'You have fun now, won't you boys?'

2:3

They crossed the boardwalk. Jacob spat into the seamoss that made the slipway beneath Adam's glasshouse perilously slick and they descended the pier.

Night had all but fallen. The harbourscape was smeared with a kind of low-hanging brownish blueish haze. The concrete and the steel and all the tinted glass were slowly dropping towards the same confronting alluvial shade. From several directions deep music pounded through the air. The water, normally black, was at dusk the colour of mercury. The ocean, but not a fish to be found; there were only jellyfish, which when brought by the current had to contend for space solely with garbage. In their swarms they managed almost to lighten the water to an oceanic green.

At the end of the long and meandering pier was the *Teba*. Two stories high and discomfitingly long, her windows like malevolently squinting eyes, she was black-hulled and white-canopied, sitting at berth like the floating head of a viper. Noah's mother bought her as a gift after Noah's father bought him a car. She was named after the Spanish village on the way to which Noah was conceived. His mother's only stipulation was that he let her know whenever he was going to be using her; to his mother's delight Noah turned out to be terrified of being on the ocean; the boat was practically hers to use whenever and with whomever she wished.

The chatter of a party loudened as they neared the *Teba*'s low stern. Noah and Jacob stepped onto the lower deck. Adam looked back at the vanishing sunset (at the rear of a low panorama of distant beige buildings, between the two pylons of the bridge from which most of the city's suicides leapt, mostly obscured by power lines and transmission towers) and winced.

Immediately Noah put two feet on the boat he opened a flush compartment and pulled out a life jacket. Jezebel, Noah's glib and flippant and spectacularly popular mother, watched him put it on before kissing him on the cheek. 'The boy of the hour!' she shrieked as loudly as she could. She was a decade older than Adam's mother would have been. Her raiment was confusing and of silk, her skin kept surgically from its gravitational resting points, her face only partially her own. When she spoke her lips looked like the puffy wings of a panicked sea slug. 'And Jacob, my favourite! How are you darling? Everybody,' she said, turning to the crowd of twenty, variously posed and reposed about the deck. She put an arm around Noah's back and presented him. 'Noah. My son the novelist. Congratulations!' She thrust forward her hands and with them most of the contents of her martini glass and one of her maltese terriers. The crowd joined her. 'Congratulations!' it said.

'And everyone, this is Jacob, Noah's friend. He's a little bit hilarious, somebody get him talking. Oh, and Adam. Adam, little darling, I haven't seen you in so long!'

'Hello, Mrs Dulrich.'

'Miss now, please. How's your grandmother?'

'She's very well.'

'Goo-od. Now why don't you shuffle off and get yourself a drink?'

Adam introduced himself to everybody who bumped into him as he passed slowly through the crowd. He pulled across the double glass doors which opened to the bar. The *Teba*'s interior was of unabashed plastic and of modified plastic masquerading as carpet and of adulterated plastic pretending to be wood trim. Fake ferns rested in pots in a few corners. Downlights and mirrors stripped the room entirely of any hope of attaining the elegance to which it aspired.

One shaky step at a time, Noah reached the starboard bench. He eased himself into it and gripped tightly at the railing behind him.

Adam approached the bar.

'What can I get you?' said a young man in an ill-fitting waistcoat.

'Do you have lemon cordial?'

'Yes.'

'Lemon cordial, please.'

'With?'

'Ice. Oh, actually. Is that your ice? Oh, tubes. Yes, no, I don't know why they even make these. You may as well put discs of ice in your drink, the way they melt. Do you know if there's any ice in that refrigerator down there? I'll tell you what, why don't you help these other people and I'll look in the fridge to see if there are some cubes down there.'

The bartender stared at Adam until, some time later, he concluded that Adam was indeed being serious. 'Sure, buddy. Have a look.'

Watched by all waiting at the bar, Adam found and inspected three trays of ice cubes.

'Hi, could I get some more ice in here?' said a girl. 'It's getting a bit warm.'

'It is *your* lucky day,' said Adam, standing. 'I've found cubes with rounded bottoms. As close to spheres as one can hope for in a run-of-the-mill tray.'

'Can you just top it up for me?'

'Oh yes, I see. That'll be half water by now, won't it? Tubes just melt so quickly, don't they? I don't know why they even make them. You really should always ask for cubes with rounded bottoms.'

'Cubes with rounded bottoms?' This girl looked at the bartender and gave him a sideways smirk.

'Cubes with rounded bottoms,' said Adam.

'And what's your name?' she asked. Her cheekbones glowed when she genuinely smiled. Adam told her his name. 'You're very helpful, Adam,' she said, in the same tone she used when speaking to horribly disabled children.

'Thank you, Deborah. You know you have some icing sugar on your nostril there?'

She gave a frustrated click of her tongue and rubbed her thumb at the inside of her septum. 'Thank you. How do you know my name?'

'I introduced myself outside.'

'Did you? You must have a very good memory. And very strong views on ice, I see.'

'Refrigeration, Deborah, is the benchmark of civilisation.'

'Oh is it?'

Outside, Jacob had ensconced himself among some very foppish people, all of whom thought themselves pleasant and hilarious and most of whom thought it meet to wear sunglasses in the dark. An espresso martini had been thrust into each of his hands. 'Slaves,' he had opened with. He proceeded to divulge his revelation as it came. All were finding him uproarious. 'Slaves, man, are the last step to becoming one of the really great civilisations of the world. What do the Romans, the Greeks and the Ottomans all have in common? We have to have slaves. … But you make it a free market of slaves, because that's what we believe in, isn't it? We're not barbarians. … Anybody can become one and anybody can own one.'

'Mummy these are all your people again.' Noah's most frequent tone with his mother was one of juvenile grumbling.

'They're not darling. I'm sorry. They are here for you though. I was at the studio yesterday and I told everyone about your decision and they were all so happy for you. I couldn't not invite them. I invited all of your friends as well. I'm sure they're just late. Sarah! Sarah, come here. Noah you *have* to meet Sarah.'

A young woman with peroxided waves for hair, dressed too scantily and made up too heavily to have pulled off her attempt at elegant, lowered her shoulders as she came to be under Jezebel's adulterate arm.

'Sarah, this is my son. Noah, this is Sarah, my new designer.'

'It's so nice to finally meet you, Noah! And congratulations on the novel! Why are you sitting down with a life jacket on?'

'Noah's not entirely at his ease on boats. I met Sarah through Isaac, Noah. Isn't that funny?'

'Who's Isaac?'

'Isaac does my face, darling. I've told you that.'

'Dr Webber?'

'No, darling, I dropped him months ago. Not attentive enough, remember? Always flirting with his nurses. Isaac! Isaac's incredible, I told you.'

He who had fallen into the harbour, shirtless and flabbily drooping with a towel over his shoulders, put his arm around Sarah's waist and said, 'Here's to welcome aboard. Not the ship. Ha! Welcome aboard Quim, honey. Oh, you look so elegant.' This man turned to look down on Noah and said, rather like a drunken and judgmental caterpillar, 'Who is this?'

'This is my boat and my party.'

'Noah, you remember Francy?'

Francy turned to Jezebel's ear and did not whisper, 'I thought this was the Welcome Sarah party. It's a good one. Sarah, welcome. Welcome, Sarah,' he announced to the rest of the boat.

'No, darling, it's for Noah, isn't it? He's decided what he's going to do with his life. Remember?'

'Has he?' said Francy. 'Oooooooooh! Welcome Aboard, Sarah!'

'I'm going inside.'

'The poor darling,' said Jezebel to Sarah as she watched her son hobble off.

'It used to be fire,' said Adam. 'But we're past that now. Anybody can keep things hot, you just need fire. But to keep things cold, Deborah! Hello, Noah.'

'Are you making drinks?'

'He's icing them for me,' said the bartender. 'Aren't you buddy?'

'Get me a beer.'

'Me?'

'In the fridge underneath,' said the bartender, readying eight espresso martinis.

Noah noticed Deborah. He opened his posture to her and said, 'What's that?'

'My drink.' She smiled to herself and put her mouth to its straw.

'It's lovely.'

'Thank you.'

'You're lovely.'

'Thank you.'

'And *very* chirpy.'

Deborah smiled again. 'Am I?'

'Have you ever gone out with a novelist?'

'I can't say that I have, no.'

'My name's Noah.'

'Why are you wearing a life jacket?'

'I can't find my captain's hat. And I have to show people that this is my boat somehow. So what are you doing Wednesday night? You're free?'

'I'm sure you're very nice, and thank you for having me on your boat, but I *have* just started seeing someone.'

'You've just started seeing someone?'

'I have *just* started seeing someone.'

'I suppose that's why you're so chirpy then.'

Deborah nodded apologetically. Noah took a step away from her as the glass doors slid open and Sarah, laughing, plodded in. 'Noah, there you are! What's taking you so long? I want to get to know you. Jezebel Dulrich's son!'

'Sarah, this is Deborah. If you're wondering why she's so happy it's because she's just started seeing someone.' And Noah took his beer up the flight of steps beside the bar.

'A new boy!' said Sarah, rising to her toes. 'How exciting! I'm just going to order a drink. Could I get an espresso martini? Thanks.' Adam stared blankly at Sarah and then looked to the bartender. He was still very busy. 'So tell me all about him then. Where did you meet?'

'At work. You've got some, ah...'

Sarah brushed at her right nostril. 'Oh thanks.'

And they proceeded to exchange the peculiar sentences, creaking always with at least one inordinately elongated word, of clucky Australian girls talking about boys.

'So at work? That's exciting! Are you colleagues then?'

'Yep.'

'And what do you do?'

'I'm a nurse.'

'Oh, I love nurses! How many times have you been out then?'

'Three.'

'Oh, only three! I love that excitement. Don't you love it? Where was your first date?'

'He took me to this little tiny sidebar in St Kilda to see a jazz band.'

'Claypots!?'

'*That's* what it was called!' she said, remembering. 'Claypots!'

'That's where my boyfriend took me on *our* first date! How funny! And did he outdo himself on the second? He did, didn't he?'

'Oh, yes. A picnic in a rowboat on the river.'

Sarah became most excited. 'At the Studley Park Boathouse?!'

'Maybe. We hired it from a boathouse. In Kew?'

'That's so funny! That's where my boyfriend took me on our second date! What! Are! The chances?! If he's anything like my boyfriend, well he must be if they think so much alike, then you are one lucky girl. Now where was the third? The third's important. If he's still trying on the third...' she sang.

'You know, he really just blew me away. He called me out of the blue at midnight and came and picked me up and took me to a secret bakery on Lygon street.'

'A se–' Sarah's enthusiasm had evaporated. 'A secret–. A secret bakery?'

Deborah chirped, 'Mm-hm.'

Sarah's words became uniformly brief. 'What does your boyfriend do?'

'Well I don't know if he's my boyfriend *just* yet.'

'What does he do?' said Sarah, suddenly impatient.

'And I know it sounds clichéd because I'm a nurse but he's a doctor. A surgeon, actually. The fourth date's tomorrow,' she exhaled. 'I can't wait. But he hasn't told me where he's taking me.'

'The botanical gardens,' said Sarah, staring into the distance.

'Oo, do you think so? That'll be nice.'

A young man came in from the deck and kissed Deborah's lips. 'I'm just going to the bathroom. You don't know where it is do you?'

'I think it's down that way,' said Deborah.

Instantly and greatly relieved Sarah said, 'That was him?'

'No,' Deborah sighed. 'That was someone else. But shh. Anyway, it was *so* nice talking to you. I'd better go and mingle now that I've got all this ice. Thanks Adam.'

'You are most welcome, Deborah.'

'My espresso martini?' said Sarah.

'Well doesn't it sound like there are *two* very romantic young men out there?'

'*No* gin?' said a girl at the other end of the bar.

'All out, sorry,' said the bartender. 'How about an espresso martini?'

'No gin,' the girl called out to her friend who was playing with the necktie of an excited young man on the other side of the glass doors. 'Nup, she can't hear me.'

'Espresso martini?'

'Errrr, vodka,' she groaned with a dawning sense of inevitability. 'I am anybody's after vodka.'

'Espresso martini!' said the bartender, putting the one he had just prepared for Sarah onto the bar. 'So should I show you the rest of my boat?'

'*Your* boat?'

'Mm hm.'

'I think you should definitely show me the rest of your boat!'

The bartender patted Adam on the shoulders and said, 'All yours, buddy,' as he shuffled along behind him.

'Could I get that espresso martini now?' said Sarah, impatient still.

'Oh. Ah, that young man was the bartender. I was just looking for some ice. And you'll be very happy to know that I've found cubes with rounded bottoms.'

2:4

In the doorway to the forward deck Noah Dulrich was busy convincing himself that he absolutely did possess the courage to take one more step up, to cross despite almost certain exposure to the elements the expanse of his boat's bow and then to stand astride it like the novelist that he was.

A feminine hand rose slowly over the starboard gunwale, its fingertips barely managing to touch the lowest rail. In its second attempt the whole hand gripped. It was quickly followed by another. Then a young woman's face appeared, straining from pulling herself up. Deciding that the time to act was at hand, Noah strode towards this damsel and reached over the railings and pulled her up.

'Thank you so much!' said the girl. 'Oh, I didn't think I was ever going to make it up.'

'What were you doing down there?'

'So I am *not* invited to whatever is going on on this boat.' Beside most other males the girl would have looked awkwardly tall. The width of her shoulders betrayed that she had once been very serious about her rowing. The skin of her face, pockmarked and littered with a permanent cycle of pimples, was distinctly not uniform of colour. She had a smile that could have been through kindness described as big; at full stretch it made her look daft. A small flower behind her left ear kept back that side of her uninspiring brown hair.

'Are you not?'

'No,' said the girl in a long syllable. 'My friends and I were out for dinner and then we were walking past up on the boardwalk and they heard a party. They do love a party.'

'And where are they?'

'They boosted each other up and left me down there. Ages ago. I think I might just stay up here and stow away until they text me.'

'You're a stowaway?'

'Probably. I'm not really the party-crashing type. Too nervous about being found out I think. And who knows whose party it is!?'

'Your friends sound interesting.'

'Ha. That's one way of putting it.'

'Have any of them ever had an affair with an aristocat?'

'Oh they've had affairs with just about everybody. I'm sure they're already at it downstairs. They love the kinds of people who party on boats. *Is* there a party downstairs?'

'Have any of them have ever gone up a tropical river?'

'A tropical river? I don't know. They do go to Thailand all the time.'

'What's your name, stowaway?'

'Rachel.'

'I'm Noah. This is my boat.'

'Your boat?'

'My boat.'

'You must be rich.'

'I'm a novelist.'

'What's your last name? I'll look you up. I love reading!'

'Dulrich.'

'Like Jezebel Dulrich?'

'Mummy,' Noah groaned.

'Mummy?'

'She's my mother.'

'Jezebel Dulrich is your mum?'

'Do you want to meet her?'

'Oh. … Oh, I nearly threw up. Are you serious?'

'It's her party. It was meant to be mine. But it's hers.'

'I think I'd be too nervous. Can I hear monkeys?'

'Mummy keeps two of them in the bedroom on weekends. They play with them when they're drunk. What do you do, Rachel?'

'Me? I work for the Department of Multicultural Affairs.'

'Mmm,' said Noah, incapable of feigning excitement.

'In the settlement coordination unit. You're falling asleep?'

'No, no. What about your friends?'

'The ones here?'

'The interesting ones.'

'One's a model and one's a lawyer. I can't believe your mum's Jezebel Dulrich! I love Quim! I have one of her dresses and I wear it *all* the time! I. love. Quim. Just love it.'

'I like this dress.'

'Really?'

Purple, plain and with thin shoulder straps, it was not an extraordinary garment.

'You look striking.'

'Striking?'

'Striking. Will you have a drink with me?'

'Why are you wearing a life jacket?'

'I had to jump in and save somebody before. I'm staying prepared.'

'You're not wet.'

'It's my boat, remember? Change of clothes on board.'

Another hand preceded yet another at the lowest rail behind Rachel and was followed by the thud of a risen foot. Very soon a second young woman was stepping over the rail and onto the bow.

'Dinah?'

'Hi Noah.'

'What are you doing?'

'I can hear Jacob from the pier. I can't deal with him when he's like this.'

'This is Rachel. Rachel, Dinah. My best friend's wife.'

The young women smiled at one another and shook hands.

'We were just about to go in for a drink.'

Jezebel, chortling, slid open the door to the bar and walked in backwards. 'Oh, don't let him stop,' she called out to those watching Jacob. 'He's just too much fun to listen to.'

Jacob was orating now from the lower deck's long dining table.

'We should all be allowed to own slaves! Even slaves can own slaves.'

'Sarah!' said Jezebel, closing the door. 'Where *have* you been? Adam have you been keeping Sarah from us? Sarah?'

She was staring blankly into the harrowing distance beyond her empty martini glass. She had broken down halfway through explaining to Adam the process of making her drink. 'It's the deceit and the disrespect of the whole thing,' she kept saying to Adam. She had been fighting her shuddering jaw ever since. 'How can people be so cruel to one another?'

Jezebel put a hand at her shoulder. 'Sarah?'

'Jezebel. I'm sorry. I'm really not feeling well.'

'Are you not? You poor dear.'

'I'm really sorry.'

'Don't be ridiculous. You're not seasick are you?'

'I could be. Yeah, maybe. I'm not normally good on boats. I've got Isaac waiting for me at home, I think I'm going to go. Is that all right?'

'Of course, darling. Go home and sleep it off. You poor thing.'

'Thank you so much, Adam. Bye.'

'Yes goodbye, Sarah. Do feel better.'

Sarah kissed Jezebel quickly on the cheek and opened the doors and hurried across the lower deck. She disembarked without saying goodbye to anyone.

'Not the inferior peoples of the world or anything like that,' said Jacob. 'I'm not racist. But all I'm saying is that slavery should be an option. People who get into debt, people who refuse to work.'

'Where's my bartender?' said Jezebel.

'He left some time ago, with a young woman.'

'Left? Who's going to make me my martini, Adam?'

'Oh, God, he's still at it,' said Dinah, coming down the steps.

'Dinah, my darling! How are you? Your husband is hilarious. I absolutely love him.'

'Somebody has to.'

'Strength should be the lord of imbecility,' Dinah's loveable husband was saying. 'Their glory would be in serving us, in contributing to us surpassing the greatest civilisations ever to grace the earth. *Then* we'll become one. No, not one. We'll become *the* greatest civilisation ever to grace the earth. Do you see? Does everybody see?'

'What does he do?' yelled a stoned marketing manager.

'I'm guessing he is writer,' yelled an emaciated old screamer who all night had been telling others to call him *Ha*-nibal. (This person's costume was a child-sized orange polo tucked into torn-in-the-centre-of-the-buttocks acid-washed jeans and an octogenarian's purple velvet dinner jacket mostly hidden under a keffiyeh.)

'He bloody is not,' yelled Noah.

'He's a genius, whatever he is,' said Francy.

'I am a divorce lawyer, you.'

'I knew it!' said Francy.

'Get his card. I'll want him for mine.'

'Can a you help me with a my CVay?' said *Ha*–nibal, a question he had asked at least once of everybody on the boat (and it by no means an inconsiderable task – its opening sentence contained the phrase, 'Always big successful').

With a self-made espresso martini accompanying another of her maltese terriers, Jezebel went back outside and used her elbow to close the door behind her.

'Hello, Dinah,' said Adam.

'I could hear him from the boardwalk,' she lamented.

'He has taken a very strange turn. Stranger than usual. Would you like something to drink? I have plenty of ice.'

'No, thanks. As soon as he's done we're off.'

Noah introduced Rachel to Adam.

'Noah's got a new friend, I see? Oh, I like your bellis perennis.'

'My what?'

'Behind your ear. Your bellis perennis. Everlasting beauty. It's a daisy. And pink, for youth and innocence. And a very fine one indeed.'

'All right, mate. Don't bore her to death.'

'It used to be called Mary's rose. Do you know where its

common name comes from?'

'Where?' said Rachel.

'The day's eyes. The whole flower closes at night and opens again at sunrise to look upon the day. It's the day's eye. The daisy.'

Rachel's mouth was agape from a mild sort of wonder. Never before had she been so passionately inundated by so much pleasant information. 'I love him,' she said to Noah. She went behind the bar and gave Adam a hug. 'This is your best friend?'

'No,' said Dinah. 'That is.' She knocked across one of the sliding doors.

'Conscience is a word that cowards use,' yelled Jacob, crouching down and sweeping his pointed hand around the boat. He pointed at himself. 'Devised to keep the strong in awe. Our arms are our conscience and swords our law. March bravely, let us to it hells-bells. If not in heaven, then hand to hand–, wait, no. Yes. No!'

'All right,' said Dinah, trying to wrap up the production she had been allowing Jacob to star in. 'That's enough.'

'Enough what, woman?' said Jacob.

'How do you know so much about daisies?' said Rachel.

'He has a greenhouse full of flowers,' said Noah.

'That's amazing.'

'Would you like to see it?'

'No she wouldn't.'

'Absolutely.'

'Really?' said Noah.

'Of course!'

'We could go and look at them now if you'd like.'

'Now?'

'I live just on the harbour there.'

'Yes! Let's do it, let's go! I'd love to see them. I'll just tell my friends I'm leaving for a bit.'

The back of a man's head was being pinned against the window by pressure applied to his lips. The applicator was one of Rachel's friends. 'Kari, where's Mel?'

'On the vodka,' said Kari from the side of her mouth.

Rachel clicked her tongue. 'You two! I'm going on shore for a bit. I'll be back soon. Will you be here?'

'Mm hm,' she mumbled.

'Jacob, will you come down from there please?'

'This, ladies and gentlemen, is my wife. Dinah, these are people. Rich and famous and influential people. Come up here and help me. These people like me and I like them too.'

'Of course they do, Jacob, look at them. Now would you please come down.'

'I need to calm down? You need to calm down. We should own slaves.'

'And we'll get some on the way home. Now come on, down you hop.'

'Oh, leave him be, Dinah,' said Jezebel. 'Otherwise we'll have to get the monkeys out.'

'Where are you two going? Who's the girl?'

'Back in a minute,' said Noah.

'Good. Dinah! Don't you think that some people should be our slaves? Look what we've built!' Jacob swept his hand in a wide arc over the harbourside. 'People who don't build anything should be allowed to be our slaves if they want to. We'll pay them of course. But we can make them do whatever we want.'

'Please, Jacob.'

'Don't you believe in slavery? If you love me you'll believe in slavery.'

'Jacob!'

'My wife believes that everybody should love everybody.'

A roar of laughter, the first since Dinah had joined the performance, resounded from Jacob's audience. The stoned marketing manager was hit suddenly by a revelation of his own. With some difficulty he outlined it. 'Loving somebody … does not preclude … having them as a slave.'

'Thas aso true!' screamed *Ha*-nibal, passing along their cigarette.

'Is Leah coming?' said Jacob.

'Why would Leah be coming?'

'I'd like to make Leah come,' said the marketing manager.

'Is a Leah mun?' said *Ha*-nibal.

'I told you to invite her,' said Jacob. 'Everybody, my wife is a flight attendant. But she's going to be a wedding planner. A hippie wedding planner. Wedding planner for hippies. Dirty feet weddings. She believes that love makes the world go round. I know better. It's money. Divorce lawyer, wedding planner. Ha! You put 'em together and we cash 'em apart. And then we're going to run away together to Vietnam. In a decade. Rich and happy. Just like all of you.'

Jacob had talked too long. He had just about lost them. They were turning to each other and raising over their sunglasses their eyebrows. 'Where is Sarah?' Francy yelled to Jezebel. 'I want to feel her tits again. You can hardly tell.'

'Didn't they feel amazing?! You really can hardly tell.'

'Jacob, now.'

'Jacob, now.'

Adam pushed down the switch for the night lights in the glasshouse. 'I don't want to wake them,' he said with a grin. The greens of his plants remained unilluminated. The flowers shone. He pulled back the gramophone's plastic cover and unscrewed the horn from the base and started the record. Without amplification it sounded tinny and distant. 'To keep them dreaming,' said Adam.

Rachel inhaled deeply through her nose. 'I love that smell. Don't you love that smell?'

'I love that smell,' said Noah.

'Do you know what I like to think that smell is? It's the smell of life old and new.'

'That's beautiful,' said Rachel. She pointed at the ceiling. 'Oh, this could be our song.'

'*Our* song?' said Noah.

'No?'

Adam gave his guests the grand tour. He pointed out flowers of particular beauty or interest and told with exhausting detail everything he knew about each. He told Rachel she could pick any flower she liked and could have it. She picked a lily of the valley, endearing her to him instantly.

'And this,' he said, coming to the back corner, 'is the opposite of your English daisy.'

'My bellum perennis?'

'Almost. This is an epiphyllum oxypetalum. The queen of the night. Instead of blooming every day at sunrise it blooms once a year at night, and the flowers wither before dawn.'

'A single night?'

'And they're one of the most supernal flowers you've ever seen.'

'That's incredible, Adam.'

'That's actually pretty cool,' said Noah.

'When's it due to bloom, do you know?'

'A month from today.'

'A month from today? Adam, do you think I could come and watch it when it blooms?'

'Do you really want to?'

'I'll come,' said Noah.

'I'd be so happy to have somebody to watch it with.'

'What do you do with all these flowers?'

'He sells them.'

'I sell about half of them. Some of them are very valuable. They should be shared with people who love them enough to give away their beloved money for them. But I don't sell the wild roses or the lilies of the valley. Or the queen of the night. Some things are too precious to sell. Now, Rachel,' he said, stooping. 'What do you know about the queen of the night?'

'Nothing.'

'Just a few petals from a queen of the night flower will give you diarrhea, can cause baldness, and can even induce an abortion. Ingestion of a whole flower would be certain death.'

'It looks so harmless.'

'Flowers can teach us all the moral lessons the world has to teach. This one, the rarer something is that we consume, the worse are the consequences.'

'I love him,' she said again to Noah.

The glasshouse door thudded against its frame. 'Only me, dear,' said Edith. 'I saw the night lights on and I thought I'd best come out and see if you wanted anything to eat or drink. I didn't know you had guests. Hello lovely. Hello again, Noah. That's a very fancy life jacket.'

'Mrs Athelstan, this is Rachel.'

'How do you? It's lovely to meet you. Now who would like some cheese and port? Rachel, won't you have something to drink?'

'No, thank you so much. I ate *so* much at dinner. I'm really full.'

Edith smiled and put her hand onto Rachel's arm. 'And you're keeping your legs closed I hope?'

'Grandma!'

'What, dear?'

'What kind of a thing to say is that?'

'I'm giving the girl a history lesson, dear.'

'You're not, you're being outrageous. She isn't drunk. Leave her be.'

'History is made by women, Rachel. Men do whatever they do only to impress us, and in whatever they do they'll only go so far as we let them. We turn the world. Don't ever listen to the economists who tell you otherwise. The love which women exact of their men makes the world go around. And no love was ever exacted from easily opened legs. All the wisest people have known so.' Edith poked Noah in the stomach. 'And certainly don't let this one tell you any different. Or Jacob. You didn't let her meet Jacob did you?'

'I think I love you too,' said Rachel, wondering now at Edith with moistening eyes.

'Well, I just thought I'd come and say hello. There's some cheddar and stilton in the fridge, dear, if anybody changes their mind. It's lovely to meet you, Rachel. Goodnight.'

'I love her,' said Rachel when Edith had gone.

'She's quite lovely most of the time. Sorry about that.'

'We should get back to the boat,' said Noah.

'Yes, enough debauchery for me for one night,' said Adam. 'Thank you so much for coming over.'

'Thank you for showing me the flowers, Adam.'

'Oh, my pleasure.'

'And I'll get hold of you in a month? To watch the queen of the night?'

'That would be something quite wonderful, Rachel. I'm looking forward to it all the more now.'

Adam was winked and nodded at as Noah ushered Rachel from the glasshouse.

2:5

For an hour Sarah had been waiting in the kitchen of the home she shared with Isaac, fighting the urge to snoop with her phone and telling herself that it was just her being paranoid. When eventually Isaac walked through the door she took a deep breath and, knowing he would come into the kitchen to drop his keys on the table, listened to his footsteps resound in the hallway. He went straight into the bathroom and started the shower.

She knocked quietly on the bathroom door, opened it a little and called to him. 'Oh, you're home,' he said, surprised. Sarah sat on the toilet seat. Isaac lathered and rinsed.

'Where were you?'

'What's that?' said Isaac, leaning back from the showerhead.

'Where were you tonight?'

'What do you mean?'

'You said you'd wait at home for me.'

'You said you wouldn't be home before midnight.'

'It's a quarter to.'

'Exactly.'

'So where were you?'

Isaac peered around the shower screen. At thirty-five he was balding. It was the sole outward indicator of the prestige which his profession otherwise bestowed.

'What's the matter?'

'Nothing. Where were you?'

'I was out with a few of the uni guys.'

'Just uni guys?'

Isaac momentarily returned his face to the water. 'Hey is that dress finished yet, for my sister?'

'Not yet. Tuesday.'

Isaac turned the water off and dried himself. 'You all right?'

'Do you remember where you took me for our fourth date?'

'Of course.' He dried his thinning hair and bent down to kiss her lips. 'What's wrong? Was the party no good?'

'Where have you been?'

'What do you mean? I told you.'

'Were you out with nurses?'

'Sarah.'

'What did we do on our fourth date?'

'We had a picnic.'

'Where?'

'Sarah.'

'*Where?*'

'In the botanical gardens! What's the matter with you?' Isaac streaked his toothbrush with toothpaste.

'Do you remember what I said to you on our fifth date?'

With his toothbrush readied Isaac repeated what now seemed to him a tired mantra of an anecdote. 'You said that if it wasn't for the exact order of the dates I took you on you probably wouldn't have fallen in love with me. Each one was more grand than the last, like climbing a mountain of …? It was the worst line I've ever heard that wasn't in a movie. It still is the worst line I've ever heard.'

'Can we go for champagne brunch tomorrow? Como house?'

Isaac shimmied his toothbrush around and spat.

'I can't tomorrow. I have a patient.'

'On a Sunday?'

'I know. Her operation's on Wednesday and tomorrow's the only time I could see her before then. Funny little old lady. Said she wouldn't see anybody on a Sunday until after church. Isn't that funny?'

'And that's what you're doing tomorrow?'

'Around late brunch time, yes. We can go out for dinner though if you want.'

'What time's her appointment?'

'What's with all the questions?'

'What time's her appointment?'

'At one! I'll see you in bed.'

And Sarah was left by Isaac to fret on the toilet seat.

2:6

The downlit bedroom below the *Teba*'s deck was upholstered largely in red velvet and stank of bait. Rachel stopped at the bottom of the stairwell and waited with a nervous smile. Noah took a few steps into the room and turned around. Immediately he recognized the exact moment at which the films and television programmes that wholly determined his behavioural catalogue dictated that he should kiss her. He went to her and did so and they shuffled towards the bed. Rachel began unclipping his life jacket. One of the monkeys rattled at a bar of its domed cage. Noah broke off to put a sheet over it. The second he recommenced the sheet was pulled down by tiny fingers. The two monkeys cackled and Noah got up again and one of the monkeys clapped. They were enshrouded again. With uncanny timing one of them pulled down the sheet exactly as Noah returned his hand to Rachel's cheek. Both monkeys bared their teeth and stood, their hands clasped, smiling sovereigns of the bedroom.

'Monkeys,' said Noah with atypical remorse.

Stomping could be heard then Rachel's friends seen at the bottom of the bedroom steps. 'There you are!' said Kari.

'There are no boys left on this boat,' said Mel.

'We're leaving.'

'I think I might stay?' said Rachel, scrunching her nose.

'Finally!' said Mel.

'Yes! Have fun!' said Kari, and the girls thundered back up the stairs.

'Have they ever played Russian roulette?'

'Like at the casino?'

'Anywhere.'

'In Vegas they partied with Kenny Powers at a casino once. A *lot* of vodka that night. Vodka's Russian.'

'Vodka is Russian.'

Then Jezebel came giggling lewdly down the steps, towing two men by their neck ties. 'Hello darling.'

'Mummy!' said Noah, most annoyed.

'Sorry darling.'

'Maybe I should catch up with the girls,' said Rachel.

'No darling, you two stay down here. This is Noah's party and Noah's boat. We were just leaving. I was coming to say goodbye. Goodnight darlings. You two, congratulate my son. I'll just take the monkeys with me? They get very disruptive.' Jezebel lifted the cage and said one last goodnight and made one of her men carry it up the steps.

Noah pressed his face against Rachel's. Very shortly he was squeezing at her chest with his fingertips. She pulled aside. 'Can we wait a bit? I feel awkward now your mum's seen us. Can we just talk for a bit?'

Noah huffed gently through his nose. 'Of course.'

They both looked around the room for a few immature seconds.

'Oo, do you want me to show you the bridge?'

'What's that?'

'So this,' said Noah, 'is apparently called the bridge. Hang on a second.' He eventually hit the right switch. The room lit up and they stood, sheltered perfectly behind tinted perspex from the frigid and blustery night, over the control panel. 'Now what do you think we call this?'

'The steering wheel.'

'Very good! Is this your first bridge?'

'I've been in many bridges,' said Rachel, attempting to flirt.

Noah pointed to one of the switches. 'And this is the...?'

Rachel read the sticker above it. 'The ignition.'

'The ignition switch.'

She looked up at Noah and smiled, trying to catch his eye.

'And this is the...?'

'Hm?'

'No, I don't know either.'

'So are we going to go for a sail?'

'No, I don't have my boat licence.'

'Really?'

'And which one's this?'

'That is the... throttle,' said Rachel, pointing to the label above it.

'Which makes the boat...?'

'Go.'

'Backwards *and* forwards.'

'And... this one?'

'The bilge.'

'The bilge. What's the bilge?'

'I don't know. Must be important though because it's next to the...?'

'Kiss me?'

'Nope. Wait, what? Really?'

Noah lowered his head and put his lips to Rachel's. Very soon their arms were around one another's bodies and neither of them were thinking of very much else besides getting back down to the bedroom without interrupting their embrace.

CHAPTER 3

1

A despiser of driving in cities and trapped behind an intersection of speeding traffic which ran like eight screaming meat saws between her home and the world, Edith had a car service take her and Adam to church on Sundays. After being sent a succession of variously unpleasant drivers (the most unpleasant of whom, Qedesh, was an unintelligible young man whose taxi contained three shrines to the destruction of the twin towers) she was one Sunday sent John. He played no music, made no phone calls, dressed respectfully rather than fashionably and spoke only in English. She had insisted on him ever since.

'Good morning, Mrs Athelstan,' he said, slightly lowering his head and smiling warmly.

'Good morning, John,' said Edith, always glad to see him. 'How are you?'

'Oh, very well this morning, ma'am.'

'And the family?'

'Despite having to put up with me, ma'am, even better.'

'Ha, very good, John.'

They crossed town in silence. John waited through the service at the bottom of the church steps. When reverend Newman, white-haired and decrepit, exited his house of worship and took the position from which he always farewelled his dim flock John opened the car door. Edith put her hand in the reverend's and smiled as he mumbled and nodded at her. Only his Credos and his Lord's Prayers, miraculously remembered from a time when the measure of his voice matched the fervour of his belief, were now ever intelligible. Most of the congregation thought that probably it was for the best that he was to be replaced by that young Taiwanese man. Though none had yet volunteered for the dread task of informing him of his redundancy. All Adam could pick up in his own exchanges with this primordial man were his s's, his hard c's and the occasional t. And Adam felt awful about it.

'A very nice button-hole today, Adam. Purple hyacinths?'

'They are purple hyacinths, John. How did you know?'

'I'm old, but I'm not colour blind.'

'Oh, John, you are funny. How did you know they were hyacinths?'

'You come to know a lot of things at my age. How was service today, Mrs Athelstan?'

'Very nice thank you, John.'

They crossed town a second time.

'Oh, look, Grandma,' said Adam, pointing out the window. Sunday Mass always left the both of them feeling as though they ought more to engage with the world. 'Those two men are holding hands.'

'Arabs are they?'

'I don't think so.'

'They do that in Arabia, you know, because they can't touch their women in public.'

'Perhaps they're Arabs. They look normal enough. Shirtsleeves in April though. And besides, there's a woman being touched just there. She doesn't seem to mind. Oh dear, very touched. I wonder if we should call the police.'

'No, not our business, dear. And she appears to be enjoying it very much.'

'Oh, yes. Oh, and look at those three.'

'Oh, how terrifying. Even the boy one has eye makeup on.'

'That's a lot of metal for a belt,' said Adam. 'Suppose she fell down. That'll bruise her hips.'

'And if he falls down those spikes will go right into his skull. Ooh, and they've all got things through their noses. And their lips.'

'Like dairy cattle.'

'Goths, I think, Mrs Athelstan.'

'Goths, you say, John?'

'I think so, ma'am.'

'Ostrogoths or Visigoths?'

'Hard to say, Mrs Athelstan.'

'No wonder the Romans were frightened of them,' said Adam.

'Oh look at that floating blob, dear. You can hardly tell its... Is it a...? What's in its mouth?'

'It's a hamburger I think, Grandma. I didn't know it was customary to eat two at a time though.'

'How *would* you determine its sex? Is it a –. You'd need an inspection under anaesthetic, like they do with echidnas.'

'Maybe its voice would give it away,' said John.

'Oh, yes its voice. I didn't think of that. Heavens.'

'*That*'s an Arab,' said Adam.

'Oh, so it is. I wonder if all those children are hers. Do you suppose she's allowed to go into banks in that get-up? They'd be liable to think she was in there to rob the place.'

'Now what's going on?' said Adam.

'You've driven us to Peking, John.'

'Russell street, Mrs Athelstan.'

'Is it really? How extraordinary.'

'So many shopping bags,' said Adam. 'What *do* they all buy?'

Then Edith shrieked and pulled her purse in close. 'Look at *those* filthy people. There on the lawn. They look as though they've crawled out from the dust of an apocalypse.'

'Hippies, Mrs Athelstan.'

'Ohhhh, hippies, yes, I remember them. Look at their hair though. It doesn't look as though they've combed it since I last saw them.'

'I think their hair is in dreadlocks, ma'am. It's a style.'

'Dreadlocks? Hmm. Well they certainly are dreadful.'

John pulled in at the kerb. Edith waited for her door to be opened. 'Best of luck, ma'am.'

Upstairs Edith and Adam were greeted at the door to his rooms by the precocious Dr Isaac Krass.

'Afternoon, Mrs Athelstan. Hello, Adam. How are you both? We shouldn't be too long at all. Don't want to keep you on a Sunday.'

'Oh, no,' said Edith. 'Thank *you* for seeing us. You probably have all sorts of exciting things to be doing. Handsome young doctor and everything.'

The walls and shelves of Dr Krass's office were adorned by surprisingly few cumbersome books and by surprisingly many plastic life-sized moulds of multitudinous cups of breast, all pleasantly formed and nipples centred. Two huge glossy posters displayed an exhaustive catalogue of lips and necks; before-and-after photographs of sagging buttocks and scarred and bruised lifted ones processed in pairs around the room.

'Did I see you pull up in a driven car, Mrs Athelstan?'

'You may have done.'

'Do you have a chauffeur?'

'No, no, not a chauffeur. Nothing as fancy as that. I just can't stand driving in the city so I have John drive us on Sundays.'

'A very gay little black man,' said Adam.

Dr Krass's wobbling pen was suddenly stilled. 'Is he?' he said, smirking.

'Mmm,' said Adam.

Dr Krass moved his smirk across to Edith, who was looking calmly at him. 'All right then.' He opened on his desk the manila folder which pertained to Edith. 'Today's just a final briefing session. I want you to ask any and all questions you might have about Wednesday. You have to be completely at your ease going into it. It makes a very big difference to the success of the procedure and to the speed of your recovery. So, as you know your operation is called a coronary artery bypass, or a CABG. Cabbage, for short. And what that means is that I'm going to open your chest at the sternum, stop your heart, and then graft an artificial blood vessel, just like this one, onto your heart in order to bypass the obstruction in your left main coronary artery.'

Adam winced and stood up and went to the window.

'It's not a very risky operation, despite your age – not in my hands. The biggest risk comes from infection. The most important thing is that the chest cavity is open for the shortest time possible. Brevity is paramount. In a normal cabbage the chest cavity is open for around thirty minutes. I try and keep mine down to fifteen. But that's all on my side. Now, one concern I've come across in the past is that you might be wondering why *I'll* be performing your operation. Well the undeniable fact is, Mrs Athelstan, is that the modern heart is exactly like the parts of the body that I am quite expert in dealing with. It's composed of tissue, you see, that's very similar in malleability and behaviour to the breasts, to the lips, and to the buttocks. Has anybody ever told you, Adam, that you are an exceptional whistler?'

'Why, thank you, Dr Krass. No they have not.'

'What song is that?'

'Well actually that's not entirely true. I have been told a few times that I can whistle a tune. That was Goodnight Sweetheart by

Al Bowlly.'

'Tou whistle a lot, do you?'

'No, not usually. Well no, I suppose I do, yes. I'm just feeling very gay today.'

Dr Krass smiled again at Edith and almost laughed. 'Now, the company that manufactures these vessels appoints their own head surgeon, in this case me, and they send their own specialised perfusionist to oversee every operation in which their vessels are used. Do you know what a perfusionist does? A perfusionist uses what's called the heart-and-lung-machine to keep your body supplied with blood while your heart is stopped. And Halberd has a zero mortality rate, so far. I've asked that they send Dr Grace Monroe. An exceptional woman. I've worked with her before. She'll be standing beside me through the whole thing.

'Now, I have a list here of things you absolutely must not do before the operation. And on the back is exactly what you'll be going through on Wednesday. I'll perform the procedure at one o'clock, and you should be back at home by Friday.'

'It all sounds so easy.'

'In a way it is. And now that you know everything there is to know from my end, are there any questions from yours?'

'I don't think so, no. I feel perfectly comfortable in your hands.'

'Good. Then I think we can all head out and enjoy the sunshine. Have you got much on for today?'

'Tea at Mrs Gladstone's.'

'Tea at Mrs Gladstone's?'

'She makes the most sensational shortbread. Doesn't she, Adam? You wouldn't believe.'

'Well you make sure you go easy on the full cream milk and the butter, won't you? Adam, how about you? What's on for you for the afternoon, matey?'

'It's so unbelievably gay outside. One of the gayest April days I can remember for a long time. Grandma, you'll be all right getting around with just John, won't you? I think I'll go for a walk. It's just too gay to say no.'

3:2

An hour later Adam was in the Royal Botanical Gardens, waist-deep in agapanthus and angling his cheeks at the sun. He caught the scent of jasmine on the breeze and broke into song. '*Have you ever been lonely? Have you ever been blue? Have you ever loved someone just as I love you?*'

'Mummy look,' said a little girl, pointing from the footpath. Terrified, her mother put a protective arm around her and walked away as quickly as the girl's tiny legs would allow.

Thin cloud smothered the sun and took away what was pleasant in its warmth. Adam opened his eyes. 'Pesky stratocumulus,' he said and continued wading through the shrubbery. Presently he saw some peroxided waves amongst the long leaves. He neared and then recognised them.

'Hello, Sarah!' She was crouching in between the two rows of bushes, surveying the open lawn like a tigress watching a clearing she knew to be tapir-trodden. 'Sarah?' His slightly raised voice startled her.

'Oh!' she said, putting her hand at her chest. 'Oh, God, hello. Adam? It is Adam, isn't it?'

'It *is* Adam, that's right. Now what on earth could you be doing in agapanthus this afternoon?'

'In what?'

'That flower you're tearing to pieces in your hand. You look as though you're hiding. Are you hiding?'

'Shh, get down.'

'You are hiding! How fun.'

'It's *not* fun. My boyfriend's cheating on me. Get down.'

'If he's cheating you shouldn't be playing with him then. That's not fair.'

'No, it's not fair, is it? Thank you, Adam. I'm glad you agree. You're so nice. Are you here for a wedding or something?'

'A wedding? Why?'

'The suit.'

'This? Oh no, I would never wear this to a wedding. What would people think?'

'What are *you* doing in the bushes?'

'Ah, you're right! If he sees me talking to an agapanthus he might think something's up and he'll come over and find you, won't he? Well, good luck. And don't you let him go on cheating.'

Adam stepped out of Sarah's cover and looked to see if there were an imminent chance of the sun being delivered of its shroud. Then he remembered the loropetalum in the Southern China garden, just around the first corner of the lake, and set off for it.

Soon enough, at the far end of Sarah's hunting lawn a young woman stepped cautiously, for she was wearing very tall heels, onto the lawn. Soon Sarah saw that it was Deborah after all. The lesser criminal in the conspiracy, but a criminal nonetheless, and wading towards her as a very tapir through mud. Sarah waited until her prey was in the centre of the lawn. Then she ambushed her.

'Do you have any idea what you're doing?' said Sarah, racing across the savannah. She was unheard. 'Do you have any idea what you're doing?!'

Deborah pointed to herself. 'Excuse me?'

'Where is he?'

'Oh, Sarah. It is Sarah, isn't it? Hi. From the boat.'

'Where is he?'

'Where's who?'

'Isaac,' Sarah growled.

'Who's Isaac?'

'*Who's* Isaac. The man who's been taking you on *our* dates. The jazz bar, the rowboat, the bakery. And now here you are, date four, the Botanical Gardens. Now where is he?'

'Sarah, I'm here for a wedding.'

'Oh you have a wedding to go to together. How nice.'

'I'm here alone, Sarah. My date cancelled on me at the last minute. I think I'm on the wrong lawn though. It starts in half an hour. They'd be here by now if this was it. And the guy I'm seeing isn't Isaac. His name's Mark.'

Over Deborah's shoulder Sarah spied a couple begin joyfully their stroll into her wilderness. She recognised a few peculiarities of movement and shortly filled out the whole man. Unexpected prey, but prey nonetheless. She stormed past Deborah.

'Hello, Andy. Gone away for the weekend have you? I suppose the trip was cancelled?' Sarah looked at the woman whose arm was threaded through his. 'More important things to be *doing* than seeing me on a Sunday afternoon have you?'

'Sarah, I told you already, we can't be seeing each other. Not now that Isaac's working out of the same hospital as me. It's not right.'

On the path behind all this Adam was on his tip toes. His face had been buried in a pink camellia for some time now. He felt a tug at his sleeve. It was the tug of a woman in dark green shorts and heavy boots. 'Oi,' she said. 'Where did you get that from?' She tapped at her own breast.

'You're referring to my magnolia denudata,' said Adam, exuberantly. He so enjoyed curiosity about flowers.

But her interest was a very stern one. 'Where did you get it from?'

'Why just from the Southern china garden, just down there. Have you been down there today yet? They're bursting forth like joyous rockets. I had a purple hyacinth for my button-hole this morning but I saw this and I was breathtaken. It's lovely, isn't it?'

'It's a federal offence to transport endangered flowers out of the Botanical Gardens.'

'Is it?' said Adam, uncertain of why this woman was so ready with so boring a fact.

'Now hand it over.'

'I'm sorry?'

'The Yulan magnolia you're trying to steal.'

'Steal?' She offered Adam an impatient palm. 'Should I not have picked it?'

'You should not have picked it. It's a federal offence to transport endangered flowers out of the Botanical Gardens.'

'Is it really? That's funny, I am sorry. I donated the denudata cutting to Dr Moors when I had to change glasshouses. In a small way I always thought the tree was partly mine. But I suppose, if you insist.'

Adam pulled the flower from his lapel and gave it to her.

'Vandal.'

'I am not a vandal.'

'You are a vandal.'

'I am not a vandal.'

CHAPTER 4

1

When three years ago Jacob Barron proposed to Dinah Manthorne one of the few things they agreed upon was that only they had long engagements who did not really want to get married. She organised their whole wedding in four months. The Botanical Gardens ceremony preceded a sordid reception at the rooftop and oceanfront function-room of their favourite St Kilda bar.

It was persistence which initially endeared Jacob to her. Sick of the kind of man she was meeting as a flight attendant Dinah was tricked into giving Jacob her number at a night-club. For two months Jacob thought he was being rejected by Dinah's sister, Leah. Dinah kept up the digital correspondence because Jacob, two years a lawyer and advertising himself copiously, seemed at least to have things together. When tricked again by a builder into thinking she had found someone only secondarily interested in her flesh Dinah convinced herself that Jacob's forwardness might just be an extension of his honesty. By the time they met in person Jacob had forgotten what Leah looked like. He certainly did not remember her chest being quite so large. So he persevered until he found that he did not half mind Dinah. His protectiveness she reasoned down to passion, his whininess she downgraded with not very much effort to sensitivity. Thus convincing herself that Jacob was after all something of a catch, she announced to him a vague intention of permanence and they moved in together.

Quickly and one by one Jacob's small efforts—those which manured Dinah's belief that he possessed the attributes which she told him she thought he possessed—dwindled, until, almost three years married and committed to one another by Dinah's self-written vows and a mortgage, they took each other entirely for granted and spoke even in the most benign exchanges as though they were bickering.

Sleep offered little respite. Jacob kicked and Dinah snored. Their Middle Park townhouse only calcified their problems. Its walls were of very bright tones selected and painted by Dinah in a single weekend—so averse had Jacob been to their colour that he refused to have any part in their application. The living room, the bedroom, the kitchen, the bathroom, all were littered now with Dinah's things—an Audrey Hepburn poster, the autobiographies of several singers of popular music, green Moroccan tea glasses, his and hers dream-catchers, the best-sellers of half a dozen eastern gurus and mystics, a photograph of Dinah excitedly stroking a sedated tiger, three wooden elephants, two teak buddhas (one enormous, one slightly less so), a silken banner with two oms and the English inscription, 'You Are Truly Special'. Jacob's contribution to the décor, beside the study into which Dinah was now fast encroaching, was limited to an ashtray in the form of a skull (Jacob was no longer permitted to smoke), the wall-mounted television, and a very grim poster that was curling from moisture on the back of the bathroom door of a band with a very gloomy name whom he had adored in adolescence.

All to Jacob sources of grievous frustration.

Only a single routine betrayed a preference for one another's company before anyone else's, or to solitude. They took it in turns whenever Dinah was at home (and not in a Balinese hotel or waiting upon bogans in the cabin of a 737) to make one another breakfast. When it was Jacob's turn Dinah showered with excitement, knowing that breakfast would be ready for her when she got out. When it was Dinah's he showered with the relief that a chore was temporarily off his hands. The first day of Dinah's unemployment (as Jacob called it) or her new career (as she called it) and it was Jacob's turn.

From the bathroom Dinah could smell bacon. She hoped that it was Jacob's private accompaniment to any one of her favourite breakfasts.

'Morning, babe,' said Jacob, turning from the kitchen bench. He kissed Dinah on the cheek and reached around her back to push at the side of her towel-covered breast. He was trying to be especially affectionate. After a sleepless night of overreacting to her rebuffs he thought it his best chance (despite infuriating mountains of evidence to the contrary) of being allowed between her legs that night, or, as had mythically happened once in their first year of marriage, invited into them before leaving for work.

Jacob had cooked practically nothing besides bacon.

'No quinoa.'

'Quinoa's not food.'

'Well it's the food I wanted for breakfast, isn't it?'

'But you love bacon.'

'I haven't eaten bacon in a year. You love bacon.'

'And what better time to restart,' he said, smiling.

The abandonment of bacon had been Dinah's final step to full veganism. She had dropped all animal products, cheese even, with ease; bacon had lingered as too tempting for a full conversion. Veganism, she was once told by a stallholder at a healer's market, was the ultimate way to bring out her true inner hippie, a bringing-out to which she desperately aspired. Jacob vigorously mocked her gradual adoption of a vague kind of spiritual assertion. She proclaimed that she was just trying to be happier with herself, a right she figured he could not refuse her. He could not at all see why being happier with oneself should involve teak buddhas, dream-catchers, and dinner gongs. The latest and most grave manifestation of her descent into nirvana was an extremely unwelcome refusal to groom.

Dinah took another plate from the cupboard and slid her bacon onto Jacob's. She spread some ebony toast with an olive spread then sliced some fruit onto it and drizzled it with honey.

'Babe, when I make you breakfast I don't wanna just pour you a bowl of cereal or cut up some fruit. That's no effort. I want to go all out for you, babe. My breakfasts for you should be elaborate and labour-intensive.'

'Then make me what I want for breakfast! That's the effort I want. The most labour-intensive thing that you can do for me is to give me the breakfast I want when it's your turn. I know how hard it is for you to give me what I want.'

He put an egg on his toast and made a sandwich with the bacon. He put his tie over his shoulder and dug in.

'How about this—I go to work today and make real money, and pay for bacon, and eat the bacon, and you go to work today...'

'You're an arsehole.'

'I know, I'm sorry. Here.' He reached across the table and kissed her cheek.

'You need to stop giving me shit about this. I can either go on being a flight attendant until I'm forty and then have a mental breakdown and you can deal with that…'

'I know.'

'…or I can give this a shot now and if it fails I get back into it before I'm thirty-five.'

'I know.'

'But I have to use my life to make other people happy, Jacob. It's one of the four immeasurables.'

'I know! And you better make it huge. That's what she said. I want to be out and in Vietnam by forty.'

'I know you do, Jacob.'

'Have you read about what's going on over there?' Jacob flicked through a newspaper to find the article he had been reading as their marital bacon sizzled. 'Villagers hacking each other to bits. Warlords springing up. … Look at these pictures. They're barbarians. We should just leave them to fight it out until there's none of them left. If it was up to me–.'

'Oh, but it is up to you,' said Dinah, pouting. 'You should go over there. And you should go up a river and track down whoever's causing the killings, and you should kill them.'

'Maybe I will.'

'You should. With nothing but a machete. Maybe it'll be a skinny bald girl.'

'Ha! I wish. At least--.' Jacob saw opening before him a tired course of a morning. He broke off. 'So what's today then? Day one.'

'You don't care.'

'Of course I care! This is our future. Why would I ask if I didn't care?'

Dinah wanted to tell him anyway. 'Hmm. Well. I think I'll start off with the big stuff. I have to get a venue. They want this Buddhist temple out in the western suburbs so I'll have to see if they even allow weddings there. And then I think catering. They want Indian so I'll have to shop around for that. Ooh, hopefully I get to taste all the food.'

'And flowers?'

'No, flowers are the easy part. I've already got that florist at South Melbourne. But, I can assure you that I will not be leaving that office until five o'clock. Full working hours. It's the only way to make a proper go of it. Hard work and long hours. If you're in your office, I'm in mine.'

'Well you'll be working late tonight. One of my clients wants to mediate after work.'

'And what happened with these two?'

'He slept with her sister.'

'Oh, God. How can people be so cruel to one another? All right, so you'll be home late. Just Leah and I for dinner then. I'll order you extra.'

'Leah's coming round? What time?'

'Dinner time.'

'Oh. ... Well I'll see if I can get done a bit earlier then. Or I might just see if they want to postpone. It's never good after work. People are tired and vindictive.'

'Don't stress. She's just popping in for dinner and then popping out. She wants to tell me all about her new boyfriend.'

'She has a new boyfriend? Why didn't you tell me?'

'Why would I tell you?'

'I like to know what's happening with your family. They're my family too.'

If Dinah were not certain that Jacob was not at all Leah's type, she being very cherishing of things which Dinah knew he barely possessed or habitually mocked, she might have worried that he held more than a groveling interest in her.

'Mmm. Well I'll see you later tonight.'

'Mmm,' said Jacob, kissing her on the collar bone. 'Can't wait. I'm looking forward to seeing you in a towel again.'

'Is that right?'

'Mm hm.'

'And I just want to tell you again how grateful I am that you're letting me do this career change thing.'

'Letting you? I'm not your boss.'

'I know. But you're working hard, you're doing all the extra hours. I just want to know how happy I am that you're letting me have a new start. Maybe I'll even see if I can make it up to you a little tonight.'

'Anus tart?'

'Jacob!'

'What?'

'Stop making fun of me!'

'I'm not making fun of you! It was funny.'

'It's not funny. It's my life you're mocking. You're an arsehole. Go to work. You're gonna be late.'

Jacob looked at his watch 'Oh, shit. Kiss? I'll try and be back by six-thirty.'

The front door closed at Jacob's back and Dinah went to the bedroom and got ready. She put on her full make-up and spent half an hour on her hair. She put on a sun dress and heels. She stood at the desk in the workspace she had set aside for herself in Jacob's study and picked up a business card and keyed its number into her phone.

'Hi, I was just wondering if you allow weddings at your temple. … You do? Great. And do you have many openings in November? … All of November's free? … No, that's great, thank you. … Yep, will do, bye.'

She put her phone in her handbag and checked herself one last time in the bathroom mirror on the way out. She unchained her bicycle from the cast iron railing of their front fence and walked it out onto the footpath; she clipped her helmet at her chin and threw a leg over and rode away.

4:2

Jacob stepped off his tram and walked what had now become his semi-daily eleven-block detour. When he reached his destination he put his satchel down and leaned a shoulder against a tree and stared across the street.

Closest to the large windowfront of the Happiest Garden Kindergarten were a dozen small children cross-legged in a half circle. They were putting their hands in the air and clapping. The source and focus of their energy, with long blonde curls and a tiny waist, smiling and laughing and full of every joy which those possess in their company who do not loathe children, was their teacher. They were allowed to call her Miss Leah.

Jacob had no meetings until ten and the walk to his office was half an hour. Thirty minutes of watching. Leah led the children in an ecstatic succession of sing-alongs then had them all stand at easels as she wandered among them, encouraging, instructing, and smiling. Jacob, envisioning what he would, given the chance, do to the hot young thing in the window, let out a quiet animalistic growl. A voice interrupted the slightly louder follow-up to this noise.

'Morning.' It was one of two police officers now looming beside him.

Jacob inspected their faces and nodded. 'Morning.'

'On our way to work are we?'

'We are.'

'And is this tree your office?'

Jacob gave a sarcastic smile.

'We got a call saying somebody had been ogling a kindergarten, for the last half an hour.'

'Ogling?' The vocal officer nodded. 'I wasn't ogling. And I wasn't ogling the kindergarten.'

'Ogling the children then were we?'

'No. Why would you think that?'

'Because paedophiles ogle children,' said the other officer.

'Are you a paedophile?'

'What's your name, paedophile?'

'What's your name and rank, officers? I'm a lawyer. I was—. It's the teacher. Not the children. I was not ogling the children.'

'And she knows she's being ogled does she?'

'Was it her that called the police?'

'Just move on, smart arse. Or we'll go and tell her that you're out here. Maybe she'd like to come and say hi.'

'You're doing a great job, you know that? I'm so glad to see the law that I practice, the law that I love, the basis of our great civilisation, is being enforced by two such proud slobs. You have a good day, uh?'

'Paedophile, we just added this tree to our morning patrol. If we see you again we take you in for questioning. That means you go on to a list of suspected sex offenders. Hard to keep a secret for a lawyer, no?'

4:3

In South Melbourne Market a thirty-five-year-old man with a large head and already-greying hair was cramming with profound disdain bunches of yellow roses into a white bucket when two sweaty palms came from behind to cover his eyes.

'Guess who,' said Dinah.

He seized Dinah's wrists and lifted them as he turned around. 'Hey sexy!' He pulled her in and pushed one of her breasts against her body as they kissed.

'I'm finally free, Slob. I have all day to myself. I can come and see you whenever I want.'

'Whenever you want, huh? You know I still have work to do?'

'I know. But some of it'll be work with me, won't it? Don't you love that I can pop down and come and see you whenever we feel like it? I think you can put work down just for a couple of minutes for these.'

'I definitely can for those puppies.'

'When can you get away? I've missed you.'

'I was about to send Vuong on a delivery. You want me to do it and we can go together?'

'Oo, in the van. I love it in the van.'

Slob called out to the loading dock, 'Vuong!'

A young man hopped down from the back of a delivery truck and front-and-centred himself. 'Hello.' He was wearing a uniform of green polo shirt and white polyester track suit. His baggy trousers and jacket were covered in flowers of green, magenta and blue.

'Calm down,' said Slob. 'No word from Tao?'

'No he no call.'

'Do you think he'll turn up or what?'

'I think maybe no. Tao know many bad people. Maybe he cannot leave he house. Maybe he hide.'

'Well if he calls, you tell me, yes? Yes. I'm going to run this delivery. You stay here and look after the shop.'

'Look after shop. OK boss.'

'Don't call me boss.'

'OK boss.'

Vuong looked on as Slob led Dinah to the passenger side of the van and reached under her dress as she hoisted herself into the cab. She squealed and Slob closed the van's back doors.

4:4

Noah Dulrich had spent all of his Sunday with Rachel Clam, getting to know her as he thought he ought to, what with these new feelings churning his insides. He was finding her to be a wealth of material for this novel of his and he had spent the greatest deal of their morning asking about what all her friends got up to. They had done some variation of every single thing which Jacob and Adam had insisted were the necessary components of a novel, and a great deal of other, far more outrageous, things. After twenty minutes of discussing Mel—her friend from university who had skinny-dipped in fountains not only all over Italy but in Paris, Luzern and Barcelona; Mel the Carabinieri-pashing exhibitionist who kept flats in her handbag so that she could do runners on taxis and who had indeed played roulette in Vegas from a Russian billionaire's pocket—Noah accidentally called Rachel by the wrong name and she asked that they stop talking about her friends for a while.

Halfway through a dreamy kiss-filled lunch Noah discovered that Sarah's colleagues, many of them public figures, were privately just as interesting as her friends. He got stories of brothels and expense accounts and bribes and string-pulling and orgies and human trafficking – all, Noah thought, nothing short of gold for the revolutionarily liberating novelist. He spent most of their afternoon in the park taking notes in the small notebook which he had purchased solely because it professed to be the heir to those which Hemingway used. He promised Rachel that he would not write down or remember a single name or profession and took a break between every other page in order to roll around with her on the picnic rug.

Come Monday and Rachel had to work. Noah spent the day at home, rereading her stories in search of a common theme and a main character. He gleaned from it all one startlingly unifying thread—utter mayhem. Then he thought that, when you look at it, the establishment, the system, the man – those sempiternal enemies of the liberated individual – were all deeply obsessed with getting people to be monogamous and to earn money and then to spend it, weren't they? A line of poetry vaguely recalled –

something about earnings and expenditure – seemed to spring forth from his creative recesses in order to vindicate his revealed purpose: he was to show the reading public plainly and for the first time that there was more fun to be had than all that. One could even contend, he concluded, excitedly following his ill-tracked train of thought, that there was on earth more fun to be had in one year of one lifetime than most people had in ten, and that it was everybody's damn right to have that fun. And who on earth was better qualified to be the sole vanguard in bringing that right out into the glorious light of acceptability?

And then he realised, by now quite feeling that his novel was being granted to him by some higher power (and in the course of a single day) that there was no better way of achieving his original goal of becoming himself an excitement than by planting a thinly stylised version of himself as its hero. It would be Noah Dulrich by another name who would liberate the world from the humdrum and the routine, Noah Dulrich to live those ten intense and liberating lifetimes in one fictional year—Noah Dulrich immortalised. Then every girl he met would recognise instantly that their present company was indeed the so-longed-for remedy to their perpetual ennui, the outrageous young novelist Noah Dulrich.

He asked Rachel if he could meet her outside her work to take her for a stroll before dinner. He leaned against the cold stone of her Victoria Parade office building and watched its revolving door, taking notes about facial features and body types. (He had a theory that exhaustive description was the key to this best-seller. And there was no doubt that the novel would be made into a movie. He wanted no mistakes about who should be cast as who, least of all himself, and so he would get to know noses and acquaint himself with builds.) Five o'clock neared and the outward flow of the doors increased until Rachel emerged. She kissed Noah as though she had not seen him in a year.

'I never want to spend the day apart from you again.'

'Quit your job.' She moaned at the glory of the notion and kissed him again. 'Once I'm famous you'll never need to work again.' They set off for Carlton Gardens.

'How was your day?'

'Good. How was yours?'

'Oh, you know, same old, same old.'

'Do you remember that story you told me about one of the guys getting kicked off the pirate ship?'

'It was one of the girls. What about it?'

'Could you tell it to me again? I forgot it.'

'Can we talk about something else?'

'I know, I just need this one story. I'm sorry. But I've been trying to remember it all day.'

Rachel retold the story with frustrated haste. 'Steph went out drinking in Barcelona and ended up down at the water and the boy she was with was too scared to go on this replica boat. Steph climbed up to the crow's nest and the owner of the ship woke up and came on deck and started yelling at her in Spanish and kicked her off.'

'Kicked off a pirate ship. It's incredible.'

The oak-lined boulevards of Carlton Gardens hissed softly in the dusk wind. All manner of employees were using it as a calming promenade on the return to their homes. Some were exercising on its lawns. Tourists were up at the Exhibition building taking photos in front of its fountain. Noah stopped at the first corner. 'Wait.'

'What?'

'Possums.'

'What about them?'

'It's getting dark.'

'What are you scared of them?'

Noah stared down the darkening path. It appeared as a wooden tunnel infested with lurking, hissing, long-snouted, claw-wielding monsters. He scanned the lawn's edges for marsupial silhouettes. Then, with a novelist's defiance, he shook his head and strode on.

'And what was the one in Vienna with the threesome. Something about a dildo?'

'Noah! Who are you more interested in, my friends or me?' He could not but see her point; he put away his notebook. 'Now what's in the bag?'

'Oh, I forgot. Look.' He pulled from the unmarked silver bag a smaller paper bag with black text on a yellow ground. This Rachel knew and loved as a Quim shopping bag.

She sensed a surprise of no small awesomeness and was

smiling again. 'What's that?'

'Mummy got you something.' Noah handed her the bag. She peeked inside and saw white tissue paper. Her jaw well and truly dropped.

'Oh my God. Is this? Oh my God. Oh my God. Can we sit down?'

The bench on which they sat seemed a doll's dining chair beneath their combined physical magnitude. She pulled out the folded and wrapped dress and unfolded and unwrapped. Orange daisies; a blue hem bordered with white triangles; studded with amber circles. She held it up and had trouble breathing and then put it to her chin and looked down at it. She turned to Noah. 'I love you.' Noah's jaw well and truly dropped. His eyebrows jumped. He said, because it was the only response he knew to the phrase, 'I love you too,' and they hugged. She broke off and stared for a while at the dress, turning over in her mind all the parties she had coming up and thinking about how she could get away with wearing it to all of them.

'I love this dress.'

'I'm glad. Rachel, can I ask you just one more question?'

'Yeah.'

'It's about your friends.'

'Oh, I don't care. Look at this dress!'

'What was the one you told me about your friend the model? Something about having an affair with a cripple?'

'I really love this dress.'

'Rachel?'

'What?'

'Your friend the model, and the cripple?'

'Oh, yeah. So, she lives with her boyfriend, who's a pilot, and once a week when he does the overnight flight to Denpasar, she goes and strips at Wonderland.'

'Ah, that's right! And he doesn't know about it, does he?'

'No.' Rachel held the dress to her face and inhaled its very essence.

'And what was the bit about a cripple? … Rachel?'

'Him? Oh, I know she's gone into the back room a few times with really rich clients, and one of the really rich clients is a guy with only one leg and one testicle who can't have sex and he pays just to touch her.'

Noah shook his head slowly. 'I had no idea people were so cruel to one another. No wonder I haven't been able to write a book. What people get up to!'

'Oh, Noah, I just love this dress.'

'I can get you as many as you want. Mummy's happy to give them away to somebody I love.'

This made Rachel's bottom lip momentarily quiver. 'Oh, Noah. We're going to be so happy together.'

'And rich. We won't even *need* money. I'll be a famous writer. We don't book and pay to stay in hotels, hotels invite us to stay with them. Royalty, too. When Hemingway went to Venice he stayed with a count.'

'A count? Really?'

'I looked it up.'

'Royalty,' said Rachel, suddenly dreaming. She became overwhelmed and kissed him. They took up where they had that morning left off in acquainting themselves with one another's mouths. When eventually they had to breathe Noah said, 'We should leave before the possums come out.' Thinking this an adorable joke Rachel returned to tonguing the backside of his teeth.

4:5

In the main mediation room at Michael & Tasman Partners, Jacob Barron was trying his best to move things at so rapid and haphazard a pace that either his opposing counsel would ask for the session to be adjourned or his own client would. He had been unable to reason with Mrs Tinder, very soon to once again be Miss Creamer, that meeting with her poor husband after a long work-day would almost certainly mean that negotiations through exhaustion would be heated and that, though her husband was of course at fault, the exorbitant settlement which she would no doubt attempt to exact of him would be repented further down the track. Vengeance, Jacob failed to convince her, was not to be sought after a thing like this. He had seen it countless times – otherwise kindly and rational clients becoming tyrannical in after-work mediation and a year later, the sharpness of the pain faded and the shared memories glowing all the brighter, phoning to ask if he could lessen the blow of their settlement. Undoable, he pleaded with her. These things were binding. But Mrs Tinder wanted to get it over and done with. Though not, as was so painfully evident to Jacob, by six o'clock.

'You're being very harsh,' said Jacob, whispering behind Mrs Tinder's ear. The second she had looked across the table at her husband she had decided, just as Jacob had warned her she would, that her previous offer was extravagantly generous and that the bastard deserved to bleed. She told Jacob she now wanted seventy-five percent of their net worth.

'I'm not being harsh,' whispered Mrs Tinder. 'He fucked my sister.'

'Are you're sure it's entirely his fault? What about your sister? Is she flirtatious? Alluring? Do you think maybe you're taking your anger at her out on your husband?'

'No I am not, Mr Barron. He approached my sister and seduced her with an insincere confession of love. It had nothing to do with her.'

'Did he?' said Jacob, and was momentarily lost to the room. 'Mr Tinder, how did you initiate your affection for your wife's sister? How did you go from her thinking you were just her brother-in-law to getting her to consider sleeping with you.'

'Don't answer that,' said Mr Tinder's counsel, an obstructive and unhurried foe. He looked and lawyered like an oxen. 'Irrelevant to proceedings. And seventy-five percent is unprecedented, even in fault-admitted cases. Mr Tinder's offer of fifty-percent is a generous and an acceptable one.'

Jacob leaned back to Mrs Tinder's ear. 'How did he approach her?'

'What?'

'Was it premeditated? Did he seek her out solely to tell her he loved her or were they both at a dinner party or something and it came out, like because of alcohol?'

'I don't see how that's relevant. You burn him.'

'It's relevant because if it was premeditated then I can get you your seventy percent.'

'Seventy-five percent. And yes it was premeditated. He wrote her a letter and put it in her letterbox and waited outside her house in a bush until she opened it. He watched her and when she did not wince or express horror he popped out of the bush and talked his way into her home. Into the kitchen as a matter of fact.'

'That's ingenious.'

'What?'

'Hm? … And he didn't tell you about it did he?'

'No!' said Mrs Tinder, worked now into something of a fury. 'She did.'

'I'll get him.' Jacob turned back towards her husband and rested his elbows on the conference table. 'Mr Tinder, my client, your wife, who you vowed to love and honour forever, do you remember that? Will not be accepting anything less than seventy-five percent of your combined net worth. And you will give it to her, Mr Tinder, because you went to your wife's sister's house with the express intention of having an affair with her. Premeditated adultery. Malicious premeditated adultery. You contrived an ingenious, a malevolent plan, to seduce your wife's sister, which included ambushing her after putting her into a state of heightened emotional sensitivity and then you kept the transgression from your wife until her sister, out of guilt, a human guilt which, given your lack of confession and your premeditation of a sin which you could not have doubted would cause considerable hurt to countless people as well as permanent damage to a quite reputable and blissful family, I can only believe that you at no stage felt. Anything less than your wife's offer is an unsatisfactory recompense. And to be perfectly honest, Mr Tinder, this small sum, given your considerable wealth, would perhaps be the first step towards making amends not only for the people whose lives you have destroyed but for your soul, Mr Tinder, which I imagine lies now in quite the precarious state. Part with this your devastated, fragile wife, by an act of generosity and repentance.'

It was this mastery of improvised emotional blackmail that had prompted Michael & Tasman Partners to scalp Jacob as the youngest divorce lawyer they had ever taken on.

Mr Tinder stared sheepishly at his wife's counsel. Jacob had comprehensively put him in his place. Not even Mrs Tinder, his wife of thirty-five years, when he came home that traumatising afternoon to find her weeping, had so moved him to regret. He looked at her and attempted to say a long and sincere sorry with his eyes, which were not very expressive. He looked at his lawyer, who he saw now as an agent of extortion, a seller of indulgence, a promiser of false remission. He looked back across the table, and gave a small nod.

Jacob looked at his watch and shoved his papers into his briefcase. 'You've done the right thing, Mr Tinder. Mr Bison, the settlement will be on your desk Wednesday morning. Mrs Tinder, congratulations, I have to run.'

He shook his client's hand and sprinted out of the mediation room and into an elevator. His foot tapped as the contraption descended thirteen floors. At the sixth it stopped. He checked his watch. Half past six. He could be home by seven if he got to the tram stop quickly enough and there was one waiting for him. Hopefully the Manthorne sisters had gotten drunk and lost track of time as they talked about how good Jacob was to Dinah and how bad was this new boyfriend to Leah. The elevator opened and he pushed his way from its rear and sprinted onto Victoria Parade.

4:6

Unusually peckish, a possum had descended its tree and was crossing the lawn towards the bench on which Noah and Rachel were still fondling. Cautiously it sniffed its way across the grass in search of a dusk breakfast until it found itself directly beneath the enmeshed couple. Noah's ankle looked in the possum's favourite light not really very much like food, but it thought it might have a go anyway. It swiped a set of claws out and was disappointed. Definitely not food. Noah shrieked with deathly horror and whipped both legs up onto the bench. Rachel screamed at Noah's shriek.

'What was that?' Noah squealed. 'What was that? I think a possum touched my leg. A possum touched my leg. Oh my God it hurts.'

'Oh, grow up,' said Rachel. 'You scared the bloody hell outta me.'

'I think I'm bleeding.' He inspected his ankle. Then sounded the thumping of human footseps, running towards them in the darkness. 'That guy runs exactly like Jacob,' said Noah. 'It is Jacob. Jacob?'

Jacket trailing behind him and tie stuck by the wind over his shoulder, Jacob ignored his inquired name from so unexpected a place and tore past his best friend.

A tram had just stopped at his stop and he leaped aboard. He tapped anxiously on his briefcase as it took off far too slowly, eased to a halt, stopped, slowly took off again, for seven stops, and then he bounded out of its doors. He stopped running when he reached the end of his street and took a moment to wipe the sweat from his face and take off his tie.

Three houses from his he could hear Dinah and Leah farewelling one another in the courtyard. He hurried to his gate.

'Hey, look who it is!' he said, trying to hide his heaving chest. 'Hi, babe. Hi, Leah.'

'Hot, Jacob?'

'I always sweat on trams. I don't know why. How are you?'

'I'm good. Sorry I missed you.'

'You didn't miss me. I'm right here.'

'I was just on my way out.'

'Oh, were you? You don't want to stay for a drink? I haven't seen you in ages.'

'Last week? Oh, I did need to ask you though, what's the law regarding stopping paedophiles from looking through our window at work?'

'I don't know, why?'

'We had some woman come in today and she said she called the police this morning 'cos some guy was standing across the street ogling the kids through the window.'

'Ergh, that's terrifying,' said Dinah.

'I know. Perverts.'

'I'm not sure what the law can do, really. Not unless he flops his dick out.'

'Jacob!'

'You'll probably just have to tint the window.'

'Hm.'

'So you're leaving? Where are you off to?'

'My boyfriend's playing just around the corner.'

'Playing? What's he playing?'

'Guitar.'

'Oh he's in a band is he? Of course he is.'

'Very funny, Jacob.'

'Thank you. And which of the very loud instruments will he be playing? The drums? Or is it one of the stringed ones? The bassoon?'

'He plays lead guitar and he sings. But he got a new tattoo on his hand last week so they're getting the rhythm guitarist to play lead tonight.'

'You like hand tattoos do you?'

'I *love* tattoos.'

'I was thinking of getting a tattoo.'

This was too much for Dinah. 'No you weren't. You hate tattoos. You said only members of barbarian tribes tattoo themselves.'

'That was a joke. I'm always joking, you know that. I really was thinking of getting one.'

'Really interesting conversation, Jacob, but I do have to go. I'm late as it is. Dinah,' Leah blew her sister a kiss as she walked out the gate, 'Love you, and I'll see you soon, Jacob, enjoy the leftovers.' Jacob's attempt to lean in and kiss her went unseen by Leah as she squeezed past him at the gate.

'You're an arse,' said Dinah.

'I am not. Why?'

'You're thinking of getting a tattoo?'

'I *was* thinking of getting one.'

'When?'

'For ages.'

'Of what?'

'Of your face, over my heart. What did you get for dinner? It smells like Thai.'

'Mongolian.'

'Mon–. I fucking hate Mongolian. You know I hate Mongolian. It's Thai's crappy–'

'Thai's crappy flavourless cousin. I know.'

'So why didn't you get Thai?'

'Because I didn't want Thai. Thai's bad for you.'

'Since when? Thai's not bad for you. They're tiny. Thais are tiny. … You don't eat the breakfast I make for you, you order dinners you know I won't eat. You always do this.'

'I always do what?'

They argued for half an hour about the familial relationships of the cuisines of Asia. Then they argued for half an hour about Jacob's obsession with categorising by one bigoted word whole nations of people. Dinah made no attempt to make it up to him that night.

CHAPTER 5

1

Lying in a hospital bed in a paperthin backless gown and greatly intruded upon by machines, Edith was not her unusually stolid self. She put her hand on Adam's, he resting it on her bed as he read.

'I am sorry for keeping you from the flowers for so long, dear.'

'I don't think they'll mind, Grandma.'

'No?'

'No. Sometimes I get the feeling they don't actually need me all that much.'

'Is that so?'

'Yes, sometimes I think it's my water they're after.'

'The traitors.'

'I half expect to arrive home this afternoon to find they've commandeered the water supply and barricaded the glasshouse against me.'

Edith stared across at him, her old, glistening eyes small in their pink sockets; she smiled and rubbed her hand along his forearm. This was the game they most often enjoyed with one another. Early in her guardianship she saw that it was through his flowers that her grandson channelled his small measure of imaginative perception. Where she could she encouraged it. Were he even slightly more worldly it might have made him an artist. But Edith was happy knowing that his unassailable innocence meant that he would never follow so fruitless a path. She had kept him as best she could from the intrigues of the marketplace and was supremely comfortable knowing that he would be happy long after she was gone.

She had checked in at ten that morning and Edith was shown to the room in which she was to spend two nights recovering from her operation. It was as any other private hospital room, tinged through its curtains by a yellow glow which sharpened the smell of cold urine inexplicably pervading the cardiology wing.

A nurse slunk into the room.

'Mrs Athelstan? Good morning. How are you feeling?'

'Wonderful, dear.'

'That's very good to hear. I'm Chloe.' (A very attractive young girl, kind-eyed with bobbed blonde hair and a voice more befitting a pediatric nurse. Men other than Adam never failed to notice, even beneath the amorphous drapery of her medical scrubs, that she was in possession of excellent endowments.) 'They're prepping the operating theatre for you now. Dr Krass tells me he's given you all the pre-op briefing you need?'

'Yes, we had a delightful meeting on Sunday afternoon, didn't we, dear? He's put me quite at my ease. I think any more information would only be detrimental to my comfort. Let's just get it over and done with, dear.'

'That's what I like to hear. Dr Krass is great, isn't he? You're in very safe hands. Now after the operation you'll be down in intensive care until at least tomorrow morning so that we can keep a close eye on you, all right? And when you're strong enough we'll bring you back up here.'

'Nurse Chloe?' said Adam, 'Am I allowed to come and see her while she's in intensive care?'

'Grandma will be under for an hour after the operation and we'll leave her be for another few hours after that, so the grogginess from the anaesthetic wears off. But if you want I can come up here and get you when she's ready to have visitors.'

'That would be lovely, nurse Chloe. I have nowhere else to be so I'll stay right here waiting. And *they* are angel's trumpets.'

'What are?' said Chloe.

'On your uniform there.'

'Are they?'

'Mm-hm.'

'I just thought they were flowers.'

'They are flowers. But they're angel's trumpets. Brugmansias.'

'Do you like them?'

'You look very pretty in them, dear,' said Edith.

'Thank you. Oh, you're both so lovely!'

'Very poisonous though.'

'The flowers are?'

'Angel's trumpets. Ingestion can cause paralysis, migraines, terrifying hallucinations.'

'That's awful.'

'Yes it is awful. But then look at them. Flowers can teach us all the moral lessons the world has to teach.'

'Mrs Athelstan, do you think you're ready to go down now?'

'I'm always ready, dear. And don't let my grandson scare you with his toxicology. They're beautiful flowers. Now, the sooner the better. Let's go.' The nurse began unplugging tubes to make Edith portable. 'Then no more worries about my heart. And no more worries about you, dear.'

'Oh, don't worry about me, Grandma. I'll be sitting up waiting for nurse Chloe to come and get me and then we'll have a little catch up, all right? We'll see what you dream about in that special little sleep you're about to have.'

'I love you, dear.'

'Yes, I love you too, Grandma. And you'll say hello to Dr Krass for me won't you?'

Two floors below, in the viewing room beside his day's theatre, Dr Krass was inspecting for one last time before it was brought to him the x-rays and MRI scans of Edith's heart.

Dr Isaac Krass, through his student days and early career a brash prodigy, had been chosen as the face and scapegoat (pioneer was the word they used) of the cosmetic surgery industry's first foray into cardiology. When that industry, or rather two Australian cosmetic surgeons working in it, accidentally discovered the applicability to infirm hearts of the synthetic material they used to re-establish rectums in homosexual patients, they chose a manufacturer, founded Halberd Pharmaceutical, and went about establishing the zero mortality rate that would make their fortune. Too busy spending their rapidly increasing fortunes to oversee each and every operation in which a Halberd vessel was used they now contracted the services of seven very renowned perfusionists, flying them around the world to stand over each plastic surgeon entrusted with the delivery and installation of a Halberd product.

Dr Krass was checking his watch as often as he was the images of Edith's chambers. Dr Grace Monroe, the perfusionist he had once again especially requested of Halberd was very late. She ought to have been there for half an hour by now, running through the steps of the procedure with him, testing him on anatomy, allowing him to put his hand on her arm when she caught him pretending to make a mistake.

On the other side of the glass Mrs Athelstan was wheeled in on a gurney. Mechanically was her body attached to the machines that would maintain and monitor her life while she was under.

Dr Krass began to worry about whether or not he might have to start without Dr Monroe. The decision was his. Halberd trusted him fully. And he had a two o'clock facelift and a three o'clock buttock liposuction that would have to be postponed if he did not begin right away. These were to be the deposit on his new boat. But any possible blemish on Halberd's perfect mortality rate would mean the loss of his contract—a very much larger financial setback.

He received a text message. '*In traffic. There in ten. We trust you. Start without me.*' He gave the nurses a nod and scrubbed up. The anaesthetist injected things into Edith's chest. Fully garbed, Dr Krass walked out into the theatre and stood over Edith.

'Dr Monroe has informed me that she will be arriving in the next five minutes and has given us permission to begin. Let's get this sternum open. Saw.'

He was handed and then started his miniature angle-grinder and divided Edith's sternum in two. Then he and another nurse each slid eight fingers into one side of the central incision and two nurses eight fingers into the other and they all pulled. They lifted her ribcage until it sat like an open drawbridge and there they clamped it in place.

Ten minutes passed without sign of Dr Monroe. Dr Krass had a nurse change gloves and reach into his pocket to check his phone. She had not messaged. Then there came a tap on the glass of the viewing room. Dr Monroe was rushing to kit up.

'I'm just going to consult with Dr Monroe.' Isaac took off his bloodied gloves and went into the viewing room. 'Grace,' he said. He allowed the beauty of her name to echo in his ears. She ignored him and went on getting changed. 'What took you so long?'

'Traffic in this city! I don't know how anybody could live here.'

'Don't put that on yet. Come with me. I got you something. We've got time. I only just opened the chest.' Isaac picked up a flat yellow box and held up an index finger to the watching nurses as he and Dr Monroe walked out of the viewing room and down the hall.

'You wore it,' said Isaac.

'I always wear it for you. You know it's my favourite dress.'

Isaac opened the door to a supply closet and ushered Grace in. 'Do you like Quim?'

'Shoosh, you. You know I do.'

Isaac handed her the box. She pulled from its white tissue paper a long blue and orange dress covered in white daisies, cinched at the waist and hemmed with blue and jagged white.

'Isaac,' she said, slowly and deeply, as though she were disappointed. 'You shouldn't buy me such expensive dresses.'

'I told you, I don't buy them. I know the designer.'

'At Quim as well? How do you know so many designers, hmm? And I really wish you wouldn't get these for me. They really make me feel obliged to keep seeing you.'

'You need to feel obliged to see me?' He pulled her towards him.

'You know what I mean. It makes me feel guilty. Like you buy me things just so that I'll see you.'

'Why are you so late? We usually have the whole morning.'

'I had an operation in Sydney this morning. I came straight from the airport. The traffic in this city! Really, it's ridiculous.'

'I'll tell you what's ridiculous,' he said. Rather than telling her anything he put her hand over his inner thigh. Grace meowed like a kitten.

'We should get back to the patient,' she said.

'She'll be fine. I only just opened her up, we haven't stopped her heart yet. She's a stubborn old gal, full of life. You can't kill people like that if you tried. When do you leave?'

'This afternoon.'

'This afternoon?!' he whined.

'I've got an operation in Singapore tomorrow. I'm straight out of here. I'm sorry.'

'When are you back?'

'I'm not scheduled for Melbourne until next month.'

'Well then we'd better make the most of it now.'

'Now?'

'Mmm,' said Isaac, going for her neck.

She lifted her head and groaned. 'What about the patient?'

'This won't take long,' said Isaac between boarish breaths. She groaned again and enveloped him.

The nurses over Mrs Athelstan's body watched the doors and the long window for any signs of a returning doctor. The anaesthetist monitored the needles and beeps of a dozen dials and screens. One of the nurses writhed with a shiver.

'There are like four breezes in here,' she said.

'How long is the chest allowed to be open?' said the youngest nurse.

'How old's the patient?'

They checked Edith's admission bracelet. 'Seventy.'

'Never more than sixteen minutes.'

Adam was upright in a very uncomfortable chair, trying to get through his favourite scene from *As You Like It*. It had started well enough, that very tangible joy in words coming easily as he rolled around in his mouth his most cherished combinations of pleasant phrase and syllable. But then he found that trumpets would not be shooed from his mind.

'Troublesome trumpet, tell me why you ruin,' he sang quietly as Orlando and Jaques exchanged their insults. 'He saith among the trumpets, Ha, ha,' he repeated a few times as Rosalind was informing Orlando of her expertise in ridding men of their pointless affections, 'He saith among the trumpets, Ha, ha.' And then his mind began to really wander. 'Oh billiard parlour walls come a-tumblin' down! Seventy-six trombones led the big parade. … The famous fabled walls of Jericho, oh billiard parlour walls come a-tumblin' down! … Troublesome trumpet. … There were thunders and lightning's and a thick cloud upon the mount and the voice of the trumpet exceeding loud, so that all the people that was in the camp trembled. … Trumpet,' he annunciated like Blackadder. 'Trumpet. Strumpet. Oh, most true, she is a strumpet. In the secret parts of fortune? Most true, she is a strumpet.'

Nurse Chloe peeked into the room and in her silent pink-and-green running shoes glided slowly until she was standing over Adam.

'I am he that is so love-shaked, I pray you tell me your remedy. I am he *who* is so love-shaked. Who.'

She kneeled down and spoke almost in a whisper. 'Adam.'

'Hello, nurse Chloe!' Adam was very glad to see her.

'Adam…'

'I've been trying to read. I can't get very far though. Can I see Grandma already? That was very fast. I was expecting to be waiting for at least four hours, and I only brought one book.'

CHAPTER 6

1

'Not at all, Rachel. I was glad of the invitation.'

'I'd just be too nervous to come to a place like this alone.' Rachel found overhead the sign for the salon.

'A Joy For Ever,' said Adam, reading.

Rachel stepped up to open the front door. 'Oh, Jesus. Have a look at it.'

The wall-to-wall mirror on one side of the room was framed in chunky floral gilt daubed with crimson. The ceiling was high and from it suspended on fishing line were various objects of industrial extraction—girders, a cartwheel, a bellows, a smiley face, the bottom half of a female mannequin, an oversized asexual Lego family. Fake ferns and miniature palm trees, brown and brittle, sat in small plastic pots on the benches and in the corners. Two hairdressers, one in a long black dress, one (sordid old *Ha*-nibal) in a tight green t-shirt tucked into a long and high black skirt, were more insidious than any of their clients. Where the room intimidated Rachel it confused Adam. In her blue and orange Quim dress Rachel approached with shrunken shoulders the unkind-looking woman standing behind a lectern.

'Hi … I think I have a one o'clock appointment. Jezebel Dulrich made it for me?'

'Oh, Miss Jezebel! How awesome! Of course!' The silt of her orange make-up suddenly filled the creases of a smile and she ceased to appear snooty. 'Rachel?'

'Yes!'

'Welcome, Rachel. Anything for Miss Jezebel. My name's Anastasia. Put your stuff down and I'll get you a glass of champagne. Two?'

Adam was staring. A shrivelling woman with a hooked nose was already so shrivelled that she appeared to be floating in the barber's chair. She was admiring herself in the mirror while the two hairdressers worked long combs along both sides of her head. Two Asian women were set on low stools at her hanging arms doing all manner of things to her fingernails.

'Adam? Glass of champagne?'

'Oh, no. No thank you.'

'Rachel, have a seat in the second chair there. Today you'll have Amy perfecting your hair and the two ladies doing your nails. I'll be back in a second.'

Rachel took her seat and smiled excitedly into the mirror at Adam. She shrugged with glee her humungous shoulders. Presently Amy appeared, precisely as beautified as her co-workers, from the back room. She introduced herself and threw an apron around Rachel's ghostgum trunk of a neck. 'I love your dress!'

'Thanks!' said Rachel. 'I love it too.'

'I looooove Quim.'

'Me! Too!'

A basin was slid across the room and put behind Rachel's chair. The two Asian women set their stools on either side of her and brought over their expandable make-up cases.

'Now what are we thinking for today?' Amy put her hands through Rachel's hair and spoke to her reflection.

'I don't really know. I've just always had it like this.'

'Well, how about... We lighten, with some very subtle highlights. We layer, just a little bit, for volume. Heavy layers are ten years ago. You should *never* be able to tell you've got them. We'll trim to get rid of the ends here and I think I'll curve your bangs away from the centre like this.'

'Just make me pretty. I've got a boy to keep.'

'All right! I love your attitude!' Amy reclined the chair and Rachel lowered her head into the basin. A gently streaming hose was worked around Rachel's hair as Amy massaged her scalp to allow the water in.

Adam took a hand from the pocket of his dark charcoal suit and ran his fingers under the frond of a palm that was dying beside a hair-dryer. He put a single leaf between his thumb and first finger and squeezed. It turned to dust.

'Do you like them?' said Amy.

'You need to water these.'

'No, they're like that on purpose,' she enthused.

'To what purpose?'

'Everything dies.'

'That's very grim.'

Adam stroked the cool underside of the yellow tulip he was wearing as a button-hole. One of the women scurrying around his legs came to rest on her stool and yanked Rachel's hand from its rest.

'It really was such a lovely funeral, Adam. Adam?'

'Hm?'

'It really was such a lovely funeral.'

'Yes. It was very nice.'

'It really seemed like your grandma was loved by everybody that knew her. I wish I got to know her better. But just from that one meeting I could tell how special she was. And I've never seen so many beautiful flowers. I cried almost as much from looking at the flowers as I did from listening to the eulogy.'

'Yes, they do that to you sometimes.'

The hairdressers beside Amy, long finished curling the shriveling woman's hair, had become fervent in their discussion.

'You might think that is the worst,' said *Ha*-nibal. His beard was short and trimmed in straight lines above his emaciate throat. 'But it is not the worst.'

'You can think of something worse than me sitting at a restaurant with my boyfriend,' said the one in the dress, 'and a girl comes in and says she's caught *my* boyfriend with *me*?'

'Thass nothing darling.'

'Are you sure you're all right?' said Rachel.

'I really am fine,' said Adam.

'You're all alone in the house now.'

'I was once a-sitting in de restaurant,' said the skirted one. 'And –, are you sure you wanna hear deece?'

'I'm never alone if I have the flowers,' said Adam. 'They're all the company I need.'

'Oh, you must be so sad. I'm so sorry.' Rachel's eyelids welled with tears.

The Asian women, talking to one another in their own tongue, worked on Rachel's hands in between pointing and cackling at the raging foreign hairdresser. Amy put a towel under Rachel's head and gently dried her hair.

'Won't you get lonely?'

'Lonely's a very modern word, Rachel.'

'Yes, I want to hear it, *Ha*-nibal! Just tell me.'

'But flowers can't be everything you need, Adam. What about a girl? Don't you want to find a girl and settle down?'

'So I was a-sitting in de restaurant with my boyfriend and a man coom in, who I have been-a fucking, with his wife. But he no telled me have a wife.'

The basin was taken away and the chair returned to upright. One of the Asian women pointed at *Ha*-nibal and said something very loudly and she and her colleague chuckled.

'What language is that?' said Adam.

'They're Vietnamese,' said Amy, ends of Rachel's hair between her first and second fingers. 'You wouldn't use anybody else.'

'Vietnamese?' said Adam, thinking the name very exotic.

'I've always wanted to go to Vietnam!'

'Oh so have I!' said Amy. 'It's meant to be *so* beautiful.'

'That's what I've heard! But I don't think I would now. Not with what's going on.'

'Awful, isn't it?'

'You're very happy to be here?' said Rachel, talking down to the women attending the tips of her fingers.

'Hm?' said one of them.

'You're happy to be here? And not in Vietnam?'

'Hm!?'

'You're happy to be here?'

'Aaaahhh.' Nodding, one of the women answered with a very choppy sort of an accent. 'We are not all alone unhappy.'

'What?' said Rachel. 'No, are you happy? You two. You, happy to be here, not in Vietnam, with conflict, with war?'

'Yes, we are not all alone unhappy,' said the woman.

'This wide and universal theatre presents more woeful pageants than the scene wherein we play in,' said Adam.

'What?' said Rachel.

'It's As You Like It.'

'What is? My hair?'

'What they're quoting.'

'What who are quoting?'

'Them.'

'Are they quoting something?'

'As You Like It.'

'As I like what?'

'Never mind.'

Amy snipped away at Rachel's hair.

'We're all just a bit worried about you, Adam.'

'How's Noah's book coming on?'

'Pretty good, I think. He said he'd loved to have come today but he's working too hard on it. You know even I hardly get to see him at the moment, and we're engaged! He's so devoted to it. He says he needs to hammer all the stories I gave him into a novel before they become stale, whatever that means. And he's half finished already. Thirty thousand words.'

'Is he really?'

'Sent it off to a publisher and everything. Didn't want to waste any time. And they've accepted it.'

'Cap'n Billy's Whizzbang, he's done it! You are having a very good effect on him. I've never known him to do anything he says he's going to do. What's it about?'

'He says him.'

'It's about him?'

'Yeah, he put himself in the middle of all these wild stories and, there you go.'

'Have you read any of it?'

'I don't think I need to, they're mostly stories he got from me I think. But he did let me look at one chapter. One character I don't like at all though. The main character's editor.'

'An editor?'

'So the story's about a guy turning all his experiences into a novel, and he sends it off and then the editor who reads the manuscript assumes the stories must have been lived by the author and she starts trying to sleep with him even though she has a husband and he has a fiancé. I do not like her *at all*. Bit of a slut if you ask me. Probably shouldn't say that though, she's probably based on one of my friends.'

The two hairdressers saw the shriveling woman to the door. 'I love harr,' said *Ha*-nibal, turning around.

'She is such a bitch.'

'I knoeww.' *Ha*-nibal stopped and put his face in front of Adam's. 'Can I-a jussa sayyiy, you air is a so bew-tivul. Look at theez hair, darling.' He held up one of Adam's curls on his fingers.

'I love it. You know what? Can I straighten this for yo-ew? Because you no have a good bardy, you bardy smowll, you bardy not fat, but you no have a good bardy, and a-straightening ova the 'air make yo-ou look sue mutch bedder.' *Ha*-nibal slapped Adam on the bum.

Frightened, Adam stared.

Ha-nibal clicked his tongue and rolled his eyes. 'Donor you won to be better purson? No, you know what? Now I'm anot taoking to yo-ou. You so rode.' And his skirt swung as he stormed off to the back room.

Half an hour after Rachel's nails were finished Amy patted her on the shoulders and said she was all done. Rachel's hair looked shinier, cleaner, neater – altogether more feminine, than it ever had done. She thanked everybody involved and bounced with confidence. They told her she should come back in a week to get it all done again.

Jezebel had invited her to visit the Quim store a few doors down from the salon and there to pick out whichever dress she liked.

She flicked through the clothing racks hardly able to speak as she came to terms with the idea of owning a third Quim dress. She asked Adam if he would help her pick one out. He stood in the corner beside the changing rooms with his hands in his pockets as she came in and out from behind the curtain. He thought all the dresses hideous – one made her look like a Wild West whore, two like an Egyptian labourer, three like an Apache's overfed wife. He pronounced judgments to her based solely on how enthusiastic was her beaming as she twirled.

Seven dresses, two cardigans and one playsuit in, Rachel was spotted from the far side of the store by a young man who was almost as tall as Noah and a great deal handsomer. He was shopping with a girl. He abandoned her at the necklace racks to meander towards the changing rooms. Rachel emerged in her eighth dress and beamed wider than ever. Adam nodded, 'I think that's the one. It looks quite fantastic on you.' Rachel smiled again and spun around to look at her boulderish behind in the mirror beside Adam.

'You do look fantastic in that dress,' said the towering young man.

'Oh,' said Rachel. Then she nearly threw up. When eventually certain that nothing but words would come from her mouth she managed to say, 'Do I now?'

'Good enough to eat,' said the young man, simpering.

'Adrian?'

'What?'

'Adrian Flaherty.'

'Do we know each other?'

'We went to high school. Together. We went to high school together.'

'Did we?'

'Rachel Clam. We were in the same year. And most of the same classes in year eleven *and* twelve.'

'I think I would have remembered you.'

'No, you never really noticed me.'

'Well I'm definitely noticing you now.' The bottom half of Rachel's face faltered momentarily. 'And now I'm trying to imagine how fantastically you'd be noticed *out* of that dress.'

Rachel's eyes widened from disbelief. She could say nothing. She almost ran at him and leaped into his arms. Then she looked at Adam and condensed into a moment six long years of bitter anonymity. Then she thought of Noah.

'You're free Saturday. Tell me you're free Saturday.'

'I'm not, no. I'm having drinks on my boat.'

'You have a boat?'

'Doesn't everybody?'

Adrian Flaherty looked Adam up and down and then looked back down at Rachel's body. 'I'll look you up. I'll ask you again, you'll say yes.'

'You might not find me,' said Rachel in a meek and childish voice.

Adrian Flaherty grinned one last time before turning around and going back to the girl he had walked in with; they both walked out.

It took Rachel a few moments to recover. 'So this one?'

'I do think so, yes.'

'I think so too. I love it already.'

She went back into the change rooms and soon presented the dress proudly to the cashier. 'So Jezebel Dulrich said that I could come in today and pick anything I liked?'

'Rachel?'

'Yes,' said Rachel, bouncing on the balls of her feet.

'Your hair looks amazing!'

It was dark outside.

'So who was that lewd young giant?'

'*That* was the boy that never paid attention to me at high school.'

'Who.'

'That boy. Is that who you meant? He was the boy that never paid attention to me at high school. But, he didn't want me then and so he can't have me now. I have a soon-to-be-famous writer as a fiancé. Oh, and it's getting late and I have to meet him for a drink. I have to go home and change. Maybe they'll let me change in the store. You're going that way? All right. You'll be fine won't you, Adam, alone at home? I promise I'll visit when I get a spare afternoon. And I'm coming to see the Queen of the Night bloom next weekend, yes?'

'You remembered.'

'Of course! I'm *so* excited for it. I can't wait to see it. Oh, I really have to get going. You're going that way, yes? All right. Thanks again. I'll see you.'

She kissed Adam on the cheek and hugged him and went back into Quim.

6:2

At home Adam sliced and reheated the last withered corner of corned beef and boiled some peas. He popped six spheres of ice into a tall glass and filled it with lemon cordial. He went and sat in silence in his glasshouse. He stared at his most beloved cluster of pink roses. He had over-mustarded his arid dinner and his nostrils singed until his eyes watered. The lemon cordial he had made was full of pips and far too sweet. He disgorged it in a dribble from his mouth. Soon he fell asleep. He awoke, shivering, an hour later and went slowly inside and to bed.

CHAPTER 7

1

Jacob Barron was in the second mediation room, going one by one through the marital possessions which his client Mr Spiller had agreed to divide evenly with his wife. By the concession of a dinner setting he secured the possession of a large television. He conceded the more expensive of the two cars and gained his client a weekend a month with his children. Then Jacob's phone vibrated. Its screen read *Home* and he asked for a five minute recess.

'Hi, babe.'
'Hello?'
'Who's this?'
'This is Adam.'
'Adam?'
'Yes.'
'What's up?'
'I just thought I'd let you know that I'm at your home.'
'OK.'
'I arrived to find nobody here, and I had a vast hunger and I thought it easier if I try your back door rather than walk home for lunch and then have to come back again. I thought I'd just let you know that I'm inside and that I've eaten a ham and cheese sandwich. It was quite sufficient.'
'Wow. Is um, is Dinah not there?'
'Not that I can see, no.'
'She should be. She should be working. She's not in my office?'
'No, I did look there. And I rang the doorbell quite a few times. Should I check your bedroom?'

Dinah walked out of South Melbourne market breathing in the slight odour from the day-old orange roses that Slob had given her. She put them in the basket of her bicycle and unlocked and mounted it as her phone rang.

'Are you not at home?'
'I am. Why?'

'I sent Adam over and he said you're not there.'

'No, I just popped out to do some work stuff. I'll be home in a minute though. Why did you send Adam over?'

'It's not good for a man to be that alone. He spends his days with flowers. I called him this morning and he said he hadn't left the house in a week. Noah's busy with his friggen book and I'm at work and we're his only friends so I thought he could come over and see you for a bit. He knows a lot about flowers, maybe he could help you with the wedding stuff.'

'Well tell him I'll be home in two minutes. I just had to see somebody about flowers actually.'

'And you're coming to dinner tonight, yes?'

'Dinner?'

'Oh come on, Dinah. Noah's thing. I've told you about it twice.'

'You haven't.'

'Yes I have.'

'Then why don't I remember it?'

'Because your memory is a selfish retard. You don't remember anything that's not about you.'

'Goodbye.'

'Wait.'

She pushed a foot against the asphalt and coasted downhill. 'What?'

'I'm sorry.'

'Good.'

'But you're coming tonight, yes?'

'I can't tonight. Leah's coming over for dinner.'

'Leah can come. Bring Leah. She's met Noah before. A few times.'

'She won't be in the mood, Jacob. She went for her second round of tests today.'

'I don't want to go to dinner alone. You have to come. It'll be fun. We're celebrating. Get Leah to come. It'll take her mind off things. She can meet Adam. Adam'll cheer her up. He's got this healing power around unhappy people.'

'She's not unhappy. You're unhappy.'

'Piss off.'

'I'll see if she wants to bring her boyfriend.'

'He can't come.'

'Why not?'

'The table's reserved for six.'

'Isn't Leah the seventh? What's an eighth? They won't mind.'

'No, we've got five and I reserved for six in case somebody else wanted to come, so Leah'll be the sixth. Anybody else'll throw the whole restaurant out. It'll be chaos. They plan their nights on accurate reservations.'

'They do not.'

'Yes they do.'

'How do you know?'

'Because I used to work in restaurants.'

'You worked at McDonald's. They don't take reservations at McDonald's.'

'I worked at other restaurants. Would you stop arguing with me?'

'I'm not arguing.'

'Yes you are.'

'Just because I ask you a question doesn't mean I'm arguing.'

There was a short silence as Jacob forced himself to calm down. 'So I have to come straight from work. Will you bring Adam along? He'll already be dressed. It's at Akkadia. Do you know it?'

7:2

Dinah opened her front door and called out to Adam.

'In here, Dinah.' He was browsing through Jacob's small library. It consisted entirely of popular military histories and biographies of prominently mischievous Nazis and peculiarly resilient Jews.

'Hi, Adam.'

'This stuff is truly awful. I don't know how Jacob reads it.'

'Oh, I know. I think it's why his brain's so warped. I don't know how people could be so cruel to one another. Sorry I was out. I got these for you.' She gave Adam the browning bouquet of orange roses. He took them with the same horrified look that had sat upon his face since getting to the photographs in *The Architects of the Final Solution.* 'How are you doing, Adam? Are you all right?'

'I helped myself to a sandwich. I hope you don't mind.'

'Of course not. And Jacob said you're coming out for dinner?'

'I am, yes. I'm quite looking forward to it.'

A long pause ensued. Dinah hardly knew Adam. Before she and Jacob were married she had met him only a handful of times and always when she had been very drunk. Since then she saw him at most three times a year and always at a birthday party, occasions she typically took to get very drunk. From Jacob's account of him she thought Adam was a great deal more sensitive than he was and she was overly careful about what she said around him. The ensuing superficiality made easy conversation elusive and Adam perceived indifference in their stunted exchanges. They had certainly never been alone together for as long as was their present encounter.

'Adam, you know it really was a beautiful funeral.'

'Thank you. So you've started the wedding planning? How's that going?'

'Oh, pretty well, I s'pose. I've got two clients now which is good. One wedding in November and one in September. I was actually just at my flower supplier's now. You know he's looking for a delivery driver if you're interested. Might get you out of the house a bit more? Get your mind off things? I could get the job for you. Could be good for you.'

'I'm quite all right, Dinah, thank you. My flowers are keeping me busy as it is.'

'Well you know your grandma's spirit lives on inside us all now that she's in the spirit realm. And we're all here to help keep your spirit warm with friendship.'

Adam looked blankly at Dinah. Each time she spoke on spiritual matters she became to Adam's mind slightly more incomprehensible.

'Yes, I'm not terribly impressed by tonight's choice of restaurant, but I am looking forward to trying the food.'

'And you've never met my sister Leah, have you?'

7:3

Dinah, Adam and Leah arrived first at Akkadia. They were told that their table was not quite ready yet and they stood waiting in the shop-lined hall onto which the restaurant opened. Dinah and Leah gossiped intermittently. Shortly Rachel arrived. When she recognised Adam among this small crowd her obviously sullen mood lightened. She hugged him and asked him affectionately how he was doing. Adam introduced her to the Manthorne sisters.

'We met on Noah's boat. Briefly. My husband was being obnoxious.'

'Oh, yes. The slavery guy.'

'The slavery guy.'

Leah said that she liked Rachel's dress.

'Thanks.'

'That's Quim, yeah? I *love* their dresses. This'll keep Noah on his toes, won't it? How *does* it feel?'

'How does what feel?'

'Being the girlfriend of a soon-to-be-very-famous writer? You must be nervous.'

'Nervous? Why?'

'Well you met each other when he was nothing, so to speak. He's gonna be famous. You'll have to fight them off with a stick.'

'Fight who off?'

'The women.'

'Will I?'

'Do you think he'll be able to handle it?'

'Do I think he'll be able to handle what?'

'The temptation.'

'We're engaged.'

'Are you?!' said Dinah.

'Mm-hm. And we'll be married soon, so he won't be tempted at all.'

Leah was still looking blankly at Rachel when Jacob arrived. He kissed Dinah on the cheek and tried to do the same to Leah. He introduced himself to Rachel and said that it had taken them too long to meet and shook Adam's hand. He asked with as much sympathy as he was capable of, 'How are you doing buddy? ... And Leah. How are you?'

'Did you get that tattoo did you, Jacob?'

'Ha. I was kidding. I would never get a tattoo. Barbarians tattoo themselves.'

'I'm a barbarian then?'

'I'm kidding, Leah! Everything I say is a joke. Hasn't Dinah ever told you that about me? How long have we been waiting? I'm fucking starving.'

'Relax. Five minutes.'

'Any word from the doctors?'

'Jacob,' said Dinah.

'What?'

'It's fine, Dinah. No, Jacob, I haven't heard yet. Thanks for your concern. They were meant to call this afternoon.'

Down the long corridor of the enormous riverside complex in whose top corner Akkadia was nestled there came a loud and undeniably Noah-like laugh. He was sauntering with a tall woman, leaning so closely towards her as they laughed that their arms touched.

They reached his waiting friends and Noah introduced them all to Annie Goodman. 'Annie's my editor. We've just come from a formatting meeting. Hilarious, wasn't it, Annie? They spent the whole meeting trying to convince us that the front cover and the font and the layout and stuff like that has more influence on whether or not the book sells than whether or not it's any good!'

'They really have no idea what we're sitting on,' said Annie. 'Oh, I like your dress.'

'Good,' said Rachel, in as bubbly a tone as she could.

'How you doin', Adam?' said Noah.

'I'm perfectly well, Noah.'

'All right, calm down. Jesus. Now why are we all waiting out here?'

'The table's not ready yet,' said Dinah.

'The table's not ready,' said Noah, mockingly. 'In a week's time every table in the city will be ready for us. Won't it, Annie?'

'Probably not,' she said, and they both laughed.

The *maître d'* came out and told them their table was ready.

'See,' said Noah. 'Oh, and we have two extra people for the booking.'

'Of course. Come right through.'

'Chaos?' said Dinah to Jacob.

Noah let Annie go ahead of him. He passed Rachel and she

said, 'Hi, honey,' and put her arm around him. He bent down and offered her his cheek.

'Remember Annie thinks I'm the one who lived all the stories in the book. So if anything comes up just play along. Is that all right?'

'Anything for you, honeybuns. I love you. Come here.' She tapped her lips with her finger. Noah kissed her on the cheek and walked ahead of her as they were led out onto Akkadia's terrace. Hell-bent on ensuring that in the procession he would be between his wife and her sister, Jacob pulled Adam from between them, asked him if he was sure he was doing all right and then stepped ahead of Leah to interrupt her and ask Dinah how her day was. They pulled out their chairs and took their seats.

'I don't even need to look at a menu,' said Adam. 'I know exactly what I'm having.'

'Have you been here before, Adam?' said Annie.

'I certainly have.'

'And the food's good?'

'I have no idea.'

A waiter came to the end of their table. Noah ordered the second cheapest bottle of red wine. Adam asked for a large lemon squash.

'With extra ice?' said the waiter.

'You remembered.'

'The biggest cubes I can find?'

'The biggest cubes you can find. Thank you so much.'

'So the book is finished?' said Jacob.

'Seventy thousand words.'

'You wrote seventy thousand words in three weeks? Isn't that kinda quick?'

'Three weeks does seem very rapid, Noah,' said Adam.

'It is rapid. But I had so much material. It was like I didn't have to make anything up. I just had to fit it all together. Writing that fast is all about conquering fear. I learnt that. Fear of yourself. I used to be afraid of so many things. Boats, I was afraid of blood. And once I–.'

'You're afraid of possums too,' said Jacob.

'Yes. And of possums.'

'You're afraid of flying.'

88

'Thank you.'

'Of flying fish.'

'Yes, Jacob.'

'Of regular fish.'

'Thank you, Jacob.'

The waiter brought Adam's lemon squash and the bottle of wine. He unscrewed its lid and poured a dash into Noah's glass. Noah passed it on to Annie who swirled the glass, sniffed its contents, swirled it again, sniffed it again, drank, swished it around her mouth as though it were mouthwash, tilted her head back and let it rest at the back of her throat for a time, swallowed and then said, 'It's all right.' The waiter poured out six glasses and said that he would be back shortly to take their orders.

'And it's out tomorrow?'

'Ten a.m..'

'What's it called?' said Dinah.

'Fantastical Apish Shallow.'

'What kind of a name is that?!' said Leah.

'I got it from Adam, didn't I, Adam? I wanted to use something from Shakespeare, you know, 'cos he did kind of the same thing I'm trying to do, and Adam's the only person I could think of who would have read any Shakespeare. He told me to read some scene from some play and I skimmed it and I found that phrase. Sounds good though, doesn't it? Fantastical Apish Shallow.'

'Well, here's to Noah Dulrich,' said Jacob, raising his glass. 'The newest and greatest novelist that I think any of us know. Well maybe not Annie.'

They entangled their arms to touch glasses with one another.

'So, Rachel,' said Annie, talking across Noah. 'Tell me about dating a guy like Noah. How do you keep him pinned down?'

'We're engaged. We're not dating.'

'Oh, how domestic. You're not worried he might want to relapse into his old adventures?'

'Into *his* old adventures?' Annie stared at her, smiling. Rachel looked straight ahead. Annie eventually nodded once. 'Does he get up to adventures in the book?'

'And you are coming to the launch party, tomorrow aren't you? Make sure you finish the book before you come though.'

'Annie,' said Noah.

'Everyone will be discussing it.'

'Annie.'

'Mm?'

'Change the subject.'

'I think it'd be better if Noah was alone tomorrow night. Nobody wants to meet a playboy novelist with a fiancé do they? And plus I want to watch Adam's flower bloom.'

'Watch his flower bloom?' said Annie. 'Is that a metaphor?'

'Adam grows rare flowers. And this one only blooms once a year, and at midnight, and the flower withers before sunrise.'

Leah asked what the flower was called.

'It's my epiphyllum oxypetalum.'

'The Queen of the Night. It makes you bald and causes abortions and diarrhea. Doesn't it, Adam?'

'Rachel,' said Noah, mildly admonishing her for looking at Annie as she spoke.

'What?'

'Please.'

'Please what?'

'Please stop it.'

'Stop what?'

'You're being rude.'

'You're being rude.'

'How am I being rude?'

The waiter appeared and asked if they were all ready.

'Yes!' said Adam.

'I think we might need a few more minutes,' said Noah. 'Thanks.' Adam watched him depart.

'Leah, what do you do?' said Rachel.

'I'm a kindergarten teacher.'

'Oh, good on you! That sounds like so much fun.'

'It's *so* much fun. I love working with kids.'

'And. How 'bout you? Boyfriend?'

'All right,' said Jacob, loudly. 'Who's ready to order?'

'I am,' said Adam.

'Jacob,' said Dinah.

'What?'

'Don't interrupt.'

90

'Interrupt what?'

'Rachel and Leah were talking.'

'Were they? Sorry.'

'Jacob.'

'What?'

'Don't start.'

'Don't start what? You don't start. Just let me talk.'

'I'll let you talk if you let everybody else talk.'

'I was letting everybody else talk, Dinah. But I thought maybe we should order first. Otherwise we'll be here forever.'

'It's not a terrible idea, Dinah,' said Adam.

'It is if Jacob came up with it.'

'Marrying you.'

The waiter returned and sensed immediately that he had not left them long enough an interim; he turned without breaking stride and went back inside.

'Well I know what I want,' said Annie, closing her menu.

'So do I,' said Adam. 'The khouzi ala timman. Lamb with prunes and mint.'

'I know what I want too,' said Rachel.

'It all sounds so delicious,' said Noah.

'What do you do again, Rachel?' said Annie. 'You're a public servant?'

'I work in the Settlement Coordination Unit for the Department of Multicultural Affairs.'

'Well that sounds rewarding. I always say that people should make something in their work. I told you how much I liked that dress, didn't I? You know I just realised, it's almost exactly like the tunics on those guys on the walls.' In pointing to the Persian Immortals on the frieze beside them Annie knocked Noah's wine glass over. Its contents bounced across the table cloth and ricocheted in splatters across Rachel's dress. Rachel gasped and pushed her chair back from the table.

'I am so sorry,' said Annie, very adamantly.

'Oh my dress,' said Rachel, standing up to inspect the extent of the desecration.

'You know it does look like their tunics,' said Jacob, able now to compare the costumes side by side.

'You did that on purpose,' said Rachel.

'Oh, God, no, Rachel. I really didn't. I'm so sorry. It was an accident. It'll come out. I'll pay the dry cleaning bill. I'm so sorry, really. I do like that dress, a lot. Are you crying? Why are you crying? It's just a dress.'

'Noah gave me this dress.'

'Rachel, I'm so sorry, really. Crying's a bit much though, don't you think?'

'Annie,' said Noah.

Leah was exchanging concerned and hungry glances with Adam when her phone rang. She pulled it from her purse and looked at its screen and excused herself as she stood and put the thing to her ear.

'I think I'm gonna go,' said Rachel.

'No, Rachel, don't go,' said Dinah. 'Here come with me, we'll get some soda water and some salt and we'll go into the bathroom.'

'No, no, I don't feel well. I'm gonna go home. I'm not in the mood to watch this. I'll leave you two to it.'

'What does that mean?' said Noah.

'Adam, I'll see you tomorrow. I'm really sorry everyone.'

Rachel picked up her purse from the table and walked into the restaurant. Noah looked at Annie and then Jacob and Dinah and then stood up. He took his jacket and followed her.

'Well he drove me here,' said Annie. 'It was so nice to meet everyone,' and she went after him.

'Now look what you've done,' said Dinah.

'What *I've* done?'

'I'm joking, Jacob. Calm down. Hasn't Leah ever told you that about me? Everything I say is a joke.'

'Now would I be grossly incorrect in saying that that was rather awkward?' said Adam.

'That was awkward,' said Dinah.

'I don't think couples ought to come to this restaurant.'

'Do you think Noah's switched it up there?' said Jacob.

'He better bloody not have. That girl's the best thing that's ever happened to him.'

'I think he might have traded out, the little bastard. And traded up, too.'

'Don't be such an arsehole.'

'You know what they say?'

'Jacob.'

'You only cheat if she's hotter.'

'Jacob!'

Leah returned to the terrace. She had a hand over her mouth.

'What?' said Dinah.

'Can we go home?'

'Home? Honey, why?'

'I just want to go home.'

'Of course.'

'The tests?'

'Jacob!'

Leah nodded and gasped. She stopped herself at the brink of crying. She stood up straight and took her hand from her mouth. 'I–.' Dinah stood up and embraced her. 'The first round of chemo starts next week.' She began to sob. 'I'm going to have the first round ... then go home to be with Mum for a bit.'

'Oh, honey, I'll come with you. We'll all be up there. The three girls again. Jacob, grab my purse.' Dinah turned Leah around and insisted sharply that Jacob pay for the drinks.

The waiter returned to Adam. 'Is everything all right? Where's everyone gone?'

'We aren't going to be ordering,' said Adam, forbearingly. 'Thank you for the lemon squash. It was very cold.'

CHAPTER 8

1

Rachel arrived at Adam's at half past five, four and a half hours earlier than she had told him she would.

'I thought it might be nice to have dinner together? I'll leave you alone for the evening. You do what you have to do. I've brought Noah's book to finish.'

'Are you all right there, Rachel? You don't seem to be your jubilant self. Are you upset about something?'

'No. … No, not really.'

'Last night?'

'No, that was just embarrassing. It's Noah's book, Adam. I don't like it at all. It's so horrible, knowing that what he's put in there are things that people actually get up to. How can people be so cruel to one another? And he's put all my girlfriends in here, and my bosses. And he did *not* disguise them as much as he said he would. If any of them read it… But I've told them all that their stories might make an appearance, so they will.'

'I'm sure it's not as bad as you think, Rachel. It's probably all obvious to you because you know what he's put in there. I'm sure nobody else will recognise your stories.'

'*Their* stories. Oh, God.'

Rachel offered to go out and buy ingredients for dinner and she made them both pasta. She asked Adam to tell her more about the Queen of the Night. When he mentioned that it was most commonly found in Mexico she told him the few inoffensive details of her girls' trip to Cancun—the white sand beaches, the cenotes, the Mayan ruins, the margaritas, the food. She cleared the table and washed the dishes and Adam said he had a little bit of setting up to do. Rachel said she would read out on the patio. Adam made her a coffee and gave her a jumper and a knitted quilt and then switched on the night lights in the glasshouse. The door closed behind him and Rachel leaned back in a patio chair and put her feet up on another. She spread the blanket over herself so that only the hand which held Noah's book was exposed.

Throughout Rachel Clam's life she had been acutely aware that everything about her lay somewhere between the sixtieth and seventieth percentile. The rating she found out the boys had given her at school, her final score in year twelve, her body mass index, her IQ, her income—all fell within that decent but unimpressive range. In Noah she thought she had met somebody as comfortable being thusly situated, in all but height and privilege, as she was. But with the publication of his novel had come an obvious desire, simply because for the first time in his life he sensed that he could rise, to rise perhaps to somewhere as high as the eightieth percentile. With Annie menacing at his side he was hobnobbing with somebody who possessed all the attributes of the eighty-fifth. And global fame as an artist, to which he loudly aspired, would put him at least in the ninetieth, a place in which Rachel was certain she did not belong. She opened Noah's book to where she was up to, about half way, and took a worried sip of coffee.

An hour later Adam conveyed some candelabras to the glasshouse and lit their candles. He pulled the cover from the gramophone and played his record. He pushed open the glasshouse door and called gently up to Rachel. 'Rachel, you should come and see this.'

Her tears were pouring into the absorbent, recycled, pages of *Fantastical Apish Shallow: a novel by Noah Dulrich.*

'Rachel, what is it? Is the book that good?'

'It's over,' she said, wailing a little.

'You've finished it? It must have been *very* good if you're crying just because you've finished it. Or does it have a sad ending? I do hope he hurries up with my autographed copy.'

'Oh, Adam, no,' she said between crumbling whimpers. 'The main character has an affair with his editor. He breaks up with his girlfriend by putting what he's been getting up to in the book that he writes after all his adventures.'

'Ooo, that's a juicy one. Very convoluted. Is it one of the stories you gave him? I can't imagine Noah inventing something as complicated as that.'

'Oh, Adam.' Rachel stood from her chair and hugged him. 'It's mine now.' She sobbed on his shoulder. 'I have to go. I'm sorry. I'm just going to call some girlfriends and have a bit of a cry. Is that all right? I'm really sorry.'

Exhausted and hysterical, she lumbered across Adam's patio. Her arms hung at her sides as though a bucket of water had been thrown over her. She opened the back gate and went to her car. She pulled out her phone and called Kari, her oldest and most sympathetic friend.

'How dare you?' said Kari before Rachel had even asked her if she was free to join her to watch heartbreaking films and eat ice-cream.

'What?'

'Everybody's read it, Rachel. You know Andy'll find out about the stripping now, don't you? He said he's gonna read it on his layover in Bali on Tuesday, so that's over for me. Are you happy? I'll have to find somewhere else to live.'

'Oh, Kari.'

'And what happens when Mel's bosses find out about the cocaine in Mexico? She'll lose her practising certificate. I really hope you're happy. Don't call us. I hope you die.'

'Kari, I'm–.' But Kari had hung up.

Rachel's phone lit up with 'Alexander'. 'Hello?'

'You do know what this means, don't you?'

'What what means?'

'You do realise what'll happen if the press finds out about Tung? How could you do this to me, Rachel? After everything I've done for you. You're fired. Fuck off. I hope you die.'

Rachel had never before been so despondent. Presently she thought that nobody on earth had ever been so despondent. Up to this point she had been happily unaware that such depths of anguish existed in the human mind. Not even people in the seventy-fifth percentile were capable of such appalling despair, she thought. She opened the address book of her phone. The first number was Adrian Flaherty's. It had been hotly debated through six years of high school which of the boys was the hottest. Adrian Flaherty always ranked in the top five. Out of one hundred and thirty students, roughly sixty five boys—that was at least the eighty-fifth percentile. A huge jump for Rachel Clam. He had messaged her a couple of times but received no reply. So in love with Noah Dulrich had she been she could not really say why she had saved his number at all.

8:2

At half-past eleven Adam was sitting alone in near-darkness before his epiphyllum. He had bought some cinnamon-bun ice-cream especially for the occasion and was scraping his teaspoon around the inside of the paper tub, harvesting its softened edges. He watched closely the dangling flowers for signs of blooming. Suspended from crooked stems like upside-down flamingo heads, facing all directions, motionless among its broad leaves, the light burgundy sepals like tendrils grasped their own long white petals. He listened intently, knowing that he would hear the crack of that joyous first unfolding before he would see it.

8:3

Across the chill air of the harbourfront Rachel Clam was pushed backwards at the lips towards the pier. Adrian Flaherty held her firmly at the waist as they descended.

'Which one's yours?' he asked as he turned its first corner.

Rachel opened her eyes to search sideways. 'Mmm… that one.'

Adrian turned her around and squeezed the seat of her jeans as she stepped onto the rear deck of the *Teba*. She took his hand and led him up to the bridge. He hoisted her onto the control panel. So long and loud was her delighted shriek that neither of them heard the engine start.

'Keep your eyes closed,' said Rachel, moaning as she had her jumper then her shirt then her bra thrown to the floor.

'Mmmm,' moaned Adrian. 'Why?'

'Because I don't want you to see me.'

'But I want to see you.' Adrian growled and put both his hands on the control panel.

Rachel unbuttoned his trousers. 'Keep them closed.'

'It feels like we're moving.'

'Oh, we're moving.'

'No, the boat.'

'Mmmmm,' Rachel purred.

'It actually feels like we're going pretty fast.'

'Should we stop?'
'I like going fast.'
'Not too fast I hope. I want to enjoy this too.'
'You're dirty.'
'Sorry.'
'No, I like it.'

8:4

After ten minutes Adam heard it. That soft, sweet, organic crackle. He leaned forward in his chair and was soon on his feet and hunching. The white satin petals yawned slowly apart, waking from pleasant slumber. They forced the sepals back until all at once they sprung open to give the petals room to show off. He watched the first flower burst and then cupped it in his hand as it opened. Then there was another crack; and another.

The first flower to smile was half-way open when Adam thought he heard an engine being overrevved in the harbour behind him. He ignored the noise. The last flower's petals cracked and it seemed to try to catch up with the others. Then Adam was certain he could hear an engine being overrevved.

'I do wish they'd keep it down at this time of night. And tonight of all nights.'

He looked into the cream-coloured pistils of the dozen flowers opening before him, this adagio of new life, soft and white and glorious; very soon the whole plant was in full bloom. He fell back into his chair and found that he was quite breathless. Then the revving engine became overwhelmingly bothersome. So loud was it in fact that he could have sworn that the engine could have been just outside his glasshouse and not been any louder. He turned frustratedly towards the noise, as though his glaring reproach might persuade whomever was revving their infernal machine to ease off for a while. In the light of the street lamps along the boardwalk he saw the hull of a boat in the air. He quickly discerned that it was, after all, just outside his glasshouse. Rather more alarmingly, it was flying very much towards him. Quite immediately he overcame his disbelief and raced out of the sanctuary and made it almost to the back door of his apartment when the crash came.

His glasshouse and its frame of teak and iron crumbled beneath the hull of the *Teba*. Shattered glass crashed in every direction against the composite walls. The boat's bow rested on the top step of the sunken section of the patio; the rear half of its hull, almost twice as long as Adam's greenhouse, dangled over the boardwalk.

Rachel and vulgar boy from Noah's mother's dress shop were standing naked in the bridge. Adrian, looking around at the mess beneath them, was startled; Rachel, staring down at Adam, was mortified. She scrambled for some clothes with which to cover herself. She held her shirt at her chest with one hand and opened a window with the other.

'Adam,' she said, very feebly. 'I'm–. This was an accident.'

'Yes, I quite gathered that. Are you all right?'

'Your flowers.'

'No, no. Half of them were on the ground or the first shelf. Most of them should have survived. Ought I to call the police? How does one get a boat off one's glasshouse?'

'I'm so sorry, Adam.'

'How do you go in reverse?' said Adrian Flaherty.

'I don't know, it's not my boat.'

'It's not your boat?'

'It's my boyfriend's.'

'You have a boyfriend?'

'Well, no, a fiancé. Ex-fiancé I think. It's a long story. And I don't think you can go in reverse if you're not in water.'

Two monkeys peeked cautiously over the gunwale. Surveying their surroundings they found no obvious predators or possible captors. They jumped ship, cackling with freedom, and sprinted across Adam's patio and made for the breach in the walls.

'What about this one?' said Adrian Flaherty. 'What's "bilge"?'

'I don't know. Just see what it does,' and she hit the button for him.

Four large flaps opened along the hull. From them poured forth like squalid fountains the contents of the *Teba*'s bilge tank. Murky seawater filled the sunken recess and all the flowers and all the plants were covered and died that moved within the glasshouse.

'Wait, no, here,' said Adrian Flaherty. 'That's it.' He pointed to the button labelled 'Reverse' before pushing it. Something clunked in the great mechanical depths beneath them but still the boat was aground.

The cascade of bilge water began to slow. The water prevailed exceedingly upon Adam's patio and began to trickle over onto the boardwalk. Then the waters slowly bare up the *Teba* and she was almost floating again. After a few loud creaks the *Teba* lifted from its terracotta reef and slunk back, first onto the boardwalk and then with the flow of the receding deluge, stern-first into the harbour. Her hull hit the water with a thunderous slap. Within seconds she had found her balance and was afloat again, her underside scratched and scraped but unbroken, floating higher and easier than before.

THE SECOND BOOK OF ADAM ATHELSTAN, CALLED
EXODUS

CHAPTER 1

1

Given the black podiums crammed with flower-stuffed buckets
and the cold concrete floorspace blanketed with cellophane-
wrapped bouquets it would have been reasonable to assume that
the owner of Rad's Flowers at South Melbourne market loved
flowers. Almost an accurate assumption, for the founder of Rad's
Flowers did indeed hold a special affection for them—they made
his small fortune.

Uninterested in his Socialist Federal Republic's ethnic pot-
boiling, Rad left Croatia in 1973 with nothing but three small and
ancient hopes – to start a business, to find a wife, to raise a family.
Somebody from his village who had done as much thirty years
previously took Rad on as a delivery driver. After twenty years of
devoted service he was bequeathed the whole shop. Proudly he
rechristened it with his own name and was blessed with ten years of
prosperity, turning his South Melbourne shopfront into one of the
city's larger suppliers of occasion flowers. Then he was begged to
hire Slob, that posthumous vindication of the demise of the
European village. For it was to that tenuous form of kinship which
Slob's mother pleaded in asking Rad to give her son a job.

Instantly Slob took a disliking to flowers. He glowered at
daffodils with especial disdain. Excellent at nothing but putting a
kind face to extortion, within three years he had amassed enough
knowledge of the business to threaten to start a devastatingly cheap
rival. He one day mentioned this fact to his boss and a short while

thereafter benevolently offered to buy Rad's Flowers. Slob kept the name and the more profitable accounts, and set about modernising and expanding. He doubled his prices and halved his staff and put a stop to the tradition of providing refuge for people from his own village, partially because he would have felt a shade of guilt paying them what he now paid his employees, mostly because he strongly suspected his village of being little more than a breeding ground for workshy malevolent geniuses. So he looked around for cheaper workers with better work ethics. A cousin who worked with fruit told him that the Vietnamese were tireless, reverent and affordable.

Slob went through the services of eleven young Vietnamese men, all vaguely related. The brother of his third worked at the ill-famed Hotel Dothan. When that young man's parents found out about what their son was getting up to in Australia he committed suicide. Slob was asked to supply the flowers for the funeral and got drunk at the wake with a man who said he was the deceased's mentor. This man introduced Slob to his own boss, who got Slob even drunker. So impressed were they by Slob's imperviousness to whisky, this boss two days later paid Slob a visit and proposed a deal—constant and lucrative business plus his own special enticements in exchange for absolute discretion. The business cards which advertised the anonymity and secrecy offered by Rad's Flowers now littered the lobby and the rooms of the Hotel Dothan; Slob's services were heavily recommended to the distraught.

His livelihood rotting under the sea on his patio and the shattered remains of his glasshouse still strewn dangerously across the terracotta, Adam Athelstan had been confined for a week to the indoors of his apartment. Edith's incomes were confiscated by all levels of government. What would have been Adam's cash inheritance disappeared on the death duties. Her sole legacy to her grandson turned out to be the ground floor apartment, for whose annual maintenance was needed an income almost exactly equivalent to what Adam had earned, on average, since he had sold his first flower. Entirely unaware of how to apply for a job and having concluded that he probably needed one just for the time being, Adam remembered something Dinah had mentioned to him.

At six o'clock in the morning he was standing in a white polyester track suit covered in flowers of blue, magenta and cyan and many colours besides.

'Keep it and keep it clean,' said Slob. 'Now, do you know anything about flowers?'

'I rather think I do, yes.'

'What?'

'What?'

'Anyway. These are packing slips. One packing slip is one order to the same place. To start you off I'll get you to pack and Vuong to sort the orders into the truck, all right? Now see this code? 12–236. 236 is yellow daffodils. You'll get to know the codes. 12 is the quantity. So that's a dozen yellow daffodils. Easy, no? With 1–8054, anything with four digits is on the plush wall.'

Slob showed Adam the sealed concrete wall covered with protruding racks from which were suspended on little plastic hooks dozens of variety of stuffed animal and plush toy. Teddies holding love hearts dangled below variously shaped cushions embroidered with messages of how cherished the deceased would always be; a row of misshapen cherubs bore scrolls of, 'You'll never understand how much I love you'; red heart-shaped balloons, glittering with 'Forever Loved', were stuck on long plastic sticks amongst them all.

'So see how these two aren't separated by a space? That means they have to be packed together. So a dozen yellow daffodils and one 'I'll miss you forever' swan in one wrapping. Now,' he said, walking Adam to the long bench in the centre of the stall. 'We wrap them here. All flowers go in standard paper, and standard packaging is clear cellophane with yellow ribbon. If the customer asks for anything different it'll say it under the order. See here?' He ran his finger across the packing slip and translated. 'Two dozen orange roses and two white lilies and there, white fillers, red box, green cellophane. Everything's in front of you here on the packing bench. Easy, yes? Now, this is the weekend Dothan order, yeah? It's always the biggest order of the week. Three pages is normal. I'll give you a hand with this one and then you should be right with the smaller ones. Now, this column has the *To:* and the *From:* info. We write that in our best handwriting. Show me yours. *To:* Tung. *From:* Alexander, with love. … Shit that's nice handwriting! All right, you're doing the cards from now on. Then once they're packed up, you put them at the end of the bench, and today Vuong'll put them in the truck for you. And this is the only packing slip so far so I'll get you to ride along on the delivery, see how that works. Vuong's a good kid. His English is a bit suspect but you'll get used to it. Vuong!'

From pottering around at the rear of an emblazoned van in the loading bay a small young man wearing the familiar tracksuit came and, seeing the uniform on an unfamiliar body, held out his hand to Adam.

'Vuong this is Adam. He's starting today.'

'Nice to meet you.'

'And you,' said Adam.

'I'll show him how to pack with the Dothan order. We'll leave everything up on the bench for you. Take him along on the delivery, yes?'

'OK boss,' and Vuong returned hurriedly to the open doors of the van. For another hour Adam was shown how to pick and pack flowers.

'How do you know Dinah?' said Slob.

'I was at school with Jacob.'

'Who's Jacob?'

'Dinah's husband.'

'Oh, that guy, yep.'

'How do you know her?'

'I pollinate her flower.'

'You what?'

'Flowers. I supply her flowers.'

'Oh, for the wedding planning? It is always wonderful to hear of flowers bringing people together, isn't it?' Adam was being enthusiastic again.

'What did you do before this?'

'What did I do?'

'Yeah.'

'Before I got here?'

'Yes.'

'I woke up, shaved, bathed and dressed. I had some breakfast. Fruit mostly. The bananas were a bit old but then-'

'What did you do for a job?'

'Ohh. No, I didn't really have a job. I grew flowers and I sold some of them.'

'You were a grower? What'd you grow?'

'Very rare flowers.'

And the conversation stopped. Slob knew less about flowers than do most men who are not florists and he was wary of participating in any conversation that might betray his ignorance. He had memorised the names of all the flowers that Rad sold from the time of his first employment and since then kept up with the trends simply by walking around the stalls of his competitors to see if they had introduced any bloom which he did not recognise. When an unfamiliar flower became ubiquitous he would ask its name and begin ordering it from his suppliers.

When Vuong had loaded the last of the Dothan order into the truck Slob said, 'Now Adam, this is important. The Hotel Dothan is our best customer and their business with us relies on total discretion. Do you understand? Anything you see on one of their orders – names, nicknames, changing names – you keep to yourself. You don't even mention them to me. Anything you see while you're there you keep to yourself. It's tempting to gossip I know. You're gonna see some fucked up shit. But our silence is literally money. While you're there you don't look at anybody strangely or with judgment. And I'll see you in a couple of hours, all right?'

Adam got into the van and Slob pressed a button to raise the rickety steel door of the loading bay.

1:2

The sun, shining fully, was without any real warmth; the sky was of an unimpeded blue. At the first corner Vuong said, 'What your name?'

'Adam.'

'Ad-am?'

'Yes.'

'My name Vuong.'

'Vuong?'

'No, Vuong.'

'Vuong?'

'No. Vuong.'

'Vuong?'

'*Vuong.*'

'Vuong.'

'Yes.'

'Oh.'

'Where are you from?'

'Where am I from?'

'Yes.'

'Australia.'

'I am from Vietnam.'

'Oh, yes?'

'Have you been to Vietnam?'

'I haven't, no.'

'Vietnam is very beautiful country.'

'Is it?'

Vuong nodded. 'You like Slob?'

'Do I like him?'

'I like him not.'

'No?'

'No. He is very fat and very lazy.'

'Is he?'

Vuong nodded, once and with certainty.

'Well I'm sure I'll come to know him in time.'

'What?'

'What?'

Vuong pointed out the window and cackled loudly. He closed his eyes and threw his head back. 'Look at man so big so fat.' He cackled again. 'He good luck to many people who rub his belly. Look like Slob. So big so fat.' He banged at the steering wheel and smiled for the remainder of the drive. Soon he eased the van into the kerb. 'Here Hotel Dothan.'

Vuong opened the back doors. 'Now we take everything inside and we put against the wall. Here, take this and this, then come back you.'

The Hotel Dothan was in a tall and slender building on a busy road in Toorak, on one side of two opposing blocks of commercial shopfronts. It was for miles surrounded by blocks of large mock-Tudor houses and high-ceilinged modern apartments all occupied by people who vociferously thought themselves to have reached the highest peak of respectability ever to have been attained by unfallen man. Its seven oft-raided floors had been privy to more grovelling, more confessions of the powerful, more tyrannising, more sordidness, so much more modern selfishness than any other building in the city. For the deaths which gave it so rapid a turnover of workers it was in the news about twice a year. Stonewalling staff and illicit and fantastical favours ingeniously offered ensured that the underlings who were sent to look into the hotel's goings-on never launched the full investigation that would have uncovered the total and frequent patronage of their superiors.

Adam walked through its automatic glass doors with a box of yellow roses in one arm and some cactus dahlias in the other. The lobby looked much like that of any other medium-sized chain hotel. A round wooden table in its centre supported a vase of birds of paradise; clocks behind a reception desk of dark green imitation marble gave the time in various commercial centres; photographs of the city, all for sale, cluttered most of the walls. At the rear of the lobby a large floating imperial staircase of scuffed almost-white paint rose to a landing with a similarly coloured balustrade. It led in both directions to the interior of the first floor. The back left corner of the lobby opened onto the restaurant; doors for two elevators were embedded in the right.

'Here you put,' said Vuong, walking in behind him. He yelled something in his own tongue to the middle-aged woman standing straight-backed in her ao dai behind the reception desk. Writing something down, she yelled back at him without looking up. The wall opposite her and reception had three black free-standing shelves – the highest against the wall, the lowest a foot from the ground – all already cluttered with bouquets and gift-boxes and plush cushions. Among these were several framed headshots of Asian people of varying age, gender and complexion.

'This Wall of Love,' said Vuong.

'There are so many flowers on it.'

Vuong chuckled and yelled over to the woman. She nodded and then shook her head and said something which betrayed mild disappointment.

'She said, yes, was not good weekend.'

'*Not* a good weekend?'

'Shhh,' said Vuong, gently.

Adam put the box of roses in a gap on the second shelf.

'No. Here.' Vuong moved them to the lowest shelf. The flowers on this lowest were simply arranged and most were wilting and turning brown. 'See,' said Vuong, pointing to the three levels. 'You learn. On Wall of Love most expensive at top, most cheapest at a bottom. Otherwise Slob phone call. So just you look. If you see same size same type, you put there. Come. More flower.'

When they had made the last of the trips from the van Vuong said, 'Now we give invoice to Madame Ho, and she knows who has wall flower and she tell them when they come, and we finish delivery.' They left the lobby and Vuong yelled what might have been a farewell to Madame Ho.

Vuong pulled out into traffic. 'You no ask so many question. Madame Ho she hear. We no look or hear or see anything in the Hotel Dothan.'

Back at Rad's Flowers Slob said, 'How'd you go?'

'A very strange place.'

'Yep. So I did get a phone call from Madame Ho. She said you made a comment, but I've calmed her down, I told her it was your first day. You need to remember, no looking, no staring, no questions, no judgment, all right? Unless you're on a freebie. Then you can do whatever the fuck you want. And Madame Ho's the key to freebies. Get on her good side and she'll throw something your way soon enough.' Slob winked. 'You might even get a white bird. Here. Now this is today's Dothan order. I'll get you to pick it and pack it by yourself and then come and get me and I'll inspect it and then you and Vuong can go back out.'

An hour later Slob inspected Adam's work and found it faultless. Four small orders came through while he was preparing the Dothan order and Vuong showed Adam how to arrange the van so that it was loaded according to their delivery route.

They delivered an enormous arrangement of native flowers to a nursing home, a bouquet of unrelated flowers of clashing colour to the office of an unsuspecting and excitable young woman, red roses to a residential address, a simple arrangement of pink lilies with a small thank-you cushion to a doctor's office.

Then they were back at the Hotel Dothan.

Its lobby was now aflutter with people. Porters took bags up the staircase ahead of newly arrived guests; people sat in one another's laps on the green couches beneath them. The Wall of Love was surrounded by people inspecting the *To:* and *From:* tags. Some were almost weeping, some overcome with joy and smiling. Madame Ho had two young girls beside her in ao dais. She clicked her fingers at one of them and the young girl led a guest into an elevator. Another girl in identical dress came immediately from the back room and took her place at Madame Ho's side.

Vuong transferred four bouquets from his arms to the middle shelf. 'Remember what I tell to you?' he said to Adam. 'And see this? The number on the end of picking number. 7 means to front desk for room delivery. Very important.' Adam veered to the front desk with his three bouquets. They were taken by one of the girls at Madame Ho's side. She screeched a single word then checked the *To:* and *From:* labels. She handed the bouquets to a porter and told him harshly which room to take each to. Adam followed Vuong back out to the van. He was handed an elaborate basket of mimosa, palm frond and tulip, arranged to look like a peacock's tail, and bore it to the Wall of Love. He set it on the top shelf. The surrounding guests took turns in inspecting its tag and sighing with gladness. At the top of the stairs Adam caught sight of a little pharaoh driving a man in a coarse kaftan and sandals from one side of the landing to the other. The Hebrew almost skipped before the lash of a whip. He giggled as he frolicked, 'Rich and godless, sensuous and violent, the world.'

Adam was staring.

Then emerged from the elevator a young Asian girl wearing a suit of red leather straps which covered not much besides her necessities. She was followed to the reception desk by a middle-aged man. 'I'd like to check-out, please.' The leatherbound girl said something in her own tongue. When she had finished Madame Ho turned to the man.

'Everything is in order, sir, OK? I hope you have a wonderful day,' and she and the girls beside her and the girl in the leathern net waved him goodbye.

Through the lobby's glass doors a thin man in a cheap suit trailed in a large suitcase. He took in the arrangement of the lobby and went straight to the desk. 'Do you have a room for tonight?'

'I am sorry but we have full tonight.'

'Oh, all right. Umm... Nothing at all?'

'No. This time very busy of the year.'

He thanked her and walked out. A man trailing an almost identical suitcase crossed him on his way out.

'My wife's away for the weekend,' he said to Madame Ho.

'It is not good that a man should be alone. Of course we can take care of you.' Madame Ho yelled a single short word and a porter appeared from the rear of the lobby to take the man's suitcase and lead him up the stairs.

Vuong walked into the lobby with armfuls of plush cushions. He ran them into Adam's back. 'No! No staring you! No, no, no! You stare how long? Slob will get phone called. Wait here. Turn around. Look only at Wall of Love.' Vuong took the cushions into the back of the lobby and shortly returned. 'Now, time for you to lunch, time for me to freebie. Lunch in there. Anything you want. Rad's Flowers very good cutomer.' And Vuong sprinted up the staircase.

1:3

Suddenly looking forward to eating, Adam walked towards the back of the lobby and found the restaurant. Its floor was taken up by round and uncovered wooden tables among wooden round-backed booths. Against the far wall was a long line of bains-marie, not yet turned on. Behind these was a chrome kitchen. The lights were off and the vast room silent. Adam found that he was alone in the room except for the pharaoh who had started off his forbidden stare.

'Hello,' said Adam.

Hunched over and looking vacantly at the emptied plate in front of him, the pharaoh looked meekly up at Adam and said nothing.

'Is this the restaurant?'

'This is the restaurant.'

Adam could see no waiters, no chefs, no sign that any surface in the kitchen was as much as warm.

'Do you mind if I sit?'

The pharaoh shook his head.

'And what's your name?'

'My name Tung.'

'Tung?'

'No, Tung.'

'Tung?'

'Tung.'

'Tung?'

'Yes.'

'Why are you dressed as a pharaoh?'

'Hm?'

'Your clothing.' Adam pulled at his own jacket and pointed at Tung.

'This my uniform.'

'Oh, it's your uniform. You know I had to wear a uniform today for the first time ever? Apart from school. So you work here do you?'

'No. I slave here.'

'You slave here?'

'Yes.'

'I have often heard people comparing their jobs to slavery. Mine doesn't seem too bad though, not just yet. But it is my first day. What do you do here, Tung? Is there some sort of matinee or something?'

'What?'

'What do you do here?'

'My whole family in Vietnam. My sister, my sister, my mother, my father. It's not now safe in Vietnam. Many bloodsheds. Soon maybe my whole family may they fall prey to foreigner. So every money I make I send to my wife to bring here. We come for free-dumb here. Mo-ral-ity,' (he struggled with the word) 'of western world much better. We come for free-dumb.'

'Well that sounds lovely doesn't it?'

'Then when she come here, she go away from me.'

'She's already been?'

'Yes. She come. Then she go. She take.'

'She take?'

'Because she is illegal.'

'She's illegal? You mean she's a criminal?'

'No! Not criminal! Never! They say she is illegal. But she should be free. With me so we can be happy. But she cannot come out. Master Alexander always no-no application of she.'

'You should to go to her, Tung.'

'What?'

'You should go to her.'

'Go to her?'

'The world's a very large place. And while we're in it we should be with the ones we love, no matter where they are. If you love her and she can't come to you, you should go to her.'

Adam's simple romanticism had bridged the many gaps between them. 'I go to her? I love her. She cannot come to me, I go to her.' Tung stared at him, astounded and emboldened. 'Today I do! I make him public. I go in, I see my wife again.'

'Don't you talk about your wife behind my back,' boomed somebody who was storming into the room. It was the Hebrew— tall, solid, pot-bellied, wispy-haired.

Pharaoh's frightened eyes darted to him. 'No,' he insisted. 'Not my wife. Somebody else.'

'You were. You were talking about *her*. You know I hate hearing about her. You cannot be happy with her. Do you understand? She's locked away. She shouldn't have come here. And you know what'll happen if I catch you talking about her again.'

'Sorry master.'

'Oh, hello,' said the Hebrew, looking at Adam and feeling instantly erotic. 'I love that uniform on you.' He ran a finger along the shoulder seam of Adam's jacket. 'Are you coming to work here? I'll tell Madame Ho I'll take you. Tung, you'd look *fantastic* in this. Now come on you. We've got work to do. The pyramids aren't going to build themselves.'

'Goodbye,' said Tung, sorrow pouring from his eyes.

'Yes, goodbye,' said Adam. 'It was very nice meeting you. Have a lovely afternoon at work, won't you? I just have to wait here for my colleague to be done… wherever he is. You don't know if there's a waiter anywhere around, do you?'

But the pair were gone. And before any waitstaff materialised Vuong came bouncing and laughing into the restaurant to collect Adam.

1:4

Back at South Melbourne Market Adam was shown the numbering system which Slob had devised. He was taught how to operate a cash register and instructed on how to curl a ribbon. He was asked to inspect the unsold flowers for signs of decay and told to rotate them so that any brown spots would be hidden from tomorrow's browsers. Then he hosed down the shopfloor. In this single afternoon he missed the point of two dozen filthy jokes, and three about the holocaust.

CHAPTER 2

1

At five minutes to six the next morning Adam returned, uniformed, to find the shop locked. An hour later Vuong arrived to open up. He was out of uniform, in a t-shirt with three large black words, 'This Dreamer Cometh,' printed alike on its front and its back. 'Slob not here today. He has freebie at hotel. Not back till tomorrow. You stay. We have easy day.'

Vuong told Adam to sit with him in the office. He played on his phone for two hours and smoked and drank black coffee while Adam, phoneless and disinclined to both, stared. Eventually Adam heard the printer start. 'Vuong?'

'What?'

'Does that mean we have an order?'

'What?'

'The printer.'

'I no hear nothing. Slob no here. No order.'

Soon the printer started again. 'Are you sure there are no orders? Doesn't that printer *only* print out orders?'

'No order today. Slob no here.'

Adam wandered among the flowers, sniffing at some of his favourites and wondering why they were unscented when they should have been bursting with pleasant odour. The printer went off a few more times. He went into the office and flicked through the sheets of paper in the mouth of the thing. 'Vuong, this is the Dothan order. Won't Slob know that we haven't delivered the Dothan order if he's staying there?'

'He comes out not for whole day. We deliver later, on way home.'

'Ah. But see here, isn't this one for a bouquet of yellow roses, *To:* Slob, *From:* Dinah. Won't that be for Slob? And it has a seven on the end of the picking number. That's a room delivery. He'll know if he doesn't get it delivered to his room, won't he?'

Vuong let out a screech of frustration. 'OK. You smart. We pick. But you go. I look after shop. Maybe girl come in. I give her flowers, she love me.'

Adam picked and packed the morning's Dothan order while Vuong played on his phone. He loaded the van himself and drove slowly and disruptively to the Hotel Dothan.

Its lobby was bustling again. He carted in all the flowers that were to adorn the Wall of Love. Tung was at the reception desk talking with Madame Ho in their own tongue. No longer dressed as a Pharaoh, Tung seemed distressed. He stormed off as Adam presented to Madame Ho those arrangements which were to be delivered to the rooms. Adam's last trip between the van and the reception desk was with Slob's flowers. He handed Madame Ho the invoice. 'Lunch where you want,' she said, pointing in the direction of the restaurant. Sitting in one of the green couches under the staircase was the man formerly costumed as a Hebrew. He was now brooding in shirtsleeves. A waiter walked among the tables. Adam sat down and was brought a menu. He immediately ordered the roast of the day, lamb. At the far side of the restaurant Adam saw Tung gobbling hungrily at a plate of rice and went over to his table.

'Hello, Tung.'

'Hello you.'

'Did you get a new job then?'

'What?'

'Your uniform. You've changed uniforms. Did you get a job as a florist's delivery driver as well?'

'What?'

'What?'

'What you say?'

'Did you get a job as a florist's delivery driver? We're wearing almost the same uniform.'

'My master he see you in your uniform. He decide he want me to wear same same.'

'That's very peculiar. But you're not a delivery driver?'

'No. I did it.'

'No you did what?'

'I tell somebody.'

'What about?'

'Shh. You hear something?'

'No. What?'

'I thought I hear soldiers.'

'Why would you hear soldiers?'

'Shh. There. Hear it again?'

Adam and Tung both turned their ears to the entrance to the restaurant, from where, shortly, a dozen lethally armed and impenetrably clad police officers rushed in formation into the restaurant, scanning their machine guns from side to side.

'There he is,' said one of them.

Tung put down his chopsticks and sat back in his chair. He was overcome with serenity. 'I go to see my wife.'

'Wait,' said one of the officers. 'There are two of them.'

'Which one of you is dressed as a delivery driver for a florist?'

'That would be me,' said Adam, raising his hand. Then his raised hand was gripped at the wrist and forced behind his back. His head was slammed onto the tabletop and a black cotton bag placed over it. With impressive speed were his hands tied at his back with a cable tie.

'No!' said Tung. 'I am delivery driver. You take me.'

'They're both dressed like delivery drivers for florists.' The officers barely vacillated. 'Take them both.'

And Tung was similarly apprehended and the backs of their lowered heads were struck with extendable batons. They were lifted off the ground and carried limp by the legs and the armpits to the lobby. Adam's waiter brought his roast lamb to his table and, finding nobody around to claim it, returned it to the kitchen. Adam and Tung joined a procession of similarly bound people. Between a centurion and a sultan they were filed out of the Hotel Dothan and dropped into the seats of a waiting bus.

Most of the hotel's guests had descended on the lobby to observe the abrupt captivity of their roommates, their lovers, their sometime dainty overlords. Alexander was standing underneath the imperial staircases coldly watching the carrying out of his orders.

'Big day tomorrow,' thought Slob.

'Slob?'

'Dinah? What the fuck are you doing here?'

'Why are you dressed as a tiger? You—.' She gasped. 'You're here doing *it* aren't you? I told you I would do it with you. I can't believe you! I just needed to find the right time and the right place. Who are you doing it with? Slob?'

'What are you doing here, Dinah?'

'I wanted to say goodbye before I left. I'm leaving for Kerang today. I sent flowers but I thought I'd come and say goodbye in person. I'm such an idiot! I find you doing *this*? I told you I would do it with you, Slob. What would your wife think if she found out?'

'I don't have time for your shit right now, all right?' Slob went into an elevator.

All of Dinah's preconceptions about Slob's goodness, however wildly illogical, had been shattered. It was to her that he claimed he had first opened up about his fantasies, she who had assured him that they were not weird, she who had taken the first small steps towards making them a reality. And now she it was discovering him seeking their fulfilment beyond her, dressed as a tiger quite in her absence. No doubt the shy tortoise he so longed to nuzzle was somewhere within the confines of this boutique hotel (actually she was unconscious and sitting behind Adam on a bus). Dinah stood staring at the Wall of Love. She might have sobbed if Alexander had not put his arm around her.

'I don't know how people can be so cruel to one another,' he said.

CHAPTER 3

1

When Adam came to he was immediately aware of a throbbing ache at the top of his neck.

'Hello?' he said groggily and in the dark.

'Shhh,' said a vehement pair of teeth.

'Hello?' he said, and was struck on the back of the head.

When two hours later he came to again he thought better of attempting to greet whomever was around him. He could feel that his hands were tied and he thought that probably he was on a bus and that a bag, a soft bag rather like the ones his brogues came in, was over his head.

Soon the bus slowed and turned and came to a stop. A guard walked from the back row to the front and pulled the bags from the heads of the passengers. Not a very nice bus, thought Adam, looking around.

Outside was a plain of golden sunburnt dust. A high wall of chain link fencing was crowned by an unbroken coil of razor wire. Beyond it a low cover of grey-green shrubbery ran to the forbiddingly distant horizon. The sky was vast, unwelcoming, cloudless. Guards in light blue uniforms and with black holsters stood waiting in two files at the front door of the bus. Beyond them lay what could only very tenuously be labelled anything other than a compound; its administrators called it a facility. It consisted of six long beige-green sheds constructed of sheet metal, slightly raised off the ground with a single door and three concrete steps at their closest end. At tiny windows set every three feet into their sides little dark faces huddled to watch the new arrivals.

The frontmost passenger was picked up by the shoulder of his shirt and pushed towards the footwell of the bus. His cable-ties were snipped and thrown into a plastic tub on the dashboard. The sluggish remainder of men, women and children were kicked into following him outside.

The sun hit intensely on Adam's face and the breeze was hot. Feeling rather as though he was in a kiln he took off his tracksuit jacket and held it in his hand. A few steps into his trail a woman dressed as a tortoise tugged at it from behind and said something excitedly in a foreign language to those around her. On both sides of the slowly closing compound gates a tall date palm swayed. Littering the grounds were hundreds of little dark brown spots which occasionally jumped. One made for Adam's leg. He edged it with his shoe and it, a cane toad, hopped away. The passengers walked past the line of guards until, in an open yard, they could not know where next to move. When the bus was empty more guards emerged from a smaller shed set apart from the longer ones; with stern waves of their hands they summoned over the multitude.

A third of the way into this squarer shed two long trestle tables were stacked high with plastic-wrapped bundles. When the passengers had finished shuffling in only the whirring and clicking of three yellowing ceiling fans could be heard. A guard of obviously superior rank soon followed them in and yelled repeatedly, 'Two staggered ranks,' as his men picked up and pushed around the passengers until they had been formed. Then each of the inmates was patted down and their phones and wallets confiscated. Adam had neither on him. The guard yelled, 'Ready, Captain.' The passenger beside Adam snatched the kaleidoscopic jacket from his hand.

The flyscreen door which all were now facing creaked open; in walked a large man in blue uniform walked in. Carrying a flywhisk, each of his epaulettes had a small golden jackal with a forked tail. By no other mark was his rank distinguished. 'Thank you, Officer Rotte,' he said as he entered fully the room. He was about fifty and heavyset without a belly. His deeply wrinkled skin was fair and shining red from too much sun. His head was roughly shaven and his stubble flecked with copper, his eyes deepset and menacing. Following closely behind was an overweight middle-aged Asian man with thin eyebrows. He wore a loose short-sleeved straw-coloured shirt with mandarin collar and loose trousers and rubber sandals.

'I am Captain MacAynall,' said the man in uniform. 'Welcome all to Kerang Immigration Detention Centre, of which you are now all guests. I am your primary caregiver while you arc here. This is my facility. This is Dai Thanh, my translator. Those of you who do not understand English will be told what to do through him.'

Captain MacAynall paused. When no response came he looked at his translator. 'Go on!'

Dai Thanh nodded and in a bendy Asian accent said, 'He is Captain MacAynall. Welcome all to Kerang Immigration Detention Centre, of which you are now all guests. He is your primary caregiver while you are here. This is his facility. This is Dai Thanh, my translator. Those–'

'Not in English, you idiot. I just told them that in English. Translate it.'

'Oh, yes. Sorry.' Dai Thanh spoke at length in his own halting, tonal language and then nodded over to Captain MacAynall.

'There is to be no talking except in your quarters and in the exercise yard.' He waved his hand at Dai Thanh; his prohibition was translated. 'If you speak, in any language, other than when you are allowed to speak, you will be relaxed.'

'I'd never thought of that,' thought Adam. 'Speaking does have something of a soothing effect on the speaker.'

As Dai Thanh translated two inmates sniped to one another and then chortled.

'Relax those two,' said Captain MacAynall, pleading rather than ordering.

Two guards stepped to the offending pair and stuck tasers into the rears of their respective ribcages. The men convulsed for a time before going floppy and hitting the ground.

Slouching slightly from the pain in his neck, Adam suddenly bolted to upright and looked with fright on the two limp men.

'That… is being relaxed,' said Captain MacAynall.

Adam snapped his horrified gaze towards the front of the room.

'That is being relaxed,' said Dai Thanh, and Captain MacAynall shot him a sharp glance; he apologised and translated.

'Now I do not *want* to have to relax any of you, but order must be maintained. … Until your stay with us is concluded you must follow my orders and the orders of my guards.' Then came his first genuine order. 'Guards, su-uuunn-smart!' Each of the inmates was dispensed from the trestle tables a plastic-wrapped bundle. 'Your legionnaire's hat, your bottle of sunscreen, your inmate credit card. … Your schedule will be as follows. … 7am—breakfast, sunscreen, work. … Midday—lunch, sunscreen, work. … 5pm—

sunscreen, exercise, internet, dinner. … 9pm—lights out, no talking. … You will of course be paid for the work that you do. … Your credit cards will be deposited with your wages each week and you can spend them however you wish. … You will find that you have already received your welcome bonuses. … You will wear your hats whenever you are outside. If you lose your hat you will be made to sew yourself another one from cardboard boxes. … That is all. Welcome to Kerang Immigration Detention Centre. I do hope you have a pleasant stay.'

As his final sentiment was translated the guards pushed their batons at the inmates until they filed out through the flyscreen door. Adam, certain by now that at least one mistake had been made somewhere along the line, resisted as best he could their prodding until he was last in the room. As he passed the Captain he pointed vehemently at his eyes and shook frantically his head. When finally Captain MacAynall caught him doing so he asked that Adam be brought back to him.

'Inmate, what's the problem?' said the Captain.

'I –'

'Ah!' The Captain raised a finger to his lips. 'Shhh, shh, shh, sh, sh, sh. No talking or you'll be relaxed.'

'Hm?'

'*Shh*!'

Adam pointed with still more vehemence at his eyes. Then he pointed to the flyscreen and pulled back the corners of his own eyes and shook his head. He pointed to himself and then circled his index fingers around his own eyes.

'Are you being racist?' said the Captain.

'What? No.'

'Sh.'

'Mm mm.'

'Are you suggesting *we*'re racist?'

Adam shook his head.

'Just because you don't have slanty eyes doesn't mean we can treat you any differently, son.'

Adam shook his head and pointed at his eyes again.

'All right, you can have ten words. Make 'em count. And you can't wish for more wishes.'

Adam sighed from relief. 'I'm an Australian citizen.'

'Where's your passport?'

'Now why would I have that?'

'If you don't have your passport how can I know you're Australian?'

'I don't–'

'Ah! That's your ten words. Speak again and I'll relax you.'

Adam drooped. He pointed again at his eyes and shook his head but his fervour had waned.

'What would the newspapers say if they found out that we were being racist? Now come on, out you hop.' He took Adam's hat from his hand and put it on his head. 'Quarters with the rest of them.'

Adam's quarters were in the fourth of the long sheds. Inside, two interminable rows of double bunk beds were being ambushed by the new arrivals. Ceiling fans hung pointlessly between each bunk and a chest sat at their end. Holding his bottle of sunscreen and his credit card Adam ambled warily down the length of the aisle. People argued over who was to have the top bunks. Those who had already resolved the issue were settling in to their new homes, yelling and laughing around the room. Adam passed Tung, who waved at him without emotion, and eventually found an empty top bunk. He put his hat and his sunscreen on it, and then hoisted himself up and lay down. Presently Captain MacAynall walked through the door with Dai Thanh.

'Five pm, idiots. Exercise.'

'Five pm, idiots. Exercise,' yelled Dai Thanh.

Beyond turning their heads to the front of the shed nobody moved. Their silence brought Dai Thanh to account. 'Sorry,' he said, and translated.

3:2

Bunks were unhurriedly descended and the aisle was in two files trekked as the inmates made their way at gunpoint to a larger yard behind the sheds. Three other long files were waddling along beside Adam's—the inmates from the other quarters sheds. Adam compared their lot to his. They did not appear to have suffered any great degradation of condition. Adam realised that they could just as easily have arrived that morning. There was a woman in dilapidated Restoration costume, a man in an untorn t-shirt which read 'Waste Howling Wilderness,' a young woman in an eagle costume with holes cut in the wings so that her hands were free. Perhaps they too had been rounded up from the Hotel Dothan, Adam thought.

Beside the yard into which the inmates were pouring – that in the eastern corner of the compound – there stood a grand house with a verandah running all the way around. A rocking chair was still at its front door, a clothesline at the centre of its very grassy back lawn. Adam noticed for the first time that the compound had six watchtowers looming over its high fence; three of them overlooked the corner in which this house was nestled.

Underfoot the exercise yard was soaked wet. It sloped very gently towards the house until it ran off into a shallow bed which separated the yard's brown gravel from luscious lawn. Bulrushes grew on either side of this indentation, to cross which no bridge was needed. It ran out to the fence of the compound. Days ago a hole had been cut to prevent rubbish from again gathering and causing a flood.

Squelching around in the mud were around three-hundred men, women and children, all to Adam's unworldly eyes of the same race. He saw Tung embracing a woman and supposed she was the wife he had longed so desperately to see.

In the highest corner of the yard – that nearest the compound's main gate – a kneeling group of people were drawing things in the mud. Conspiring, thought Adam. But with a bee and a cow? One of them got into a rage and stood. Taller than Adam, taller even than Noah Dulrich, where the rest of his countrymen were shorter than Adam's grandmother, he looked like a giant. His hands, feet and jaw were disproportionately large. His forehead soared and his eyes were puffy and almost entirely lid-covered. He yelled in his own alarming idiom and then shoved the man dressed as a bee. A guard rushed over and he threw up his arms but the submission was too late. Relaxed, he crashed to the ground and sent up a spray of mud.

Adam turned and found that ten feet away from him some other people had gathered. They had their heads turned sideways, as though they had been walking by and had spotted Adam and stopped in their tracks. Eerily were they smiling at him, staring from beneath their brows. Quickly Adam realised that they were ogling his polyester trousers.

Their number soon swelled to include a few more haggard and simple-looking people. One of them, and then all of them, pointed. His concern was almost immediately superseded by their chanting. 'Deliverer,' a man dressed as a winged lion seemed to say. 'Deliverer,' followed another, in Adam's multi-coloured jacket. Soon they were all saying it. Then they were saying it, and striding towards him. Wary of what running away might induce in such a strange host Adam stood very still.

'Well yes, I was a delivery driver,' he said, appealing in his own way to stop their advance. 'For a florist's shop. But—'

'Deliverer!' They struggled for a place close enough to enable the stroking of his trousers. Those who could not reach ran their fingers through his hair or pinched at his thorax, all of them saying again, as though they had not heard his explanation, 'Deliverer.'

A young man in a white t-shirt and muddied white trousers, at his back a decrepit pair of wings made of coat-hanger and stocking, passed on his way around the exercise yard.

'They say you are The Deliverer,' he called.

'Yes, thank you,' said Adam. 'I did manage to gather as much. I *was* working as a delivery driver for a florist's shop before I came here. I don't know how they know that though. I've never seen any of them before. And I don't see what in that necessitates their touching me.'

'What?'

'Could you ask them to stop?'

'You are the Deliverer. The Deliverer will lead them to freedom.'

'To what? To freedom?'

'The Deliverer will lead them to freedom.'

'No, definitely not me. I'm a delivery driver. And I'm quite certain there's been a mistake about my being here at all. I don't expect it will last long. Do you think you could tell them that. Or will they understand if I tell them?'

'What?'

'Ought I to tell them?'

'They pick Deliverer every time new busload.'

The young man made an electronic-sounding warble and then sloshed off on his lap around the yard. A few hands grasped at the elastic waist of Adam's trousers. One of them found and another untied the drawstring.

'Ah, no!' said Adam. 'No, not that. Oh, I shouldn't be here.' He began trying to shrug them off. Captain MacAynall yelled from the steps of the fifth long shed, 'Five-thirty, idiots. Internet.'

Across the yard all activity ceased, including that of the hands on Adam's person. The inmates filed enthusiastically as though through a funnel towards the fourth shed. Adam decided he would plead once again with his primary caregiver, this time categorically. He lagged through the mud, timing it so that he was the last to reach the door.

'I see they've decided on you as their new Deliverer,' said Captain MacAynall.

'Don't worry about it too much,' said Officer Rotte, standing beside him. 'Last week it was Zipper.' He pointed to the far corner of the exercise yard. A lone young girl was standing wistfully at the fence, staring out with perfect posture towards the unending plain of spinifex and dirt.

'She's an idiot girl,' said the Captain. 'Can't talk. But she definitely knows what she's doing in there,' he said, pointing to the house. 'Can't see why they would choose her. Maybe idiots are magical where they come from, like in Russia.'

'Captain MacAynall, I wonder if I could have a word about my present detention. You see I think—'

At the commencement of Adam's flagrant insubordination the Captain's eyes had swelled. 'Exercise is over, inmate. No talking. This is your last warning. Next infringement and you will be relaxed. Do you understand?'

Adam seemed not to.

'Oh where the fuck's Dai Thanh?' Captain MacAynall leaned his face in towards Adam and slowed down his sentences. 'Exercise finish. Exercise over. No talking after exercise. Zip it. Now internet. You talk again, relax,' and in order to demonstrate he momentarily let his upper half go floppy. 'OK?'

Adam pointed, this time almost with anger, at his eyes. He shook his head in desperation and then pointed out the distinctly round shape of his very open eyes.

'Oh, I think I know what he's on about!' said Captain MacAynall. 'Why didn't you say so? The Deliverer needs glasses. Bloody hell.'

'Why didn't you say so you idiot?'

'You'll miss out on internet time,' said the Captain.

Dai Thanh came to the door. 'They're all ready.'

'Can you tell him that if we take him to get glasses now he'll miss out on internet time?'

Dai Thanh spoke to Adam in Vietnamese. Adam shook his head, first at Dai Thanh, then at the incomprehension of those around him, then at the proposition of his needing glasses. He pointed to his eyes again and waved his hands across one another in a gesture of refusal.

'Yes, I know. We'll take you to get some now. Rotte, take him to the medical shed would you?'

3:3

Adam was led by this murine-faced figure to behind the last long shed, where stood the two smallest sheds he had yet seen in the compound. He was led into the smaller and put before the compound doctor, who also ran the gift shop. Informed of Adam's frequent complaining, Dr Sidney went to his other dispensary and brought back a revolving display of reading glasses. He took Adam's hat off and asked if he would look at a chart on the wall. He put two pairs of glasses at a time onto Adam's nose and had Adam read through the lyrics to Advance Australia Fair as he said, 'One or two?' while switching magnifications. After Adam had said, 'One,' twice, Rotte decided that words were not necessary for the examination and told Adam to hold up his fingers in response to the doctor's question. When the ordeal was concluded Rotte said, 'Now. You've been fitted with these glasses at the expense of the federal government. If you take them off we will relax you.'

Outside, internet time had finished and the inmates were filing from the fifth shed into the sixth.

'Dinner time,' said Rotte. 'I hope you like Australian food. No talking. And don't take your glasses off.'

Adam beheld the long stretch of the last shed. It was stifling inside. He tried all manner of contortions above and below his eyes in order to find a squint that enabled him to see with his glasses on. The shed was a sort of mess hall. Along the right hand side were a series of trestle tables laden with the plastic means to eat and drink. Adam joined the long queue. Soon he came to plates, cutlery and napkins; then a bain-marie.

'How are you love?' said a perspiring fat woman in a hairnet. 'Four pieces per inmate. Which ones d'you want?' Sitting under heat lamps behind the glass, moist and drooping from steam, were eight round orange blurs on metal trays, grouped in four pairs. Adam leaned in as far as was possible to the case and tried to read the little placards. The woman pointed with her spatula and said, impatiently, 'Aussie, hawaiian, meatlovers cheese.'

'Hawaiian, please,' said Adam.

'Shh,' said the fat woman. 'No talking. Point.'

Adam pointed at what he thought was hawaiian and held up four fingers. She held her hand out for his plate and slid the remaining half of the frontmost tray onto it. She pushed the pizza behind it to the front and yelled to the far end of the room, 'Defrost hawaiian.'

'One hawaiian,' was returned her in acknowledgment.

Next came a table of small plastic cups and then a large machine which dispensed soft drink. Adam eventually discovered that the middle cylinder dispensed ice. He filled two cups with broken tubes of it and turned to behold with a squint the vast rows of seating.

He banged his way through the maze of plastic chairs and found an opening in a back corner. He sat opposite three young men who he found he could not distinguish from one another save by their clothing. One wore a blue t-shirt with small peeling lettering which read, 'Ravin as a wolf,' and another wore a back-to-front soccer jersey with the number 1 and the name, 'Lam Cappucchino.' They took occasional unenthusiastic bites from their dinner. Adam quickly found that this was the only way he could stomach the stuff – one bite, force it down, wait for his body to remind him that he was hungry, one bite, force it down. His face dripped with sweat. He had never less enjoyed a meal. On his second piece he bit down on something hard and pulled a thorn from between his teeth.

Half an hour later the inmates were called away from their half-eaten triangles. 'Seven o'clock, idiots. Quarters.'

Adam followed with a strange feeling of emptiness and quite blindly. In his first ever act of open rebellion he slid his glasses down his nose so that he could comfortably find his bunk bed. With a splitting headache, a still-throbbing neck and a knotted stomach he heaved himself into bed, took off his hat and lay down. He noted to himself how very long his day seemed to have been. Then he felt a sharp nick at his forearm and jerked his elbow from the bed. He took off his glasses and found a tiny round bite mark. As he scratched it he felt the same pain at his ankle and reached down to scratch that. Scratching and flinching about his bed he wondered what his new boss would be thinking of his absence. 'Fired from the first job I ever had,' he despaired quietly to himself. And there were cucumbers in the fridge that needed to be used by this afternoon. If he didn't get home tomorrow they would be soggy beyond utility, rotten even. In sorrow did he catalogue his worries until he was interrupted by a head, popped up above his mattress. It was the young man who had that afternoon pointed out that the set who were chanting 'Deliverer' at him had designated him their deliverer.

'They say you are the English Speaker,' said the man, still dressed as a haggard angel.

'I speak English, yes. So do you.'

'I speak, but not so good like you. And I cannot read it. My name Bao.'

'My name Adam. My name is Adam. How do you do?'

'What I do? I cook.'

'*How* do you do?'

'How I cook?'

'What?'

'What? ... Here please. I have something for you read. You tell to me what it say. Please you.'

Adam's arm jerked in pain from his blanket and into his hand was thrust a sheet of paper. It was a letter. Adam took off his glasses and pulled himself up onto one elbow. 'Oh, it's you.'

'My name Bao.'

'Ow! Something's biting me.'

'Flea.'

'Fleas?'

'Please you read?'

'All right. … *Dearest Bao, I am so glad that you might be able to help me. Now that I trust you I can tell you more about my situation.* Do you understand?'

'Yes. I understand. She tell me more.'

'*I have fallen deeply in love with you.* Are you sure you want me to be reading this?'

'Yes, you read.'

'All right. *I am a princess.* I am a princess?'

'Princess, yes.'

'*I am a princess of Mubjheruda. I trust you have heard about what has been going on in my country. My father was murdered in the revolution and I never can go back to my country. Now I am in Indonesia. A refugee, like you. My father was rich and I am very rich but my money is being held by the bank.* Ow,' said Adam, bitten again at the elbow. '*I don't know if it is too much to ask, but if you love me too you will understand. I only need five-hundred dollars, just to pay the processing fee, and then all my family's money will be mine. If you help me out with this small amount I will be able to reward you greatly. Then my money will be free and I can start applying for political asylum and I will be able to come to Australia to be with you and we can be rich together.* … Cap'n Billy's Whizzbang. How did you meet this woman, Bao?'

'Oh, I so in love! So in love. She send me e-mail.'

'She sent you a letter?'

'E-mail, yes.'

'That's quite the stroke of luck, Bao, having a princess in love with you.'

'Yes. I love her. Could you read something else for me?'

'Oh, anything to help.'

Bao called across the aisle to a young girl, standing nervously at the end of the opposite bunk. 'This Ngong. She have letter. Please you read. I translate for her.'

'Of course. Hello.'

Ngong put a foot onto the railing of the bottom bunk and stood beside Bao.

'*Dear Ngong. I am so glad that you might be able to help me.*' Bao translated for her. '*Now that I trust you and have fallen deeply in love with you I can tell you more about my situation. I am a prince of Mubjheruda.*'

129

Bao translated. Ngong smiled and bounced on the spot, shaking Adam's bed frame. She was bitten on the chest and slapped and scratched her breast and laughed.

'*I trust you have heard about what has been going on in my country. My father was murdered in the revolution...*' and Adam read the whole letter through. Ngong looked as though she might cry from happiness. She took the letter from Adam and embraced it in both arms. 'That's extraordinary,' said Adam. 'I wonder if they're brother and sister.'

'Ngong not my sister.'

'No, not you and her, the prince and the princess. Either way, if you both help them you could pretty soon find yourself a prince, and she a princess.'

'Yes, I help her. Ngong too. Thank you.'

'Oh, anytime.' And the pair walked off, talking to one another with a youthful bliss evident even in their unknown tongue.

Adam returned his head to his pillow and tried to think. Every time he got part way into a decent line of thought something bit him and sent him from it. Captain MacAynall soon announced lights out. The chatter around him ceased but it was hours before Adam's mind stopped attempting to race, and before the fleas, having found and abused every exposed part of his skin, allowed him to sleep.

3:4

There were no curtains in the shed and Adam woke at dawn. There followed two hours of some of the most frightful worrying he had ever done. Finally he managed to convince himself that the quaint little mess he seemed to be in would no doubt work itself out in the course of the day. Then the solution appeared to him as if in a dream. Talking was allowed during exercise, exercise which Captain MacAynall oversaw. He had wasted yesterday's exercise in gawking and in being harassed. As soon as exercise was called he would march over to this Captain and tell him all about his rotting cucumbers and his worried employer and the mix-up over his uniform and everything would be straightened out.

At seven Captain MacAynall announced that it was seven

o'clock, idiots, and that they had ten minutes until breakfast. Adam jumped down from his bunk. Three other people were brushing their teeth over the basin between his bunk and the next. He found a dry toothbrush in the plastic holder mounted on the wall and concluded that it had to be his. He brushed his teeth and put on his hat and glasses and stumbled out the door and across to the mess shed.

The bain-marie was gone and in its place a trestle table set with plastic containers of cornflakes, cartons of long-life milk, trays of cold toast and packaged portions of vegemite. The soft drink dispenser was replaced by jugs of an orange liquid labelled orange juice and two metallic towers, one dispensing a warm murky liquid labelled coffee and one dispensing a warm less-murky liquid labelled tea. Adam started in silence on his sugared cornflakes and very quickly pinned down the taste of his milk as that of aluminium foil. Captain MacAynall announced Sunscreen and Adam and his fellow inmates left their plastic plates of black once-bitten pieces of toast and soggy plastic bowls-full of cereal to return to quarters and apply their lotion. Then it was time for Work.

Outside, every corner of the compound was alive with labour. People were clearing the gutters of the shed roofs, polishing the frames of the watchtowers, brushing cobwebs from the shed windows, weeding the dust, gathering litter – all in perfect silence.

The day was ubiquitous of light. It was that perfect sunniness which in inhabitable climates induces an hysterical race for the discomforts of the seaside. Adam was assigned first to raking the dust of the arrival yard then to watering the gravel of the exercise. For this there was between the first and second quarters sheds a large water tank from whose tap extended two lines of inmate, one passing full watering cans one way, the other empty watering cans the other. These branched off into twenty-four more lines. Beside eleven others Adam began, at the closest edge of the exercise yard, to empty a watering can in a slow arc in front of him. Emptied, he passed it to his left, took one step forward, and received a full one from his right. He swung it around and tilted it and soon with ever-lengthening supply lines behind him he reached the fence and was ordered to walk back to the beginning of the yard, where he and his eleven co-waterers were shifted across and made to water the next sixth of the gravel. When the whole area was sodden and the stream beside the house steadily flowing Adam was assigned to weeding the bulrushes.

A small patch of mud was pointed out to him and he was told to kneel in it. The spindles pricked at his arms and the spores made his neck itch but he knelt among them and searched the bank for weeds. He squinted as hard as his cheeks would allow. Neither he nor those he could perceive kneeling on the opposite bank could find a single unwelcome plant in the ochre mud.

Officer Rotte, patrolling on the opposite bank, halted behind a young girl who wore a loose t-shirt printed with the words, 'Master Wotteth Not'.

'Inmate,' said Rotte. 'Are you talking?'

The girl began frantically picking up clumps of mud and rifling through them before throwing them into the stream.

'Inmate,' said Officer Rotte, descending on her. 'No talking or you *will* be relaxed.' She threw a few more clumps into the stream. 'Right! Come with me.' He picked the girl up by her arm. With an unconvincing scowl she allowed herself to be pulled across the lawn and taken into the house.

'She Nung,' whispered a voice among the bulrushes. Adam raised his glasses and saw Bao's face peeking through at him.

'The girl with the letter?' whispered Adam.

'No, that Ngong. She Nung.'

'Oh.'

'He boyfriend.'

'Officer Rotte?'

'He boyfriend.'

'Oh.'

'In the house they get Vietnam food. But also boom boom.'

A small teenager floated serenely down the stream, buoyed by an improvised ark of long white chalky balloons tied together beneath him.

'Where on earth is he going?' whispered Adam.

'No worry,' whispered Bao. 'His mother float him down river. She hope he go to safety. But at end of stream, where it gets to river, there always wait two guard.'

The boy on the prophylactics straightened his legs and put his hands at his thighs and floated neatly through the hole in the fence. He looked back into the compound and held a triumphant fist in the air.

'And they bring them straight back?' said Adam.

'First they ask him, Who sent you? Tell us or we relax you. Then he tell them, then they relax him. Then they bring him back. Then they relax his mother. But–'

A short buzz preceded Bao's silence. He flopped over in the bulrushes and his head came to rest at Adam's feet. A guard stepped back up onto the exercise yard. 'Shh,' he said at Adam, and Adam hurried to pick up clumps of mud and throw them into the stream.

'Midday, idiots. Lunch,' was yelled from somewhere and the inmates stood from the bulrushes and gravitated towards the mess shed.

The bain-marie was back and in it two wooden boards loaded with what Adam was told by the sweaty woman was roast lamb. Rejoicing, Adam handed over his plate and as best he could silently implored the woman to fill his plate with as much meat and as many roast potatoes and peas as her generosity allowed. Beside the machine which dispensed soft drink there was a metal tub of mint jelly. Adam nearly fainted from happiness. He put an enormous dollop of it on his peas and filled two cups with ice and began his squinted search for a spare seat. He thought he spotted one at the far end of the shed and banged his shins through to it. He set down his tray and drank what had already melted of his ice and sliced in half his first dry piece of meat.

'All right, idiots. Stop eating.' Dai Thanh immediately translated for Captain MacAynall. With his flywhisk at his back he walked the mess shed, watching for anybody disobeying his order. Dai Thanh followed closely behind. 'I have just received word that the Minister for Multicultural Affairs is on his way to your very fine facility for an inspection. … He has heard of the exemplary nature of our inmates and wishes to observe them in action for a few days. … As such … Work will commence immediately.' Dai Thanh's translation was followed by pained exhalations. 'And will consist of getting this place looking kinder and more hospitable than it ever has before. … We will be in a bit of a rush but as a reward we will feast tonight in his honour. … Everybody, up!' Dai Thanh mimicked his cadence and the inmates stood. Adam looked down at his uncommenced lunch and lamented.

Captain MacAynall said he wanted the stream flowing at full height for the occasion. Adam was again assigned to rewatering the gravel of the exercise yard. When that was done he was handed a pair of blunt scissors and made to crawl in a straight line across the vast lawn surrounding the officer's house, shearing as evenly as he could.

Bao crawled confusedly beside him for most of the hour. Ten minutes before Exercise was called Captain MacAynall stepped down from the verandah and loomed over a prostrate young girl.

'Inmate.' She stopped snipping. 'Have you put your sunscreen on this afternoon?' The girl looked up. Her face was white with it. She shook her head. 'I didn't think so. Right. Come with me. Come on, up you get.' And the Captain led her up the steps and into the officer's house.

'She Ngung,' whispered Bao.

'The girl with the love letter?' whispered Adam.

'No, that Ngong.'

'Oh, the girl from this morning?'

'No, that Nung.'

'She's a different one?'

'Yes, she Ngung.'

'Bao, how do I get in there?' said Adam.

'What?'

'I need to talk to the Captain. How do I get into the house?'

Bao's eyes widened from terror. He shook his head. 'You want not in there to go.'

'No, I do want to go in there. I need to talk to the Captain. And you said they have food in there. I'm starving. We've been working all day. And I haven't eaten since–. I can't even remember.'

'In there boom boom,' said Bao, thoroughly spooked.

'Boom boom?'

'Boom boom.'

'They shoot you? They don't shoot you in there.'

'Boom boom,' said Bao, repeating his dour warning.

Then Officer Rotte called Exercise.

The inmates squelched around the yard and chatted harshly with one another. Adam stood at the stream's edge, squinting at the officer's house, waiting for the emergence of a silhouette resembling Captain MacAynall's.

Soon an enormous hand dropped onto his shoulder. Adam turned around and craned his neck. Even in the blur of his imposed blindness he could tell that it was the gigantic inmate.

'Are you the one they call the Speaker of English?'

'That again. No, I–. Well, yes. I can speak English. But I wouldn't call myself *the* speaker of English. You can speak it. So can Bao.'

'What?'

'What?'

'And you are The Deliverer?'

'That again. Now, I've been through this with a few of you already. I *had* just started a new job as a delivery driver for a florist, yes. But–'

'We must to escape, you lead us to freedom.'

'Well I'm not going to lead anybody to freedom. I was working as a deliver*y driver*. Not deliver*er*, deliver*y*. Not a deliver*er* in any other more general or profound sense.'

'I hate here. I belong in outside. Always they do relax me because I talk. We should be allowed to talk. I have to get out. I have princess wait for me. I love her and we will be happy rich together. You deliver us.'

'I really don't think I can, I'm sorry.'

'I have escape plan, Speaker of English Deliverer. Is not the stream, is excursion. But my people not follow me. They only follow Deliverer. *You* are Deliverer.'

'I am not the Deliverer. Deliver-*y*, driver.' Adam returned to his watch across the stream.

'Yes,' said the giant. 'Deliver*er*. The time come, soon, when we look to you to deliver us.'

'I have never delivered people. I had only made three deliveries, of flowers, before I was brought here. Flowers.'

'Flower?'

'Yes.'

'Thank you.'

'What? Thank you for what? Please leave me alone.'

Officer Rotte came to Adam's other shoulder. 'Thinking of escaping, inmate?'

'Me? No. Not escaping. I just want to–'

'What's the giant asking you to do? He tries to escape every week.'

'No, nothing, honestly. He was just talking a bunch of rot. Sorry, not rot. A bunch of rubbish.'

'And why are you staring at the officer's house?'

'I need to talk to Captain MacAynall.'

'Is it about your glasses?'

'No it is not about my glasses.'

'What's it about then?'

'It is about my–'

'Shh,' said officer Rotte, his watch beeping. He yelled across the yard, 'Five-thirty, idiots. Internet. Ts ts,' he said to Adam. 'Internet.'

Adam joined the crowd and filed into the fourth shed. It was the coolest building he had been in since arriving. Ceiling fans kept moving the intoxicating zephyr of air-conditioners, wall-mounted every ten metres.

The inmates rushed to find an empty seat. Walking among the hurried, Adam passed several vacant cubicles before an officer made him sit in one.

'I–'

'Shh. Internet. No talking.'

For a time Adam squinted at the glowing screen. Then he looked down at the keyboard. On a small square mat beside it was a little black bubble-shaped thing. The inmate beside him was moving this bubble-shaped thing around and pressing on its button while looking at his screen. It did have buttons, Adam discovered – two of them. He pressed one. It made a pleasant enough sound. The inmate on his other side was tapping very quickly at his keyboard. Adam looked down at his and pointed out the letters of his first name and then wondered how he would insert a space before Athelstan. He leaned back and looked at the screens beside him. They were both websites with photographs of devastated cities surrounded by Vietnamese text. The only word Adam recognised on either was 'Mubjheruda'.

Dai Thanh, pacing the rows of cubicle, was leaning into people's screens and running his finger across them and saying things in Vietnamese. One girl pulled out her credit card. Dai Thanh showed her how to enter its details. Soon he came to Adam and waved an urgent hand at his screen.

'I –'

'Sh.'

Adam sat forward in his chair and mimicked the inmate to his right, swirling the bubble-shaped thing around and clicking its buttons. He pressed some letters with his index fingers. Dai Thanh said something very commanding in Vietnamese.

'English?' said Adam.

'Shh. Check your e-mail.'

'My mail?'

'Sh. Your e-mail.'

'My what?'

'No talking. Shh. Check it.'

Adam offered Dai Thanh two palms of ignorance. Dai Thanh leaned in and clicked the bubble-shaped thing a few more times. Adam saw that the little arrowhead on his screen corresponded exactly to the movements of the bubble-shaped thing. 'How clever,' he thought.

'What's your e-mail address? Whisper.'

'My address? 14/36 Gennesaret Way, Docklands, Victoria, Three zero zero eight.'

'Not your home address you idiot. Your *e-mail* address.'

'My what address?' Adam shook his head and pouted. Dai Thanh huffed and slapped Adam upside the head and then stood back and moved on.

Near the end of Internet time, through which Adam sat watching his entranced fellow-inmates, Captain MacAynall appeared at the end of the shed and announced that their esteemed visitor was half an hour away.

3:5

Through dusk they were painstakingly formed into straight rows and files for the Minister's arrival. 'What a long day,' thought Adam as he was held at the shoulders and put into line. Trestle tables and hundreds of chairs had been arranged in a u-shape around the arrival yard and the tables set tightly with cutlery. Headlights soon appeared along the highway. The gates were opened. The car came to rest where Adam's bus had stopped the previous afternoon. The driver got out and opened the back door for the honourable

Alexander Comeshotte. He put foot onto the facility's dust and was greeted enthusiastically by Captain MacAynall. Officer Rotte asked if he could take their picture with his phone; they held hands and smiled at the camera.

'I'm going to need a small favour,' said Alexander as the Captain led him on an inspection of the inmates.

'Anything, Mr Comeshotte.'

'I need to go into town a bit later.' He paced along a row of inmates, smiling and nodding at them. 'I have an important meeting and I'll need a driver.'

'You have a driver, Mr Comeshotte.'

'I need one who doesn't speak English. And I need a car if you have one. I can't take mine, it's got government licence plates. Or a van, if you have one.'

'We've got the laundry van.'

'Perfect. And find me a driver. The only secrecy you can rely on is the secrecy of the dumb.' The minister gave an inmate a paternal tap on the shoulder and shook his hand and smiled at him.

'Of course, minister.'

Alexander reached Tung and glowered at the woman beside him, clenched his teeth, and walked on.

Then it was time to feast. Alexander took his seat in the middle of the arrangement between the Captain and Officer Rotte. A bonfire raged in the centre of the tables, singeing the shins of any who wore shorts.

Fifty inmates had been chosen for waiting duties. They brought out one bottle of beer for each of the inmates and placed ice-buckets full of them in front of the guards. Most inmates took one sip before offering it to the person beside them.

Captain MacAynall rose and clinked his bottle with a knife. He made a speech welcoming the Minister and said he trusted that the inmates would make his visit a pleasant one. Then he suggested to Dai Thanh that perhaps some of the inmates would like to show the Minister one of their traditional dances. Dai Thanh said that of course they would and yelled at length at them in Vietnamese.

Twenty or so inmates rose and assembled between the Minister and the bonfire. They talked amongst themselves for a time and almost broke out into an argument. Then Dai Thanh started clapping a beat. The guards joined him, then some of the inmates.

Soon the dancers began randomly pointing their hands in the air and, with a total lack of coordination, moving their bodies around not really to the rhythm of the clapping, until one of them turned and clashed noses with another and the minister snickered and applauded. This they took as permission to stop.

Dinner was called for. The guards ate first; plush green salads and plates piled high with suckling pig. Adam watched them slather apple sauce all over the place and looked greatly forward to eating again. A dessert of chocolate mousse was served in plastic champagne coupes until finally the Minister and Captain MacAynall and the other guards fell back in their chairs and blew out huffs of engorgement.

The Captain waved his hand and the assigned inmates cleared the tables. Soon they returned to the arrival yard and dropped salads in front of the inmates. They started at the ends of the tables first. Adam looked down the length of his table then up to the guards. He was half way along. Sweet, sweet tomato would be on his tongue in a matter of minutes.

'All right if I take that van now?' said the honourable Mr Comeshotte.

'Of course,' said the Captain. 'Officer Rotte, the Minister needs a driver from one of the inmates. Can you suggest anybody? Preferably someone a little slow, but a good driver.'

'They're all pretty slow, Captain. And they're all Asian.'

'Shit yeah.' He thought for a time. 'Well which one's this week's Deliverer?'

'Umm,' said officer Rotte. 'Oh, it's four eyes. And I reckon he's got the hots for Ngung, too. I caught him eyeing off the officer's house while you two were in there.'

'Can he drive?'

'No worse than the others I don't reckon.'

'Yeah, take him. At least we know he can see properly.'

'You. Deliverer.' Officer Rotte grabbed the wrist of the waiter who was handing Adam his salad. 'Up you get.' Adam pointed to himself. 'Yes you, come on.'

He was taken to an unlit shed behind the processing shed and told to sit in the driver's seat of a van. Captain MacAynall appeared from the shadows and tapped at his window.

'Deliverer. No talking. We need you to drive this van into town.

Town's that way. You take your first left after the fifth McDonald's and then pull into the third KFC. In the carpark a girl'll be waiting beside a bin. She'll be wearing a loose blue top and purple jeans. You stop the van beside her and she'll get in the back. Drive it back to the second McDonald's you saw and park it in a corner with the back facing away from the restaurant. Get out of the van and here, get yourself something to eat, and wait for an hour before getting –'

Three quick bangs sounded against the wall of the cab.

'What?' said the Captain to it.

'Twenty minutes.'

'Huh?'

'An hour's too long. Make it twenty minutes.'

'You wait twenty minutes in the restaurant and then get back in the van and drive it back here. Now it's pizza night tomorrow night. If you pull this off without any funny business you can have two extra slices. Dai Thanh, tell him.'

Dai Thanh said a few words in Vietnamese and then waited until Adam thought to acknowledge his comprehension. He gave him a nod and Dai Thanh ngin-ed and ngang-ed at length. When Dai Thanh gave the Captain his own nod the van was slapped. Adam reversed as straight and as slowly as he could.

When he was beyond the gates of the compound he put his glasses on the passenger seat and sighed loudly with relief. He drove slowly along the deeply cleft road with his headlights at full beam. When he passed the first McDonald's he found himself singing for the first time in weeks.

'*The very thought of you … and I forget to do … the little ordinary things that everyone ought to do. … I see your face in every flower … I'm happy as a king,*' before three loud bangs on the wall behind his head told him that his cargo wished him to shut up.

It seemed as though there was a McDonald's on every block. After quickly counting five he turned and five blocks later drove into a carpark. He slowed the van around its edge until he saw the girl in the blue top and purple jeans standing beside a bin.

'Dinah?' he said, pulling in beside her.

She took this as the cue that this van of all the vans that had approached her since she had been standing beside the bin was the one for which she had been waiting. She scampered to its back. Adam heard the doors close. Soon two thuds at his head bade him continue his assignment. He returned to the second McDonald's.

There came the loud slap of a human cheek being struck.

'It feels like it's been forever since you did that to me,' whispered the male voice behind Adam.

'I know. But I have to be up here. My sister.'

'I've come for you.'

'And I'm so happy. Now come for me.'

'I've never seen anybody so beautiful and so free, Dinah. And to think you walked into the Hotel Dothan to see somebody else. I didn't believe in love at first sight.'

'What?'

'Can't you see what I'm trying to tell you? I love you.'

'Oh, Alexander. I love you too.'

'Now come for me.'

'Ooh! My big, bad, overseer.'

Adam heard the same violent slap repeated and sped up. He rushed to reverse the van into a parking space and hurried out of the cab and into the restaurant. He took a seat and looked around for a waiter. A young man in a uniform passed his table with a spray bottle and a cleaning cloth. Adam held his hand out to him.

'Hi. Excuse me, hello. May I please have a menu?'

'What?'

'A menu. May I have a menu?'

'You serious?'

'And I've only got twenty minutes. Do you think your chef could get something out to me in twenty minutes?'

'You are serious.'

'Adam?'

'Jacob?'

'What the fuck are you doing here?'

'I'm waiting for a waiter to bring me a menu.'

'What the fuck are you doing in Kerang?'

'Well! There has been a very great misunderstanding. Why are you wearing sunglasses inside?'

'No, wait! This is perfect. Come with me.'

'I have to stay here. And I'm really very hungry.'

'Come on, come on. I need your help.'

'Help? With what?'

'Adam, I need your help. Isn't that enough for you to know, to help one of your oldest friends?'

'Well I suppose. But I do have to be back in twenty minutes.'

'Twenty minutes is plenty of time. This won't take long.'

Jacob held the door open and let Adam go through first.

'What's on your arm?'

Jacob held out the inside of his forearm. Swollen and red was the outline of a vine-wrapped well. 'This? It's my tattoo.'

'What on earth did you get one of those for? And what is it?'

'Leah likes them.'

'Leah Dinah's sister?'

'Yes, Leah Dinah's sister. Now, I need you to drive this ute around for a while.'

'I really do have to be back in twenty minutes.'

'All right. So you drive us around for twenty minutes.'

'Us?'

'I was going to get a kid to do it but you're even better. Saves me twenty bucks.'

'Jacob, I'm starving.'

'All right, all right, I'll get you dinner. What do you want?'

'I haven't seen a menu yet.'

'It's McDonald's. What do you need a menu for?'

'I don't know what they serve.'

'What do you mean you don't know what they serve? It's McDonald's.'

'I've never been to a McDonald's.'

'Are you fucking serious?'

'Is that so incredible?'

Jacob groaned and went back into the restaurant, soon to return with a brown paper bag and an enormous paper cup. He saw Adam to the driver's side, handed him his dinner, and then lifted the door to the back tray and hopped in.

'What are you doing?' said Adam, whispering with some force.

'I'll be back here. The cops don't tolerate parking in this town. So just drive around, slowly. Let me know if you're coming up to any speed humps. Thank you friend.'

Adam drove out of the car park and ambled the car around. He opened the paper bag with one hand and found in it a hamburger. He returned to scrounge for a second and unwrapped both and steered with his pinky fingers. When he came to a straight length of road he beheld their shrivelled anatomy and leaned forward to take a bite. Almost immediately did his face become as distorted as his dinner. His tongue ejected all from his mouth and he shook his head in disgust. 'What is that?' he said, and put the thing back in the paper bag.

Driving slowly around the darknesses of the town he soon heard a muffled giggle. Then he heard an amorous sigh.

'You have no idea how long I've waited for this,' said Jacob.

'Tell me again,' said a female voice.

'I fell in love with you instantly. And then I found out you were already taken and I knew I had to keep you in my life. I knew that one day our time would come.'

'Let's come together.'

Adam took a bite from the other hamburger. His disgust only compounded. He returned it to its bag and he swung his tongue around, trying to remove from his mouth the chemical and dry sensations. He passed the McDonald's to which he had shortly to return. Its carpark and the whole barren area was glowing with the blue and red of spinning police lights.

'You were really with Dinah this whole time just so you could be near me?'

'I was a nervous wreck every time you came over. You couldn't tell?'

'I can't believe we'd met before you started seeing Dinah. I really don't remember.'

'You were so drunk that night.'

'Oh, keep going. Right there. Yes. Oh, Jacob. Nobody's ever done anything so romantic for me.'

'Can't you see what I'm trying to tell you?'

'What?'

'Can't you see what I'm trying to tell you? I love you.'

Adam tapped at the ute's brakes.

'Oi,' said Jacob. 'Would you calm down up there? … And you've had boyfriends ever since so I've never been able to tell you. Then when I found out this one left you because you went bald I just had to tell you, Leah, I love your baldness.'

Adam pressed down fully the brakes and got out of the car and pulled open the door to the ute's tray. Wrapped in a blanket, Jacob had a hand resting on Leah's bald scalp, shining in the streetlight.

'This isn't right,' said Adam. 'I can hear what you're doing back here. This just isn't right. Twice I've had to do this this evening and I can not be party to it anymore. I have to get back to the car park.'

'You're right, Adam.'

'We're sorry, Adam, really,' said Leah. 'We know what we're doing's wrong, but we haven't found the right time to tell Dinah yet. It's hard with what the family's going through. With what I'm going through.'

'It's not my business and I'm sorry for intruding. But I do have to get back to that car park and drive that van back to–. Where's the van? The van is gone.'

Leah asked Adam where he was staying while he was in town.

'The van's gone.'

'What van?'

'I have no way of getting back.'

'Getting back to where, Adam?' said Jacob. 'Where are you staying up here?'

'I don't know now. I think I've escaped. Oh dear, I've escaped.'

'Escaped from where?'

'I can't be an escapee. And an escapee can't go back to where he's escaped from and then apologise for escaping. Not without frightening consequences. They'll relax me. Or worse. Boom boom.'

'Adam, what the fuck are you talking about?'

'Oh, dear heavens.'

'Adam, why don't you come and stay with us?' said Leah. 'We've got plenty of room in the house. It'd be lovely to have you. We can show you Kerang.'

CHAPTER 4

1

Long after sunrise Adam extricated himself from the vasty depths of a sagging mattress.

With distaste did he put on Jacob's tight shirt and prohibitive trousers. At the end of a long and narrow pine hallway of indistinguishable closed doors he found the kitchen, abandoned but for Jacob.

It was divided nominally from the open-plan living and dining room by a high counter and a pantry. Adam was surrounded by glass walls, the two sliding doors on either side given away by a crocheted floor mat resting before them. A grand piano had sat unplayed for a decade against the lowered curtain of the north wall. Anonymous reproductions of eucalypt glades hung on the walls among startling photographs of the girls in their modish adolescence. Country kitsch littered every raised surface: a numberless clockface on a grotesque slice of redwood trunk, wooden boxes printed in a stencil font with 'Bread' and 'Tea'; barely stained pine furniture; chiffon curtains across the small high kitchen window; a white chiffon table cloth embroidered with little daisies. Facing the enormous television was a reclining chair of heavily cracked brown leather and a sagging black sofa. A mohair rug lay between repose and entertainment. Nothing but the photographs was more than five years old.

There was a black teapot of imitation iron on the plate of a black wood-stove which took up half the kitchen; from this emanated the redolent smell of redgum smoke and far too much warmth.

'I thought I'd let you sleep,' said Jacob, stacking dishes in the sink. 'Dinah and Leah have just gone to the shops to get stuff for dinner. They'll be back in an hour. We didn't have much for breakfast. Do you want some toast?'

Adam soon had a glass of orange juice and two pieces of toast in front of him. He folded the toast in half and devoured them.

'Dinah's mum's outside with the sheep. Do you want to meet

her?'

'I should, yes.'

'She's hot and she knows it so watch her.'

'Watch her what?'

'Actually, no don't watch her. Dinah always catches me looking at her ti–.' Jacob remembered who he was talking to. 'Sorry.'

'And Mr Manthorne?'

'Don't ask.' Jacob slid open the door between the piano and the dining table. After six feet of terracotta paving a short emerald lawn ran until it was patchy with golden and eventually turned to the dry yellow which swept underneath low wire stock fences as far as could be seen. He walked Adam around to the other side of the house. A tethered mule and a dark blue ute in the granite gravel driveway were the only break in another vista of flat, spiny, thirsting, pasture.

At the far corner of the first field a woman was bent over sideways at a grey wooden fence post. The sleeves of her immaculately white cotton shirt were rolled up and she was in jodhpurs and gumboots. A single length of wire fencing lay limp on the ground. She picked up its end and pulled it taught and nailed it to its post. She stood up and gave a high moan of satisfaction.

'Judith,' said Jacob. 'Judith, this is Adam, one of my very good friends. Adam, Judith.'

Judith's frame was slight and what was visible of her body against her shirt youthfully firm. Her hair was in a high ponytail. With her forearm she moved her brown sweat-stuck fringe from her brow. She slid off one of her gardening gloves and held Adam's hand.

'Sorry I couldn't see you at breakfast. I had to get this done before we moved the sheep through. And Jacob couldn't hit a nail with the head of a hammer the size of his own giant head. How's your room?'

'Most pleasant.'

'Most pleasant? Why can't you talk like that?' she said to Jacob. 'Some people find the mattress gives too much and you can't do anything in it besides sleep.'

'Oh I need only to sleep. And I was so tired I could have slept on a hot gridiron. Thank you for having me. I shouldn't be here for too long. Just a couple of days I imagine. I have quite a few very preposterous issues that I have to take a few steps back from.'

'You stay as long as you like. I love having men around who aren't Jacob. Can I show you the place? Do you like sheep?'

'I've never met one I didn't get along with.'

'Ha. Come on, I'll show you this first flock. Jacob? Sheep?'

Jacob shook his head and waved them goodbye. Judith folded and picked up the open tool bag at her feet.

'Of all the things to be afraid of my daughter's husband is scared of sheep.'

'One bit him, didn't it, when he was younger? Our other friend's afraid of his own boat.'

'Not men nowadays, are they, Adam?' Judith unlatched a chain and swung back a gate. Adam relatched it. 'How was the bus ride?'

'The bus ride?'

'Jacob said you caught a bus from Melbourne.'

'Oh yes. I was unconscious for most of it.'

'Best way to be on a bus. And there's not much to see between here and there anyway. Are they Jacob's clothes? God, he dresses like a bloody idiot.'

'I only had one suit of clothing when I was taken. And a very strange suit.'

'Taken?'

'One of the preposterous issues I mentioned.'

'Well, I ask no questions and expect no lies. I have *never* seen that before.' The flock of forty or so sheep was moving slowly and with raised heads towards the pair of approaching humans. 'Normally they run away.' The front of the flock reached Adam and one of the animals raised its head to his hand. Another pushed in beside it and nudged its head over. Soon Adam and Judith were surrounded.

'Who are you, Adam? That's incredible. My grandfather always said you should trust them more than you do people. You must be all right. I hope you'll stay a bit longer. I haven't played the game in such a long time. Somehow I feel like you've come to Kerang for a reason. What do you think? Do you like to play, Adam?' With one hand Judith widened the open top of her shirt.

'That depends on the game I think. But I daresay I'm always up for it. Nothing too violent though.'

'I can be as gentle as you want.'

'And I do find that the pleasure of a game is always tied to the quality of the other players.'

'I'm high class, Adam.' Sensing a strange tonal shift in Judith's voice, Adam nodded in response. 'And I cannot wait to start playing.'

'Did we already mention which game we'd be playing?'

'Ooh,' said Judith, twitching her legs suddenly at the thighs. 'What?'

'This burning sensation. I'm going to have to–. Oh, yep.' She wiggled with discomfort. 'You'll be all right if I leave you to it?'

'Leave me to what?'

'Ooh, whatever. I have to go to the chemist. This is too uncomfortable. Sorry to have to leave you. I'd stay out here if I were you. I know I'd prefer the company of sheep to Jacob's.' The flock shuffled out of her way as she walked off. 'I'll see you at lunch?' she called back.

'I haven't eaten in days.'

'Any requests? I'll call the girls.'

'If there were cucumber sandwiches I would be more grateful than you could know.'

'Whenever we have guests. Bit of a Manthorne girls tradition. And we're going to the Royal tonight for dinner with one of Dinah's friends.'

And she shimmied off like a penguin towards the house.

'This is no good at all, is it?' said Adam. 'Oh, little sheepies. Where am I? I don't think that going back to that place and telling that Captain MacAynall that in fact I am *not* a Vietnamese immigrant will work at all, do you? Do you ever get the feeling that the way you look at the world is not entirely like how everybody else looks at it? Yes, I'll bet you do. What would you do in my situation? How about you, little fella?' The closer sheep stared up at him. 'Yes, I suppose you're right. A good walk does give me my best thinking. Outside the glasshouse, that is. You wouldn't believe what happened to my glasshouse. You would. You look credulous.' Adam smiled and set off among the sheep, singing in a voice both American and angelic,

'Carry me back to old Virginny,
There's where the cotton and the corn and taters grow,

There's where the birds warble sweet in the springtime,
There's where the old darkey's heart longs to go.
There's where I laboured so hard for dear old master…'

And for a few hours he ambled through the barren fields attended by a silent and strangely comforting entourage of Poll Dorsets.

4:2

The cucumber sandwiches at lunch (cucumbers unpeeled and sliced too thickly, the butter unsalted, mintless) were hardly inducive of the rapture to which Adam was used. The ice appointed to Adam's glass of water (they had no lemon squash) was wretchedly lamentable. The Manthornes sat in the shade of the copse of ghost gums which shared the gentle western slope with the brick barbecue and the clothesline. Dinah and Leah talked about Shan, the friend whom Dinah said she had last night gone into town to visit. Bit of a rough patch with her husband— struggling to afford keeping three children all at once at private school, a month ago he had struck her. Judith outlined Shan's pedigree of women who chose abusive men for husbands.

'How can people be so cruel to one another?' said Leah when told of the girl's father. Adam spent most of lunch trying not to stare at the shining side of Leah's ridgy head as she conversed.

Dinah smiled and said, 'D'you remember where Shan lost her virginity?'

'Oi. Shut up you,' said Leah.

'Where?' said Jacob, for the first time in an hour interested in what they were talking about.

'The same place Leah did, and on the same night!'

'Dinah, shut up! Or I'll tell everyone about yours.'

'We started to think the Three Monkeys was blessed after that night.'

'Oh, did you now?' said Jacob, teasing Leah.

'Better than by the well,' said Judith.

'Mum!' said Dinah.

'Well don't make fun of your sister.'

Jacob smiled. 'By the well! Oh, God. Which bumpkin dropkick was that with?'

'The well?' said Adam.

'The oldest thing on the property apart from me. Totally dry now. Do you want to see it?'

Uninterested in the current conversation Adam almost said yes.

'He doesn't want to see the well, Mum.'

'I'll take him to show him the other side of the property. Come on then. Have you had enough to eat?'

On the driveway Judith asked if Adam wanted to take the mule down.

'Likes it down there does he?'

'Oh you're too adorable, Adam. I thought you might like a ride.'

'I've never ridden a mule.'

'You see? Hop up. He's used to riders. It's all right.' Adam mounted the unsaddled beast. 'Shimmy back. … Bit further.' Judith threw a leg over and put Adam's hands around her waist. 'Hold me as tight as you want. You can't hurt me.' She thrust her hips forward and the mule plodded off towards the road that led into town. In a dry field, closer to the road than to the house, was a large willow tree shading a low bluestone well.

When they were half way there Judith said, 'You're not holding me very tightly.'

'The mule's not going very fast.'

'Should I kick him?'

'You probably don't need to.'

'Do you like riding impure things, Adam?'

'Do I like riding impure things? I can't seem to think of anything else that could be ridden that you would consider impure.'

'I can.'

'Is this a riddle, Mrs Manthorne? I don't like riddles. I like puns. I can never solve riddles. I knew a boy at school who used to come up with them. He'd plague me with the things. Ask me the question and then walk off and then appear throughout the day smiling at me like Rumpelstiltskin. It used to drive me mad.'

'It's not a riddle, Adam.'

'Ooh, a liger. That could be quite dangerous though.'

'Can't you see me getting lonely around here, Adam? Mr

Manthorne's been gone for a long time now and the country hardly abounds in intelligent people.'

'Do you think intelligence is tied to being able to solve riddles? I don't. I think they show a frivolous mind.'

'My husband's dead.'

'. . .'

'He killed himself.'

'Umm…' Adam looked down at the dry field on either side of him. 'I'm dreadfully sorry.'

'No, no. It was my fault.'

Eventually Adam said, with little conviction, 'I'm sure it wasn't.'

'He found out that I was fucking the stationhand.'

'Ah.' Adam withdrew his hands from Judith's waist and hung them at his sides. Judith reached back and pulled one up onto her thigh.

'And ever since then I've resolved to make this farm work alone.'

'To alone make this farm work.'

'What?'

'You said you've resolved to make this farm work alone. As though there were other farms on whose assistance the farm previously relied. But I gather you meant you've resolved to make it work by yourself.'

Judith said nothing. Adam saw that he may have treated a weighty conversation with undue frivolity. He did not think this an entirely bad thing, given its very awkward weight, but he thought that perhaps he had been facetious. Yes, he thought, he had been rude. 'And so what became of the young man?'

'The stationhand? Long gone. Why? Do you think you're up to the job?'

'You know, I *have* often considered rural life. The Athelstan's used to be in the country. Graziers. I daresay I wouldn't start out as a stationhand though.'

Judith stopped the mule a few paces from the well and waited for Adam to hop down before holding out her hand. When he took it she pulled a leg over and jumped off the animal and down into Adam's arms.

'The position has a lot of benefits,' she said. 'Well, I suppose that depends on the position, doesn't it? … And the other person's competence to perform it.'

Adam did his best to not look at Judith's eyes. But they were three inches from his own.

'Yes, I do think my inexperience might preclude me from… from becoming an agricultural labourer. At this age, anyway.'

'I'm always looking for somebody to groom if you're interested in starting from scratch. Then you'd know exactly how I like it.'

'I think I'll get back to rare flowers again. It'll be a tough slog, getting all the seedlings again. But I do think the Botanical Gardens might help me out. I've given them so much over the years. I'm sure they could spare me a few exotics. That's the well there is it?'

Judith sighed and said, 'Yes, Adam, that's the well,' and she gave it up. She left his very immediate vicinity and set off for the house. 'We leave for dinner at five.'

4:3

They drove into town in one car and parked beside the Royal Hotel.

In the doorway a life-sized plaster bull stood to greet the patrons. Its body and its wings were painted brown and covered in large pink polka-dots. From the entrance to the dining room, carpeted as one simply-patterned Turkish rug, Dinah spotted somebody already seated and walked in ahead of the others. The man rose from his seat and kissed her on the cheek. The rest of the party crossed to his table and Dinah introduced him as Alexander. When Adam reached the table he saw that he was to dine with the honourable Alexander Comeshotte, state minister for multicultural affairs. The jig, his jig, was up; Adam froze. Dinah introduced him as Jacob's friend.

'Adam,' said the minister, taking his hand and shaking it vigorously.

Adam sat and waited to be apprehended. He watched the doors for the ambush; his heart sank and his stomach ached every time he spied a figure at the doorway.

'And you're up visiting the detention centre?' said Judith.

'Yep,' said Alexander.

'Why's that?'

'I work for the department of multicultural affairs.'

Leah said, 'Ooo-oo.'

'It's just part of the routine. The state's getting the biggest influx of Vietnamese since the war and they just brought a couple of hundred of 'em up here so I thought I'd come up and see how they're getting on. Sensitive issue, you know. People don't want them to be free but people don't want them mistreated, so we have to stay on top of it. I was only supposed to be up here for the weekend but now we've had an escapee so I'll be here until we track him down.'

Alexander's eyes came to rest on Adam. It was as he thought. He was a fugitive. But why his chief pursuer, sitting two people over from him, was glaring at rather than apprehending him, he could not understand. Perhaps he was a sadist, wallowing, while watching at so close a range his own prey, in the same sensation which Spaniards derive from a bull sacrificed over the course of a sunny, blood-soaked hour. Adam smiled as innocently as he could and meandered his gaze towards the front windows.

'You look familiar,' said Alexander.

Adam shook his head and pouted.

'You do.' Another tormenting jab of the spear; Adam hung his head.

'An escapee?' said Leah, and Adam's head shot back up.

Alexander looked for some time at her scalp and then lowered his eyes to hers. 'Happens all the time apparently. Normally they bolt when they're taken on excursions. Then they reach town and the locals dob 'em in.' Alexander looked again at Adam. 'So if you see a little Asian guy in floral pants wearing glasses, make sure you call me straight away. Or the police.'

Adam closed his eyes and exhaled. Floral pants and glasses. He was safe.

'Why so are many coming?' said Leah. 'You said hundreds.'

'We think it's 'cos of these Tourist warlords they've got springing up. You heard about them?' Judith shook her head. 'Anyway, villagers are killing themselves to get into the service of these Tourist warlords up in the highlands. They don't know their ends from their arseholes these idiots. But anybody with any sense is trying to get here. They're better off in Australia but so many of 'em end up as sex slaves. So really they're better off in detention as well. And until we can figure out which of them can go home safely and which of them have to stay here as refugees we have to keep the bastards in detention. And then I remembered I knew someone from Kerang, so I thought I'd look her up. And bang. She's here while I'm here.'

'How exactly do you know Dinah?' said Jacob.

'We've known each other for years,' said Dinah.

'Have you?'

'I helped Alexander out on a flight once. His wife –.'

'Ex-wife.'

'Oh,' said Judith.

'His ex-wife went nuts at him in business class. Exploded right in the middle of a flight and I had to calm her down and then separate them and then I slipped a xanax into her meal.'

'Saved me from a complete public relations disaster. So I gave Dinah my card and told her that if she ever needed anything…'

'And six months later I got a speeding fine and I thought Alexander might be able to get me out of it. And he did.'

'That's illegal,' said Jacob.

'Gotta be able to return a favour, don't you?' said Alexander. 'Otherwise what's the point in power?'

'You never told me this story.'

'I don't tell you everything, do I? It was ages ago. Way before we met.'

'And what *do* you think about slavery, Al?'

Dinah moaned from exhaustion. 'Jacob.'

'Alexander.'

'And what do you think about slavery?'

'What do you mean, what do I think about slavery?'

'It seems to me like people are killing each other to get into it over there and the ones that come here end up as slaves anyway. All the great civilisations in history have been slave societies. What if we brought it back?'

Dinah reprimanded her husband with his own name.

'That's the stupidest thing I've ever heard. Freedom's the foundation of Australian society.'

'And trading in human beings is one of the five livelihoods forbidden by the eightfold path,' said Dinah.

'What does that even mean?'

'You wouldn't understand,' said Dinah.

'I just think slavery should be an option, no? Get rid of the dole, that's bullshit, and you have an optional slavery system. A free market of slaves. You pay 'em but you can tell 'em to do whatever you want and they can work for their freedom. They'll appreciate it more if they have to work for it.'

'Can we just change the subject?' said Dinah. 'I think we all want to order dinner.'

'I'm talking, Dinah. You just can't say, "Can we change the subject?" whenever I'm talking.'

'Oh, I can.'

'You can? Do you see why?'

'Do I see why what?'

'Nothing.'

'What?'

'Just drop it, Dinah.'

'All right you two,' said Judith.

'Do they come to us?' said Alexander, spinning his head in search of a waiter.

'No we have to go up,' said Judith.

Adam offered to mind the table while everybody else went and ordered. Five minutes later they sat back down. Jacob said that he had ordered for Adam. 'Everybody just got parmas so I got you one. Is that all right?'

'Oh.' Adam looked wistfully back at the menu board. 'Oh I suppose so.'

'You want a beer?'

'Lemon squash please, with a glass of ice on the side.'

Jacob went through to the bar to order drinks. Thirty seconds later six behemothic plates were brought out. Upon five of them sat steaming cheese-covered breasts bigger than any adult performer, let alone a chicken, had ever possessed.

'Wowzers,' said Judith.'

'Look at the size of those,' said Leah.

'Jeez, that was quick,' said Dinah.

They waited until Jacob returned with a jug of beer, five plastic cups and Adam's lemon squash. 'I saw the ice. You won't like it.' And they dug in.

'And you'd own a slave, Jacob?'

'Leah!' said Dinah. 'Don't encourage him.'

'You know what I think?' said Leah. 'I think that if you believe in freedom then you believe in slavery. If we were really free we'd be free to choose slavery, free to be slaves. If it's not an option then how are we free?'

'See,' said Jacob to Dinah. 'Why can't you think like that? Clearly your sister got all the brains. I would own heaps, Leah. Dinah wouldn't have to do any dishes. We'd get one to drive us around. And we'd be good slaveowners, they'd love us. They'd want to stay our slaves, we'd be so good to them. Better than being dirt-poor in the rice fields.'

'No, it isn't,' said Dinah.

'Have you ever been dirt-poor in the rice fields?' said Leah.

'Have you ever been a slave?'

'You're always naysaying what Jacob has to say, Dinah. You should listen to him every once in a while. He's smart.'

'Alexander,' said Judith. 'Have you been looking for another woman since you split up with your wife?'

'Mum!' said Dinah.

'What?'

'That's private.'

'It might be. Let Alexander decide. You don't have to answer my question if you don't want to.'

'Not at all. And yes, Judith, I have been looking for another companion.'

'Aggressively?'

'*Mum!*'

'I wouldn't say that.'

'What exactly are you looking for?'

'I decided I'm looking for youth.'

'Oh,' said a deflated Judith Manthorne.

'I can give a girl stability, money, status. The least she can do for me is make me feel young.'

'And do you think you need a young girl to make you feel young? Some of us old gals can be pretty vital.'

'I'll bet they can.'

'Mum, would you please shut up?'

Alexander's lascivious eyes shot over to Dinah. 'They do start 'em pretty early nowadays though.'

'Beside wells,' said Jacob.

Very soon all were stuffed and languid from deep-fried food. Judith invited Alexander back to the house for coffee and cake.

'Why don't you two girls go with Alexander? I'll take the ute back with Jacob.'

'Sounds good to me,' said Jacob. 'Adam?'

'I'll go in Alexander's car if that's all right.'

4:4

Dinah was in a rush to use the bathroom and walked briskly up to the house. Judith put the back of her hand at Alexander's stomach and they slowed as Adam wandered up the drive.

'My husband's been dead for ten years.'

Alexander said that he was sorry to hear it.

'It was my fault.'

'I'm sure it wasn't.'

'He found out I was fucking the stationhand.'

'Oh.'

'How long have you been divorced?'

'Three years.'

'And you've found yourself a young girlfriend then?'

'I've found a few. Youth has its drawbacks. They're not very smart.'

'And here *we* are,' said Judith. 'Two free, smart, adults.'

'Mmm,' said Alexander. Judith was slowly succeeding in arousing his curiosity.

Judith took a chocolate mud cake from the fridge and lifted its translucent plastic lid as she put it on the dining table. She sliced it into eight and asked how everyone took their coffee.

'And what are you doing up here, Adam?'

'Just visiting friends. Jacob and Dinah are up here visiting Leah, so I thought I'd come and keep Jacob company.'

'What do you do in Melbourne?'

'Not very much at all at the moment.'

'Between jobs?'

'Something like that.'

Judith put the last small log of redgum into the wood-stove. 'We need more firewood. Oo, Adam, do you know what we could do tomorrow? Alexander, you can come too if you'd like. The world's biggest compass. We could go and see that.'

'Nobody wants to see the compass, Mum.'

'I think Adam would love the compass.'

'The last time we went there there was a giant dildo stuck in the middle of it.'

'There was a dildo, telling you which way was north?' said Alexander, losing control of his chortle.

'Aboriginal kids,' said Judith.

'You don't know it was them,' said Dinah.

'Would you excuse me?' said Adam, rising.

'I gotta use the bathroom,' said Alexander.

'Oh. You go first.'

'Oh, you were gonna go as well? No you go, it's all right. I'll wait.'

'Are you quite certain?'

'Yes, yes, go on.'

'No, no, it's all right. I can wait.'

'All right, you two gentlemen. There's more than one bathroom.'

'I'll show Alexander where the other toilet is,' said Dinah. 'And I'll get some more firewood while I'm at it.'

'I wonder where Jacob and Leah have gotten to,' said Judith.

'I bet you Leah let Jacob drive and she fell asleep. He can never find his way here from town.'

'He really is hopeless, Dinah,' said Judith as Dinah and Alexander disappeared into the corridor.

Adam counted with confidence the doorways on his right. Laundry, his bedroom, Leah's bedroom, lavatory. He opened the lavatory door. Instantly the two people behind it disengaged and began straightening and rebuttoning their clothing.

'Adam,' said Jacob regretfully.

'Wrong door. I'm sorry. Sorry Jacob. And that's not–. Nope. That's not your wife. I'm sorry. I'm so sorry.'

Adam's eyes alternated between Leah's head and the floor as he backed sheepishly out of the room and closed the door.

He stood in the hallway and took full stock of the identical wood-laminate doors. He had either miscounted or that was the bathroom and it was occupied. He could remember neither the room's size nor its furnishings. He went back two doors and recounted. Laundry, his bedroom, Leah's bedroom, lavatory. He was certain. If the door he had tried was the lavatory then Alexander was in Dinah's room. If that were not the lavatory then it was Leah's bedroom and so the next door was the lavatory. Yes, that made sense. He opened the door to his bedroom to make sure he was beginning his count at the right place. Then Leah's bedroom, lavatory. Or had he misremembered the order of the rooms? Then he found that he had lost count again. Which was the door he had just opened? Perhaps he had opened the door to Leah's bedroom. Yes. When he came to think of it the room whose door he had opened was a spacious one and not at all a lavatory. He could vaguely remember a vanity table. So the next door was the lavatory. He tried its handle and found it locked. It could only have been Alexander. Dinah had shown him to the lavatory after all and so the bathroom in Dinah's bedroom was the unoccupied one.

He turned and opened the door. The other Manthorne sister instantly recoiled and began rebuttoning her shirt. Adam cast down his eyes and apologised profusely as he backed out of the room.

'I'll go and get that firewood,' said Dinah as she came out of her bedroom. 'I was just showing Alexander how the plumbing worked.' She winced at her choice of words. 'Country plumbing, you know. Takes a bit of getting used to. Then one of the taps broke off and wet me. So I had to take my shirt off to change it. Alexander was just checking how wet I was. Oh no, I'm sorry.'

Adam could not look Dinah in the eye as she passed him. She went out through the laundry door and Adam waited in the corridor until Alexander emerged. He grinned at Adam and bulged his eyes a little and nodded his head and then Adam went into the bathroom.

A few minutes later he went back to the kitchen and found Judith sitting on Alexander's lap. He began slowly reversing into the corridor but found that he had to hear what was being said.

'And just how are you going to get rid of my loneliness?' said Judith to Alexander's neck.

Alexander snickered. 'I can think of a few ways.'

'Oh,' said Judith, looking up from Alexander's saliva-sodden shoulder. 'How was the toilet?'

'What?'

'What?'

Dinah called urgently from the laundry door, 'Coming through.' Her chin resting on an armful of heavy firewood, she reached the doorway as her mother stood from Alexander's lap. Judith and Alexander stared dumbly at her.

'What's going on?'

Judith shook her head.

'Were you just on his lap?'

'No.'

'You were.'

'I wasn't.'

'She wasn't,' said Alexander.

'Mum, he's a guest in our house! What are you doing?'

Adam took another step away from the dining room. It went unnoticed so he took another. Then Jacob's hands grabbed his shoulders and pushed him back in.

'Sorry we're late. Leah fell asleep and I got a bit lost. What'd I miss?'

'Mum in Alexander's lap.'

'Go Judith.'

'No, Jacob. That's disgusting. There's a time and a fucking place.'

'The well?'

'I think I should probably go,' said Alexander.

'No, stay,' said Dinah and Judith.

'Thanks for the cake and the coffee. I'll see you again. Adam, good to meet ya mate. You're staying here for the night, aren't you? Good luck with that.'

'And you, Alexander.'

And Alexander went out the sliding glass door and to his car.

'I love how you say his name,' said Judith.

'So if it's not Leah, it's you,' said Dinah, putting the firewood at her feet. 'Neither of you can leave a man alone. I mean, you're left for two minutes with one and you're in his lap. And every time I leave Leah around a guy I like he's in her lap within the hour.'

'Well maybe if you were a bit more interesting,' said Leah, having squeezed through the congregation at the kitchen doorway.

'What's the big deal, Dinah? They're both adults.'

'At dinner?'

'We're not at dinner.'

'You know what I mean.'

'You should say what you mean. If you didn't mean dinner you shouldn't have said dinner.'

'Shut up, Jacob!'

'Stop yelling at him, Dinah,' said Leah.

'And Adam's here. He's fragile. His mum just died.'

'Grandmother,' said Adam. 'Just died.'

'His grandmother just died! He's fragile.'

'I'm not fragile. Please don't amend your behaviour just for my being here.'

'This is too much Manthorne drama for me,' said Jacob. 'Night everyone.'

'I've got a doctor's appointment at nine,' said Leah. 'I should get to bed as well.'

'Adam, I'll see you in the morning, buddy.' And Jacob and Leah returned to the corridor.

'I think I might take a walk,' said Adam. 'It's a clear night. The stars are always abundant in the countryside. I think I need a bit of rehumbling after tonight's discoveries.'

Dinah went to bed in a huff; Judith soon walked out after Adam.

The night was brisk; a thick streak of silver cloud in the west but otherwise clear and sparkling. Adam crossed the western lawn and headed out into an invigorating field.

Judith quietly caught him up. 'I am sorry you had to see all of that.'

'Oh, no. … No, I'm sorry if I interrupted.'

'You didn't interrupt anything. He was a sleaze. You're so polite, you're such a gentleman.'

'Was he?'

'He pulled me onto his lap and then he started saying dirty things to me.'

'Did he?'

'Politicians.'

'Yes.' Adam looked up and found that the stars had very suddenly been smothered by a vast black cloud. He felt a drip of water on the back of his neck.

'I think it's gonna rain,' said Judith.

'I think you're right!'

A droplet of ice hit the lawn and glistened among the grass. Another followed; then the things started to tap at the roof of the house. Soon they were pelting it. Adam and Judith shielded their heads and ran back towards the house. They reached the shelter of the ghostgums.

'I don't see the point in hail,' said Adam.

'The point of it?'

'Snow is beautiful and rain is captivating. But hail?'

'Adam, I'm wet,' said Judith.

'It's only hail.'

'Adam,' said Judith, beckoning him to look at her. 'I'm wet for you.'

'You don't look wet. You do have a few little hailstones in your hair there. May I?' Adam brushed at the top of her head. She closed her eyes and grinned and moaned.

'I want you.'

He waited for Judith to finish her sentence. 'You want me to what?'

'To do everything.'

'That sounds quite taxing now, doesn't it? You mean as a stationhand? I mean, I could do some work for you tomorrow if you'd like. But I don't know how long I'll be here for.'

'Tonight.'

'Tonight? It's hailing. Or should I wait until the hail passes? What exactly needs doing?'

'I don't want to wait any longer. *I* need doing. Don't you think it's romantic out here?'

'Rain is romantic. Hail hurts.'

'Don't you want my burning bush, Adam? It means you'll never forget me.'

'Your burning bush? Where's that? I know it's not rain but I don't expect any bushes will be catching fire during hail. Not unless there's lightning.'

A whipcrack of thunder crashed above their heads, startling

them both.

'Oh,' said Adam. 'Perhaps one might catch fire.'

'*My* burning bush.' Judith took Adam's hand and squeezed it down the front of her jeans. 'I'm wet for you, Adam.'

'Oh, dear,' said Adam, jerking his hand out from fright. 'Cap'n Billy's Whizzbang. What are you doing, Mrs Manthorne?'

'Judith. You know exactly what I'm doing. You got me all worked up today, didn't you? Playing your little games. All this evading me, making me chase you. I want to give you my burning bush, Adam. Don't you want it?'

'I really don't understand what you mean.'

'Cut the crap.' She took a step in and whispered in his hear, 'I want you to lie with me.'

'To whom?'

'What?'

'What?'

'Are you rejecting me?'

'Mrs Manthorne. Judith, I'm really just very confused. How could a bush burn during a hailstorm and what does that have to do with us lying to somebody?'

'You're making fun of me.'

'I'm not.'

'You think I'm a slut, don't you?'

'Oh no. I definitely–. No, I do not think that at all.'

'It's natural for a woman to have desires, Adam. I've been alone for ten years. You're a little snob, aren't you?'

'I've been called many things before, but never a snob. Oh wait, that's not true. Twice, but that was at school.'

'I thought this was all charm, you talking the way you do and your politeness. But you think I'm beneath you, don't you? Beneath you, but you won't have me beneath you. How dare you? What age do you think you're living in? I've done my hard work, I've done my sentence and now I wanna have fun. How dare you make fun of me for being me. You need to leave.'

'Well it is hailing. I think we should probably both leave.'

'My farm. Nobody has the right to make me feel the way you're making me feel. I want you gone, tonight. I won't have a judgmental little prick sat at my breakfast table tomorrow.'

'Sit.'

'What?'

'Nothing. I'm sorry.'

'Did you just correct my English?'

'No. Yes. I did. I'm sorry.'

'Oph,' she growled. 'I don't care where you go or how you get there. How dare you reject me? No. I don't really want you to leave, Adam. I want you. Come to me, please. I'm gonna leave the door to the house open. But if you come into my house you had better come into my room. Either you come and I get to know your dick or you leave.' And Judith moved her hands from cupping Adam's groin to sheltering her head and she ran up to the house.

Adam stood for a few minutes beneath the trees. He looked out from under the lowest branches. No clear sky was approaching. He looked up at the house. The light in Judith's bedroom came on. Hail rattled on the cover of the barbecue and pinged off the garden furniture. But he was certainly not going into the house if those were the stipulations.

He hunched his shoulders and walked slowly over to the mule and untethered and mounted it and set off down the drive.

CHAPTER 5

1

An hour after a sunrise onto almost-darkness Adam passed between the palm trees of the gates of Kerang Immigration Detention Centre.

A short time into his journey the hail had subsided and rain taken its place. Only an hour ago had the heavens closed. As he and the mule entered the compound a car rolled in, streams of dirty water jetting up from its tyres, and overtook him. Cane toads had swarmed the grounds. The mule's hooves squashed the things into the slurry as it sauntered.

Captain MacAynall came from the welcome shed and waved Adam down. The hour of his reckoning. He had been preparing himself for immediate relaxation; he put his hands in the air. The Captain kicked toads from his path as he splashed through the mud. 'You here about the job are you?'

The Honourable Alexander Comeshotte stepped out of his driven car. 'Adam?'

'Oh, hello, Alexander.'

'I said, are you here about the job?' The Captain grabbed the mule's reigns.

'Job?' said Adam.

'I only put the ad up last night. That was bloody quick.'

'Good on you, lad,' said Alexander. 'Out of work in Melbourne, and here he is.'

'I've never seen a man turn up to a job interview on a mule,' said the Captain. 'Or soaking wet. Why *have* you come on a mule?'

'Walking would have taken me days.'

'That is drive if ever I've seen it!' said Alexander.

'Come on then we'll get you a towel and we'll have an interview.'

'He doesn't need an interview. I had dinner with the lad last night. I know him. Unemployed in Melbourne and he makes it out here on a mule in the rain. I'll vouch for him. Hire him, MacAynall.'

'Welcome aboard then. Captain Reuben MacAynall. Let's get you started. I'll show you the Palace and we'll get you out of these wet clothes and into a uniform.'

'Those Manthorne girls are something else, ay Adam?' said Alexander, accompanying them across the several yards.

'They certainly are uniquely charged.'

'Who's that?' said the Captain.

'Remember that girl I was telling you about? Her mum and her sister. The three of them. Firecrackers.'

The downpour was still trickling off the exercise yard into the stream. It was so high that its meagre banks had just broken. A ladder had been laid across it at the closest corner of the officer's house.

'They're like that around here. Especially when they meet somebody civilized like us. Go nuts for 'em. Now, Adam,' said the Captain as they sloshed their way across the rungs, 'The thing you'll get to know about me...' Captain MacAynall hopped off the end of the ladder and turned around. A small red blister beneath the corner of his mouth bubbled with white seeping pustules. Adam laboured to pull his eyes from it. '...is that I'm a moralist. Do you know what that means?' The Captain pulled out a handkerchief and daubed at his chin.

'I have something of an idea,' said Adam.

The dark wooden barely-walled interior of the Palace was buzzing with blowflies. Several men were on couches and at the dining table, all facing the television. Each had a fly swatter and was waiting for one to land within range. 'It's the bloody rain,' said the Captain. 'Brings the toads out *and* the blowies, in swarms.' The Captain waved his flywhisk around. Two flies landed on either of Adam's cheeks and hurried to the sides of his mouth. He made a raspberry sound and shook his head and waved his hands at them.

'So this is the Palace. Kitchen there. Lounge room. I can see what you're looking at. It's the rain. It always brings them out.'

'It looks like the young umbels of a lantana camara.'

'What?'

'It's a flower.'

'What is? My cold sore?'

'No, no. Never mind.'

'Good. Now there are rooms upstairs for the guards. It's up to you if you stay the night. Most of the guys are married so they tend to stay. And you've only got the mule?'

'I've only got the mule.'

'Then I guess you'll be staying. Now, we've got Levis, allergic to denim, that's Jew, self-explanatory, Dan, Benji, Ash, and Gaddo. And there are three more out on duty, you'll meet them a bit later. First things first, each guard's entitled to pick two inmates. The inmates get Vietnamese food in here and the hope of refugee status and we get small tokens of our own in return. I'll show you which ones are taken when we're watching Exercise. Now, remember I was saying I was a moralist? Don't do what Simmo did. He's the guy you're replacing. It's not right and it's a waste. One of our brightest, but he couldn't keep it in his pants.'

'Couldn't keep what in his pants?'

Alexander laughed and went over to the couches and slotted himself into a gap between two guards.

'I like that. We need someone funny around here. Use your own condoms, all right? And don't buy them from the gift shop. The inmates get in there and they prick 'em. If you're not careful you'll end up with herpes and a little Asian baby as well. Just not right, is it, what some people do to one another? People they're supposed to care about. So we take our meals in here. Now we have a couple of older ladies who come in and cook for us. Benji there and Naf-Naf, Naf-Naf's in the tower this morning, they like 'em old. Perverts if you ask me. But the older ones *are* better cooks. So I'll get you your uniform. You look like a small? Back in a second.'

The Captain ran up the wooden stairs.

A short time later Adam emerged from the Palace bathrooms in the powder-blue uniform, black belt and boots of his new employment.

The sky was blue-grey, cloud-covered, ominous—early morning but as morose as dusk. The heat was moist rather than blaring.

'Gaddo, go out and announce sunscreen, would ya? I gotta show the new kid around. Now, as for your job, specifically, Rotte had two duties. He ran the Prince scam with Dai Thanh and he took the inmates on excursions. Work's about to start, so let's jump in. I'll show you what's what. All right, boys. Work.'

167

The five guards dispersed across the compound and the Captain removed the ladder bridge. He leaned beside Adam on the wooden railing of the verandah and gazed out over the exercise yard. The compound was soon bustling with human movement.

'Nothing like hard work,' said the Captain.

Files formed at the water tank and spouts began to oscillate. 'See the toads? When they first arrived the inmates tried to eat them. Horrible, horrible scenes. Sick for days. A dozen dead. Idiots. Anyway, they're only allowed to talk during exercise, that's at 5:10 in the afternoon, and in quarters. It just saves us a whole lot of trouble. None of us can understand what they say and when they try to talk to us in English it's gibberish. So I say there's no point in hearing it. Limitations are important for people. Especially prisoners. We let them talk for half an hour a day and they only want to talk to each other. Now what they're doing here is they're watering the exercise yard. See how it runs off into the stream? That's my little pet project. I love the sound of trickling water, especially at dusk. One of the refinements I allow myself. Reminds me of being young. I call it the Pithom river, after my grandpa, John Pithom. I had the inmates dig it a few weeks ago. Next I think I'll get 'em to build me a pyramid. Gotta give 'em something to do. My other grandpa's middle name, Grandpa MacAynall, was Ramses. Not sure why. But it's important to reverence your forefathers, Adam. One of the things the inmates have really taught me. Don't forget it.

'Now, you see the giant one there, half way along the fourth line? That's Khong. Watch him, he's always trying to escape. And I know he's come up with a new plan. I reckon it involves the river. Escape attempts always involve the river now. We just had an escapee, actually. Or we thought we did. He'd taken his glasses off before he tried to escape so we couldn't recognise him. But he forgot to change his floral pants. They really are stupid. He'll be relaxed almost all day. Oh, shit, that reminds me.'

The Captain bounded back across the verandah and shortly returned from inside the house. 'Your taser.' He handed Adam a holster. 'These are what we use to make sure the inmates stay relaxed. Anywhere on the body. Neck is easiest but not the safest. If you don't like 'em, neck. But just below the ribcage if you can manage it. Here, come with me.'

The Captain relaid the ladder. 'Go and relax Seb. See how your new toy works.' A guard was standing at the corner of the exercise yard with his back to the house. 'Go on. He loves taking it from behind.'

'Will it not hurt him?'

'No! He's used to it. The boys are always stuffing around with them.'

'I don't really think I ought to. Not without warning him perhaps.'

'Of course you should! If you warn him he'll tense up beforehand and it'll do him some damage. How else are you gonna know how your only weapon works, hm? What if you catch an inmate talking this arvo? You gotta know how to defend yourself. Here.'

The Captain walked Adam across the bridge and silently pointed out to him the only button on his taser. He motioned for Adam to dig it into Seb's ribs. After silent, nodded exchanges of reluctance, of encouragement, of despair, and finally of vehemence, Adam said, 'Sorry,' and Seb's head turned just as Adam with eyes closed touched his taser into his ribs. His eyes fluttered before he flopped down into the mud. The Captain let out long snickers of laughter. 'He'll be up in a minute. Just watch out though, 'cos now he's allowed to get one back on you.'

'Oh.'

The Captain continued his briefing on the verandah. He pointed down at Tung, who, hazily walking around in circles, caught himself being singled out. Frightened, he looked instantly away. Then he realised who he had just seen beside the Captain. He snapped his head back to the verandah.

'The idiot staring at us. That's Tung. Comeshotte's boyfriend, the politician. He's the one that tried to escape yesterday. Hourly relaxation for him. Fuck he looks funny, doesn't he, that relaxed? I think he's why the minister's come up here. Comeshotte doesn't know I know that though. Funny name, isn't it? I'd never vote for anybody called Comeshotte. He's only here for today now and then he's going back to Melbourne. Thank God. He's a pain in the arse. Hate politicians. They're not honorable people, you know? Now that's Bao, see in the line closest to us? He talks too much, so watch him. He's so relaxed he's gonna end up more retarded than he already is. And next to him's Zipper. She's a mute and she's got a bum lip, but she's the best piece of arse in the compound, so stay away from her, she's mine. Along with that one, Ngung. Now, do you see the pregnant one there? She's the reason you're here. She was Rotte's. She'd been wearing pyjamas for the last four weeks and then yesterday she comes out for work in a tight t-shirt and stares at him until he sees her. Then she jumps in the bloody stream and tries to drown herself with his unborn baby. Traumatised the bastard so much he quit on the spot. Said he's moving to Bali with his wife. His wife's infertile as it is and this goes and happens to him here. Some things serve as a warning to us all. D'you ever think that, Adam?'

'Mmm.'

The lines of inmate had lengthened to the fence. The six watering cans ran dry and the inmates wandered back to begin at their new positions. Khong tapped Zipper on her posterior and had his hand swatted.

'That little giant bastard,' said Captain MacAynall.

With two fingers Khong lifted the girl's hair. She recoiled and the Captain said, 'Right.' Seb, covered in mud, was slowly regaining consciousness. 'Seb, relax Khong, would you? ... Seb!'

Seb turned his head over in the mud and looked up at his commanding officer. He gurgled.

'Get up! Go and relax Khong.'

He eventually managed to stand. The instruction was repeated. He stumbled across the yard and fell into the giant inmate as he relaxed him. Khong's long body dragged easily through the slush and Seb deposited it beside the water tank. Zipper took up his watering can and continued where he had flopped off.

'Now,' continued the Captain. 'That's the Internet shed. See the fat shady bloke smoking on the steps? Dai Thanh his name is. He was a refugee here. Well he is a refugee. But he came to me during Exercise one day and he blurted out a little scheme he ran at home. We'll get to that later.'

Adam luncheoned in the Palace. Three middle-aged inmates served a sweet-brothed beef noodle soup which Adam rather enjoyed. During Exercise he had pointed out for him all the females who were already taken and was informed of the prowess and the pitfalls of those who were not. Then Internet was called.

Adam and the Captain shadowed Dai Thanh up and down the cubicles of the Internet shed. 'And this'll be your main job while you're with us. It's very important. It's the reason we have such a big TV. We pay the inmates for the work that they do and then we sit them down here for an hour every evening and we convince them to give us most of it back. We send them e-mails from Mubjherudan refugees, do you remember that country? and we get them to fall in love with them, then we tell them that they're princes and princesses and whatnot and tell 'em they need just a little bit of money to unlock their giant fortunes, which they'll of course share with their one true loves as soon as they can get it. That's the power of love. You like that song? I like that song.'

'I'm not quite sure I've heard it,' said Adam.

Dai Thanh stopped at each of the cubicles and inspected the computer screens. Occasionally he rested his hand on a female's shoulders, smelled a head of hair, tickled an ear.

'And the money goes back into our staff account and we divide it among the officers. Dai Thanh gets his cut and we use the money for anything really. Mostly for furnishing the Palace. Part of it goes into a kitty and once a month we have a big piss-up in town. Izzy saved up his share and bought his girlfriend fake tits. You can do whatever you want with yours.

'Now your job will be to keep them going. You have to stay on top of where all the inmates are at. Who's in love but cautious with their money, who's struggling to fall in love. You'll have to hook new ones, keep current ones on the line and close bigger on old ones. Rotte had templates, you'll look them over tomorrow. I'll keep you out of the yards and get you to familiarise yourself with his material. I think they were getting a bit stale to be honest. His numbers were dropping. Probably a good thing that girl got pregnant. Yours'll be a fresh mind, so we'll see what you can come up with.'

Dinner in the Palace was a feast of barbecued pork and rice paper and herbs which Adam had never before tasted. The officers drank cans of beer and watched television as they ate. They talked filthily of what they had been doing with their inmates, their girlfriends, their wives.

'Movie night tonight,' said the Captain, stuffed and slouching in his chair. 'Anything you wanna watch?'

'You know I didn't really sleep at all last night so I was thinking I might try to get a good night's rest. There's been a lot to take in today.'

'No worries. Bunks are upstairs. I'm not sure which ones are taken. Just check the bed sheets. Any red stains and they're taken. Asian girls. Tight like a tiger. Breakfast's at seven. Somebody'll wake you up. Probably with a toe in your ear.'

'Oh.'

At the top of the stairs Adam went into the first bedroom and inspected the closest bed to the doorway and found in its sheets marks of red. He pulled back the covers of the second bed and found there a fading blotch of ruby. Only on inspecting the fifth bed of the third bedroom did he find bedsheets of an acceptably stainfree nature. He put his head on his pillow and stared at the knots in the ceiling. The obscenities downstairs abruptly ceased when a film was put on. Adam heard the flitting beat of a helicopter, then an undistorted electric guitar; a drum beat, a tambourine, a singing voice proclaiming the end, more helicopters. Somewhere during a narration about Saigon, the jungle and divorce he managed to ignore the microscopic things that were chomping at his skin and he fell asleep.

5:2

He woke with faint memories of having dreamt of grown men giggling and to a warm sulphuric smell. After a lurid breakfast he was shown to a small office on the second floor of the Palace and handed a plastic-bound document entitled *Prince Scam*.

He flicked back and forth, saw pages of sums and pie charts and bar graphs and then a sheaf of letters. He dropped it on the desk and looked around the room and despaired. Then he thought of Judith Manthorne. He took the book back up and read the thing thoroughly and an hour later was in full comprehension of precisely what his primary job as an officer at the Kerang Immigration Detention Centre was to entail. He decided that absolutely he would not do it. He would tell the Captain exactly what had happened since his employment at Rad's Flowers and would bear whatever punishment was meted. Fortuitously enough the Captain knocked quietly on the office door and poked his head in.

'How'd you find it?'

'Finally I understand what's going on here, Captain.'

'Good. Very good. A man should know his job and then every day perform it to the best of his abilities. What do you think of that? Now it's time for your second job. Come on.'

'Now, I need to talk to you about something.'

'Of course. When you're back from the excursion I'll sit down with you and we can run through any ideas you've got.'

'Excursion?'

If an inmate wished to go on one of Kerang Immigration Detention Centre's bi-weekly excursions he or she had to put a week's wage into the lottery. If there were any spaces left on the bus once the officers' girlfriends and any inmates who had done some other favour for the staff were counted, the winners could hope for either an undemanding afternoon at the world's largest compass, a perilous swim in the Murray river, or a trip to the carpark beside a brackish lake where they were told to watch for birds. Such were Kerang's touristical delights.

Outside, Adam's shirt was straight away a rag. The day was already of molten sunshine, invasive and oppressive. Flies flocked at his orifices, cane toads to his lower appendages.

'Now, they're allowed to talk on excursions,' said Captain MacAynall, breaking off to turn his head in irritation. He daubed a handkerchief at the bulbs of the two white sores on one side of his mouth and at the enormous lone stigma on the other. 'I can't scratch 'em! They're driving me nuts! … So yes, they're allowed to talk on excursions so go easy on them. They won't try and escape.'

'To escape.'

'No. They've done it a couple of times but now they know. I've shown them the map again, reminded them there's only one town within forty days walk, and they know that the people in town hate Asians and'll just call the police. Now, you can't relax them in public. I'll take your taser, just in case the reflex kicks in. But here…' The Captain knelt down and selected five round stones from the banks of the stream. 'It's too graphic to relax them in public so if any of them do try and escape just throw a rock at them. Aim for the head. A small taste of freedom's good for them.

Reminds them of why they should work hard.'

Seated on a minibus, buoyant and unsuspecting, were twenty inmates. Behind Tung and his wife was an inmate in a flannelette dairy-cow costume. Khong was beside a rotund pin-headed bee. There was a tortoise, a shoddy lion, a headless bear. Beside Ngung, who had her hands at her belly, was Zipper poised with a straight back, her hands in her lap, gazing with all serenity out the window.

The Captain lowered his head under the doorway and looked the passengers over.

'Take them down to Gunbower and walk 'em around the Lagoon Circuit for a bit and then let 'em swim in the river. Most of them won't 'cos they can't. And have 'em back by five-thirty for Internet, all right?'

Adam turned the minibus onto the dirt road. Immediately those inmates who were capable of speaking spoke. The bus bounced in and out of potholes and its passengers filled its cabin with the jolting syllables of their choppy tongue. Adam drove the mirthful little gang the hour into Gunbower with the map unfolded over the steering wheel. He located the carpark to the Lagoon Circuit and pulled up the handbrake. They were surrounded by eucalypt forest – sparse, high tree trunks, a floor of grey dirt littered with grey spinifex and fallen branches. A few brown billabongs bloomed red with algae. A wooden picnic table covered in bird droppings and lichen was beside two green bins, fastened back-to-back to a steel pole and overflowing with rubbish; the brick toilet block could be smelled from a distance of furlongs. A front was sweeping over them, a blue and black-streaked pillar of cloud rolling in and bringing with it a cool and gusty breeze.

Adam stepped onto the sandy gravel and waited for the inmates to assemble around him. Rather they swarmed.

'Thank you,' said Tung. He had an arm around his wife; they were both jubilant.

'You are most welcome, Tung.'

'I knew you would come back for us. I knew it is true.'

'True? What's true?'

'Thank you, Speaker of English,' said another inmate, raising the back of Adam's hand to his inclined forehead.

'I do hope you enjoy your excursion. Have any of you been to the bush before? It's a bit hot up here but it's a nice enough landscape once you're used to it. Does it look like this where you're from? I imagine not.'

Khong took Adam's other hand in his; he looked down at him and nodded a stern and grateful nod.

'All right. Are we all ready then? Let's take a walk down to the water?'

'No, we not go to water,' said Khong.

'What's that?'

'We not go to water.'

'Well, I have been instructed to take you to the water. It wouldn't sound very good to the captain if I took you all back and not one of you had even tried to go for a swim now, would it?'

'You won't be taking us back,' said the inmate dressed as a bee.

'The language barrier again.'

'You have delivered us,' said Tung.

'We have escaped,' said his wife.

'Thank you, Speaker of English,' said Khong.

'Not that again. No. Do you know what an excursion is? You haven't escaped. You're just on an excursion. Do you understand?'

'We have escaped,' said the dairy cow. 'We have been delivered of the detention centre.'

'You have delivered us.'

'No, I haven't. I brought you here, yes. But that's because I had to. Bring and deliver have very different connotations in English.'

'Rotte never brought us,' said the bee. 'He make us wait in bus while he go to motel with Nung.'

'You are our deliverer,' said Tung. 'You brought us.'

'Yes, and I have to take you back in an hour.'

'You no take us back.'

'I yes take you back. Yes, I will be taking you back.'

'It is foretold.'

'Foretold by whom?'

'You no see?' said Tung. 'Captain want you to deliver us because he no want the firstborn of Ngung.'

'We have come to find a herb in the forest,' said Tung's wife. 'We give to Ngung and she no have baby. Then you lead us to free.'

'Now you take us to Indonesia,' said Khong. 'I see my princess. She love me.'

'Indonesia?'

'My princess wait for me there too,' said the dairy cow. 'We go to see them. We be happy together.'

'We go to Indonesia.'

'We go to find herb for Ngung then we go to free.'

Khong said something in Vietnamese which sounded like a rebuke to Tung's wife. She sniped back and very quickly most of the inmates were quarreling. Khong spoke to Adam beneath the din. 'If you will not lead us to Indonesia, I will lead us. Tell them to follow me, Deliverer.'

'No follow him,' said Tung.

'Khong, I'm not going to tell them to follow you. Please none of you try to escape, all right?'

'If you will not deliverer us then none will make it to river.' Khong yelled in Vietnamese then said, 'I take them all and they be our slaves. They come with we or they no go anywhere.'

'You're being very dramatic. Please would you just come with me for a walk around this footpath here and then we'll have a nice swim, all right? Doesn't that sound nice?'

'We go to princesses,' said Khong.

'And our princes.'

'Internet can no do more for us.'

'In Indonesia. Beyond the water.'

'I can assure you that Indonesia is *not* beyond the river.'

'We are in love,' said Khong. 'We go to be with our princesses. We in love. All we can royalty.'

'Oh dear,' Adam sighed.

'Come,' yelled Khong to his fellow inmates. 'We go this way.'

'No,' said Tung, very gruffly. 'We go with Deliverer to the water. We find herb for Ngung. Then Deliverer deliver us to freedom.'

'No!' yelled Khong. 'You follow us. You follow me. We have been delivered. Now it is for us. This is way we go to Indonesia.'

'We go with the Deliverer,' said Tung.

'If you no come with us you no go anywhere. We go to find Indonesia. Then we come to find you, and you will be our slaves and serve us.'

'You leave us to follow Deliverer,' yelled Tung.

'If you no follow me you no follow anyone. We find river.'

Then we take you!'

Khong and the bee and the dairy cow and several other costumed inmates backed towards the pathless forest. They stepped off the gravel of the carpark and turned and sprinted off into the bush. Adam looked upon the remainder of his excursion. They were thoroughly spooked. Then all at once they too sprinted off, down the wide path of trampled dirt that was the Lagoon Circuit.

Adam called after them and asked where they were going. He hesitated between the two groups. He ought to chase one of them, he thought. He remembered the stones in his pocket but decided against attempting to clock anybody in the head. Eventually he chose the less belligerent of the two and ran after Tung and his wife. He quickly caught them up and overtook them. He stopped and turned and outstretched his arms. 'Please stop,' he pleaded, and they did. 'I will take you to the river.'

'OK,' said one of them.

'Just please don't run away again.'

'OK,' said another.

'Do you promise?'

'OK,' said another.

For twenty minutes they strolled past lagoons pleasant with grass and lilypad, puddles luminescent with maroon algae. Adam thought about which of the bush plants the inmates would be looking for in order to intervene in Ngung's pregnancy. Probably a quinine bush or a buttercup orchid. He searched carefully for both, intending to prevent them through diversion from seeing and ultimately using either. Soon the inmates made it tiresomely clear that they had developed a thirst.

'Did you bring water, Deliverer?' said one of them.

'Please just call me Adam. And no, I did not bring any water. Was I supposed to?'

'If we no have water, how we drink?'

'We won't be out here for very long. I'm sure you can go without water for an hour or so.'

'We will drink at the river,' said another inmate. Then he murmured something in Vietnamese.

They walked, all of them quite bored, along the dusty track for another twenty minutes, occasionally snapping at one another in

Vietnamese. An inmate told Adam she was hungry.

'You can get us food?'

'Not presently, no.'

'We no want present. We want food.'

'But if present is food, we want.'

'You cannot get us food. He cannot get us food.'

'How will we eat while we are in the desert?'

'You're not in the desert. And we won't be out here for long. You'll be back soon enough. I'm sure they'll let you eat at the compound. Can't you go forty minutes without eating?'

'So hungry,' groaned another inmate.

'I want to go back,' said another, then something in Vietnamese.

'Is Work time,' said Tung.

'I no care. When we work we have food. Now we die in desert. Deliverer cannot feed us.'

'He has no food for us.'

'Maybe he is not Deliverer. Deliverer would have brought food.'

'And water.'

'I think he is not Deliverer. I think you are not Deliverer.'

'I've told you I'm not the Deliverer. I've been telling you that days.'

'He is Deliverer. Look!'

'He take us to river.'

The detritus beside the path dwindled to leave exposed a ground of light clay which soon turned to auburn sand. It sloped gently down to a straight length of brown river, not very wide but flowing steadily.

'River,' said an inmate, angrily.

'How we cross river?'

'You're not supposed to cross it, you're supposed to swim in it.'

'Swim? No,' said one inmate, horrified by the idea.

'You bring us to nowhere, Deliverer.'

'I brought you for a swim.'

'No,' repeated the angered inmate.

'Come on, I'll show you.' Adam stripped to his boxer shorts and waded into the water. Half way across it was still inches below his knees. 'There, see?'

'We cross river,' said Tung. Clothes in hand over his head, he copied Adam's demonstration. His wife followed. Soon all but Zipper were down to their underwear and standing nearly up to their knees in light brown water. Zipper stared with folded arms across the river. The inmates stood around Adam and waited for him to lead them further into the depths. They patted water onto their necks and gazed around. Then one of them, a petite young man, looked wistfully back at the departed bank and immediately screamed in Vietnamese and pointed to the tree line. A huge flock of cockatoos squawked and fled their boughs. Zipper jumped from fright and turned around. Now all were looking back into the forest.

'He say he see person,' said Tung.

'Up there?' said Adam.

'There, yes.'

'Why is he so scared?'

'Because Khong.'

'Khong?'

'Because Khong. Khong say he take us if we no go with him. He see Khong. Ad-am, deliver us please.'

'He won't take you, would you relax? He just wants to go to Indonesia. Let him try. It's impossible from here. It's thousands of miles away.'

'Khong very bad. He leave Vietnam because police they look for him. He come here and he get arrested already. Send to detention.'

'I'm sure it isn't him. He's probably half way to Indonesia by now. Well he's not half way, but I'm sure he's at least on his way to Indonesia.'

'What?'

'What?'

'Khong come.'

'Khong take us. Make us serve him.'

'Why would he take you? Why wouldn't he just leave?'

'You no understand Vietnamese.'

'No I don't. Now, look, why don't I go and see what's spooked your friend. You stay here, and don't cross to the other side of the river, OK?'

'Don't go,' said Tung. 'You are Deliverer. If he kill you all of we gone.'

'But I really would like to stop his screaming.'

Tung snapped at the screamer; it halted nothing. An even slighter young man waded from behind and lowered his extended arm. The screaming ceased. 'Do no be afraid,' said the slighter, looking at Adam, 'because I am not afraid. I will go and search the land.'

'I go too,' said Tung. 'He should go not alone.'

Tung kissed his wife on the cheek and the two men ascended the bank and went warily into the forest; very shortly the backs of their heads could no longer be seen among the trunks.

Those wading stood transfixed on the treeline. No words were exchanged; heads were turned slightly to ensure the ear caught any alarming sound. Only the water trickling around their shins and two or three bird calls marked the slow passing of time. The longer they had to wait the heavier became their breathing. Then came yelling in Vietnamese, the cracking of branches, the thud of sprinting feet. The slighter man scrambled down the bank. He yelled something in Vietnamese and screamed, 'Milk and honey! Milk and honey!'

'Milk and honey?' said Adam. 'What on earth do you mean?'

'Tung?' cried Tung's wife. She pulled at the slighter man's arm and they spoke in Vietnamese. 'Tung?'

'Milk and honey,' said the young man as he splashed into the river.

More branches cracked and there rose again the thud of sprinting feet. 'Giant!' yelled Tung as he fled the bush and leaped onto the sandbank and into the water. 'Giant!'

'Giant? What do you mean? He came out yelling "Milk and Honey".'

'Not milk and honey. Cow and bee! Cow and bee! Giant here. Khong come.'

There emerged from the bush to loom at the eroded bank the giant and his costumed friends. They had each a menacingly thick stick in one hand. Without hesitation they stepped onto the sand. Zipper backed away from them but stopped at the water's edge. Khong turned her around and grabbed her by the throat. He yelled in Vietnamese and then to Adam, 'Out of the water.'

Slowly they all obeyed. The bee and the dairy cow took the two other female inmates by their throats.

'Where are the other inmates?' said Adam. 'The ones who went with you.'

'They died from thirst and starvation,' said the giant.

'They did not. We've only been out here for an hour.'

'They were very thirsty and very hungry.'

'Are they really dead, Khong?'

'No. But they come. Milk and honey and we run for Tung and Phat. The others come soon. Now, Deliverer, you choose a man and let him come down to me.'

'Up.'

'What?'

'Up to you. You're above us.'

'Hm?'

'Never mind. Look. There's something I have to tell you about your Mubjherudan princesses.'

'We go to Indonesia. We in love. But first we give your body to bird of air and beast of field.'

'I'm not really sure what that means, Khong, but there really is something I need to tell you.'

'What?'

'All right. Well… Wait, first let the girls go.'

'No. You tell me.'

Adam put his hand in his pocket and readied a smooth stone between his fingers. But there came from above a great wind and then a deep woosh that caused all ears to be blocked by fingers and all eyes to be closed. The women, released, stepped out of the reach of their captors and into the arms of Adam, of Tung and of the once-frightened, secondmost-petite inmate. The other inmates arrived at the riverbank just in time to join in the astonishment at the helicopter that was dropping with unbearable turbulence towards the river.

From its loudspeaker came, 'Chao?' Zipper burrowed her head into Adam's breast.

The waters of the river receded under the blades of the helicopter. Its whirlwind sent up a cloud of debris, including a stone which hit Khong in the temple. He fell upon his face to the earth. The skids touched down and sank a foot into the mud of the river bed. The inmates cheered, though they were heard by no one:

'Deliverer!' and all except Zipper jumped into the mud and sank to their shins and laboured to lift one foot out after the other as they scrambled past the helicopter. They soon made it to the other side of the river and into the denser bush disappeared.

A voice came slow and firm through the loudspeaker. 'Chao, get in the helicopter.'

Zipper looked up at Adam. Her lip was no longer sagging. She looked beautiful, though no longer serene.

'Your face?'

'If you are pretty many officers take you for boom boom. If you are ugly maybe only one.'

'And you can talk?'

The turbines of the helicopter's mast squealed off and the blades slowed to resting and drooped at their ends. Silence returned to the riverbank.

Zipper's eyes were teary. 'I no want to go with them,' she said, softly but clearly and with a thick accent.

From the helicopter a man with a suntan and dark hair, in a khaki shirt and shorts, stepped out into the replenishing stream. He sank to the knees. He put an arm against the helicopter's nose and took off his golden-mirrored sunglasses. With deep crow's feet at his eyes he glared rock-faced at Zipper.

'Chao, let's go. I'm bringing you back.' His voice was deep and patriarchal and Australian. 'Van wants you at home with him.'

Zipper looked again to Adam. 'I do not want to go back.'

'Chao, listen to me. Come with me now and Van will forget about you running away. He won't hurt you.'

'Who's Chao?' said Adam.

'I am Chao.'

'And who's Van?'

'Van is a man. I am not his wife but he pays to have me.'

'Chao, your family is missing you. Van misses you!'

'He does not miss me,' she said to Adam. 'He wants to own me.'

'He doesn't want to own you, Chao. Van loves you. We both know that.'

'Take me back to detention.'

'Detention's horrible,' said Adam.

'He's right Chao. Listen to him.'

'Do you have a big family, Chao?'

'I have a mother and a father and a sister and a brother.'

'So yes, you have a big family. You should be with them. Family's important. I would give anything to have one again. You should be with yours. Won't they be missing you? Think about them. Don't you think they would prefer to have you near them, so they can see you? So they can feel your life?'

'But they have found out about Van. They say I am living life of sin.'

'Sins repented of are forgiven, Chao.'

'What?'

'Go back to your home and tell this Van how you feel. He'll understand. He's human. He won't keep you against your will. You belong where your family and your friends and your country are. Think of how much they need you in *their* lives. You certainly don't belong here, not in detention, not in Australia.' Chao stared up at him. Adam was still in his boxer shorts and she longed to believe. 'And once the sin is ended, it will be forgiven. You'll be forgiven, Chao. Don't go back to detention. You don't belong there.'

Chao looked long up at Adam. She backed solemnly from his arms and turned towards the helicopter. The older man trudged forward and held out a hand. She reached for him and he carried her to the helicopter. Adam went ashore and put his trousers back on. The man hoisted Chao up into the helicopter then waded decisively back across the river. His hair was oiled and combed back, its line high at the temples. The hairs on his thick forearms were beginning to blonde. 'How would you like to come and work for me, son?'

And the blades started up and reparted the water. After a brief struggle with the riverbed the helicopter rose and turned and flew away.

THE THIRD BOOK OF ADAM ATHELSTAN, CALLED
REGNUM

CHAPTER 1

1

In the opulent cabin of Paul Tyrus's aeroplane Adam rested his head against his plush leather headrest and reposed his elbows on the soft white arms of his seat. After five hours in the air he at last ceased to be alarmed by the whir of the engines. Opposite him, Chao was hunched and huddled, staring forlornly out at the tiny ripples in the unending ocean.

The cabin, with fold-out tables between facing armchairs, was furnished with cupboards and compartments of burnt oak. The ceiling was of hanging white silk. Two crystal vases on fold-out shelves each encased six peach tiger lilies. After the sole flight attendant, a Vietnamese girl with surreal English, brought out a second three-course meal Paul emerged from the cockpit and took off his reading glasses and sat beside Adam.

'How's everything?'

'Very nice. Thank you very much.'

'If you need anything – if you're hungry, thirsty, anything – just press the bell and Carly'll get you whatever you want.'

'Thank you so much.'

'Now tell me, where did you come up with that stuff?'

'Come up with what stuff?'

'All that stuff about forgiveness with Chao. Your words were like a harp, soothing. It was brilliant. I've never thought about using stuff like that before.'

'Oh, I didn't come up with that. It's quite old.'

'And what are you doing working at an immigration detention centre with a brain like that?'

'*That* is a very long story.'

'It's five more hours to Saigon.'

'Is she all right?'

'She'll be fine once we get her back where she belongs.'

'With her family?'

'She's the mistress of a very important Vietnamese man. She goes straight back to him. The rest is up to her.'

'Oh. … Now what's this job you're offering me?' Adam lifted his soup bowl and spooned from it.

'Jungle extraction. Mainly. I own a company called I Love My Family. Ever heard of us? … No. Well, we rescue people who've abandoned their families, their countries, their civilisations, for Asia. Eternal tourists, deluded expats, defective artists. Business has never been better, now that we have these new tourist warlords, and I need another negotiator with me on the ground in Vietnam. And now I find you. Sometimes I doubt the nonexistence of the big fella upstairs.'

'A negotiator?'

'The most common deserter goes to Southeast Asia and decides that western civilisation's not for them. And then, and I can't figure out where they get the idea from, they go up a river as far as they can and become a hermit. Their families of course get worried. They think they've gotten addicted to drugs or something. And they find me and we go in and bring 'em back. That's where negotiating comes into it. In the past we used material incentives. They're becoming more and more ineffective. The parents don't realise that a lot of the time it's material things that their kids are turning their backs on. They can't understand it. And now I've got you. Mr Spiritual.'

'That sounds like quite a noble profession, Paul.' Adam put down his empty bowl and leaned over his pork chop. So much mint, he thought. How did they know?

'Yeah, it's all right. You should get some sleep. We start work on your first client tonight. When you've finished call Carly and she'll show you how your chair turns into a bed. Chao, you should eat something. Chao?'

'There are *two* types of mint in here!' said Adam, elated.

Adam slept soundly enough under a cashmere blanket and was woken to mangoes and yoghurt and bread and eggs. The aeroplane was taxied to a bay and a staircar driven to its door. Paul handed a piece of paper to the man on its platform and said, 'Call this number.' Half an hour later the suited official returned.

'I am so sorry sir but our phone is no working.'

'Your phone's not working. Why isn't your phone working?'

'It appear to have broken down. It is a very old phone. Vietnam very poor country.'

Paul took a wad of American dollars from his pocket and handed the official a single bill.

'I see if we can fix as soon as possible, sir.'

Half an hour later a different official knocked at the cabin door. 'Hello, sir. Sorry sir. We are able to get phone working for you, and we call number you give, but then cleaner she walk pass and lock the door for room that have phone in. It have no window and soundproof. We must call a man to come and fix. The man who fix is three hour away. But there is another man just ten minute away, but he make a very high price.'

Joylessly Paul parted with another bill and the official and two of his friends ambled across the tarmac to the terminal. 'It's one of the most corrupt countries on earth,' said Paul. 'Van, the man who sent me to get Chao, is the only reason I can even do business here. If I didn't pay him off every month my house would be burnt down. Sit tight. We'll be good soon.'

Half an hour later a different official. 'Welcome in Tan Son Nhat International Airport. Can I have you flight paper please?'

'Never mind, you. I've already got two men sorting it out.'

'Two other men? I Ho Chi Minh City Airport's only flight manager. I greet every flight when arrive at Tan Son Nhat International Airport and make sure they have correct paper. I am a very busy job. Please you paper.'

'I'm not giving you any more money. I've already paid two men.'

'Oh no. This happen a more and a more. Were they same height me? Straight hair? Black hair? Look my age? Yes, they no work for Tan Son Nhat International Airport. They bad men. They take you money.'

'Well I'm not giving you any. Call this number. He'll sort everything out.'

'What?'

'Call this number. Tell him Paul is here.'

'Oh. Of course you. So sorry about this. I call.'

And thirty minutes later he knocked on the cabin door.

'I really am so sorry about what happen. And now it look to me that the two bad men who take you money have broken phone and broken lock of door in office that have phone. We have to pay to get a man for to fix and we have to pay for man to repair telephone. Vietnam so poor country.'

Paul stared with a sense of impatient futility that was very familiar to him. This latest official was eventually handed two green bills and Paul dropped into a chair.

'I don't know how they can still claim to be so poor, the amount of money they take from me.'

After a locksmith opened the door and after a snake coiled itself around the airport's broken telephone and after a sackless and stickless snake-catcher was called and then locked in the office with the snake and the broken telephone; and after the locksmith was called out again and after the snake-catcher's equipment was purchased and after the snake-catcher's equipment was delivered—all involving seven more knocks on the fuselage by five different officials—the telephone was repaired and Paul's telephone call made and his aeroplane allowed to depart for Da Nang.

1:2

They landed and descended the staircar. Immediately Adam became aware of heat. Unladen, he felt as though he were being made to carry two bags of concrete through the desert with loud hairdryers pointed at him. The bright light of midday could not have been called sunshine. It was simply the unadulterated sun, to which Adam had never felt closer.

Beyond the glass doors of the arrivals hall, waiting among the taxis, a short chubby man in a shiny black suit and sunglasses was flanked by his several attendants, all taller and chubbier than he and all huddled around a shiny black van. Chao saw these discomfiting figures and made a single step towards running in the opposite direction. Paul caught her firmly by the elbow.

'Thank you for returning to me what is mine.' The man greeted Chao sinisterly in his own language.

'It was very nice meeting you, Chao,' said Adam, waving to her as she was put into the back seat of Van's van. 'I do hope all goes well with your family.'

'Van, this is my new agent, Adam. Adam, this is Van Cu Trinh. He's a very important man.'

'How do you do?'

'Paul, you car have flat tyre while your driver wait for you arrive. We bring him new one. It was three-hundred dollar. We pay for him from his money. Make sure you pay to him back. Vietnamese people very poor.'

'Thank you, Van. I will.'

'Thank you for bringing to me Chao. Now we get back to business. I see you later.'

The natives got into the van and it was driven away. Immediately Paul and Adam were swarmed by taxi drivers. 'Where you go?' … 'You want taxi?' … 'Skew me, sir.' … 'You go Hoi An?'

Paul rushed Adam to his car, parked a short way down the concourse.

'Thuc. How are you, mate?'

'I good, Mr Paul. How you?'

'Had a flat tyre did you?'

'Yes. Sorry. I drive to here and then I park and then police say to move. I move and tyre is flat. But Mr Van he get spare for you. Three hundred dollar, and he make me to pay.'

'Yes, here you are. Sorry about that.'

'Thank you Mr Paul. Sorry. Sorry.'

'Business is strange here. The locals never let you forget that you're in their country. I can only work because of Van, and two weeks ago Chao ran away and he asked me to find her. *Asked me*, of course. Now we can get to work, right in the middle of busy season too. This is Da Nang. The fourth biggest city in Vietnam. My son teaches English here. You'll meet him. Jonathan. He won't work for me anymore, he doesn't agree with it. We're going to Hoi An, half an hour south. We'll need to get you some clothes before we start.'

'Actual clothes?'

'What do you mean?'

'I've worn nothing but a polyester tracksuit and then my friend's tight trousers and then this, for the last week.'

'Part of your very long story?'

'Part of my very long story.'

'Actual clothes. Hoi An's famous for its tailors.'

'Tailors? Goody.'

They were driven out of the shade of Da Nang's strange concrete erections. Hulking garbage trucks careened about them and hundreds of motor scooters overtook. Every thirty seconds Thuc beeped his horn to remind the indifferent road of his presence. The densely green marble mountains sat like rocky mistakes among the thin four and five-storeyed houses. The procession along the wide and unbending highway which stretched before them was one of vast new resorts, some in imitation of Roman temples, some as American casinos; of immaculately kempt and wastefully unattended golf courses. Once colourful shrines, dust-covered and littered with dead offerings, lined the roadside as teeth on an ancient lady's gums. Smoke rose gently from the gutters before brick shanties, sweetly perfuming the air with the smell of burning charcoal from an unfamiliar wood. Billboard advertisements for cloth shops and tailors and resorts and restaurants poked like giant croquet hoops out of the sandy orange scrubland.

Thuc slowed and turned onto the road into Hoi An. Crouching old ladies hawked seafood in shallow pans at the roadside. They passed through more grassland, crossed a bridge overlooking clusters of sticks embedded as alluring shelters for small fish; in the distance mountains rose blue. Soon low rice fields were on both sides, a patchwork of springing green and scythed yellow and mud, a high plume of smouldering smoke, a farmer on crutches pestering his herd of two cattle, tourists dismounted from their bicycles to photograph water buffalo. Tour buses commanded the road in both directions until they reached town; there the traffic was at a standstill.

The tailor shops began, and the hotels and the restaurants. Tourists sweated on bicycles; those on foot were hounded by women in floppy hats and pyjamas. Shoals of school children in blue neckerchiefs and white shirts rode merrily, two to a bicycle.

'Just here, Thuc.'

Thuc pulled in outside a dark and dingy store. Plastic-wrapped backpacks overlapped plastic-wrapped backpacks, thongs and singlets were crammed side by side, until the musty store was filled with them. A woman came running out from its unlit depths and flopped her raised hand at Paul and Adam.

'Hello you! You look my shop! Happy hour! Hello you! You come back my shop!'

'Yes,' said Paul.

'What you look today?'

'We need singlets –'

'Singelet, OK.'

'Shorts.'

'Short OK.'

'Thongs.'

'Thong OK.'

'Sunglasses.'

'Sungelass I no have. But you wait.' Barely lifting her feet, she jogged off down the street and very shortly returned with a man bearing at his chest a board of sunglasses.

'Sungelass very cheap,' said the man. 'Happy hour. Two sungelass thirty dollar.'

'Things are cheap here,' said Paul. 'And they're even cheaper if you know how to bargain.' He turned to the salesman and asserted himself, 'Twenty-eight for two.'

'OK.'

The salesman became ardent with gratitude as Paul chose two fluorescently framed pairs, then he scurried home to his family.

'Now what you need?' said the shop lady. 'Here.' She held a singlet, red with a yellow star, up to Adam's frame. 'Happy hour. Two singelet... forty dollar.'

'We only need one.'

'One singelet, thirty dollar.'

'Twenty-eight.'

'OK.' And she put the singlet aside and punched 28 into her calculator. When soon Adam had had pairs of shorts and thongs chosen for him she converted the total into dong. 'One million,' she said, and Paul gave her five plastic bills.

'You did say actual clothes?' said Adam.

'Yeah, not these. This is your disguise for tonight.'

Paul dismissed Thuc for the afternoon and he and Adam walked to a bland new shopfront. A Vietnamese man looked up from clipping the inseams of a pair of trousers. 'Hello you again my friend!' He rose and hurried to turn on four large chrome floorfans as Paul and Adam ascended the steps to 'Coco'. 'Who your very handsome friend?'

'Coco, this is Adam.'

Coco yelled: 'You so handsome! You come for to me to make a suit?' If ever this man's enthusiasm had been leashed, it was certainly now loosed. 'Paul one my very good cutomer. I make a best suit in Hoi An. Make you look so funky. How many suit you want?'

'Pick your fabric and tell Coco exactly what you want. He's good.'

'I no good. I *fucking* good.' And with great familiarity of hand Adam had his measurements taken while Paul briefed him on his first assignment.

'It's a young kid, a run away, obviously, but he's not in the jungle. I think he's in town. We'll find him once we're done here and then see what he gets up to of an evening. Then you'll figure out the strategy for getting him back to his parents. They fly in tomorrow morning.'

'You pick a so very nice suit!' said Coco. Adam had given very detailed instructions as to the specifics of his garment. 'You look a very smart gentleman. So funky my suit. And Adam, I make for you not good. I make you for you *fucking* good! And I have for you ready tomorrow.'

'Tomorrow?' said Adam.

'OK for you? I deliver Paul house tomorrow in around… eight a.m. Paul my very good cutomer!'

Paul paid double what he had paid for Adam's disguise and they left.

'I've never heard English spoken like that,' said Adam.

'He's the gayest man in Vietnam.'

'He was rather gay wasn't he? You'd think it would be hard to be gay in this heat. I know I'm finding it hard.'

Paul eventually said beneath a raised eyebrow, 'Shoes and a belt.' Adam chose from a store the pair of brogues whose burnished tan most resembled his favourite pair.

From each of the stores that lined both sides of the street – tailor, clothing, souvenir, travel, grocery – a person rushed and tried to attract them with some combination of the already familiar cries: 'You buy something,' 'Happy hour,' 'You look my shop,' 'You very handsome man.' They were followed to the first corner by two women each bouncing baskets of fruit over a shoulder. They listed again and again what they were selling. One of them tried to sell Adam avocados by the kilometre. Paul and Adam turned right at an ignored set of traffic lights and were harassed by a woman on a bicycle who begged them to come and look at her tailor shop. Paul shooed her away as they passed polished wooden lobby after polished wooden lobby. A man lying on the seat of his motorscooter became animated from his dozing and asked Adam if he wanted boom boom.

The back of Adam's shirt was dark with sweat. Enveloping the entranceway to one polished wooden hotel was a gushing arch of white and pink bougainvillaea. Only when Paul reached their next turn did he realise that Adam was still halfway down the street, staring happily up at the mass of ebullient paper-thin bracts.

He had raised himself onto his toes and buried his face in the greenery.

'Oi. … Adam? Keep up.'

'Oh, sorry.'

'We've got work to do, mate.'

'Sorry. I've just never seen such an abundance of bougainvillaea.'

Adam's jubilant gaze refused to turn with his body and he nearly walked into a telephone pole built of end-on-end cinder blocks.

'An abundance of bougainvillaea?' said Paul.

They passed a water-logged field of fish-mint and turned down a road which, Paul was constantly assured, might soon be paved. They coughed and spluttered from the hot dust until they very shortly came to a high wall of sealed blue-grey concrete. Trees and hanging vines loomed high over it. Paul keyed a code into a metal panel and an iron gate drew across. A short drive of smooth white pebble, verged by two lawns, ran through a garden of banana palm, frangipani and tropical almond to a house built entirely of darkly stained teak. It had no windows and no walls. Tall bifold panelled shutters were drawn and a thatch-adorned roof rested on dozens of thin posts. Paul took off his boat shoes at the threshold and Adam followed with his boots and his socks. Terracotta tiling was cool underfoot.

'Make yourself at home. Treat it like it's yours. My kids live here too. They'll be in and out'

Cushion-covered divans and tall vases of lilies and orchids furnished the first two dark, facing rooms. A fountain surrounded by lawn lay in the open centre of the house, its simple baroque basque trickling peacefully to its basin. There was a shining modern kitchen above one side of this atrium and a dining room over the other. Paul led Adam through to the rear of the house and the bedrooms. The guestroom had a large bed set with sumptuous linen. The glass shower screens of the dimly lit en-suite seemed to him partitions in a gneiss firmament.

'You'll stay with us until I find you a place of your own. That wall opens up onto the backyard if you want to try to get a breeze. Just open the other wall and the air'll rush through. Get showered and into your tourist clothes and we'll get going in halfa, all right?'

Dirt sat in millimetres upon Adam's skin. He threw his filthy clothes into a corner and took the longest shower he had ever taken. He put on his new fluorescent shorts and tied their drawstring. Against their bright magenta his white legs shone like two fluorescent tubes. With even greater reluctance he put on the first singlet he had ever worn.

He pulled back the first of the back wall's shutters. The backyard was a thick lawn of fervent green verged with nubs of bamboo. Ground-covering flowers then shrubs, bushes and large-leafed tropical trees, ascended to the high wall. Four white gardenias, Adam noted. He unbolted and folded back the second shutter. In the centre of the lawn a wooden pergola dripped with vines of blue flowers like stringed bells. Shrouded by its tendrils was a white cast-iron ladybench. Adam stepped down out of the bedroom to fully take in the garden. A terracotta path led from the centre of the house. The tropical hedgerow ran all the way around the backyard walls and there, in the furthest corner, stood a small greenhouse of translucent plastic. Green blurs blotched through its walls. Presently Adam thought he saw movement among them. The silhouette shifted again and Adam thought that perhaps it resembled a head inspecting a bush at chest height. He crept crossed the lawn. When he reached the path he saw clearly a silhouette, luxuriating among the flowers.

'Adam,' said Paul, standing in the open hall between the atrium and the backyard. 'Ready to go?'

'Ah, yes. I'm ready. I'll just get my thongs.'

'And your sunglasses.'

'And my sunglasses.'

1:3

He and Paul were driven at a leisurely roll past a temple with a moat, a church trimmed with neon lights, a small carnival at rest, before crossing a river. There was a long row of restaurants on their right and a chequered field of concrete on their left. Then, before them, back across a low-arched bridge strung with lanterns, was the diminutive old town – proclaimed by the Vietnamese and the ahistorical multitudes as ancient – of Hoi An.

It has in common with the ancient places of Europe only that it is no longer vital. It serves now as a contrived display-funnel down which can disappear the undeserved cash of purpose-deprived tourists. And the streets of this simulated fishing village heaved and screeched with them, sweating and strolling.

Restaurant- and party-boats and old women hawking half hours in their dwarf sampans and, temporarily, in the weeks before the birthday of Buddha's mother, seven giant pink lotus flowers—all cluttered the dirt-green river. A stout Japanese bridge, the town's most frequently posed in front of object, was surrounded by cameras. Locals were preparing the traditional bingo, played nightly for and by the tourists, under a cluster of thatched rotundas. Single- and two-storey buildings, high-roofed and painted yellow, half in the simple local idiom, half graced with columns, were either emptying of tourists or filling with them according as they peddled clothing or food. Some were strung with lanterns, others had balconies overflowing with creeper. Vietnamese flags flew from high flagpoles every twenty feet on both riverbanks and hung from most of the shopfronts. Trite Western songs were broadcast from loudspeakers through the low streets, their melodies played on Vietnamese instruments and interspersed with messages from the Communist Party. The hazy sky was beginning to purple and a breeze to pick up. At any moment dusk would wash over the place.

Paul and Adam took a table on the street outside the restaurant that was closest to the lantern bridge. They sat beside one another and faced the river. Menus were brought and Paul ordered two fresh beers with ice. He pulled from his backpack a photograph of a young man with a preposterous quiff of blonde hair.

'Nick Absálom. Twenty-seven. English. He's gone backpacking around Southeast Asia and he was last heard of in Hoi An. One of my sources says that a kid that fits his description–'

'Who fits.'

'What?'

'Who fits his description.'

'This kid does.'

'Yes, never mind.'

Four glass mugs were brought, two filled with beer, two with single blocks of ice which took up nearly the whole mug. Adam raised the vessel containing his rectangular prism.

'It's almost perfect.'

'What is?'

'In a glass like this nothing could possibly keep the drink colder.'

'What are you talking about?'

'Except for a cylinder. It's almost perfect.'

'It's ice.'

'Exactly! Refrigeration is the benchmark of civilization, Paul.'

'Just drink your beer.'

Adam poured from his full glass into the iced and then sipped. It tasted faintly of fish and very faintly of beer.

'Now a kid that fits his description has just started working for Volcano.'

'Who fits.'

'What?'

'*Who* fits.'

'Who fits what?'

'Your description.'

'This kid does.'

'Again, never mind.'

'Volcano's a nightclub, the only nightclub in town. They get young kids to hand out flyers for them on the bridge there. So we'll sit and watch and see if that's what he's getting up to. You hungry?'

Adam took off his sunglasses and browsed the menu. A page of local specialties was followed by fifteen dishes repeated under headings of Cow, Chicken, Porks, Ducks, Ocean. Adam marvelled at the 'Spaghettis' page. He might have chosen spaghetti barbonara, spaghetti with groand beef or spaghetti bolongesse. A page each of burgers and pizzas preceded the list of chicken burgers, given at the bottom of a short list of available cigarettes. He decided on porks with chilli and lemons glass.

The dusk was long and punctuated heavily with people hawking peanuts and dried fruits and greeting cards and ponchos and cigarettes and tiger balm and little plastic dragonflies which balanced on one's fingertip. Adam was told a dozen times that he was handsome and began to wonder if there was a time when it was not happy hour.

Night fell and the riverside glowed red and yellow, seemed a wondrous nook of multicoloured lanterns; the warm and intense rainbow of the quaint and welcoming orient. Then the Eastern-sounding music wafting from beyond the river was replaced by unmistakably Western. The restaurants lining the streets turned up everywhere their volume and heavy, deep, fast thuds bombarded the air. Its small tranquility gone, the lanterns now seemed adornments to abandon and uniformity.

A thick-thighed blonde girl approached the bridge and began handing out flyers to the younger tourists, addressing them as they passed. Soon she was competing with a tall younger man who patrolled the span of the bridge, walking beside his targets and explaining what was offered by the bar in whose flyers he abounded. A Vietnamese boy stood in the middle of the street in front of Paul and Adam and gave flyers to unlistening tourists as he repeated an unintelligible blurb. Several more flyer-bearers arrived to work the vicinity of the bridge until there appeared, in a white singlet printed with fluorescent triangles, following tourists along the riverbank, smiling at the young girls with one raised cheek as he talked, the blonde quiff for which Paul had been waiting.

Adam cross-checked against the photograph. His hair and vulpine face were unmistakable. He neared their table and his London accent rose above the din.

'Hellow. How are you you all right? Thinkin' of goin' out tonight? Yeah? You should check this place out. Huge dance floor, sick DJ, girls drink for free all night. … Yeah for free. Yeah, it's a good deal love. Free pick up from anywhere in town. I'll be there from ten. Have a think about it, yeah?' And he left these two girls to continue their ambling. He caught the first group of girls coming from the opposite direction. 'Hellow, how are you you all right? What you doin' tonight then?'

They watched him repeat his patter for an hour. He altered it slightly depending on his audience, exaggerated to boys the number of girls that would be in attendance, prolonged his attack on lone males, emphasised the cost of drinks and the size of the dance floor to the girls. Couples he refused to say Hellow to and he approached no group whose average age might have exceeded thirty-five.

'Go and see exactly what he's saying. Walk up the street then come back up here and time it so that he stops you. Put your sunglasses back on.'

'It's night time.'

'You see that stopping anybody else?'

Adam used Nick Absalom's luminescent bouffant as a beacon in the throng of tourists. Nick turned around and planted his feet just as Adam reached him.

'Hellow, how are you you all right? Do you know what you're doing tonight then?'

'I don't, no,' said Adam, overexcited.

'Check this place out. Really cool club just outside the old town. Volcano.' He handed Adam a flyer. 'Loads of girls every night, man. Girls love it there. Drinks are buy-one-get-one-free all night and there's free local rum between ten and eleven, yeah? So come down if you're thinking of going out. Great place to pull man.'

'Great place to..?'

'To pull.'

'Pull?'

'Yeah.'

'To pull what?'

Nick slapped Adam on the back and cackled like a stork. 'That's brilliant mate. Might see you tonight then, yeah?' And he turned and resumed his patrol.

Adam handed Paul the flyer.

'Volcano people get stuck for months. They give you a free meal, free accommodation, free drinks. His overheads go down to a meal a day. And girls get smashed there. He'll be having a field day. We have to get him out before he starts hating himself.'

Half an hour later the last of the restaurants had turned up their music and the riverside was an intolerable cacophony. Australians squealed over one another to have heard their flabbergasted discussions of the differences between things at home and things in other countries. The lights on the footbridge were switched off and it might have been any riverside in the world.

Nick ran out of flyers and walked to his motor-scooter. Paul called a waiter for the bill. 'Keep an eye on him. I'll go in and pay.'

Nick retrieved his helmet from under the seat and clipped it at his chin. Paul and Adam hastened around the corner and got into the waiting car. 'Follow that motorbike, Thuc.'

Cars moved much more cumbersomely through Hoi An's traffic than did scooters. Only Thuc's daring enabled them to keep up. He held down the car's horn and overtook buses and clusters of scooter with maniacal abandon. They reached the road running through the rice fields and Nick pulled away. Almost instantly his tail light was indistinguishable among the others.

'He's gone to the beach. There's only two bars there. We'll find him.'

'There *are* only two bars.'

'Yes. That's what I said.'

'Well not really.'

'Huh?'

Thuc parked in the sand beside a one-wall shed built of bamboo. Adam and Paul went down a sparsely paved walkway between huts with no walls and vacant wooden restaurants. Reggae music rolled ahead. The ocean crashed softly down beyond the tables. They went into the first bar. Paul walked around the bamboo sofas and the umbrella-sheltered tables and found only families and couples.

'He's not here.'

Banyan Bar, the last structure on the beach proper, was better lit than the first. The two were separated only by a high fence of coconut thatch. Its uneven ground was of patchy lawn and sand. Long dining tables rested wonkily beneath thatched shelters; low tables and chairs sat beneath canvas umbrellas. Bamboo-framed daybeds and banana lounges faced the ocean. At the far end of the grounds a high-ceilinged thatched marquee sheltered beneath its golden light a tall bamboo bar and a pool table speckled with sand. Two couples stood with cues in hand. A few of the daybeds were occupied and one of the low tables. A dozen Vietnamese waitstaff were loitering at the end of the pathway which led back to the toilets. And on a stool at the bar, Nick Absalom, sunglasses on and with a beer bottle in one hand. He was talking intermittently to a Frankish-looking man poised at a computer screen on the other side of the bar. A cigarette was passed to him and he drew deeply from it.

'Ah, shit,' said Paul. 'He's smoking.'

'So?'

'There's not worse form of relaxation.'

Adam turned his head slowly to Paul. 'Oh, there's worse. Trust me, there is worse.'

'It gets them completely hooked on the place. They stop caring about everything we need them to care about.'

When Nick Absalom had recovered from its smoke he got up and descended the staired slope which led down to the beach. Paul and Adam stood at the sandy ledge and listened.

'Nick have you met Ian? Ian, Nick.'

'Hellow.'

Three men lay side by side on the damp and stained mat of a daybed. Nick was passed another cigarette and occupied himself with its smoking while the others talked.

'Like I love my wife,' said Ian, 'but I would *never* take her to Australia. I couldn't take her away from her family. It means so much to them here. She'd be nothing if she didn't have them close to her. And my kids can come and visit whenever they want. It's only nine hours. So here's perfect.'

'Mmm. Nick do you know we have proclaimed Hoi An as Freedonia?'

'That's awesome, man' said Nick between puffs.

'So where is your ideal place?'

'Mine? Right here, man. Right here.'

'Oh man, that's perfect then.'

'Mmm,' said Ian.

'Do you want to know where mine is? I will have a bungalow treehouse in Switzerland.'

'That sounds well cool man,' said Nick.

'Because here is good but I don't think I can stay forever? And when I go back to Switzerland I will build a bungalow treehouse. Because have one of you heard about the Shaolin monk that was chased by a tiger?'

Neither had.

'So there is a Shaolin monk, and he is being chased by a... by a tiger. And he is running, running, running really fast and all of a sudden he falls down a... a... how do you say in English? When the land stop and below is the water?'

'A cliff?' said Nick.

'A cliff. Yes, he fell down a cliff, but he grabs onto a wine and he is hanging with the ocean beneath and tiger above and the monk looks down at the ocean and then he looks up at the tiger and then he sees in front of him on the wine which he is holding, he finds a strawberry. ... And he eat the strawberry.'

His audience waited for the rest of the story. They soon realised that it was complete. They both thought it profound and exhaled long variations of the word, 'Fuck.'

Halfway through a very uninformed conversation about Buddhism Nick rose and said he had to go to work. He stumbled up the sandy stairs. Paul moved Adam into the shadows and Nick left Banyan bar and went to his motor scooter. Paul and then Adam took off their thongs and ran to the car.

Thuc reached the first intersection as Nick turned onto the road ahead of them. They followed him at speed into town. Nick slowed around the last corner before the old town and rolled into the concrete space in front of a dilapidated double story building with the word 'Volcano' protruding vertically in neon letters over its door. He unclipped and put away his helmet and slapped the hand of the emaciated man sitting cross-legged at its entrance. Then he was gone.

Stuck onto glass bricks beside the door was a piece of paper with the typed words: 'We look foreigner for work in the bar.'

CHAPTER 2

1

Adam woke to the sound of clinking crockery and sparse and reluctant conversation. On the end of his bed his new suit was folded through a hanger beneath his shoes and a belt. He shaved and showered and dressed and went to breakfast in shirtsleeves.

Paul was at the head of the dining table. With him were sitting a young man about Adam's age, and, as Adam entered fully the dining room, a sweet and delicate brunette girl in a yellow sundress. She looked like a sunflower at midday among two hunchbacks in the dark. The skin of her petite shoulders was smooth and flawless and golden brown. Her eyes were big and light and gentle. Her hair in a loose ponytail was the colour of a chestnut melted of snow, glistening. Adam had not ever beheld even a flower so beautiful. Enchanted, he walked with a turned head past the dining table and into the atrium. Paul recalled him.

'Adam. Adam? You all right? Adam, this is my son, Jonathan. My daughter, Evelyn.'

Adam soon managed to take his eyes from the girl's disarming neck and said hello to Jonathan. He immediately turned back to the girl.

'How do you do?' said Evelyn.

'Yes.'

'Hm?'

'Yes.'

'Yes what?'

'Yes please. It's the magic word.'

'What?'

'What? No. What? Nothing, dear. I'm sorry. Oh, dear. How do you do? I'm very sorry. Excuse me.'

Evelyn put a small spoon of diced fruit to her mouth and smiled. Even her spoonfuls were delicate, Adam thought as he walked back out of the dining room.

'Adam,' said Paul.

'Sorry,' said Adam, turning around again and hurrying into an empty chair.

In the centre of the table there was a white platter of ornately carved fruit, a tray of croissants, a basket of short baguettes, a bowl of muesli, a large tub of yoghurt, sat before him as a banquet. A Vietnamese girl came to Adam's side.

'Coffee, Adam?' said Paul.

'Ooh yes please. Iced, if you have it.'

'With condensed milk?'

'How did you know?!'

'How did I know what?'

'That I put condensed milk in my coffee.'

'That's how they drink it here.' Paul said something in Vietnamese to the girl and she nodded and went to the kitchen. A crying bird sounded in the distance. 'I was just telling the kids about my newest negotiator and then I realised I don't know anything about you. Now do I want to know, or would you prefer to leave it all at home?'

'Dad,' said Evelyn.

'What?'

'Personal questions at breakfast, really?'

'It's not a personal question.'

'You're so Australian sometimes.'

'Their mother was English,' said Paul. 'As I am so constantly reminded.'

Adam's coffee was brought. Its astonishingly ample ice (a single cube, each of its corners almost touching the round tumbler) and then its new and wonderful flavour brought to Adam a rare joy. 'This is absolutely delicious!'

'It's an intense country,' said Jonathan. 'And it starts with the food.'

Adam slathered a warm baguette with butter.

'Do you want anything hot? I can get Thuy to cook you some eggs. Or do you want something Vietnamese? They eat all their best meals at breakfast.'

'No, this is incredibly satisfactory,' said Adam. 'Thank you so much.'

There sounded from outside another long and desperate warble.

'Is somebody strangling a rooster?'

Evelyn smiled. 'They try to crow all day. Not the proudest of specimens. Wait until you see one.'

'Haggard?'

'Nauseating. Is that all Coco, Adam?'

'Coco? Oh, the tailor. Yes, it is. It's not bad from a distance. But if you get up close you see that none of the seams are *quite* straight.'

'That's Vietnam,' said Jonathan. 'It shows itself in everything it produces.'

'Great nations write their autobiographies in three manuscripts,' said Adam.

'What's that?' said Jonathan.

'It's Ruskin,' said Adam.

'And what are the three manuscripts?' said Paul.

'The book of their deeds, the book of their words, and the book of their art.'

'Their words are hilarious,' said Jonathan. 'It's the most inflected language on the planet. And it sounds atrocious even when they're being as kind as dandelions.'

'Sweet thunder,' said Evelyn.

'So musical a discord,' said Adam, and he and Evelyn exchanged smiles.

'And what did you think of our little Coco? He's sweet, isn't he? And those teeth! Oph.'

'I like a gay man,' said Adam. 'Especially a poor gay man. I think it shows real character. Hard to be gay when you're really poor. And in this heat. I'm finding it very hard indeed.'

Evelyn laughed. She said in a high voice, 'Oh, Adam, how is it *even* possible that you're working for Dad?'

'Well I haven't started yet. And I haven't lasted at my last two jobs. Two days each. I might not be working for him for very long.'

'Well just you be careful of Dad, won't you?' said Evelyn. 'Make sure you let him keep his pride. He gets jealous, don't you, Dad? And we all know what jealousy can drive people to.'

Paul's spoon, stirring the condensed milk through his coffee, came to a halt. He glared at Evelyn and looked almost wrathful. Evelyn turned to better combining her fruit and yoghurt.

'Speaking of which,' said Jonathan, rising, 'I have to be off.' He took his leather satchel from the corner of his chair and kissed his sister on the cheek as he walked out.

'I'd better get to it as well,' said Evelyn. 'Adam, it was a pleasure meeting you.'

Adam stood. 'And you.'

She paused and took in the surprisingly full breadth of Adam's politeness. 'I'm sure I'll see you very soon. Dad.' And she disappeared in the direction of the bedrooms.

Paul drank his coffee in one go and wiped his mouth with his napkin and dropped it on his plate. 'I'll get you to spend the morning looking over this kid's file. You'll be doing the negotiating tonight, so I'm going to let you decide how you want to get him out. We meet his parents this arvo and we'll brief them on what I Love My Family are gonna do for them.'

2:2

Paul and Adam met the Absaloms for a late lunch. Nick's mother sobbed through it. It was arranged that Paul would call them when it was safe for them to come to Banyan Bar, where from a safe distance they could listen to their son being restored to them, in spirit and in body, through the radio microphone under Adam's shirt.

At dusk Paul and Adam returned to the riverside and sat at the same restaurant table while Nick dispensed his armful of flyers.

'You ever think there's something fundamentally wrong with Poms?'

'How's that?' said Adam.

'There's just something about them. Same with Americans. And South Africans. Like they're all up their own arses or something.'

'I don't quite understand your metaphor.'

'And you bloody talk like one. Now I've got three of 'ya. And Kiwis, I mean–. No, not up their own arses. Blank. Daft. And the women… Fuck they're ugly.'

Nick left on his motorscooter and Paul rose. 'You ready?'

'I suppose.'

'Don't suppose. You be ready. This means money. This is real. I want him out and back with his parents tonight. You've got your approach down?'

'I think so, yes.'

'Don't think. Know. What is it?'

'Well, I was thinking—. No, I was knowing, that I will approach him when he's down on the beach, where he's philosophic, though rather outlandish, and I engage with his fantasies about life here and I'll refute them.'

'Good.'

They were driven slowly out to the beach and strolled into Banyan bar. Reggae meandered through the bamboo complex. Nick was at the bar, smoking and drinking and wearing sunglasses. He looked around to see if there were anybody he knew. He said something to the man behind the laptop then nodded for a time at his brief response. He looked around again, laboured to come up with something else to ask, asked it, then nodded at length. When eventually he failed to come up with another question and was not asked one he nodded to himself and walked down to the beach.

Paul phoned the Absaloms then attached a small microphone to the inside of Adam's singlet. 'It's dark, so they won't be able to see it. Just don't hug him. I'll whistle when his parents are ready. Tap the microphone to tell me you heard me. You can start any time after that. And don't talk to me. You'll look like you're talking to yourself. Go and wait in the daybed beside his.'

Ten minutes later Nick's parents walked into the bar.

'Something to drink?' said Paul.

'Please,' said a sombre Mr Absalom. 'A gin and tonic and a beer.'

Paul took his clients to an unlit table at the vacant side of the bar and called over a waiter. 'Your son'll be back with you in no time.' He put a receiver between them and had the Absaloms share a pair of earphones. He plugged in a second pair and put them in his ears and switched on the receiver. Mrs Absalom sipped nervously from her heavy tumbler. A lanky young bald man, topless and in long shorts, walked down to the beach with sunglasses on his face and a beer in his hand.

'Ho, Min,' came faintly through the device.

'Hiiii, Kevin. Kevin have you met Nick? Kevin, Nick.'

'Hellow. You smoke?' Mrs Absalom gasped at the sound of her son's name and then voice.

They next heard a determined exhalation and a groan of relief. Paul chirped a pair of two short whistles. Two muffled taps banged through the headphones.

'Kevin, we were just talking about your ideal place in the world,' said Min. 'Where would you be most happy?'

'I think right here, man.'

'Shit yeah,' said Nick. His mother sipped again at her drink. 'You know we proclaimed Hoi An as a Freedonia?'

'Yeah, right, man,' said Kevin. 'What does that mean?'

'Do you know that 'if' is the middle word in 'life'?' said Nick.

Min said, 'It means you can do whatever you want whenever you want and be whoever you want to be.'

'Who are you gonna be, Kevin?' said Nick.

'I am… I am Muhammad fucking Kevin Ali.'

'I'm Sasha Fierce,' said Nick and the others laughed.

'He was always the funny one,' said his mother, her composure faltering.

'And Min. Where's your perfect place?' said Kevin.

'I will have a bungalow treehouse in Switzerland.'

'That sounds well cool man,' said Nick.

'Because Hoi An is good, but I don't think I can stay here forever? And when I go back to Switzerland I will build a bungalow treehouse.'

'Can I come visit you?'

'Oh yeah, man. You better. You too, Kevin. We can surf all day and smoke all night.'

'Surf in Switzerland?'

'Oh yeah. Well then we smoke all day and smoke all night!'

They all laughed.

'So Nick, you're here on holiday?' said Kevin.

'I think I'm gonna move here, man.' Nick's parents exchanged long, sorrowful glances.

'For how long?'

'That's the question, man. I can't go home. I hate London. I was selling mannequin lamps. What am I doing in the world, selling fucking mannequin lamps? And the only way you can make money or afford to live in London is if you work in finance or marketing. Then I'd just be like my mum and dad. And who wants to live like them?'

His parents despaired. 'Remember,' said Paul. 'It's not your son talking. It's Southeast Asia. Asia has brainwashed him. But we're gonna get him back.'

'They've been miserable their whole lives,' said Nick. 'Chasing things, chasing shit.'

Adam became uncomfortable. Any harsher comment might cause more pain than Nick could know. His poor parents, Adam thought. He got up to interrupt Nick on his daybed. The ocean and the sky were together a black curtain dotted only by the distant but intense white lights of squid boats.

'Good evening sirs.'

Min tried to unsettle the newcomer with a few moments of silence. Then Nick said, 'Hellow.'

'Room for a fourth? It is a very pleasant evening. Warm and starry. What else could one hope for except for some company?'

'Sure, man, have a seat,' said Min. There was not enough space for four to recline. The three got up and sat with their backs against the bamboo frame. 'What's your name, man?'

'Adam.'

'Adam, Min, Kevin. I'm Nick.'

'A pleasure.'

'We were just talking about going home,' said Min. 'For how long are you here?'

'I'm not entirely sure. I think I may have just moved here.'

'See, that's what I'm talking about, man!' said Nick. 'Don't even think about it. You just do it. You don't even know you've moved here! If you think about it you'll never do anything. You'll just end up behind a desk your whole life, wishing. My parents were together for twenty-seven years, pretending to be happy. Then one day I find out my mum's cheating on my dad and I confront her about it and she begs me to keep it quiet. It's more complicated than I think, she tells me. What the fuck is that? That's not happy. And all I did was cheat on my last girlfriend. Constantly, with anything that would open her legs. That's my future in London!'

From the bar above there came a series of violent and dramatic cries. 'This is how I find out?! Who with?! Tell me now you slut! Oh, this is fucking great, isn't it? I am out of here.' They on the daybed looked up over their shoulders and then grimaced at one another.

'That's awkward,' said Nick.

'What the hell is going on up there?' said Min.

'Trouble in paradise,' said Nick. 'But how can people be so cruel to one another, you know what I mean?'

Adam saw his opening. 'Did you ever think, Nick, that maybe your parents did what they did with their lives so that you could do something great with yours?'

'Nope.' All but Adam laughed. 'And I never asked them to do that, did I?'

'Doesn't that make their sacrifice all the greater?'

'What the hell are you talking about man? You need to smoke. Here.'

'Oh, no. No, thank you.'

'Come on, man. It's weed. Look where you are.'

'Did you say you're smoking a weed?'

'Weed. Grass.'

'Oh, it's a grass. Which species?'

'It's marijuana, Adam.'

'Oh, that.'

Until now Adam had had no personal motivation for returning this ungrateful boy's soul (which is exactly what he felt he was about to do) to wherever it belonged. But illicit drugs was something to which he had the strongest aversion. He knew it to be true that they were enjoyed only at the expense of the entirety of one's dignity, and that he could not passively allow. He had once talked Noah out of smoking marijuana in his presence. In that particular instance goodness had prevailed and Noah went off to the back of the oval with the cretinous girl in front of whom he wished to smoke. Here his mandate was vastly broadened. He could get this ingrate away from the stuff and it just so happened that 'away from the stuff' coincided exactly with what Paul was expecting of him. An opportunity had arisen to do some real good in a job. He redoubled his offensive.

'And do you think, Nick, that your parents are happy knowing that you're here? What do you do here?'

'I do whatever I want. This is Freedonia, man.'

'And do you think your parents would be happy knowing that you, as you say, are doing whatever you want?'

'I don't know, man. Probably. Who cares?'

'Did you dream about doing whatever you wanted, which, if you think about it, is really doing nothing at all, when you were younger?'

'What are you on, man? You're so intense. Are you taking ADD pills or something? Are you on dexies?'

'I was just thinking about this very question earlier today. Your parents give their lives for yours. Shouldn't you be honouring that by contributing?'

'I am contributing.'

'To what?'

'To my own happiness.'

'Which is exactly what your parents forewent for you.'

To this Nick had no response. He had never heard the word 'forewent' before. He thought for a while then came out with, 'Maybe I'm here figuring out what my contribution should be.'

'Are you though? Happiness comes through having meaning. And the subordination of your own desires to something greater than ourselves is the only sure way of giving our lives meaning.'

Paul smiled at Mrs Absalom. They could both sense it. His boy was doing it. She saw hope and smiled back at him. Paul reached across the table and put his hand on hers. He looked her in the eyes and moved his fingers back and forth across hers. He nodded slightly and raised his eyebrows at her. She ignored him and rested back in her chair and pushed the earphones further into her ears.

'I think that this is not true,' said Min. 'Have you heard of the shaolin monk and the tiger?'

'If you would permit me, Min? In all your works, Nick, be mindful of your end and you will never do wrong.'

'You know about Shaolin teachings?'

'What's your end going to be, Nick? Are you going to sit here for the rest of your life? You'll kill your parents with disappointment. Place and family are two of the most important things on earth. I've been away from where I belong for a month now and it doesn't quite feel right, does it? And my time in the desert taught me that it *isn't* right.'

'Why are you picking on me, man?'

'You're the one disparaging the sacrifice of others for your own sake. I'm merely trying to outline the selfishness of your idleness, and how it can never make you happy. There are people who love you and who would hate to see you wasting your potential, wasting your life, Nick. You're young. You should be using it.'

'What should I do then, oh wise one?'

'I think you should come with me.'

'Where?'

'Up to the bar.'

'Are you gonna try and touch me?'

'Touch you?'

'Are you a fruit?'

'I like fruit.'

'You like fruit?' said Nick, breathing a laugh through closed lips. 'My deliverer. You make me think too much, man.' Adam's incursions had blunted Nick's fervent desire to languish. He held his beer up to the squid boats. 'I'm empty. Can I buy my deliverer a drink. Anybody else?'

Min and Kevin both said, 'Larue.'

Adam walked ahead of Nick and passed between Paul and Mrs Absalom, both standing under the bamboo frame at the top of the stairs. She with grateful tears in her eyes held out her arms and waited for her son to look up.

'Mum? Hellow. What are you doing here?'

'I've come to bring you home, Nick.'

Nick tried to take in exactly what was happening. His mother embraced him. 'Come home, Nick. We love you.'

He soon surrendered to the maternal embrace. He convulsed with tears.

'I'm sorry, Mum. I'm so sorry. I just…'

'Shhhh. We understand.' Mrs Absalom buried her face into her son's shoulder. 'Just come home, OK?'

'Is Dad here?'

'We'll talk about that later.'

Paul and Adam walked them to a taxi. Nick got into the back seat and Mrs Absalom turned to say goodbye.

'Thank you so much, Adam. That was really incredible. I've never heard such beautiful words. I'll bet you could talk anybody out of anywhere. Really, you've made me so happy. Mr Tyrus, this young man's a genius.'

'I trained him well.'

'Make sure you pay him handsomely, won't you? I want him to

be rewarded. Adam, thank you so much. Really.'

'Maybe you and I could get a drink tomorrow and have a bit of a debriefing of our own?'

'Thank you, Mr Tyrus, but no. We'll be in touch.'

She slammed the door and the taxi rumbled off towards town. Adam looked up at the stars and smiled. He felt a cool breeze on his face and turned to look out across the ocean. After a time he thought that perhaps Paul might be enjoying the very same indescribable pleasure, what with their hard day's work at its end and the warm hush of the palm trees and the sweet air and the comforting push of the shifting ocean. He turned to look at him. Paul's deeply wrinkled forehead and weathered blue eyes, starlit and stern, were glowering very directly at him.

'Well that was *quite* enjoyable,' said Adam. 'No?'

'You did all right. But it's not the jungle. We'll just see how you go in the jungle.'

CHAPTER 3

1

Adam went to the dining room in jacket and tie. He was looking forward in his own humble way to a triumph in the form a Tyrus family breakfast. His assumption of dignitas was erroneous. The dining table was empty save for its silk runner. The sound of a spoon clinking in a bowl turned his attention to the kitchen.

'Morning, Adam.' Jonathan was shirtless and hunched on a high stool at the central marble benchtop. He was as ruggedly handsome as his father had been at his age and almost as gruff. 'Self-serve breakfast this morning. We only sit down when Dad's home. It's one of the traditions he likes to think keeps the family together. Cereal and bread in that cupboard and help yourself to the fridge. The black stuff in the water bottle is the coffee. Put the condensed milk in first if you want it like you had it yesterday.'

Adam made himself an iced coffee. The enormous cubes in the top shelf of the freezer astonished him.

'Evelyn and I were thinking of going to the beach. You interested?'

'I don't know if I'm allowed.'

'If you're allowed?'

'Well I don't know if I have to work.'

'Did Dad tell you had an extraction today?'

'I haven't seen him this morning.'

'Then you're fine. It's not an office job. I'll get you a towel.'

Adam was called for later that morning and appeared in shirtsleeves at the front door.

'You're not going like that,' said Jonathan.

'I know, I'm sorry. I just think it's too hot for a jacket.'

Evelyn smiled. 'It's thirty-five degrees, mate,' said Jonathan. 'You'll pass out before you get half way there. And what are you going to swim in? Change into your shorts. And you've got thongs, don't you? Here.' Jonathan slung a towel over Adam's shoulder. 'We'll wait for you.'

The cycle to the beach differed from the necessarily slow drive only in that the blaring horns of the trucks and the buses, alerting him every thirty seconds to their deathly proximity, were unimpeded and deeply unsettling.

Walking along the sand, menus were thrust at him by women trying to corral him onto one of their sun-lounges. He pushed his way through the swarm of head-to-toe cotton pyjamas and followed Evelyn and Jonathan to the daybeds on the sand in front of Banyan Bar.

'Too early for a gin and tonic?' said Evelyn.

'Never. Adam?'

'I would baulk at making you feel degenerate. Extra ice if they could manage it.'

'Three gin and tonics,' said Jonathan to the waiter. 'With cucumber.'

'What?'

'Gin and tonic.'

'Yes. Gin and tonic three.'

'With cucumber.'

'What?'

'Cucumber.'

The waiter concentrated on what he was being told. He attempted to repeat it. 'Coo-com-…'

'Ber. Cucumber. Never mind.' Jonathan patted the boy on the back and went up the stairs to order the drinks in French from the bar's owner.

Countless recreational engines hurtled people up and down the stretch of water before them. Jet boats lifted from the shore tourists attached to parachutes; jet skis tore up the water's surface, spinning and thrashing in front of the tourist-occupied expanse of white sand; speed boats were roared along for no other apparent reason than speed and roaring. The fishermen, struggling in their coracles through the disturbing wakes, paddled with their single oar out to the deep to lay their nets. They had not seen so many engine-powered watercraft since the American occupation.

The upper outlines of three small islands were barely visible through a haze in the distance. On clear days the skyscrapers of Da Nang, the Marble Mountains, Monkey Island, the sixty-metre white Lady Buddha, could be seen to the north. Today there was no horizon and no view.

When they had finished their drinks and were sufficiently hot Evelyn suggested a swim. They waded out to their necks.

'Don't you love the water?' said Evelyn, springing up from a duck-dive. I don't know how anybody could live more than half an hour away from the ocean. Imagine living in a land-locked country!'

'Or a double land-lacked country,' said Adam.

'Double land-locked?'

'Land-locked by land-locked countries.'

'There's not such a place!'

'There are two.'

'Where?'

'You have to guess.'

'I'd rather be dead than live in a double land-locked country.'

'Evelyn!' said Jonathan.

'What?'

'Well I'm sure they have rivers.'

'Oo, rivers. Rivers aren't the same though, are they, Adam? Nor are lakes. It's the ocean for me. How did last night go?'

'Well enough, I suppose.'

'Well enough? What happened?'

'Nothing, really. We got the young man back to his parents. Well, parent. Long story.'

'And that's *all* you're going to tell us?'

'There's not much else to tell. The rest was the young man's business, not mine.'

Evelyn pleaded. 'But the extractions are so interesting. Please tell us. People are so pathetic here. Can't you tell us just a tiny bit more?'

'So talkative, Evelyn,' said Jonathan.

'I am not.'

'I've never heard you say four words to anybody you haven't known your whole life.'

They ordered more drinks and Jonathan and Evelyn lay in the sun for a while. Adam stayed in the shade of the thatched umbrella. When Jonathan had dried off from another swim he said, 'I have to meet Olivia. Adam, I'll see you later? Remember Dad wants us home for dinner.'

'Another gin and tonic?' said Evelyn.

'Oh, heavens no. There's no telling what might happen after a third.'

'After a third? Do you not drink?'

'I drink. I love lemon squash.'

'Alcohol?'

'Oh, that. No. Not really. Just lemon squash mainly.'

Evelyn repeated Adam's favourite beverage as a laugh. 'All right, well, I'm going to read for a bit.' She put on her sunglasses and lay back on her sun lounge. She pulled a paperback from her shoulder bag and held the thing up in one hand. She was a while reading a left-hand page and then turned her wrist to read a right, showing fully to Adam the book's title.

'Evelyn, you're not going to believe this.'

'What?'

'I'm best friends with the author of that novel.'

'Are you really?'

'I can't believe you're reading it. If you knew what went into its writing.'

Evelyn further spun her wrist and looked over the front cover. 'Noah Dulrich is your best friend?'

'He is.'

'Your best friend is the worst writer whose published words I've ever read.'

'I really can't believe you're reading it. If you knew where that book has taken me!'

'I never read new books. But a friend at home said this was so bad and so badly written, and so popular, that I absolutely had to. And Vietnam bootlegs everything, I got it for a dollar.'

'Is it not very good?'

'I've disliked it from the title page.'

'I gave him the title. Well sort of.'

'Noah's not a smart person, is he?'

'Hm. … He took all his stories from the people around him. Friends and friends of friends in Melbourne.'

'I've always felt that there couldn't *be* literature about Australians. They're so one-dimensional, do you know what I mean? No sense of history, no sense even of the absence of the Divine. Materialistic, hedonistic, products entirely of modern government. Am I being too harsh? I do sense that perhaps you might feel the same. Rich without beauty, powerful without wisdom. They may as well be Turks. Perhaps that's why they're so afraid of them. They're the modern world personified and who could read about that? I read one last year. About a young man who made up a Southeast Asian country, Mubjheruda he called it, just so that he could overthrow its dictator purely in the media. Quite good I thought. But the product of an immature mind. It did prove me wrong in one way though. You can have a literature that denigrates Australians. Although if they are simply products of modern government then I suppose that any book denigrating them denigrates most of the Western world, doesn't it? So they are relatable. Hm. Literaturable. Do you like that word? I just made it up. And off I've gone on a bit of a tangent, haven't I? I'm sorry.'

'No, no. You do seem rather vehement about it though.'

'Probably my own insecurity, isn't it? Anyway. Come on. I want to show you something.'

They bicycled over the high bridge overlooking the fishing traps and turned before the rice fields. At the end of a narrow street which ran between single-room concrete houses and a small lake the colour of weak gravy they came to open fields. The road turned to a dirt path and ran above variously full rectangular pools partitioned by walls of mud. They quickly came to a crowd of people assembled at a dusty intersection.

'Watch this,' said Evelyn.

At the end of a vague queue a dark Vietnamese man in a conical straw hat and heavy pyjamas held in one hand a length of bamboo and in the other the reigns of his water buffalo. Tourists, brought to this attraction by their day's tour guides, had dismounted their bicycles and were waiting. The frontmost tourist slapped both arms across the beast's back and then hoisted himself up onto it. The Vietnamese man handed him his hat. The tourist put it on and then smiled down at his girlfriend, who took a photo of him. Then they switched places.

'Next!' yelled the buffalo's owner, tapping his stick at the knee of the she-tourist. He was returned his hat. Another tourist handed him money, hoisted himself up onto the animal, was passed the hat, smiled and then switched places with his girlfriend. 'Next!'

'Tourists,' said Evelyn.

'That water buffalo is a prostitute.'

Evelyn laughed.

'And what's that word people use for the men who tell prostitutes what to do?'

'A pimp?'

'And that little man is a buffalo's pimp.'

3:2

Dinner was thin slices of roasted pork belly wrapped with sweet herbs in rice paper to be dipped in passionfruit juice and soy sauce. They drank sweetened coconut water. Adam was handed for the first time in his life a pair of chopsticks. He used them like skewers until Evelyn caught him stabbing and leaned across to help him. She positioned his fingers along the sticks and lowered his configured hand towards the pork. She laughed when he sent a piece of meat across the table. Paul glowered at the whole intimate process.

'You'll starve if you stick with those,' said Evelyn, giggling, and fetched him a knife and fork.

'Now, Dad,' she said, 'Will *you* tell us about last night?'

'Last night?'

'Your new boy's first extraction.'

'I didn't think you liked me talking about work at the table.'

'I want to hear how he went.'

'Oh do you?'

'Yes,' said Evelyn, quite defiantly. 'He wouldn't tell me a thing.'

'Well if you really want to know, he did very well. The mother seemed to think that he did all the work.'

'And did you come onto her?' said Jonathan.

Paul's chewing mouth halted in ire. Slowly it recommenced. 'No, Jonathan. Thank you. Adam's words were like a sweet and soothing harp. No befriending whatsoever. It's… I mean, I've had agents who would have taken a week to get that kid out. And they would have had to break his heart. Must be something in your face.'

'There is definitely something in that face.'

'Evelyn?' said Jonathan.

3:3

Next morning Adam was accompanied at breakfast solely by Thuy. She had come to do the housekeeping and, seeing Adam rifling hopelessly through the kitchen drawers, refused to let him make his own coffee or cook his own eggs. Then she refused to let him eat alone. She stood smiling at him as he ate at the bench.

'You very handsome.'

'Thank you.'

'I have baby.'

'Oh, do you?'

'Yes I have baby.' She thrust two fingers towards him.

'You have two babies?'

Thuy shook her head. 'She,' she said and thrust the same fingers.

'She *is* two?'

Thuy nodded. Adam returned to his eggs.

'You have baby?'

'Nope.'

'You have girlfriend?'

'Nope.'

Thuy pointed towards the backyard and nodded. 'Your girlfriend.'

'Hm?'

'You very handsome.'

'Thank you.'

'What you name?'

'Adam.'

'Ad-am.'

'Yes.'

'My name Thuy.'

'Thuy?'

'No, Thuy.'

'Thuy?'

'*Thuy.*'

'Thuy?'

'No!' She laughed. '*Thuy.*'

'Thuy?'

'Yes.'

'Oh. Thuy.'

'No! Ha ha, you very funny!'

The angelic sound of bare feet pattering on the tiles at the rear of the house; Evelyn soon walked into the kitchen. 'Good morning, sir.' She slid off one gardening glove with her teeth and pulled off the other. A faint swipe of dirt beamed across her cheek. Her fringe had broken loose to decorate her forehead. 'Chatting with Thuy I see? Babies and girlfriends?'

'I have baby. This your boyfriend?' she said, then laughed heartily with her hand over her mouth.

'Babies and girlfriends,' said Adam. 'Evelyn?'

'What?'

'Is that your greenhouse?'

'Why?'

'Would you show it to me?'

'Really?'

'Really.'

'I'd love to have you see it.'

She unzipped its front door and held back the plastic curtain. It was half the length that Adam's glasshouse had been but, Adam thought, just as splendid. Not since his sepian days at Ilmey had he walked among so idyllic a place. He felt as though he might be wearing knickers and a lace collar. And it was cool inside.

'Nothing's tropical,' said Adam.

'No. I want to feel at home in here. What would be the point of growing plants you're already surrounded by?'

A gently winding path was paved with terracotta wedges. Adam passed beds of sweet william, burning red and softened by pink, of fluorescent cornflowers, heads of purple kale and delicate violas sitting prettily like smiling butterfly wings, precocious hollyhocks and spears of foxglove and snapdragons, a bush of mock orange, pastel rows of giotto larkspur, white candytuft floating in bushes of lavender and rosemary. A shelf running along the walls teemed with potted gerberas and petunias and freesias and fuchsias, and primroses that looked as though they were blowing him kisses.

'A lily of the valley,' said Adam, touching his fingertips to a flower.

'It is. How did you know that?'

Adam gasped. 'And a white rosa acicularis.'

'The wild rose?'

'My favourite.'

'*How* do you know so much about flowers?'

'I used to grow them. I used to have a glasshouse.'

'A glasshouse?'

'Until my best friend's girlfriend drove a boat onto it.'

'Drove a boat onto it?'

'Or fiancé, drove a boat onto it.'

'I don't believe you.'

'She did. Then she opened the bilge tank and flooded the thing with seawater.'

'On purpose?'

'I don't think so, no.'

'You're making fun of me.'

'What makes you say that?'

'That never happened.'

'It did. … How do you keep it so cool in here?'

'See at the back there?'

Hanging from the frame of the greenhouse's back wall was a voluptuous green vine bursting with round blue flowers.

'With an ipomoea tricolor?'

'A what?'

'That's morning glory. Do you know what they mean?'

'The flowers?'

'Love in vain.'

'Not the flowers, Adam. Beneath the flowers.'

On the shelf at the rear of this grove a slab of ice a metre long and a foot thick rested in front of four embedded fans.

Adam's mouth yawned open like the cave of wonders. 'Is that ice?'

'Delivered every morning. It keeps everything at twenty-three degrees.'

'That's the most magnificent block of ice I've ever seen. It's enormous.'

'I was thinking of going for a walk into town. Would you like to come?'

Adam put a hand at either end of the slab of ice and stared down at the thing.

'Adam? … Adam?'

'What?'

'Would you like to come?'

'Come where?'

'For a walk into town you silly person.'

'Oh, yes. That would be lovely,' he said, gazing upon the frozen block as though overlooking a crystal landscape from a high place.

'I'll just get washed up and then we'll go? You'll wait for me in here? Adam?'

He was too busy marvelling and caressing to hear her. A few minutes later he turned around to find her gone. He went to wait for her in the front yard.

Standing at the open house's entrance a gentle breeze washed over him. He lifted his cheek to the sunlight. He opened his eyes and noticed a resplendent fall of bougainvillea overhanging the corner of the fence. When ten minutes later Evelyn appeared at the entrance steps Adam was ears deep in pink and verdure.

She crept up on him and put her hands on his back just as she shouted his name. He pulled a leaf from the back of his mouth as he turned to face her.

'So what *is* there to do in Hoi An?'

'While I was washing up I thought of a game we can play.'

3:4

'This a so special suit!' Coco was in his screechingly brightest mood. 'Make for summer, wear on summer. You look a so beachy beachy hot. You go to An Bang beach, many giiirl. I like you so much you style!'

Adam beheld himself in the mirror. The fabric Evelyn had chosen for him was printed with overlapping repeats of a palm tree above a pink kite-board behind a green toucan. The very short legs matched the very short sleeves. 'I don't know about this.'

'Tough. These are the rules. For the rest of the day.'

'What time is it?'

'We'll look ridiculous together. Relax. Now it's your turn.'

'Now you take off a short,' said Coco. 'Have to hem you leg.'

He followed Adam to the changing room.

'Coco,' said Evelyn.

'What!?' said Coco, grinning cheekily and turning about. 'What you worry? I have boyfriend.'

'Do you?'

'No! I have fiancé! Look my ring. See?!' He held up his left hand and wiggled his ring finger.

'A Vietnamese fiancé?'

'Noo, he from Engeland.'

'And he lives here with you?'

'No, he live in Engeland. He have wife and a many children. But he want to leave for to me to marry.'

'Have you met him?'

'What you think?! Of course I met him! Oh, I so offended by you. We have a skype and he come every year for a sick week.'

'With his family?'

'Nooo!' Coco attempted to say Evelyn's name. 'And soon he leave his family to come in Vietnam with me.'

Adam emerged from the changing room and picked out a fabric for Evelyn. When she walked out of the changing room in fisherman pants cut of a fabric printed everywhere with, 'I can only ♥ money' on a background of avocados, dice and cappuccinos, she fanned the loose fabric from her legs and said, 'I cannot help but feel as though you are being cruel.'

As they walked out of Coco's shop Evelyn said, 'Did you hear all that about his fiancé?'

'Most of it.'

'How can people be so cruel to one another?'

Evelyn took Adam to a three-walled shack for lunch. They sat on stools as high as Adam's hand was long.

'Beef noodle soup?' said Adam. 'It's thirty-eight degrees. My insides will boil my outsides.'

'Just trust me.'

She held up her chopsticks so that Adam could mimic her pose.

'Are these hot?' he said, poking around in a dish of green chillies.

'No, they're sweet like capsicums.'

Adam fumbled to pick up a slice and eventually managed to hold one for long enough to get it to his mouth. Almost immediately he took the slice out of his mouth with his fingers and was standing up and circling his tiny chair, exhaling and opening and closing his mouth. 'Water. Water. Water.'

'You need milk,' said Evelyn, laughing hysterically. 'Milk's the only thing that cools it down.'

'Milk. Milk. Milk,' he said to the chef, who had stopped chopping vegetables in order to laugh at him.

'She doesn't speak English.'

'What's the word for milk?'

'Sua.'

'Sua!' Adam yelled.

'Hm?' said the old lady.

'Sua!'

'Ser?'

'Sua!

'Ahhh, sua! OK.' She soon brought him a glass of milk. He swished half of it around his mouth and spat it into the gutter before swishing the rest of it. The worst of the burning eventually subsided.

'They're not sweet at all!'

'No, they're incredibly spicy.'

'You enjoyed that, did you?'

'Immensely.'

Sweating prolifically, Adam wiped some perspiration from the upper corner of his left eye. He had used the wrong hand. He rose again and held his hand over his eye socket. He called for more milk. The old lady rushed to splash a soup pot full of cold water over his right foot. She looked up at him, anticipating with a smile his immediate relief.

'What are you doing?'

'Left eye right foot.'

'What?'

'Left eye right foot!'

'What's milk again?'

'Sua,' said Evelyn, barely able to speak from laughter.

'Sua!' said Adam.

'What?'

'Don't start. Sua!'

'Hm?'

'*Sua!*'

'Oh, sua! OK,' and she brought him a glass whose contents he patted with his right hand onto his left eye. When he returned to his tiny seat his lunch was put in front of him and his shirt fabric felt and its pattern ridiculed.

On their way to the lantern bridge they passed a shack whereunder an old woman was running an ice block through a meat saw. It was the size of the one Adam had seen in Evelyn's greenhouse. He stood enthralled. The woman's husband collected and put the two-inch cubes into blue hessian bags. When the block was completely divided she picked up a meathook and pulled a new block over a roller belt and began working on that. She caught Adam staring at her. 'Dá,' she said.

'Da,' said Adam, repeating the sound.

'Dá,' nodded the woman.

'That's heaven.'

'You're obsessed with ice.'

'I'm not. It's just… Well…'

'Fancy a beer?' said Evelyn.

'Not that iced stuff?'

'That's the cheapest beer in the world, did you know that?'

'It tastes it.'

They sat at a restaurant looking out at the lantern bridge and watched the strolling tourists. A motorscooter crossed the bridge at speed. But for its driver slamming on its brakes the vehicle would have hit an overweight and pruney couple of Norwegians. The scooter's back wheel slid out and the lid of the yellow Styrofoam box strapped to its handlebars slid off. From this suddenly halted container an eel shot out and slapped onto the road. Obviously flustered, it writhed with desperation and excitement. The driver kicked out his scooter's stand and rushed to retrieve his fish. He bent down to grab it, only to have it squirm from his reach. When soon he did pin it down and pick it up it slithered from his hands and slapped back onto the road and wriggled with even more urgency.

'It's like it's trying to evolve on the spot,' said Adam, chuckling.

The driver, now smiling, looked at the phones and the cameras that were poised at him and laughed as he continued with growing inaccuracy to chase his panicked creature.

'That was the cheekiest grin I've ever seen,' said Adam, laughing heartily. 'He knew exactly how farcical was his situation but he had no choice but to try to pick up the eel! Oh, dear heavens.'

Evelyn smiled at how much enjoyment Adam had gotten out of the episode. He looked across at her through euphoric eyes. She was a thing too beautiful to be dressed like an idiot, though he found her all the more beautiful for it. And it was dusk. Adam momentarily lost all sense of time and place and nearly cried.

'Where *did* Dad find you?'

'In the desert,' said Adam, slowly recovering from his ecstasy.

'Oh, stop it.'

'Stop what?'

'He did not find you in the desert.'

'He did.'

'Is this like your flying boat story?'

'Part of the same story I'm afraid.' Adam recounted his excursion to the river. '…And then your dad offered me a job.'

'Well whether it's true or not they do say that all you have to do is make her laugh.'

'Make who laugh?'

'Do you know what I've never done in Hoi An?'

'What?'

Evelyn called for the bill. 'Now do me a favour and keep your head that way,' she said, pointing to their left. They walked to the bridge. The crowd had grown particularly thick. A larger than usual proportion of it consisted of Vietnamese tourists. 'Do you know what night it is tonight?'

'Wednesday?'

'That too. Look that way.'

Sitting cross-legged at the top of the bridge was a young girl monitoring the wicks of a dozen candle-lit paper lanterns set before her. 'Would you like to buy a lantern? See I speak very good English. You buy a lantern and you make a wish. Where you from?'

Evelyn kneeled down and chose one. The girl attached it to a long pole and gave it to her. She lowered it among the countless others already floating slowly downstream. 'Can I look the other way now?'

'You can look down.'

He leaned against the railing and watched her lantern drift.

'It's Buddha's mother's birthday.'

'Wow. … And you made a wish? What did you wish for?'

She smiled at him then looked off into the distance. Soon she looked back to Adam. 'You can look up now.' A full moon had risen, big and burning orange and brown over a black horizon of silhouette palm trees. 'And it came true.'

'Did it?'

'Part of it.'

'Evelyn, do you ever have the feeling that things are ordered precisely and correctly for us?'

'Go on.'

'That if you look at things in the right way, if you look hard enough and see correctly, you can only see that certain things happen in a certain order in certain places, even bad and traumatic things, and if you assemble them as they're supposed to be assembled you cannot but believe that they've been done especially for you. And that wherever you are you are exactly where you are supposed to be.'

'What ever could you be talking about?' she said, though she was teasing. Unknowingly Adam Athelstan was playing his soothing harp; and she knew exactly what he was talking about.

CHAPTER 4

1

Woken by the frequent, unmistakable, wailing of a distressed mother Adam found Paul calming a woman at his dining table.

'Ah, Adam. Rebecca, this is Adam. Rebecca, Adam's my best negotiator. Rebecca? Look at me, come on. Rebecca, this is Adam. Everything's going to be fine all right?'

'You have to get my Rachel back to me,' said the woman to neither of them. 'You have got to get her back to me. I can't do anything knowing she's disappeared. I'll do anything. I'll pay you whatever you want.'

'We will, Rebecca, calm down. We need some information first, all right? Now, when did you last hear from her?'

'Umm . . . last week. I got an email.'

'Do you still have it?'

'Yes.'

Paul told Adam to get his laptop from the kitchen bench.

'What's a laptop?'

'What's a laptop? What do you mean?'

'Lap-top?'

'Yes! On the bench.'

Adam pouted his bottom lip and brought to Paul the only unidentifiable object on the kitchen bench. Paul spun it around to face Rebecca. 'Can you bring up any emails from around when you last heard from her?'

Rebecca opened her inbox and turned the laptop to face Paul. Paul waved Adam in and they read through her correspondence.

'See that?' said Paul in a low voice. He pointed at the screen. 'Rebecca, Rachel's come to Vietnam to get away from something. Do you know what?'

'I have no idea. Really I don't. She was so happy, she's always been so happy. I thought she loved it at home.'

'Rebecca, is Rachel a generous person?'

She nodded.

'And kindhearted?'

'She's so kindhearted.'

'Rebecca, I see this all the time. People like Rachel see that they have little place in the western world. See here she talks a lot about how corrupt things are and how hopeless her future seems and about how cruel everybody is to one another. These are very common symptoms of the young people we deal with. They come here and they think it's the opposite here but that's because they live like tourists. They live in a fantasyland. Once we get talking to her, when we find her, we can make her see that in minutes. Rebecca, are you listening? If your daughter is here we'll get her back to you.'

Still unable to look Paul in the eye, Rebecca nodded.

'So she's come to Hoi An, and that's the last you heard from her, yes? No phone calls? No text messages? All right. ... My Son,' he said to Adam, his finger stopping on the screen. 'Rebecca, it says here in her last email that Rachel was thinking of going to My Son the next day. Rebecca, I think that's probably where she is.'

Rebecca started nodding manically. 'Just get her back. Please just get her back. I'll do anything. I'll pay whatever you want. Tens of thousands. I'll pay upfront now and if you get her back to me I'll give you all the money I have.'

Paul tried to calm her by embracing her hand. 'That's not necessary, Rebecca. It's our pleasure and our duty to return your daughter to her civilisation and to you. It's what I Love My Family live for. Now, I'm just going to forward these emails to myself so that Adam and I can look them over. Rebecca, will you meet me at the river tomorrow morning? Do you know where the Temple of Supreme Modesty is?'

'I'll find it.'

'Ask at your hotel. It's down by the river. Can you meet me there at seven tomorrow morning? We'll go up river to My Son and we can have her back to you by lunchtime. Doesn't that sound great?'

Rebecca Mussil rose, forlorn and fragile, from the dining table and Paul put an arm around her and escorted her to his car. He had Thuc drive her back to her hotel. Paul returned pensive to the dining room.

'There's been reports of a Tourist warlord operating out of My Son. It's probably her.'

'Paul, I want to ask you something.'

'It's been escalating for weeks. Two clans from two villages are trying to squeeze each other out of serving him, or her if it's Rachel. It'll be war soon. If that happens the army'll get involved and they'll kill her and say it was an accident.'

'Paul, might I ask you something?'

'A Tourist warlord'll make my name. This is big. Even the Vietnamese will come to me from now on.'

'Paul?'

'What?'

Now that the time had actually arrived for him to ask what he had spent that morning working himself up to be able to ask, Adam froze. He stared at this unsuspecting father until saying, in one loudly blurted sentence, 'I want to ask Evelyn to marry me.'

Eventually Paul snapped out of thinking about the glory this Tourist warlord might bring and said, 'Hm?'

'I want to ask Evelyn to marry me.'

'Ergh. I knew this would happen.'

'Did you?'

'Evelyn's shy and reserved and delicate. She's mute around people she doesn't know. She spends most of her days with her flowers. I've never seen her react to anybody the way she reacted to you. You haven't asked her yet have you?'

'I would never think of doing so before asking you.'

'And what do you think she'll say?'

'I haven't a clue. But I have to ask her. I have this sudden and overwhelming certainty that it's imperative for me to do so.'

'Sudden certainty? I don't like the sound of that. Are you sure it'll last? It's not just you wanting some?'

'If it's what I think it is then it has to last.'

'Love?'

'Love.'

Paul stared scornfully at Adam. 'If she says yes then I suppose it's foolishness to say no.'

Adam offered up his hand to be shaken. Beholding what might very soon be his son-in-law, Paul was unimpressed, disappointed, and quite baffled. Eventually he shook Adam's hand. 'We'll go out to My Son tomorrow by boat. But that means we have to do somebody a favour first.'

4:2

'It's a complicated country,' said Jonathan.

The pair of them waiting on the lantern bridge, Jonathan was perfectly comfortable in the tourist livery of singlet, shorts and thongs which so appalled Adam. Jonathan had been for some time warning Adam of the evening ahead.

'Reputation and honour and face and things like that mean a lot to them. I hate it when Dad makes me do this.'

'How bad can it be?' said Adam. 'I mean I have always felt that night is a time for quiet reflection. And I do like to stay in past nine. I certainly wouldn't think of going out if I was still in at nine. But how bad can it be? Hoi An seems like such a peaceful place.'

A motorcycle sprung forth from the crowd and drove momentarily at Jonathan before halting two inches from Adam's feet. 'Ho, Jonathan! Fuck you!' said its driver. 'Who you? My name Mun.'

This round-faced whirlwind dismounted and pulled his black t-shirt down over his sagging globular belly. He spun a silver chain around his wrist. He had on his enormous melting jube of a head a dark blue baseball cap embroidered with the red words, 'Can't Stop Won't Stop.' His teeth were discordant – no two ran in the same direction – and most clashed with their neighbours for space in his reeking and eternally open mouth.

Jonathan was instantly tired of him. 'Mun, this is Adam.'

'Adam. Fuck you! Ha ha ha. Joking. My name Mun.'

Mun's head darted furtively from one end of the bridge to the other then down to check the phone in his hand. 'OK. We start?'

'Start what?'

'You get tourist come to bar.'

'Mun, you know I hate doing that,' said Jonathan, almost pleading. 'We're not doing that. You can do that. We'll go and wait at the bar.'

He mumbled softly: 'OK. I get motorbike for you.' His voice bounced loudly through the air as he yelled in Vietnamese to one end of the bridge. Then he relented and returned to his soft mumble: 'OK you go he take you.'

Jonathan and Adam went to a delinquent young man who was leaning forward on the handlebars of a motorbike.

'You want boom boom?'

'No.'

'OK. You go Why Not bar?'

'Yes.'

'OK I take you.'

Jonathan addressed the youth as though he were talking to a small child. 'For free, yes? We're with Mun.'

'Yes.'

'No money?'

'Yes!'

They straddled the motorbike and shuffled forward. Adam was hit by the fetor of tropical labour and they were conveyed swiftly to the eastern limit of the old town.

In the centre of a short street dozens of motorbikes cluttered the footpath. Their Vietnamese owners loitered about the kerbsides and glared out of the wooden restaurant opposite Why Not Bar.

In Hoi An only two places of revelry are open past midnight. One is five kilometres out of town and a fish market patronised by the fishermen and women of whom it stinks. One wades through puddles of blood and seawater to get a beer and sits on tiny stools to watch American films among an unhandsome assembly of village idiots and midget layabouts. The other is Why Not Bar. This den of a place is mentioned in most of the guidebooks and so eagerly attended by the recently-arrived tourists who live by them. By anybody who has been in Hoi An for three nights it is avoided as a source of embarrassment and as a temptation to backsliding. By all who have remained in Hoi An for any longer than that it is disparaged and lamented as the epitome of all that has gone and is going and will go wrong with the westernisation of this archaically stubborn country.

'Eighty thousand OK,' said the delinquent.

'You said no money,' said Jonathan, familiar with and impatient of this process.

'I drive you. You pay.'

'You said no money.'

'I very poor. Work hard. Bring you. For petrol in motorbike. How I pay?'

'We're not paying you.'

He· spoke calmly to the oafish gaggle who were all of overbearing dispositions. A few of them took two steps towards Adam and Jonathan.

'We know Mun. Mun told you to bring us here.'

'You know Mun.' The name-drop failed to impress him. 'Eighty thousand.'

Jonathan extracted the money from his wallet and the irate urchin pocketed it and sped off around the corner.

The window beside Why Not Bar's sliding glass door was stickered large with the phrase, 'Girls No Top No Pay.' A small pillared temple, smoking with incense and offering up a mango and five teacups of rice wine, obscured its other window. Neon lights barely illuminated its interior. Its walls were covered with the chaotic graffiti of a thousand drunken teenage tourists. A mirror-backed bar was manned by two Frenchmen and the topless and emaciated hunchback of a bar owner. A doorway led to a second room and a pool table, a staircase to the second floor and a pool table. The only other person in the bar was a middle-aged knock-kneed Frenchman standing in cut-off denim shorts at a laptop, swaying to the diva ballads of his own choosing.

Jonathan ordered two beers.

Adam inspected his surroundings with rising horror. 'Why do we have to come here again?'

'Mun works for Why Not Bar. And Mun owns the boat that Dad needs to take up the river tomorrow. Mun charges him to use the boat, but he won't let him use it at all unless he gives him something else in return. That something else is the appearance of having Western friends. And I'm the only westerner he has commercial access to.'

'Oh.'

'He'll be in here in an hour and he'll want us to talk to him in front of the tourists and in front of the thugs outside, and he'll want us to get him a girl.'

'Get him one?'

'Yes.'

'In what capacity?'

'In *that* capacity.'

They went upstairs and sat on the bamboo stools on the

balcony which overlooked the street. Tourist-bearing motorbikes began to arrive in swarms. The mobile youth of the world ascended the two steps which elevated them, ecstatic and unsuspecting, to Why Not Bar. The music soon changed from the Frenchman's awful ballads to the electronic pollution of which Adam had already heard so much. Thirteen Australians in singlets started a pool game behind them; immediately they began bawling and chanting. One of them took to yelling expletives in Adam's ear each time a ball was pocketed. Beer splashed intermittently onto Adam's neck. 'Downstairs is worse,' said Jonathan. 'Trust me, downstairs is worse. Just ignore them.'

'Would you excuse me?'

'Where are you going?'

'I have to use the lavatory.'

'Don't.'

'Why not?'

'Especially not in thongs.'

'But I really do have to use the lavatory.'

'Honestly.'

'What? How bad can it be?'

'It's next to the pool table. I warned you.'

Adam shimmied along the wall and pushed with his index finger at the rattan bathroom door. Immediately fluid ran over the top of his right thong and lubricated his foot. He lifted his left off the ground and then saw the sink. It was filled with crimson vomit. He returned his left foot to the dry ground from which he had raised it and turned around.

'Ho, Adam! Fuck you! Where Jonathan?'

Adam pointed to the balcony.

Mun screamed Jonathan's name and waved him over. 'We go downstair. You want drink? You buy me.'

'Just beer,' said Jonathan.

'No.' Mun leaned across the bar and yelled into the ear of one of the Italians. Three shots were poured at the bar and the glasses crossed with lemon wedges. 'You pay,' he said to Jonathan.

Mun handed Adam a shot glass. 'What's this?'

'This tequila.'

'What's tequila?'

'Tequila very nice. Make you happy.'

'Oh,' said Adam, quite looking forward to the stuff.

Mun licked the back of his hand then downed the shot and bit a lemon wedge. Jonathan did the same and so Adam followed. As soon as the liquid hit the floor of his mouth he sprayed it onto the floor of the bar. 'It is not at all very nice.'

'Make you so drunk!' said Mun and slapped Adam on the back.

They inched their way across the dancefloor. Oblivious girls were bobbing up and down and undulating their hips atop the pool table. Elated boys stood behind most of them. The Great Heathen Army had overrun the inside of the bar and were encamping on the street.

Mun studied the crowd from the kerb. 'You find me girl.'

'What kind of girl?' said Jonathan, extremely weary.

'Western girl. But not English girl. I have English girlfriend.'

'You have an English girlfriend?'

Mun spoke in a hastening crescendo of excitement. 'Yeah but she in England. We meet here. I get her drunk, take her to beach, but she fuck me first! You watch this.'

He handed Adam his beer and went into the restaurant. When shortly he returned he had two long strips of toilet paper. He waited behind a pair of tall tourists until one of them leaned onto his toes, when he inserted one end of the combustible between his heel and the rubber of his thong; he waited until the other tourist gave him a chance to do the same. Then he called out in Vietnamese and waited for a sufficient number of his colleagues to be watching before igniting the paper. Shortly the first tourist felt a discomfort at the back of his foot and turned around to investigate its source. The second tourist, soon laughing at the panic with which his friend was trying to rid himself of a blaze, gave an identical performance. Holding their bellies and pointing, the Vietnamese bent backwards with laughter.

'Tourists so stupid,' said Mun. 'You how long you stay Hoi An?'

'I'm not sure yet,' said Adam. 'I think I just moved here.'

'OK. You have girlfriend?'

'Do I have a girlfriend?'

'You gay?' he said, then chuckled.

'Mun,' said Jonathan, and shook his head.

'Tell you last night I work here. Two girl from Norway they

come, I bring them Why Not Bar. They party then they finish, they come out and want taxi to home. I take them home. One go inside. One, she...' (Knowing no variation of the word 'vomit' he supplemented his narration by poking his tongue out and thrusting his head forward.) 'Then...' He paused for effect. 'I kiss her. Ha ha ha.'

'Mun, that's disgusting.'

'No, not disgusting. Funny. Oo, see her?' He pointed to a short Vietnamese girl in the bar's uniform. 'She my sister.' He whacked Adam in the stomach. 'You like her?'

'I've never met her,' said Adam.

'You want to meet her?'

'What for?'

'Anything you want.'

'Mun, you're taking Dad on the boat tomorrow?'

'Tomorrow I take you father on the boat.'

'Adam's coming with you.'

'You come?' A heavyset girl, drunkenly making her way across the drunken encampment, was intercepted. 'Where you from?'

'Denmark,' she said impatiently.

'God dag. See I know Danish. These my friends.'

'This is Mun,' said Jonathan, hoping a belated introduction might count as his mandatory contribution to Mun's imaginary sex life.

'These my friends. What your name?'

'Julia.'

'Julia, my name Mun.'

'Mun?'

'Yes, Mun. Where you go now?'

'I'm looking for my friend.'

'You want to dance?'

'Thank you but I have to find my friend.'

'You dance with me. I rock you body.'

She laughed. 'Maybe later.'

'No, we dance now!' said Mun gaily. He put his hands on her flabby waist. 'Come on, I make you feel so good dancing.'

'No, thank you. Really I have to find my friend. She is looking for me.'

'We dance. Find her later. Then I have room for us.' He moved another step in and tried to sway the girl's hips. She put a knee to his crotch and promptly walked on. He doubled over and chuckled. 'She want to fuck me, but…' and he left the sentence incomplete.

Two people walked hand-in-hand out of the bar and set off up the street. Mun spotted them and became suddenly alert and quite stern.

'Where you go?' He went after them. 'Where you go now? You fuck here. … I have room for you. You fuck here. Where you go?'

The hot heaving mass of long singlets, purple baseball caps and sunglasses in the evening, of mascara from the climate running, new sun dresses and slurring femininity, had begun to waver. Some of it had realised their mistake in staying at Why Not Bar for too long and were deserting. Some of it was tired from a long day of touristing in a very foreign climate and were sitting on the gutter. A great deal more if it was too drunk to stand and were reclining in the silt of the street.

A young English girl tugged at Adam's shorts. 'Do you know where I can get some weed from?'

'What?'

'Do you know,' she said, a great deal more slowly, 'where I can get some weed from?'

'No I don't. Why would you want a weed at this time of night?'

'To smoke.'

'To smoke? Oh that again. No. I don't know whence you might procure some weed.'

'Dickhead,' said the girl and pushed innacurately at his knee.

'Adam if you ever want to quit working for Dad my school always needs English teachers.'

'Where *you* go now?' yelled Mun, another departing couple passing him on his way back to Adam and Jonathan. 'You fuck here. I have room for you! Where you go?! You fuck here!'

'I'm not sure that you could teach these people English.'

'Adam!' said a very jolly Mun, 'You fuck your girlfriend condom or no condom?'

Adam looked at Jonathan with abhorrent disbelief. It was the same look which had distorted his face when he was told about the larvae of the epomis beetle, when first he had read about the ineluctable extinction of the honeybee, when informed of Jacob's detestation of butterflies. 'Mun, I really do not care for the questions you're asking me. They are unspeakably vulgar and I will thank you very much to stop asking them.'

'What?'

'Stop asking him questions, Mun. He's not a tourist.'

'Oh, OK. You want more beer?'

'No, thank you.'

'OK I get one. You want snake wine?'

'No.'

Adam looked at the dirty street beneath him. He was utterly exhausted, as though all vitality had been extracted from him by some malevolent spirit.

'You're going to ask my sister to marry you?'

'Hm?'

'You're going to ask my sister to marry you?'

'I got your father's permission today.'

'Be good to her.'

'Absolutely.'

'I love you.'

'What?'

'Nothing. No, I don't know. I'm very drunk. But if you're going to marry Evelyn then I love you as my own soul. It makes me very… Her happiness makes me happiness. Makes me happy. Sorry. Tequila.'

CHAPTER 5

1

Adam and Paul found Rebecca Mussil waiting anxiously at the riverside entrance to the Temple of Supreme Modesty. A red obelisk, diseased with ornament as a stick of processed cheese by mould, this local-cherished and tourist-ignored construction was protected by four fiercely camp dragons carved at attention over its plinth. Its wide base, flaring at its corners with shining white swirls of stone, was fenced off beside a rarely manned wooden ticket booth and a parking lot for motorscooters.

Paul wished Rebecca a good morning. She nodded behind huge dark sunglasses.

'Ho! You know her?' Mun's head was bobbing at the river's edge among banana palms.

'Good morning, Mun,' said Paul, not bothering to conceal his immediate tiredness.

'You know this man?' said Rebecca, suddenly shocked.

'Mun? Mun's taking us up the river.'

'You keep him from me.'

'Mun, what have you done?'

'What I do?'

'What's he been saying?'

'I say nothing! But I think she no like me. She shy.'

'Mun, you leave Mrs Mussil alone. Mun? You leave her alone. All right?'

Mun closed his eyes and accepted Paul's limitation with a nod.

'Does he need to apologise?'

'No, it's fine.'

'Mun, apologise.'

'What!?'

'Say sorry.'

'Sorry you,' he grumbled, and Paul stepped down onto the boat and offered Rebecca his hand.

Mun's vessel had a long and thin hull. Attached to its steeply rising prow was a towering bamboo trawling frame draped with reeking fishing nets. A few car tyres were tied in pairs at the gunwales to protect it from knocks. A Vietnamese flag flew astern from a high pole. A third of its deckspace was taken up by a shoddily erected cabin guarded by a white door stolen from the bathroom of a foreigner's house by Mun's favourite uncle. A small table and simple wooden chair rested outside the cabin door. A short wooden bench ran along both sides of the deckspace. A ramshackle canopy allowed him to walk upright on deck almost until the cabin; the foreigners had to stoop everywhere but beside the trawling frame.

The Thu Bon river—unlike the Mekong, whose name intimates jungle-shored tributaries and inundations of fertility, or the Perfume, down whose stream at burning sunset the more romantic tourists picture tranquil shoals of lily blossom scenting the air, or even the Red, which through unfamiliarity remains pregnant with the romance of the oriental and forbidding north—is not very interesting. Unscenic, infertile and overprone to flooding, it has traditionally been viewed as a hindrance to communication, to transport, to prosperity. In the late eighteenth century the river mouth silted up entirely; forty years later a Nguyen Emperor took a short break from executing as corrupters of the hearts of men missionaries in order to forbid European ships from making landfall anywhere other than at Da Nang. So for a century and a half Hoi An and its Thu Bon were left to their own private tranquility. Bridges are still notoriously difficult to found in its infirm bed of silt and sand. Today it is used primarily as a latrine and as the cheapest means by which very remote rice farmers might conduct their produce to more gluttonous markets.

As it reaches Hoi An its wide sandy banks are shaded beneath a wild mesh of conifers. The water is a dull and sickly green. To the southwest two brief and unlofty mountain ranges are a constant companion. Sitting on the gunwales with his feet on the bench, Adam put his head towards the sun and let the hot breeze run through his hair. He almost smiled. Then he sniffed and caught the stench of festering seafood and opened his eyes. They were passing the fish market, unpeopled and at rest for the day. He heard nothing but the violent, thunderous spluttering of the engine until the river bent southwards and the wind bore most of the racket away.

Mun had been waiting all night and all morning for somebody to brag to. He chose Adam, and spoke at him. 'This Danish girl she dance with me. You 'member? I call her Melons,. She slap me.' He wheezed out a few excited chuckles. 'Then I say sorry. Dance more, then I touch her melons. She slap me. Ha ha ha. I say sorry. I very drunk but I like you. Soon, dancing, dancing, dancing, and she let me put fingers!'

Adam was being attacked by his first hangover. He had neither the energy to reprove nor to condemn.

Mun, crouched in the cabin with his hand on the rudder of the outboard motor (which was mounted inboard), was looking out past the trawling frame in order to navigate. He was the first to break the long vocal silence. 'Rebecca!'

The fourth time he called her name it became too obviously impolite for her to go on ignoring him. 'Yes?'

'You have husband?'

'Leave her alone, Mun,' said Paul.

'You have husband? I look for wife.'

Rebecca scratched the back of her head and crossed her arms and looked away.

'I be good husband. Loyal me. You look like good wife. Very nice face.'

'Mun!' said Paul, and Mun, chuckling, relented.

They shared the river only with the occasional sand barge. The sky was an intense baby blue, bursting in places with small clusters of cloud like fluffed-out balls of cotton. They passed the first pair of bridges – long, high and concrete. The shore was littered with heavy machinery still among mounds of sand. A few long boats with canopies of bright corrugated iron, low in the water, were moored at the river bend.

Paul crossed the deck to sit beside Mrs Mussil. 'Ummm,' he said, knowing that he was about to attempt to tread through what might very well be a delicate subject. He spoke quietly. 'We do need to know everything that we should know about Rachel's life, so I am going to ask you, is there a Mr Mussil?'

'There is not. I am Miss Mussil. Divorced.'

'Divorced?'

'Yes.'

'Under what circumstances exactly?'

'He left me.'

'I'm sorry. When?'

'Six years ago.'

'Your husband leave you?!' said Mun. 'I no leave you. I good husband. Treat you nice. *Very* nice.'

'Mun!' Mun smiled at Paul and nodded. Rebecca's revelation had greatly excited him.

'He cheat on you? I no cheat on you never. Mun make good husband. You want marry me?'

'Mun, shut, up!'

'No, he's right. My husband cheated on me. But I don't blame him. He was virile and gracious. Adam reminds me a lot of him. Quietly spoken, diffident. But I know what's underneath.'

'What's underneath?' said Paul.

'Hot raging passion.'

Paul looked across the deck at his impending son-in-law. Adam dismissed Rachel's characterisation with a frantic shake of his head.

'I think if anybody on this boat would be considered virile it would probably be me,' said Paul.

Came from the darkness of the cabin, 'Rebecca, you like sex no condom or sex yes condom?'

They unanimously ignored him.

'Adam's about to propose to my daughter.'

'Congratulations. *She's* a very lucky girl. You be good to her.'

Adam nodded.

'My wife cheated on me as well,' said Paul.

'I'm sorry.'

'She went on holiday without me, I had to stay home for work and to look after the kids. She met someone while she was there and she never came home.'

'How can people be so cruel to one another?' said Rebecca.

'I've been alone ever since.'

They were motoring along a low panorama of sparsely tended land – thin strips of elevated vine, of herb, of corn and wheat. Soon the river narrowed and the banks became thicker with tall vegetation. Conifers were brightened by smothering creepers and clusters of bamboo hung over the water like fishing poles. Lone fishermen in rice hats pottered about circles of shaded lilypad in their tiny sampans. Then the flow of the river dwindled until between wide shores Mun had to negotiate through a succession of narrow streams which joined shallow brown lakes. The mountains disappeared behind the trees and power lines and transmission towers became the skyline. The long dry banks were littered with debris and rubble. The grass and the weeds that had begun to overgrow the exposed bed were strung with tattered yellow-stained clothing and sun-bleached plastic packaging.

When soon the river returned to a steady flow Mun said that he was tired. 'I look so hard for so long time. Time for brunch.'

'Brunch?' said Paul.

'Yes. You no think I know brunch. I speak English good. Brunch breakfast and lunch together.'

'Brunch *is* breakfast,' said Adam, 'and lunch together.'

'That's what I say!'

'That's what you said.'

'You no make sense.' Mun pulled in at a high and long bamboo dock, its stilts almost entirely exposed, and had Adam moor the boat. They walked over a series of ponds crammed with paddling ducklings. At the top of a steep dirt path Mun began shouting in Vietnamese. He led them down the street to a shack where an elderly woman grinned and said, 'Hello,' repeatedly. They took up half the tiny stools which were the place's seating. Their knees were higher than the table top. All except Mun writhed to get as close in as they could. Rebecca turned her body so that her legs rested against Adam's. 'Cosy, isn't it?' The restaurateur busied herself at her preparation surface of a freshly hosed concrete floor. She soon brought out bowls of beef noodle soup to the roadside.

'So you're sure you're going to get my Rachel back to me today?'

'I'm sure,' said Paul, answering a question that was obviously directed at Adam. 'You and I will stay back from the complex to avoid detection. We don't really know how many people Rachel might have working for her, or how loyal they are to her, or how intolerant they are of intruders. Adam will go in, and he'll be miked, so we can listen to the whole thing.'

'You must be so brave.'

'Why?' said Adam.

'It sounds so dangerous.'

'Does it? Paul, is this dangerous?'

'No, no, it's not dangerous. Or it shouldn't be. My source tells me it's a friendly operation. If you get kidnapped they'll just try to sell you things.'

'If I get kidnapped, Paul? I don't–'

'It's not *really* kidnapping. It's like being cornered by a saleswomen in a clothing store. But cornered for a long time. And by a lot of saleswomen. But I'll keep your money before you go in so you won't be able to buy a thing from them. They should let you go if they know you don't have any money.'

Mun said, 'Now you pay,' to Paul. They were farewelled with

the biggest grin the old lady had yet given. They crossed back over the duckling farm and Mun said, 'Shit.'

'What?'

'Flat tyre.'

'What is?'

'Boat have flat tyre.'

'How can a boat have a flat tyre you idiot?'

Mun kicked one of the car tyres which hung uselessly over the bow. 'Flat tyre boat no work.'

'Of course it does,' said Paul.

'No, look.' Mun stepped aboard and went into the cabin and tried to start the engine. It wheezed and revved but would not click over. 'See,' he said, re-emerging. 'I come back soon.' He walked back up to the roadside.

Soon he returned with a small young man laughing behind him. A wide-brimmed floppy hat with a white rose sewn into its side bounced as this imp strode down the bamboo dock, fully swinging both arms. He had a puncture repair kit in one hand, a bicycle pump in the other and an inner tube slung over his shoulder.

'You want fix this or you want fix this?' He stank of beer.

'I don't know,' said Paul. 'Just fix it. Mun?'

'What?'

'What's he on about?'

'You use this, maybe tyre go flat again, then boat stop. But is cheaper. You use this is better.'

'Well you decide.'

'What?'

'You choose.'

'Is up to you. You must pay. But I think this better. Is safer. We no want to have to stop again because flat tyre.'

Paul handed the little man his asked price of the equivalent, for foreigners, of two nights of four-star accommodation.

'For you,' he said, beaming.

'No, for you,' said Paul.

'Yes, this for you. And money you and money you.'

'You want us to pay per person?'

He nodded and pointed again at all three of them.

'Mun, this doesn't make sense, mate.'

'He only can fix. He have tools. You want to keep going on the boat? We find Rebecca you daughter.'

Paul parted with the rest of the money and the little man inflated the inner tube and then checked it for leaks. When satisfied that it had none he deflated it and inserted it into the dangling tyre. He pumped it up and slapped it and yelled to Mun. Mun went into the cabin and the motor started without delay. 'See!'

Mun kept to the shaded side of the river. In the cool Adam turned his face to the breeze and closed his eyes. He had not been on a boat since Noah's party, he reflected, and this was a great deal more pleasant than spending an evening with that raucous lot. He smiled and breathed deeply just as a heavy cloud of pestilent diesel smoke passed over him. His eyes opened and he coughed and spluttered with his fist at his mouth.

'Adam!' yelled Mun. 'What your favourite country? Mine Norway.'

'I've never been to Norway.'

'Me too.'

'You've never been?'

'No.'

'Then how is it your favourite country?'

'Girls very nice.'

'Oh.'

'Good also is New Zealand. But very ugly. You been with Africa? Black lady?'

Adam gave no response and as was his intention the discussion fizzled. The trees came to an end on both banks as the river widened and deepened. The mountain range loomed again and rice fields dotted with palm trees became their foreground. A long and low barge glided slowly and loudly downriver.

Rebecca sat very closely beside Adam. 'So when I've got Rachel back do you think there's any reason we should stick around in Hoi An for a little while?'

'It's a nice enough town. Worth seeing. The beach is quite nice. Just make sure you're in your hotel though by eleven. It's quite a horrible place late at night.'

'You're not thinking you'll want to get some more of your bucket list out of the way before you get engaged?'

'My what?'

'Your bucket list.'

'Who has a list of buckets?'

'*And* you're funny. We call *these* fuck-it lists. Does a forty-eight year old make an appearance anywhere on yours?'

'On my what?'

'On your fuck-it list.'

'If you're thinking of sticking around, Rebecca' said Paul from the other side of the boat, 'maybe I could take you out to dinner. There's an *incredible* Vietnamese restaurant in the old town. One of the best meals you'll ever eat. Honestly.'

'Yes, I think we should all go out to celebrate. I'm sure Rachel will love Adam.'

Soon Mun yelled, 'We here!' and he turned the boat until it was perpendicular to the current and he ran it aground. Paul jumped off and anchored them to the sand. Rebecca pretended not to see Paul's outstretched arms and waited until Adam was on shore to ask him if he could help her down. She leaped into his arms and held her face awkwardly close to his.

'You catch me? Ha ha ha,' said Mun to Adam. He jumped onto the sand and toppled forward. His shirt came up over his head and his face scraped the sand. When he regained his composure he said, 'OK, How long you be?'

'An hour.'

'OK I wait.'

Paul, Adam and Rebecca strode up the overgrown embankment and crossed a one-lane road to a field of sandy grassland. They followed a barely discernible path the width of a foot. They walked among slender fields, a yellow and green patchwork of rows of seedling and flourishing herb and fallow. A tiny corrugated iron shack stood on wonky bamboo stilts at the end of a long lake. They came to a church – a gaudy blue and white building with a four-columned façade at the centre of which rested a statue of St. Anthony of Padua in a niche above a painting of Christ in the firmament. Inevitably Adam lagged behind. The adjacent field, hedged by a row of high coconut palms, was half of weed and grass and half of bog. Three water buffaloes were immersed in it, shaking their smiling heads.

Paul and Rebecca neared the cover of the tree line and turned back to find Adam standing still a hundred metres behind them, lost in gawking at the church's white-striped architrave. Its ends supported a statue of a winged Virgin and the Archangel Michael dressed as Superman. A recording of pealing bells blasted from speakers on the church roof. The palm trees were dancing in the hot wind and the buffalo tails swishing. Adam was called to. His face dripping with sweat, he uncraned his neck and ambled to the envelopment of the elephant grass and the edge of the jungle whose unfathomable darknesses surrounded the My Son ruins.

5:2

The canopy enclosed them. There was no visible path. Paul, at the head of the trio and the only one who had before walked in jungle, trod in big, high steps. Rebecca watched his feet and tried to match his footsteps. In the coolless shade Paul monitored their location on a GPS tracker. A tree infested with deafening cicadas temporarily drowned out the noise of the hundreds of the other insects ticking and creaking and walloping around them. Bird calls sounded their myriad hoops and hollers from every direction; some of them might have been monkey calls. Paul was unfamiliar with the local fauna.

'Adam,' said Rebecca. 'Would you go ahead of me? I'm going to close my eyes and put a hand on your shoulder. If I see a snake I'll have to scream and run away. Is that all right?'

'Oh. Well, if you must.'

He stepped ahead of her and she put a hand on his shoulder. Soon she reached her index finger across and gave a single stroke of it to his neck. She squeezed the muscles of his shoulder as though she were massaging.

'Paul, how far is it until we're there?' said Adam.

'It's just that clearing up there. ... Are you ready?'

'Quite.'

Paul miked Adam and wished him good luck. 'We'll stay here and listen to the whole thing. Now listen. Do you see that path? There through the trees? It turns right up ahead. Do you see it? Follow that for fifty metres and you'll be in the jungle directly east of the ruins. Rachel should be in there. Now, on your way into her there'll be women trying to sell you things. Ignore them. Ignore them completely. They're extremely cunning. Anything you say they'll have heard before and they'll have an answer to it. Now, Adam, if you reach the tourist warlord –'

'*If* I reach them?'

'When. When you reach the tourist warlord, and it's not Rebecca's daughter, if it's not Rachel you leave immediately, all right? Just turn around and walk straight back out. Don't run. They respond very badly to panic.'

'Adam, you're so brave.'

'We'll see,' said Paul. 'And if you find any Vietnamese men guarding her, slay them and bring me their foreskins.'

'What?'

'I'm joking, Adam. Good luck.'

Miss Mussil, overwhelmed by Adam's upcoming bravery, stepped in and kissed him on the cheek. Adam thought he felt her tongue.

And with a pat on the back Paul set Adam on his way. He plugged two sets of headphones into his receiver and gradually sidled up to Rebecca before putting a set in her ears for her.

Adam turned with the path and was shortly alone in the jungle. Instantly it seemed darker and more sinister. The roots of the banyan trees appeared as the melting lips of a wailing spirit calling out between the branches and the jungle floor. The sipo matador vines climbing the agarwoods looked as though they might snatch him by the ankles and have him upside down; the nameless trees hiding places for naked archers with vicious superstitions about white people.

His pace slowed to a wary prowl until he saw among the innumerable leaves two eyes, when it stopped. He turned his head to the other side of the path and saw another set. Now nervous, he looked straight ahead and walked slowly. He turned his gaze again and spied two more eyes, then two more, until onto the path ahead a short woman, dressed in cotton pyjamas with polyester gloves up to her elbows and polyester socks under her sandals and with a floppy hat turned up at the front, stepped. She had a large plastic colander of knick-knacks hanging from her neck. He was intent on heeding Paul's warning; he would push the woman aside if he had to. He walked on.

A smile suddenly beamed across her face. 'Where you from?' she said, in a very sweet tone.

Adam thought the question harmless enough. He slowed in order to keep his distance and answered suspiciously, 'Australia.'

'Melbourne or Sydney?'

'Melbourne,' he said, quite surprised that she had so easily narrowed it down.

'I live Melbourne two year ago.'

'Oh, did you?' He had reached the woman. She stepped to the edge of the path and Adam walked on without breaking step. The woman wound her ankles around the scrub as she kept pace with him.

'Yes. I live in Richmond.'

'Oh. There are a lot of Vietnamese people there.'

'Many Vietnamese people in Richmond.'

'Yes.'

'You stay Hoi An?'

'I am.' She seemed omniscient.

'How long you stay Hoi An?'

'I don't know yet. '

'Hoi An very nice.'

'Yes, it is rather.'

'You buy something?' And there it was. She began pulling things out of her basket and offering them to Adam. She flung open a book of fading postcards, a wooden dragonfly which balanced on the tip of her index finger. 'Tiger balm?' she said, showing him the contents of one of her small tins. Adam shut his mouth and hurried forward. 'Look, bracelet. You have girlfriend? Very nice bracelet. Two for five dollar. Happy hour.'

Ahead of him another woman stepped from the wilderness into his path. Her pyjama top was a lighter pink than the first lady's; where the first lady's trousers were red with daisies hers were blue with ducks. She wore a rice hat rather than a floppy one but her gloves and her high socks and sandals were the same.

'Where you from?' said the new lady, advancing.

'Australia,' said Adam, reaching the woman, who walked on his other side.

'Melbourne or Sydney?'

'Melbourne.'

'I live Melbourne two year ago.'

'Oh, so did she.'

'Yes, I live in Richmond.'

'Ah, so did she. You don't know each other?'

'Many Vietnamese people in Richmond.'

'Yes, they do.'

'You stay Hoi An?'

Another lady marched from the thicket and walked a step ahead of the first.

'Where you from?'

'Australia,' said the first lady, answering for him.

'Melbourne or Sydney?'

'You buy something?' said the second lady.

'You buy something?' said the third, skipping ahead in her catechism.

'You buy tiger balm?'

Two more ladies stepped onto the path and scurried from behind to pull at the hem of Adam's shirt. He turned around.

'Where you from?'

'Hello, you buy something?'

'No, I haven't got any money.'

'Very cheap.'

'Yes but, honestly, I don't have a cent on me.'

'Please you help me. I have baby.'

'You look me sell. Very cheap. Happy hour.'

'It's not–. What time is it? It can't be happy hour. We're–. No. We're in the jungle.'

'Excuse me sir.'

'You buy tiger balm?'

'You have girlfriend. Look bracelet. Very pretty.'

'You handsome boy.'

'Yes. Thank you.'

'You buy peanut? Happy hour.'

'Where you go now?'

'I'm looking for somebody.'

'Where you from?'

'Excuse me sir.'

'You buy tiger balm?'

The density of the two dozen women now following him through the jungle kept him from walking at the brisk pace which he felt might give them a hint that he was interested in something other than buying something. Overtaking one another, then falling back, then pushing forward to overtake again, the women bore him along the path. Then a male voice yelled quickly and briefly in Vietnamese. The women dropped into their baskets whatever they had been proffering and whipped back into the cover of the vegetation.

A small man in pleated beige trousers walked towards Adam. He smiled and called out, 'Hello.'

'Hello,' said Adam, softly.

'I am very sorry about those woman. It is the jungle. There are many dangers.' He wore leather sandals and a white shirt. 'May I ask where you are going?'

Adam ignored his question. When they had reached one another and the man turned to walk beside Adam he asked again, 'And may I ask where you are going?'

'I'm looking for somebody.'

'Who?'

'I'd rather not say.'

'You are looking for ruins of My Son?'

Adam said nothing.

'Then you are almost going the right way. But, please, I will show you where they are.'

'No, really. That's all right. I've been instructed to follow this path until I find… what I'm looking for.'

'But this path does not lead anywhere. It leads back to Thu Bon river. There are many dangers at the river. Are you afraid of snakes?'

'Yes.'

'Just up ahead on this path is the nest of a jungle snake. They like water and shelter, and just ahead is the river and before the river, shelter, where one thousand snakes are babies.'

'Oh.'

'And you are scared of snakes. Please, you come with me. I will take you to where you are looking for. I don't want any money.'

'Are you sure you don't want any money? I really don't have any. I didn't bring my wallet. You're not selling anything?'

'Look at me. What could I be selling? My clothe? Ha ha ha.'

Following the man's outstretched arm Adam veered onto another barely discernible path.

'Where are you from?'

Adam hesitated to answer. But the man's face was kindly enough and he was not selling anything. 'Australia.'

'Melbourne or Sydney?'

'Melbourne.'

'I live in Melbourne two years ago.'

An unsurprising claim. 'Did you?'

'Yes. There many Vietnamese people in Melbourne.'

'There are, yes.'

'What your name?'

'Adam.'

'My name Vinh.'

'Vinh?'

'Yes. And here we are.'

On the side of the path, ensconced in dripping leaf and shining vine, was a small wooden booth, painted brown. 'Here is World Heritage Ancient Cham ruins of the My Son Temples.' He pointed out the construction to Adam.

'Here?'

A man was sitting inside the booth, smoking a cigarette. 'You go My Son ruins?'

'Yes.'

'Twenty dollar.'

'Oh. No, I don't have any money.'

'What?'

'I don't have any money.'

Vinh saw that Adam was being serious. '*No* money?'

'None at all. I told you I didn't have any money. I don't have my wallet on me.'

'Ahhh, I thought you joking. Australia very rich place. Vietnam very poor. But you cannot visit World Heritage Ancient Cham ruins of the My Son Temples without a ticket.'

'I don't want to visit the ruins. I'm looking for somebody.'

'Somebody who is at World Heritage Ancient Cham ruins of the My Son Temples?'

'She's near them. Behind them, I think.'

'Yes, is all the same jungle. You must buy a ticket.'

'Ticket for World Heritage Ancient Cham ruins of the My Son Temples twenty dollars,' said the man in the booth.

'But really, I don't have any money at all.'

'Oh, maybe this will be a problem if you want to see World Heritage Ancient Cham ruins of the My Son Temples.'

'I don't want to see them. I want to find somebody.'

'Yes, who is in World Heritage Ancient Cham ruins of the My Son Temples.'

The man in the booth said something in Vietnamese, leaned out of his booth, looked Adam up and down, and then said something else.

'Your shoes very nice.'

'Thank you.'

'He will take them and you won't have to buy ticket for World Heritage Ancient Cham ruins of the My Son Temples.'

'I don't want to buy a ticket.'

'Then you cannot see World Heritage Ancient Cham ruins of the My Son Temples.'

'I don't want to see them.'

'But you want to find your friend.'

'She's not my friend. I'm just looking for her.'

'At World Heritage Ancient Cham ruins of the My Son Temples.'

'Ticket twenty dollar.'

'And you want my shoes?'

'If you cannot buy a ticket you must pay something. What about one shoe?'

'One shoe?'

'How much cost your shoes?'

'A hundred dollars.'

'Very expensive! In Hoi An?'

'Yes.'

'You get ripped off.'

'Was I?'

'Yes. It happens for tourists in Hoi An. Some people not so nice to tourists. But maybe my friend here will take just one shoe for ticket. Half of hundred is fifty. And you have already worn them, so half price. Twenty-five. My friend is very poor. He have a big family so price is OK.'

The two Vietnamese men talked softly to one another before the man in the booth gave a disgusted nod.

'Yes, he will take one. But you only get half-hour ticket.'

'Half an hour? Is that enough time to get there?'

'Yes, plenty of time. World Heritage Ancient Cham ruins of the My Son Temples just around next corner.'

Detecting but ignoring injustice, Adam slowly took off his right shoe and put it on the booth's counter.

'OK, you go,' said the official.

'Don't I get a ticket?'

'You don't need one, Adam. This only ticket booth. He know who goes in and who has paid. World Heritage Ancient Cham ruins of the My Son Temples just around next corner. Enjoy. But make sure you are back here half hour.'

'Half an hour?'

'Thirty minute.'

Adam limped off down the path. Soon it turned. After a hundred metres a man in pleated blue trousers and white shirt stepped out onto the path in front of him and flapped his hands at Adam.

'Hello you.'

'Oh, Good Lord.'

He saw that Adam was one-shoed, and laughed. 'What happened to your shoe? You lose in jungle?'

'Yes.'

'Oh, no! Jungle have many danger. Don't step on snakes.'

'Yes, I'll try not to.'

'So please, you go to World Heritage Ancient Cham ruins of the My Son Temple?'

'Yes.'

'Here you buy ticket.'

The man met Adam and pointed into the jungle beside them. A manned booth was set back from the path, made by the trees invisible from any angle other than straight on.

'I just bought a ticket.'

'Ha ha! No.'

'Yes.'

'No is impossible. This is ticket booth for World Heritage Ancient Cham ruin of the My Son Temple.'

'No, I just bought a ticket from the ticket booth. Just back there. I paid with my shoe because I didn't have any money.'

'And you get one hour ticket?'

'Half hour ticket.'

'Oh, no. That not real booth. They no work for World Heritage Ancient Cham Ruin of the My Son Temple. They make scam to you. Shoe worth one-hour ticket! Show me ticket.'

'I don't have one.'

'You no have?'

'He said I didn't need one. He said his was the only ticket booth and he knew who went in and who had paid.'

'Ohhh. Did he look like me?'

'A little bit.'

'Yes, he is bad man. Always he rip off tourist. You go back now and he will not be there. So, if you want ticket you must pay.'

'But I don't have any money.'

The man was shocked. He gasped. 'No money?'

'No. I had to pay the last man with a shoe.'

'And for half hour ticket. It is such a shame. People like him give Vietnam bad name. You get shoe from Hoi An?'

'Yes, two of them.'

'How much?'

'A hundred dollars.'

'Ohhhh,' said the man, scrunching up his nose and closing his eyes. 'So much money. You get rip off. OK, so you see World Heritage Ancient Cham ruin of the My Son Temple with one hour ticket, twenty dollars.'

'That's the same price as a half hour ticket.'

'See, I make special price for you. Happy hour.'

And soon, barefoot, Adam was pointed in the direction of the jungle, where he was mobbed by women in pyjamas. For long enough he ignored them and with force enough he pushed through them to eventually come to a clearing where stood before him underneath a blaring sun the red brick ruins of the temples at My Son.

Weeds sprouting from every crack and grass having for centuries made its way up their walls, they were set among the mountains with enough easy picturesqueness to have made it, along with a cooking class and the village where herbs are grown, onto every tourist's Hoi An itinerary. Small trees sprang from some of their tops. Some were of three solid stories, all lopsided from decay. Carved shivas faded in their niches of spiraled column and arch, elephants still wore away on architraves. Short octagonal stone columns lay strewn on the ground. Craters pocked the surrounding terrain, reminders of the week of carpet bombing which destroyed more of these ancient structures than had done a thousand years of humidity, typhoon and flood.

The women trying to sell him tiger balm stopped at the forest edge and Adam walked (in the company of a hundred long-white-socked tourists, bumbagged and backpacked bearing burdensome cameras and sporting cowboy and baseball and rice hats) among these Hindu tombs, their ornately reliefed pilasters, lichen-covered, their almost Corinthian capitals. At the jungle's edge, on the other side of the path which cut through the middle of the site, a strangely obvious black hole of an opening seemed to beckon him. Through masks of broad leaf and from behind pandan root everywhere eyes peered out at him. He passed through the temples and, wandering, returned warily to the jungle.

A swarm of ladies asked where he was from until very shortly he came to another clearing. It was surrounded by bracken. In the shade of a canopy of jasmine, bouganvillea, of thin white gardenias, a young girl was enthroned on a tiny red plastic chair atop a podium of three short steps of painted concrete. A wide stream of yellow light crossed the scorching glade. She was wearing fisherman pants. A loose t-shirt that said in a bleeding yellow script, 'Good Morning Vietnam' stretched wide over her titanic shoulders. Her hair was braided and beaded. Over her head a wicker arch had been weaved and threaded with flowers of a hundred shapes and colours. She was listening to a woman in pyjamas who had ascended the steps to be on her left. On her right a woman in pyjamas was waiting to have her plea heard.

'Please you help me,' said one of the women, extracting long stems from from the basket suspended at her neck. 'Please, you buy something. Look my orchid. Very pretty. You very pretty girl.'

'Oh, thank you.' The girl smiled and her lips like wide pink elastic bands went taught across her face.

'Two for one. Happy hour. Look,' said the woman and fanned the girl with a small palm frond. 'Very hot.'

'Yes, it is very hot here.'

'Please you look,' said the woman on her right. The girl turned to face her. The woman offered her four different flowers, their stems held between her fingers. 'Please you buy something. One, five dollar. Two for eight, four for six. I very poor, have baby. You very pretty girl.'

'Oh, thank you. Yes, those are very nice.'

'Rachel,' said Adam, calling softly to her.

'Please, I have baby,' said the first woman. Rachel turned quickly to her. 'I very poor.'

'Do you have a baby as well?'

'Yes I have baby.'

'OK then. How much for these three?' Rachel pulled three flowers from the woman's basket.

'Ten dollar. Special price for you. Happy hour.'

'Oh it is? That's lucky. I'm sorry I'm so rich. Here.' She leaned forward and searched through a backpack lying underneath her tiny red throne. She handed the women some Vietnamese money and they disappeared into the forest. She threaded her purchases into the arch behind her as two women bearing baskets of cut flowers stepped up to her.

'Rachel,' said Adam, slightly louder.

'Adam?'

'You're the tourist warlord?'

'The what?'

'What are you doing here?'

'Oh, Adam, I'm so sorry.'

'Sorry? Sorry for what?'

'For everything. For destroying your greenhouse. For destroying all your flowers. You had to get such a horrible job because of me. I'm so sorry.' And Rachel Clam began to cry.

'Well I've come to bring you back.'

'How did you know I was here?'

'I didn't. I knew someone was here, but not you. It's a long story.'

'I'm not going back, Adam. If that's what you're here for you should leave now. Not after what I did to you. And not after what Noah did to me and what I did to him. Oh, Adam. Everything is so corrupt. The jungle has taught me so much. Everybody's doing exactly what they want to do without thinking about anybody else or of the consequences of their lusts, and I just can't live amongst it anymore. The people here are so pure.'

'Rachel?'

'What?'

'I forgive you.'

'What?'

'I forgive you.'

'You forgive me? Why? For what?'

'Because without forgiveness nothing moves forward. People *are* cruel to one another, unspeakably, and only love and forgiveness can break that cycle of corruption and hatred and misery.'

'Oh, you're so lovely, aren't you? Oh, Adam. Why don't you stay here with me? These people are so poor and so innocent. They'd love you. Why aren't you wearing shoes?'

'I had to give them away in order to come in here to get you.'

'You're so good, Adam. Really you're a good person. A really good person.'

'I'm not a good person, Rachel. Not alone. Nobody is good alone. You can't be good in the jungle. You're a good person, too. But you can only be a good person when you're surrounded by your own people. Not out here. Rachel, you couldn't have known what would happen by being on Noah's boat that night. But you need to know that it happened for a reason.'

'What reason, Adam? All I did was destroy things. Your greenhouse, lives, your flowers. Oh, your flowers. They were so beautiful.' Rachel began again to sob.

'Everything we do has a meaning, Rachel, but it only has that meaning if you use it to be a better person than you were before. Use what happened to my glasshouse to make yourself see that your actions have consequences in the world, and make sure that your next action has very good consequences. Do you see? That's how the world becomes a better place. I don't blame you for what happened, Rachel.'

'But you should blame me. It was all my fault. I cheated on Noah. Because I thought revenge would make me feel better. I wanted him to hurt but then I hurt somebody good, somebody better than myself. A saint. I hurt a saint, Adam.'

'But do you see that only your return to trying to be good can break that cycle? If you keep going the way you're going you'll just be a jungle-bum, an animal.' Adam became aware of the hundred pair of eyes staring calmly at him from the thicket. 'But if you choose to forgive... If you had have chosen to forgive none of this would have happened. You judged Noah and acted on your judgment. Judgment is not ours to pass, Rachel. There are forces in the world which want us to give up hope so that we go on being bad just like the perpetuators of those forces. They want us to inhabit a jungle. But if we are good, people will be good to us. They have to be. The wickedness of the world is not to be abhorred, Rachel, but overcome by good example.'

'What have I got to go home to, Adam? I got fired by a boss who was cheating on his wife with an Asian sex-worker. A male Asian sex-worker. Why does he have the last laugh? Why does he prosper when I fall?'

'Does he, Rachel, prosper? You don't know that.'

'He didn't lose his job.'

'What's a job, Rachel? Think about his soul. Think about the guilt he must be feeling. Everybody feels guilt. Guilt's more tormenting than having to change jobs. It's getting to him, Rachel, eating at him, turning him cynical and making him hate himself and the world, bringing him to darkness. He knows he's done the wrong thing, and the outward appearance of having done the right will destroy him. If he doesn't repent and come clean and make things right he'll suffer here, and then when he's dead, for making others suffer.'

'Do you really believe that, Adam?'

'I have to, Rachel. Otherwise the world is unfair. And I can't believe that the world is unfair. I know how horrible it all seems. I've only really been in it for a week and it... it has a few things that might be said against it. But you put on a gay face and you sing despite it. Because every now and then somebody who isn't gay will hear your singing and he might smile as well. I know people think I'm a lunatic.'

'I don't think that, I think you're lovely.'

'And I've been called an idiot. And a simpleton once. I've been called a fuddy-duddy, boring. I know Jacob thinks I'm boring. But if being interesting means that I cheat on my wife with her sister, or I welcome guests into my home only so that I might molest them, or that I promise immigrants freedom in exchange for sexual favours, then I would prefer to be called very boring. What about people at home, Rachel? Won't your family be worried about you?'

'My mum's probably pretty worried.'

'She must be worried sick about you. You don't belong here, Rachel, not in the jungle. You belong at home, where you're free to do all you can to make the world a better place. I forgive you, Rachel. I understand why you were on Noah's boat that night and I forgive you for what happened.'

Rachel stood from her uncomfortable throne. A dozen pyjama ladies stepped in from the thicket and surrounded the stone steps. Not for days had their tourist warlord risen during the daytime from her mystical seat of power. They gazed at her colossal size as she descended and took Adam's arm.

Rachel and Adam were followed menacingly through the temples by two dozen of her peons. The women shuffled on among the ruins and were soon joined at the far clearing by another couple of dozen ladies in their pyjamas. They closed in on Adam and Rachel and almost blocked them from re-entering the jungle. Rachel hopped as she took off one shoe, then the other.

'Run.'

'What?'

'Run. They can only move so fast with their baskets and in their sandals. Trust me, run.' They reached the confinement of the forest and took off barefoot along the path. By the time they passed the second ticket booth the women were already losing ground. Each of them had an arm raised and a hand flopping as they called after them, 'Excuse me sir.' … 'You very pretty.' … 'Where you from?' Adam and Rachel passed the first ticket booth and looked behind them. Women from all along the jungle's edge were stepping out into the path and joining the waning chase. This plodding mass of pyjama cloth soon dwindled in their sights and Adam eventually saw the sunlight of the clearing from which he had set off.

Having listened to the whole ordeal, Paul and Rebecca were in the middle of the path, Rebecca pulling her body away from Paul and pushing at his.

'Mum?' said Rachel. 'What are you doing here? Wait, run. Run!'

And very shortly the four of them emerged from the forest into the heat of the elephant grass under the sunshine.

'Oh, Rachel,' said Rebecca when she had regained her breath.

She briefly embraced her daughter and then stepped across to Adam. She kissed him with enthusiasm, fully and with both lips. 'That was the most beautiful thing I've ever heard.'

Mun was sitting over the bow of the boat, picking at his toenails with the long fingernail of his pinky.

Paul spent the boat ride back in silence. Rachel apologised profusely to her mother and explained what had happened with Noah's book and Adam's glasshouse. She had flown to Saigon on the recommendation of a colleague, had not liked it very much, and then had taken a twenty-four hour bus to Hoi An where she immediately decided that she had found paradise.

'You *no* have boyfriend?' Mun had found a fresh victim for his advances. His eyes lit up. 'You like strong man? I strong man. Big dick. Like dick of... buffalo. You like buffalo dick?'

'Paul, would you please say something? Paul?'

'What?'

'Would you say something to Mun, he's being digusting.'

'It's his boat. He can say what he wants.'

Paul sat brooding with his hand across his mouth, staring for two hours at the passing riverbank. They returned to the concrete riverside at the Temple of Supreme Modesty and scrambled up onto the street. A frail old man was sitting on a beer crate with a *dan nhi* between his legs, bowing this extraordinarily screechy instrument.

'Thank you so much, Adam,' said Rachel.

'Oh, not at all. I would have hated to have heard that you were stuck out there in the jungle. It's not a life, Rachel.'

'Keep in touch?'

'I look forward to hearing from you.'

'I really would like to take you out to dinner tonight,' said Paul.

'I'll be spending the afternoon with my daughter, Mr Tyrus. I'll get in touch with Adam in order to take *him* out for dinner and to pay him.'

'I was thinking that maybe just you and I. Two adults. We could talk about our exes. I know I'd like to have somebody to talk to. So few people understand what it's like to be cheated on. I get so lonely.'

'Mr Tyrus, I admire what you think you do for a living, but I really do prefer younger men. I need to feel young. If Adam wasn't engaged to your daughter I'd be chasing him with a butterfly net.'

Paul thought for a few moments about the best method of finally changing Rebecca Mussil's mind. Then he went for it. He slammed his lips onto hers. She immediately tried to back away from him and he grabbed her by the arms. She squirmed and yelped and Paul squeezed a hand at one of her breasts. When finally Paul had to admit that his method of seduction might not have very much further to go he released Rebecca and she stepped back from him.

Mun's fat head, floating just above the shoreline, was laughing from his boat. 'You fuck here? Western mama have a big pussy.'

Paul looked at Rebecca and appeared to be shocked at what he had done. He fell to one knee.

Rebecca chided him as she put her arm around her daughter and walked away. 'I will be paying your fee, Mr Tyrus, entirely to Adam. You may charge thousands but Adam will be getting tens of thousands. *He* returned my daughter to me, not you. You're nothing but an old pervert.'

Paul bowed his head. Rebecca was not finished.

'A dirty, pathetic man, Mr Tyrus. And a pimp. You have him go out and do all the hard and noble work so that you can hang back and proposition vulnerable mothers. Ergh,' she said, shuddering. 'You're no better than him,' she said, pointing at Mun.

'She so angry!' Mun chuckled. 'Angry sex best sex.'

The dan nhi was still being sawn.

'Will you shut the fuck up!' Paul screamed, though the musician knew no English and was deaf and blind.

His arm resting on his bent knee, Paul looked up at Adam. At the end of a long stare, during which Adam tried to look as inoffensive as possible, Adam thought that it rather appeared as though Paul wished to very gravely hurt him.

CHAPTER 6

1

'Dad wants to kill you.'

Still on one knee in the invigorating cool of Evelyn's greenhouse Adam said, 'He what?'

'He's going to kill you.'

Evelyn, breathtaken and speechless, her right hand clasping her splayed left at her breast, found her breath and received back her speech and said, 'Oh, he's a stupid, silly, idiot!'

'But I asked his permission.'

'It's not about that. He wants to kill you and he's going to kill you.'

'He's jealous again,' said Evelyn.

'Jealous of what?' said Adam, alarmed and now with an arm around his new fiancé.

'Your negotiating,' said Jonathan. 'Your eloquence. Your way with words. Did a mum come onto you?'

'Your dad said he likes my words. He said they're like a soothing harp.'

'He's being sarcastic, Adam. He hates the harp. He thinks it's gay.'

'How could anybody hate a gay instrument?'

'Adam.'

'What?'

'He wants to kill you. There's a tourist warlord on the Hai Van pass and last night he was on the phone getting Van to organise it with the police. He's gone to see the kid's mums now and when he gets back he's gonna take you up there, today. I'm gonna go with him and try and talk him out of it. You have to hide yourself for a couple of days.'

'I really think you're being overly dramatic, Jonathan.'

'I'm not, Adam.'

'Evelyn?'

'Trust us.'

'I'm sure he doesn't want to actually kill me. People don't kill other people. I'm sure he's—.'

'Adam,' said Jonathan. 'People kill people. And our father wants to kill you. He wants you to die. To be physically dead. He's done it before.'

'He what?'

'Have you not told him, Evelyn?'

A warm air of solemnity suddenly blasted around the greenhouse. Adam looked at Evelyn, she looking very gravely back at him, and, shaking his head, he looked back to Jonathan.

'Dad cheated on our mother. With her best friend. It broke her heart, and she went to Southeast Asia to get away for a while, to try and recover, to find herself again. She met a German man while she was here in Hoi An and they went to Thailand together and became Buddhists. They decided to stay in Thailand and Evelyn and I never saw her again. The first time Dad ever went to Asia was to track her down. He did, and he killed the German. Then our mother killed herself. Adam, he's going to kill you, today, and he'll say it was the villagers. He was jealous of the German man and he's jealous of you. Are you two engaged? Is that what I just interrupted?'

The brief joy of their engagement, overshadowed since its immediate disruption, returned momentarily to the greenhouse. They both nodded.

'I'll use that to get him to change his mind. Adam you be good to her. Congratulations. Now, you need to go away for two days. Dad and I will be back tonight and I'll make sure tomorrow that he's definitely calmed down and I'll call you the next day to tell you to come back.'

Adam was a little flustered. 'Where should I go?'

'I'm going with you. If he loses you he loses me. Can we stay with Olivia?'

6:2

Jonathan's Canadian girlfriend lived in central Da Nang. She was dark-skinned and had moles, had large eyes and a larger mouth. Her students had their lunch break from eleven to one and she came back to her loft to let her guests in.

'So good to see you.'

'So good to see you, too. This is Adam. My fiancé.'

'What!?' said Olivia, flabbergasted. 'When!?'

'This morning.'

'This morning!? What an introduction. Adam! It's so nice to meet you.'

They had banh mi for lunch at a food cart down the street and Olivia said that she had to get back to school. She gave Evelyn the key to her front door. 'That's my only key. If you just make sure you're home around four, that's when I get home. And we'll go for drinks and some dinner? We have to celebrate, you guys! And I have to get to know you, Adam, don't I? I know the *best* sushi place. You'll love it. You like sushi, Adam?'

'Sushi?'

'Yeah.'

'What's sushi?'

'Is he being serious right now?' Olivia turned her head and grinned at Adam. 'Have you snagged yourself a comedian, Evelyn? Lucky you, huh? All right guys, I'm off. You have fun.'

Evelyn and Adam spent a whole hot afternoon at the beach. The dark green mountains of the Son Tra peninsula rose swiftly as a close horizon. My Khe was emptier of people than the beach in Hoi An and its winds were calmer. The sunshine was brilliant and they overpaid for an umbrella and two sun lounges and drank bottled beer in between refreshing swims.

'And you aren't ever going to hurt me?' said Evelyn, half asking, half demanding.

'I don't think I'm at all capable of it.'

'And you won't ever behave like a silly person?'

'Definitely not.'

'And you won't ever be cruel to me?'

'I've not ever been cruel and I shan't ever be cruel.'

'Adultery?'

'A sin more grievous even than murder. For it kills the heart and leaves the body intact.'

'I love you.'

'I love you.'

They dined with Olivia. Adam had sushi explained to him and was instantly suspicious of it. Olivia asked how Adam and Evelyn met and then insisted he tell her every detail of his long story. He had to use a knife and fork in order to eat his meal and left the restaurant tired, hungry, and unimpressed.

At first Olivia thought they were joking when they said they would both prefer sleeping in separate rooms. She gave Evelyn her own bed, slept on a yoga mat on her bedroom floor, and gave Adam the living-room couch and a fan.

The next day, as they awaited Jonathan's phone call, Evelyn showed Adam how to use a computer. When he had gotten something of a hold on the internet she went out to buy baking ingredients. Adam read *Val d'Arno* on the screen of Olivia's laptop until Olivia came home from work.

'You didn't hear from Jonathan today, did you?' said Evelyn, covered in flour at the kitchen bench.

'No,' said Olivia. 'Which is strange. He normally calls me at lunchtime and then pesters me with texts for the afternoon.'

'Hmm,' said Evelyn, rolling her palm over a ball of cookie dough. 'Perhaps they got stuck yesterday and aren't back yet.'

'Maybe. I'll call him now, see if he answers.' She put her phone to her ear and almost immediately pulled it away. 'It says his cell phone's switched off.'

'Well he said he'd call tomorrow morning. I'll just wait for that. Let me know if he calls you to say goodnight or anything, won't you?'

Adam and Evelyn went out to Olivia's school and met her for lunch at a restaurant.

'Still nothing?' said Olivia.

Evelyn, pensive all morning, was staring at the warm display case of unrefrigerated cooked meat. Adam shook his head.

'I'll try him again.' She put her phone to her ear and straight away lowered it. She bounced its weight in her hand then tapped the thing and then put its top to her mouth.

'I think we should go home and see what's going on,' said Evelyn. She thanked Olivia for everything and kissed her on the cheeks.

'Now?' said Adam.

'Yes.'

'Are you sure?' said Olivia.

'I'm sure. We can't do or know anything from up here.'

'All right. Can you just leave my key at the reception of the hotel next door? Adam it was *so* nice meeting you. Congratulations again. I'm sure I'll see you very soon. You call me when you find out what's happened won't you? Love you both.'

Thuc came to pick them up. The air of gloom which Evelyn exuded stifled the car and Adam thought better of trying to talk to her.

The iron gate of their house lay mangled in the dust across the street from its walls. In the driveway Van was waiting beside his van with three stout cronies.

'Mun-nee,' said Van when Adam and Evelyn rose from the car.

'What?'

'Mun-nee. Where you father?'

'I don't know where he is.'

'Where you boss?'

'I've been with her.'

'I come yesterday, nobody here. I call him, nobody answer.'

Thuy stepped out onto the short terrace. Van spoke calmly to her in Vietnamese.

'Miss Everyn, I call Mr Tyrus many time but he no answer.'

'Where he go?' said Van.

'The Hai Van pass,' said Evelyn.

'Hai Van pass. OK you wait.'

Van spoke briefly to his companions and then made a phone call. He spoke in Vietnamese and quickly rose to yelling before calmly hanging up the phone. 'You father dead.'

'What?'

'So sorry.'

'He's dead?'

'He dead.'

'Where? How?'

'He go to Hai Van pass. Big tourist there. He go to get him. But Hai Van people very bad. You Dad try to take tourist. Hai Van people say no. Tourist see he really no want to go back to Australia.

They say kill? He say kill. So Hai Van people kill you father.'

'What about my brother?'

'You brother? Who you brother?'

'Jonathan. He went to the Hai Van pass with him.'

'Hai Van pass? OK you wait.' Van made another phone call. 'He dead too.'

Evelyn fell across into Adam's arms and sobbed.

'You dad he owe mun-nee.'

'How much money?' said Adam.

'Five hundred dollar US. You pay now.'

'Can we pay you tomorrow? My fiancé's very distraught. Is it all right if we pay you tomorrow?'

'Tomorrow? OK. I nice man. You father dead you no pay anymore if no work in Hoi An. You stop work?'

'Yes.'

'She work here?'

'No.'

'OK. Five hundred US dollar you father money tomorrow. And you no pay anymore. I very nice man.'

CHAPTER 7

Shaved, bathed and dressed, Adam walked out into the dining room and, fiddling at his tie pin, chimed, 'Good morning.'

'Good morning, honey,' said Evelyn.

Thuy lifted Adam's toast from the sesame oil and covered them each with an egg. She crossed the atrium with his and Evelyn's plates.

'Thuy, when you come to Australia you have to try bacon. You will love it.'

'Yes. Bacon. You take me.'

'Yes. We'll take you.'

'And my baby.'

'And your baby.'

'How did you sleep, dear?' said Evelyn. In a white linen dress embroidered with cotton daisies at the shoulder-straps, she was slouching in her chair.

'Perfectly. Thuy, those bedsheets your parents gave us are exceptional.'

'What?'

'Sheets?' Adam put his joined hands to his ear and tilted his head. 'Sheets.'

'Yes,' said Thuy.

'Very good.'

'Shit very good.'

'Yes.'

'Good.'

'Thank you.'

'You welcome.'

Evelyn reached across the corner of the table and put one of her soft hands on Adam's. 'And what have you got on for the day then?'

'Ooh, relative clauses again,' said Adam, mildly excited. 'Who, that, and which. They *really* don't seem to be getting it though. Just when you think one of them has it, he'll go and say something like, "The selfish men *that* take away everyone from the good". They really make no sense sometimes.'

'You can't expect them to be perfect at it, can you, dear? It's their second language. And their own is so different.'

'I suppose. I'll probably be home early, too. There were only six students in class yesterday and three of them were going to higher ground this morning to be with their families. Thuy, your family's coming tonight?'

'Family come tonight, yes.'

'Thuy, we can't get much English news about it. How bad do you think it's going to be?'

'Yes.'

'How bad?'

'Yes, bad. There is one, two, three, four and five typhoon. Last year we have a four. Everything gone. Water everywhere. This one, five.'

'Mmm,' said Adam. 'And your uncles are bringing a truck of sand, yes? And bags?'

'Sand, yes. For ahh…. bag sand.'

'Yes.'

'They help you for… for flower house.'

'Yes, that would be great. And we have to board the whole place up tonight.' Adam gave a hammering gesture with his fist and saw his watch. 'Oh, I'd better go. The highway'll be packed I suppose. You take it easy today, all right darling? Don't move anything around. Get Thuy to do it. Or wait until I get home. If there are only three students I'll just run them through adverbs for an hour and give them relative clauses to study until school's allowed back.' He kissed Evelyn on the top of the head and went out to his motorscooter. He strapped on his helmet (it had come free with the vehicle and was stickered all over with little flying figures of Disney's Peter Pan) and turned the key and slowed out onto the dirt road and the street.

It was dark, cool and windy. More litter than usual was spread around the town, collected by constant wind into bundles at kerbsides and around temple pillars and at the bottoms of fences. People were everywhere covering shingled roofs with sheets of iron and weighing those down with sandbags, were arranging strings of bricks on corrugated iron rooftops, taking down and securing thatch and nailing boards over windows.

The palm trees along the road in the open rice fields wobbled in the gale. Adam heard a racket coming towards him on the road. It was some sort of procession. Four motorscooters, two men on each, neared. The foremost bore on a long bamboo pole a St. George's cross. More motorscooters, then a convoy of new cars preceded a green-canopied truck bedecked on its front and its sides with colourful ribboned cartouches. The Chorus of the Hebrew Slaves blared from mounted speakers, sung in Vietnamese, its melody played by an orchestra of screeching bowed instruments. There followed quickly a white van decorated as a red temple, its dragon-lined rear bearing a dozen men in white robes and headbands.

Adam watched the sky, one vast threatening blanket of heaving blue-grey cloud. Riding slowly against the wind under the six taught wires of the concrete telephone poles he watched a water buffalo and its calf chin-deep in mud, a white crane on each of their backs. He closed his eyes and felt the air on his face and breathed in the densely sweet scent of smouldering agarwood, and was delighted.

Made in the USA
Charleston, SC
13 January 2016